The
Friendship
Quilts

The Friendship Quilts

June Calender

atmosphere press

Authors Note

The places described in this story are the area where the author was born and lived until completing her BA from Indiana University. Her memory of the small towns, especially tiny Friendship, contains some inaccuracies.

All the characters in the novel are entirely fictional.

The information about the craft and art of quilting is the result of fifty years of pursuing the craft, purely for personal pleasure. It is her hope that readers of the novel will understand that quilting has become a sophisticated craft and art but that this novel will be enjoyed for its story.

Chapter 1

Liz had not found the subject for her thesis in the Louvre, the Uffizi or the Rijksmuseum; she might have found it in a folk art shop in Ulaan Baator. This spring day her search was taking her east on U.S. Rte. 50 through Indiana farmlands. Maybe, down a two-lane road, leading to the tiny town of Friendship, she would discover a Grandma Moses. Her little spark of hope flickered less and less brightly as she drove through wide-place-in-the-road towns to no-stoplight Dillsboro. When she pulled her third-hand Toyota into her second cousin Marjorie's drive, Liz saw a perky quartet of garden gnomes lining the short walkway. She felt like turning around and heading back to the highway as fast as the old heap would go.

Marjorie had been sitting in her La-Z-Boy watching for Liz. She hurried out the front door. "You got the right place, you didn't forget where I live after all these years," she called.

Marjorie had broadened and softened. Liz remembered her with a stiff school marm posture and control-panel polyester slacks. *English teacher* was written all over Marjorie, even sitting apart from others at family picnics gossiping with Liz's mother, Barbara. Marjorie's hair short, as it had always been, was now salt and pepper. She had put on makeup, bright pink lipstick and pink blush, in Liz's honor. Tulip shaped earrings dangled from her earlobes; she wore an aqua sweat suit with the expected Reeboks and white socks. "Come in, Elizabeth Jane, come in. How was the drive?"

"Beautiful. It's good to see you." Liz had not heard her middle name used in years. The Southern Indiana part of her mother's family was originally from eastern Kentucky and had many Southern speech habits, as well as a nasal twang that was more Appalachian than north of the Mason-Dixon line. Theirs was not a demonstrative family but Marjorie, the only one of her generation likely to pick up current fads, hugged Liz and said, "You look like the world traveler you are."

Liz had dressed thinking that she did not want to have a "city look" in the eyes of the old lady she had come to meet. She wore jeans with a white shirt under a cashmere sweater purchased inexpensively in Mongolia. She rarely wore sneakers because they did not seem appropriate for a post-grad who taught as well as studied at the University. She wore loafers and socks. Her brown hair was pulled into a ponytail. She wore no makeup and her only jewelry was the Om symbol ear studs Randy had given her. Her eyes were blue-gray like Marjorie's and her mother's.

Liz had emailed her mother asking to be reminded who was who and who had died. She asked how demented was Great-aunt Alma, Marjorie's mother. Marjorie and Barbara had been best friends as girls; they were still close.

In response to the email, Barbara called Liz, "You never call me."

"I know you're busy and work odd hours," Liz replied. This was true, although it was not the reason she didn't call.

Barbara said, "I'm glad you're getting in touch with family."

"When was the last time *you* went down there?"

"I go when things come up. I guess it was Don's funeral. That was while you were still in Europe. Marjorie's been up here a few times. She'll be glad to see you. You're the family curiosity."

"Meaning black sheep?"

"No, Sweetheart, everyone's proud of you. I hope that old lady makes wonderful quilts."

"It's a shot in the dark. Mostly I'm getting cabin fever from spending the winter in a carrel in the library. Quilting is more alive than most folk arts. I think I could write about how the craft is changing."

"All that traveling and maybe your thesis subject is right down there in Friendship," Barbara said. "Give me a call when you get back."

"I'll email you." Liz shared very little with her mother, just the facts: her whereabouts, major decisions like her return to Indiana University to get a Ph.D., and that the purpose of the trip was to look for a unique quilter to write about. Her interest in art history could equally have been astrophysics or numismatics, Russian literature or molecular biophysiology for all anyone in her family cared or understood. Only Marjorie, and now Marjorie's two adult children—both older than Liz and both, happily, living elsewhere so Liz wouldn't have to see them—had gone to college. Only Liz had chosen a hopelessly impractical field. Meanwhile Barbara had a party planning business in Indianapolis and a life as foreign to Liz as Liz's experiences in Europe and Mongolia were to her. Mother and daughter were like unused pieces of furniture stored in each other's attic.

Liz had declared she wanted to do her thesis on some niche area of American folk art. She was inspired by Professor Tom Simmons' American Folk Art seminar last fall. She did all the extra reading and slide viewing he suggested. At a bookstore sale she had discovered a huge, five-pound coffee table book about art quilts. The $75 book was irresistible at $20. The editorial in the book was informative and the quilts pictured were a wonderful variety of graphic designs. Professor Simmons, her thesis advisor, was not very interested in quilts. He reluctantly agreed she might choose some aspect of the craft for a thesis subject. "Get a broad picture," he advised. "See if something excites you from an aesthetic perspective. You have to feel an emotional connection. Think about your family. Do they have old quilts?" Prof. Simmons felt antique quilts might be more promising than the contemporary ones in the book. She left the book with him. When he returned it, he said, "Very interesting. Develop an area to write about and enlighten me. I'd love you to teach me something I don't know."

Liz took his advice and researched broadly. She found antique quilts were widely studied, including an entire subject area at the University of Nebraska. She explored their website thoroughly. They also had a museum with a vast collection of quilts. She had seen a show of quilts by some Black women from the South at the Whitney Museum in New York years ago, before she left for Europe. They had also been much written about. She researched herself into a state of confusion. In the spring she took Prof. Simmons' seminars on Outsider Artists. All the while she taught an Intro to Art class and worked ten hours a week in the library.

Liz had not been out of Bloomington since a brief Christmas visit with her mother in Indianapolis. She longed to drive through the countryside even though spring was late and the trees were still bare. Professor Simmons had said, "Folk art often requires fieldwork, more like anthropology than fine art. For me that's the fun part." Liz's trip to see this old woman's quilts was her first foray. She had a list of quilt shows she wanted to see in the next few months. She told herself she would know her subject if and when she came face to face with it.

She was getting nowhere faster than the grounded Concord. Then she remembered quilts on beds when she and her mother stayed overnight at Marjorie's house one long boring weekend. Those quilts didn't seem special and were not especially treasured as far as she remembered. Liz was bottoming out of ideas. Writing to Marjorie was an act of desperation. She asked if anyone in that very rural southeast corner of the state made interesting quilts. Did she, by some strange fluke, know anyone in the Kentucky part of the family who had old quilts?

Marjorie had called her to say the only quilter she could think of was Geneva Gardiner, a friend of her mother's, who made very odd quilts that she planned to send to a mission in Africa. "She and Mom were childhood friends, and I know she'd let you visit if we took Mom along."

"What does odd mean?" Liz asked.

"Strange color combinations, mixed up patterns, I guess. I haven't seen them. I just know people say they're odd. What are you looking for?"

"I don't really know."

"You'd be very welcome to come visit. I'll take you to meet her," Marjorie said. "It would be good for Mom."

"She lives with you now, doesn't she?"

"I guess you don't know, I had to move Mom to Sunset Manor. It's a nursing home, just down the street. Her arthritis got so bad she can't walk far. Most of the winter she was grouchy and depressed. It's hard to have patience with your mother." Liz nodded and said nothing. She simply knew very little about her mother's life and career. They had hardly seen one another in the last four years. Liz thought of the family here in southeastern Indiana as simple people with few interests. She thought of herself as an escapee.

Marjorie went on, "Mom forgets and repeats things. We got on each other's nerves a lot."

"Is it a depressing place?" Liz remembered stories—but maybe she was confusing nursing homes and mental asylums. Liz had visited very old people living with their families in Mongolian villages. They often had sweet smiles and hands busy knitting as if their fingers were machines that began to move the moment they felt knitting needles and yarn. If the family had infants, the grannies rocked and fed them and played with them when they were old enough for peek-a-boo.

"Actually it's a nice place," Marjorie said. "The building she's in is separate from the home for bedridden patients. It's a friendly place. Some people are lonely and some are grumpy and I guess Mom's some of both some of the time. There's so many assisted living places these days. In fact, it's the only thing you'd call an industry around here except for farming. And farming's changed a lot. At least they still need school teachers."

"Are you sorry you're retired?"

"I miss it. I still teach Sunday School. I'm reading those Great Books, you know?" Liz nodded. She wasn't sure what Marjorie was referring to, but it sounded like Marjorie.

On the way through the living room, Marjorie introduced Liz to the children and recent grandchildren via photographs arranged on a wall behind an old roll-top desk. Liz made appropriate responses. The ritual was like entering the ger of a Mongolian family for the first time and being told, as a foreigner, about their family photographs, their shrine to Buddha, maybe their recent acquisitions: TV with a satellite dish powered by a solar panel outside. Marjorie led Liz into her kitchen and offered donuts, sandwiches, fruit, coffee, tea. "I guess you're so slim and trim because you don't eat anything."

"I'll have coffee," Liz said.

Marjorie poured coffee and helped herself to a donut. "Since when have you been a quilter? I would never have expected it of you."

"I don't quilt. I have a needle and a little bit of thread for fixing buttons, that's it. I got curious about the designs and now that there's a field of art quilts—"

"Really?" Marjorie asked. "I don't think that's what Geneva does. If her quilts are really disappointing, be polite. It's her whole life, I think."

"Really, Marjorie, I've finally learned to be less of a pain than I used to be."

"Well, I hope so. You were a difficult teen. You really were, you know?" She had an indulgent smile although her voice was teacherly stern.

"Yeah, I was a pain in the ass. Couldn't wait to get away."

"Well, you got away. Far, far away."

"I did." She almost laughed. "I can't believe I'm here."

"So, tell me about art quilts. Of course I want to know about Mongolia too."

Liz wished she had brought the big book. She explained that the subject appealed to her because she was entirely jaded with fine art. She was looking for a field that offered possibilities for a career. "I don't see myself doing preservation work on Old Masters in the bowels of the Metropolitan Museum. Serious quilt museums have spread across the US like coyotes. They need administrators. That appeals to me."

Marjorie's head bobbed in understanding. "Funny, you look for treasure in all the great treasure houses of Europe and come back home."

"Funny," Liz said. "Mom said the same thing, but you said it better. I have a feeling you two—"

"Of course we talked about you. We love you."

Liz paused a moment. Marjorie might be someone she could talk to more easily than her mother. She said, "I'm looking for one particular quilter doing something different."

"The word for Geneva Gardiner's quilting is different and peculiar—not 'particular.'" Marjorie said.

Liz remembered that Marjorie was herself particular about words and tended to correct people. After teaching English in high school for thirty-five years the habit was not easily erased. "I need to find a career that will support me and won't bore me to death."

"So, I guess you're not planning on marrying that guy," Marjorie said.

The question took Liz's breath away. Marjorie's voice had been matter of fact and even gentle, but the words felt like the jolt from a defibrillator, as if her heart had stopped but was now beating too fast. She had never spoken to any of her family about marrying Randy. Part of the reason she had spent almost no time with her mother since her return last summer had been to avoid the topic altogether. She thought of the past winter of intense college work as "denning up" like a hibernating bear or a wintering marmot.

"It's none of my business," Marjorie said quickly. "I'm sorry."

"It's just hard to talk about," Liz said.

Marjorie nodded. Liz fought back tears that were not as much about Randy as about a sudden gratitude to Marjorie for seeing the pain and apologizing. She felt an impulse to hug Marjorie but she merely touched Marjorie's arm and said, "Thank you."

"I know about missing someone," Marjorie said.

"I'm sorry I haven't said I'm sorry about Don." Liz felt she had regressed to the self-involved teen who had no empathy for anyone in the family. Whatever adult sensibility she had attained in the last six years had flown away like a gum wrapper thrown out the car window as she drove here. "I really liked him. He was the only male in the family I could ever talk to—including my brothers, you know."

"Thank you." Marjorie got up, taking the coffee cups to the sink where she rinsed them. "You know, before we get to talking too much, Mom has lunch early, 11:30 to noon. I always tell Janette, the manager, when I'm going to pick her up. They'll make sure she's ready to go down to Geneva's by 12:15, all dressed and combed and waiting. She's got the patience of a puppy that's got to pee. She keeps saying, 'Time's running out.'"

"I guess it is," Liz said and then wished she had bit her tongue.

"Yeah. For her faster than for the rest of us, though you never know. They've got two centenarians in that one home and another in the bed-ridden unit. I can't promise she'll remember you when we get there. Some days she's very clear and other days she can't find half the words she wants to say."

"How far is it?"

"Just at the other end of town. I can walk it in four minutes."

Liz had never liked Aunt Alma. Like the rest of the family Alma talked monotonously about crops and gardens and neighbors and chickens and the Sunday sermon. She called small children "little people" as if all children under school age were leprechauns or fairy folk. She seemed not to care at all for the grandchildren or great nieces and nephews between the ages of six and sixteen. "The sassy years," she had said to Barbara more than one Thanksgiving when Liz had said she hated drying dishes and didn't want to help in the kitchen after dinner. Liz remembered a large-boned, tall woman. She looked like the witch in *Hansel and Gretel*, Liz thought. She wore orthopedic shoes and bib aprons with balled up Kleenex in the pockets.

"Why don't you throw away your old Kleenex?" Liz had once asked.

"Waste not, want not. I can blow my nose three or four times on one Kleenex. Why should I throw it away 'til it's used up? Huh? Can you answer me that?"

"It's germy."

"They're my germs," Aunt Alma said. "I don't give them to nobody else." Liz saw her mother shaking her head and clamped her mouth shut. Aunt Alma chuckled, "Guess that shut you up. Kids just got no sense a-tall."

Spending this afternoon with Aunt Alma was the price Liz had to pay to meet a quilter who probably made Dresden plate or Sunbonnet Sue quilts—two of the most insipid quilt designs, but two of the most popular in this part of the country. I shouldn't be a pessimist, she thought as she refastened her ponytail. If everyone around hates this woman's quilts, then they're not the usual pastel prints.

"Thought you'd never get here," the old lady in the wheelchair said. She was bent forward as if looking for something in her lap. Her hands were gnarled with knotted joints like the roots of a tree growing on stone. She was in a sweat suit, no doubt purchased by Marjorie from the same catalog as her own. Alma's was lavender. "Whose daughter are you now?"

"This is Elizabeth Jane, little Lizzy, you used to call her," Marjorie said a little loudly. "Barbara's girl. There were the two boys and then Little Lizzy, remember?"

"Oh, the world traveler one. You're a big girl, Lizzy." Aunt Alma had a wad of Kleenex in her right hand that she worked like a worry stone.

"I'm twenty-six years old, Aunt Alma. I'm back home in Indiana for a while now."

"Well, thanks for coming to see me. Now what was it you said she wanted to do, Marj?"

"Elizabeth wants to see Geneva Gardiner's quilts, Mom. I phoned Geneva and she's looking forward to seeing all of us."

"We're going down to Geneva's?"

"Yes, Mom, we're going down to Friendship."

"Well, if I'd'a knowed that I'd'a put on my green dress."

"That new sweatsuit's just fine and it's on the coolish side outdoors," Marjorie said. "I think you need your windbreaker too."

The two-lane blacktop road wound through small farms. A couple of farmers were plowing fields near the road, turning over matted brown grass and laying out folds of damp dark soil. After a couple of miles the road snaked down a hill and flattened entering the little town of Friendship. "The crick's really muddy and high," Alma observed. "Been a long time since I seen Laugthry Crick in the spring time."

"I imagine the Ohio's pretty high too," Marjorie said.

"It's not floodin' though, is it?"

"They don't think it'll flood this year."

How many times had Liz heard the older people at the family reunions referring to the flood of '37? She hoped Aunt Alma was not going to tell again how she was just a young thing but she helped somebody, whose name she never knew, climb into a rowboat with a pillowcase full of clothes and a cat in her arms.

"This town hasn't grown, has it?" she asked to ward off any flood stories.

"Not to speak of," Marjorie said. "You turn right by the pizza place."

Friendship had one main street, a bank and a few stores. The street passed a church with a cemetery beside it and became a country road in two blocks, they passed a couple of farms. Geneva's house was back from the road behind a row of whitewashed stones. It was a small two-story house with two or three tall trees behind it. Beyond was a barn that listed somewhat eastward. Nearby was a chicken house, both had lost their paint long ago, but the house was sided in clean white aluminum clapboards. Shrubs with a faint acid green at the tips of their branches grew beside the square of concrete that was a front entryway. A big tractor tire, its center full of dirt recently dug, would be a summer flower bed. Perhaps it was already seeded.

Marjorie had helped her mother into the front seat and stowed the wheelchair in the trunk. Liz got the wheelchair out and unfolded it. "I hope we can get in the front door with this," Marjorie said.

Aunt Alma could walk a few steps. She had done so when she got into the car with a grim set to her jaw, her teeth clamped together in both pain and concentration. As Alma was being settled in the wheelchair, Geneva came from the house.

"Welcome. Welcome, Alma. It's good to see you. Marjorie, glad you could bring your mom."

Geneva was small and apple shaped. She wore a bright blue apron with a flower print and an eyelet ruffle along the bottom over a brown dress printed with small blue flowers. Liz immediately thought, She wears this on Sundays when she's fixing dinner for someone. Geneva's white hair was cropped short and straight. Her face was more lined than Alma's, but she seemed much younger because of her quick steps and brisk voice. She gave Alma a quick hug and then one for Marjorie too. "Come in, come in, it's chilly out here."

"You're looking very perky," Alma said. "See what I brung you? You know Marjorie, but I don't think you ever did see Little Lizzie a-fore."

"I'm glad to meet you," Liz said. She held out her hand.

Geneva's hand was firm and strong. It was the same size as Liz's hand. "I'm real glad to meet you. You're not Marjorie's daughter, are you?"

"No, I'm Elizabeth"—she emphasized because she hated being called Lizzy—"from the Indianapolis part of the family."

"She's Rosalie's only granddaughter. Barbara's her mother's name," Alma said. Her memory seemed to be working very well now that they were here.

"Well, you're welcome in my house. Here, let me hold the door."

"I'll push the chair, Marjorie," Liz said. Tipping it up onto the big square concrete step was easy. Aunt Alma weighed very little. But the doorway was narrow. "I don't think it's going to go through the door," Liz said.

"Well, I'll go through on my own steam then," Alma said. "Come pull me up outta this thing, Marj."

Together they managed to put Alma in a corner of an overstuffed sofa with a pillow behind her back and her feet up on an ottoman. A quilt was folded at the other end of the sofa. It immediately caught Liz's eye because it was a confusion of red, aqua and yellow triangles of different sizes and various prints. Definitely not pastel. Nothing "sweet old lady" in that quilt.

Geneva said, "You come to talk about my quilts, so I put out my newest one. I see you noticed it right off."

"The colors caught my eye. May I open it up?" Liz asked.

"Sure you can. Can I get you-all some coffee? I got it made."

"I'll help you," Marjorie said to Geneva.

"How do you take your coffee, Elizabeth?" Geneva asked.

"A little milk and no sugar."

"Plenty of sugar," Alma said loudly.

"I know, Mom," Marjorie said.

Liz unfolded the quilt. The triangles were simple, a one-block quilt, but it had been put together with sets of triangles of different sizes, something Liz had not seen in any of the books or websites she had studied during the last months. Geneva had used an enormous variety of fabrics, but they were predominantly intense hues. Colors and patterns were side by side that most people would not put together. The effect was joyous, almost manic. The back seemed a happenstance hodge-podge; it was clearly utilitarian, made with what was available, but surely the front was intentionally as loud and high spirited as a teen-age wannabe rock drummer's solo riff.

"I always wonder if there's something wrong with Geneva's eyes," Alma said. "She puts together the durnedest colors. If that was on my bed, I'd never be able to sleep a wink. The colors would keep me awake even in the dark."

"Well then I won't send it home with you," Geneva said, coming into the room with a coffee mug in each hand. "This is yours, Alma. If you drink enough coffee with this much sugar, maybe you'll put some meat back on your bones."

"All that coffee and sugar will keep her awake the rest of the afternoon," Marjorie said as she bought her own coffee and a mug for Liz.

That quilt might keep me awake tonight, Liz thought. She was eager to see what else Geneva had. She chose the only straight hard chair in the room, leaving the sofa and big recliner for the older women. "It's magnificent," Liz said. "I love this quilt."

"You like it?" Geneva asked. She sounded like a school child presenting a bouquet of wildflowers to a teacher.

"Oh, yes. The colors are very exciting. The vari—"

"You like them?" Alma interrupted with surprise so obvious Liz felt it was insulting to Geneva. "Young people these days..." She shook her head and then slurped her coffee loudly.

Marjorie gave her mother an embarrassed look. She said, "Everyone has different tastes, Mom. We can't all be like you."

"Well, that's a durned shame. I've been around long 'nough to know a few things." Aunt Alma had always had what the rest of the family called "opinions." She enjoyed voicing them. Barbara had complained on a drive back to Indianapolis after a family dinner, "She's a bigoted old woman. She still says 'nigger' and it embarrasses me to death. I wish Marjorie would put her straight. Marj doesn't mind telling the rest of us when our English isn't perfect."

Geneva said, "That's true, Alma, but I'm not that much younger than you—"

"You don't have to tell me how old you are, Geneva. If I hadn't skipped the fourth grade, we'd've graduated the same year."

"I always said you were smarter than me." Geneva turned to Marjorie and Liz and added, "But I was prettier. Still am, Alma. And don't you argue with me."

"Yes, you've always been prettier and perkier. A better shot too," Alma said.

"That I am. You never could hit the side of a barn."

Marjorie looked up at the ceiling, she had heard this routine often.

"Oh yes, I could hit the side of any barn. I just couldn't hit a flying disk."

"Geneva was a champion skeet shooter," Marjorie told Liz.

"I was and I've got a few ribbons to prove it," Geneva said. "Tho' I don't know where the ribbons got to."

Marjorie explained, "There's an annual skeet shooting competition here in Friendship. Been going as long as I can remember."

"My dad taught me to shoot," Geneva said, "'cause he didn't have any sons. I used to hunt ducks and geese with him. Squirrels and coons too."

"I'm very impressed," Liz said. "Do you still shoot or hunt?"

"Well, I got a shotgun and a rifle, but I haven't had call to use them fer quite a while. Shot at a chicken-stealin' fox, oh, must-a been more'n five years ago. Didn't hit 'im but skerte 'im away."

"Do you keep them loaded?" Marjorie asked.

"That I do. And I go shoot at a tin can on a fence post maybe once or twice a year just to check out if my eyes're still good. Livin' alone on a farm...I just want-a know I can protect myself if I ever need to."

"Ever need to?" Marjorie asked.

"Nope. I've been lucky, I guess. Not much happens round here."

Alma said, "You've been lucky with your health like I ain't."

Marjorie's mouth opened as if to correct her mother, but she closed it and sipped coffee.

"That I have, and I thank God for it every morning and night." Geneva noticed Liz had folded the quilt and held it on her lap, stroking the variety of fabrics. "People give me material; I don't go out and buy none."

"You just use what you have on hand?"

"Always have."

"Like I always say," Alma said, "waste not, want not. That's what quilt makin's 'bout. Ain't I right, Geneva?"

"That what it's always been fer me. Elizabeth, you'd be surprised how nice people can be. There's three or four at church put a bag of fabric in my hands real often. They go to a mall and buy remnants. And they put in the inter-church newsletter that I would appreciate anyone's scraps. Sometimes the mail brings me packages of fabric, little packages and sometimes big packages. It's like Christmas some days when I go to the mailbox. I never know when it's goin'na happen and it jus' lights up the whole day."

"I think that's wonderful," Marjorie said. "I'll start keeping my eyes open for you too."

"Oh, I ain't askin', I'm just sayin'—sometimes the stuff's so pretty I spread it out all over the room and look at the kind-a designs people come up with these days. I'm so grateful. It's friends and strangers alike."

"So you have a stash to choose from," Liz said.

"Oh, yes, I got boxes and boxes, all sorted out by color."

"When did you start quilting, Geneva?" Marjorie asked.

"Oh...well, I guess it was when the girls were little. I made their dresses and I'd have scraps left over. Couldn't throw good material away, had to use it up."

"Waste not, want not," Alma said again.

"My mom taught me to quilt. She sewed by hand, but I didn't have time fer that, not with three kids and all the work on the farm."

Alma slurped her coffee loudly again to draw attention back to herself, but Geneva didn't seem to notice. Liz asked, "Do you always use bright colors?"

"No, course not. People give me all kinds-a things. I never turn up my nose at what people give me, even the downright ugly. You know, if you cut an ugly piece up, take it in small enough pieces, it stops bein' ugly."

"I've known some ugly people I'd like to cut up in small little pieces," Alma said.

"Now, Mom, you don't mean that," Marjorie said.

"I do mean it. You know I mean it, don't you, Geneva? I've never been Miss Goody-Two-Shoes."

"That's true, Alma. Your mom," Geneva said to Marjorie, "was a wild thing in her younger days."

"Well, I know she ran off with Dad to Covington, Kentucky and got married and then they went to a nightclub and danced nearly all night," Marjorie said. "She always liked to tell us about that."

"My dancing days are over," Alma said. "But I was a real good dancer back in my hey-day." Liz tried to imagine Alma dancing with the husband she didn't remember. He died when she was very small. None of this family seemed like people who danced.

Geneva was nodding her head and smiling. "Many times she tried to lead me astray," Geneva said. Then she said directly to Alma, "But I stayed on the straight and narrow, mostly."

Alma looked back briefly then down at the hand with its Kleenex worry stone.

Secrets? Liz thought. She said, "I wish I could have seen you, Aunt Alma."

Marjorie was frowning and finally said, "Mom, try to drink your coffee quietly." Alma seemed lost in thought until Geneva said, "I hear Ramona Hucking is up there at Sunset Manor too." They began talking about people both knew who were in the nursing home or had been before their deaths.

Liz wanted to see more quilts, but these old ladies hadn't seen each other for months. Liz sipped her coffee and tried to be patient. She had learned in Mongolia there was a welcoming ritual when you visited a nomad's ger, a ritual not so different from this. They offered something to drink, tea or arak, if they had it, maybe something to eat; they asked after family and animals. They complained about the weather. People are the same the world over, she thought. You can't barge right in and ask to see their treasures.

After a few minutes Geneva said, "I expect you'd like to see some more quilts, Elizabeth. If you want to go in the bedroom there—that door that's partly open—there's a couple on the bed and a couple on the chair too. I put them out to show you. You can just go in and unfold them. It's all right with me."

"Thank you," Liz said.

"I want to see, too," Marjorie said. "You two can visit a few minutes without us."

In the bedroom Marjorie said, "Can you believe she's Mom's age?"

"Seems ten years younger," Liz said. The quilt on Geneva's bed was a kind of Trip Around the World with some rows of squares replaced by rows of Flying Geese.

"Geese flying around the world," Liz said.

"That's what it's called?" Marjorie asked.

"I've never seen the two patterns combined in the books I've studied."

The colors progressed from yellow in the middle, through orange, red, maroon to browns while the Flying Geese were dark and light teal. "Oh, my, I didn't expect this," Liz said.

"Not really very pretty," Marjorie said.

"Not 'pretty', stunning."

"You like it?" Marjorie looked from the bed to Liz's face.

"A lot," Liz said. "I wonder if she thinks this out or does it intuitively." She wondered if Geneva were using the traditional patterns as a way to make puns. Thesis, here I come.

"I think she's got the most god-awful taste in color I ever saw," Marjorie whispered. "You couldn't pay me to put that on my bed. I've always heard she makes odd quilts—that's why I told you about her. But I never saw any of them before. You really like it?" Marjorie picked up first one and then the other of the quilts on the chair and shook her head.

"They're really wonderful," Liz said. "I would hang it on the wall like a painting."

"Quilts are made for beds. Lots of things in this world I don't understand," Marjorie sighed. "Take your time, I'll go finish my coffee. I'm glad you're not disappointed."

"I'm happily surprised."

Liz was glad to be left alone to contemplate Geneva's choices. The quilts on a straight chair were very unusual color combinations also. They were made of random blocks, rectangles and wedge-shaped pieces. She knew I was coming and put out her wildest stuff, Liz thought. I wonder if she's showing off or trying to scare me away. She unfolded first one and then the other quilt onto the bed and stood back as she looked at each.

Why didn't I bring a camera? I was so stupid. I was sure I would be disappointed. Professor Simmons had said of folk and outsider art, "You never know what you'll find or where." Liz had expected to find timid pastels and the most sentimental, insipid patterns. These were mostly simple traditional patterns that she had become familiar with from her research; but Geneva had combined patterns or changed them in what seemed spontaneous ways—a mark of Outsider Artists. She had used scraps of cartoon prints with geometric prints; she had mixed flower patterns that were orange, magenta and chartreuse. Liz wondered what Geneva called ugly prints.

"What are you thinking, Elizabeth?" Geneva had come to the door.

"That I was an idiot to come without my camera. These are spectacular."

"Do you honestly like them?" Geneva came to stand at the foot of the bed beside Liz. She seemed a small, eager child.

But she's not a child, Liz thought, she holds her own with Aunt Alma. She felt confused by the old women. She had never seen Aunt Alma with a friend of this sort. Their relationship was very different from Alma's with the family. Something from much earlier in their lives was reflected in their voices and glances at one another. Alma was in a different world where her memory seemed flawless.

"I honestly do. Do you have others?"

"I got a closet almost more-n half full."

"You do? How many do you think?"

"Oh, probably 'bout seventy. Been piling them up for years, finally had my son build me a cedar closet in the spare room where I sew."

"Almost a hundred?"

"Not a hundred yet, that's what I'm aimin' fer. When I get to a hundred I'm sendin' them off to poor people in Africa."

"Marjorie told me that, but I don't understand."

"Three or four years ago a visitin' missionary came here for a couple weeks. He and his wife had just come back from—oh, what's that place in Africa? I forget, someplace that's got mountains and gets cold at night. I asked if they used quilts and he said they'd love to have quilts. And I said I can't give money, 'cause I don't have none. But people give me material for quilts an' I could send them some. He thought that would be good. He'd be going back in a year or so. So I set to making quilts and I jus' liked the idea more and more, 'cause I never did like all them fussy patterns in the magazines. I like to make bright happy quilts. The farm's rented out, I just got my chickens and a little garden and a few flowers in the summer. I never believed in idle hands, so I said to myself, I wonder how long it'd take to make a hundred quilts. It's kind-a jus' my idea. Makes me happy, you know?"

Liz felt as if she'd been punched in the stomach. She had found a treasure and it could suddenly disappear. "I'd love to see them."

"Well, Elizabeth, I'm real happy you like them and I don't want-a to be rude to you 'cause I'm real grateful you brought Alma here. I haven't seen her for a quite a while and I'm sad how frail she looks. You know, at my age your friends jus' drop away one by one. I'd like-ta show you some more but my spare room's not neat enough fer visitors and I think I'd better spend the time with Alma."

Liz didn't say anything, but she was thinking, like a child asking a favor, please, please, pretty please.

"You know I don't have any wheels of my own," Geneva said. "Friends take me to the store and church, so I don't get up to Dillsboro to visit with Alma. If you can maybe come back by yourself sometime, when I know you're comin' I can show you the others and you can bring your camera."

"My camera is back in Bloomington, but could I come back tomorrow morning." Liz said, "Marjorie must have a camera or I can buy a couple one-use cameras."

"Tomorrow's Sunday, Elizabeth, I spend most-a Sunday in church."

She doesn't want to show me. Liz felt her hand had been slapped like a child reaching for a second cookie. Next weekend was the annual national quilt show in Paducah, Kentucky. She planned to go, if not to find a quilter, at least to see for herself what people are making. She would have some immediate comparisons with Geneva's quilts. Maybe they weren't so unusual. Liz was aware how little she actually knew about quilts.

"I'd like to come back another weekend but..."

"Take your time," Geneva said. She went back to the living room. Liz refolded the quilts she had spread on the bed. She looked at the quilting, the straight seams, in places the thread changed colors. She must have had to thread and rethread her sewing machine as she worked. Why does she take so much time with these quilts? Habit? A perfectionist quilter? Did she ever enter them in competitions like local fairs, the Indiana State Fair? Where did she get her color sense? Where did the ideas come from? Liz needed time to look and ask questions. Suddenly time seemed limited.

Maybe Geneva didn't like Liz meddling even if she was happy to hear some praise for the quilts. What do I really know? Liz asked herself. I love these quilts, but would Tom Simmons like them? He told me to find something I love. If only I had a camera and could at least take back a few pictures. Liz looked at her wristwatch. Could she drive back to Dillsboro and see if the drug store or the grocery store had one-use cameras? Maybe, but there was Alma and Marjorie... *I was so stupid,* she told herself. *How long would it take Geneva to make enough quilts to reach a hundred? Weeks? How many more? It sounded like she didn't have a precise count. Surely time enough to come back. I'll talk to Tom Simmons. I'll see if he says yea or nay to my idea.*

Liz hated to leave the bedroom, but she went back into the living room and listened to the old ladies talking about people she had never heard of, most of them already dead. Sometimes they remembered an incident from years ago and laughed like schoolgirls. Liz tried to understand Geneva's mood, but she only saw two friends catching up and enjoying each other. Eventually Marjorie looked at her watch and said, "Mom, it's getting late. If we don't get you back to Sunset Manor, they're going to think you went AWOL."

As Marjorie was helping her mother into the car, Liz said to Geneva, "Could I come back two weeks from today? Saturday, early, maybe 9:00 or so, and you could show me some more quilts. Maybe we could talk about how you work?"

"I'm never anywhere but here," Geneva said, "'cept for Sundays and some Wednesday nights when someone takes me to prayer meetin'. You're welcome to come back."

"I will. I appreciate your letting me come today. It's been a treat."

"I have to thank you. It was a blessin' to see Alma. I'll be prayin' for her and hope to see her again."

"I wasn't, you know, thinking of bringing her next time."

"I know. You want to talk and look. That's okay, Sweetheart."

"I'll tell you what, after we talk, I'll drive you up to Dillsboro to visit her if you'd like."

"I'd like. But we'll see. Don't say nothin' to her 'bout it. Maybe you don't know what disappointment means at our age. It's a sad thing to do to a body."

"I understand. I really want to see you again."

"You're a sweet girl, Elizabeth. Nice to meet you." She gave Liz a quick hug. Liz felt the small body in her arms just a moment. *Maybe she actually likes me,* she thought. *Maybe I shouldn't worry...at least* not yet. Geneva stood at the car window and said good-bye to Marjorie and Alma.

At least four times on the drive back, Aunt Alma said, "That was a real nice visit." She had already forgotten many of the facts about Geneva's family, but Marjorie related them over and over.

At the nursing home, Liz helped Alma out of the car as Marjorie opened the wheelchair. Alma was like a marionette, a tall stick figure wearing a few clothes, so light it seemed she could easily be snapped into kindling. "You going back to see more of Geneva's wild quilts?" Alma asked.

"Yes, I want to. I just don't know when I can get back here," Liz said.

"I 'magine she likes havin' somebody to show them off to. Somebody with somethin' nice to say 'bout them. Livin' by herself like that's kind-a lonesome."

Maybe she was just making sure I'd come back, Liz thought.

When they had settled Aunt Alma in her room and were going to the car, Marjorie said, "You're going to stay the night, aren't you? You don't want to drive all the way back this evening, do you?"

Liz had been thinking of dropping Marjorie at her house and going back to Bloomington. However, not knowing how the day would go, she had packed underwear and a toothbrush. Marjorie, like the older women, was lonely. Liz knew she was the exotic visitor that brightened a routine day as she and Randy had been when they visited nomadic Mongolians. I've become interesting to my own family, she thought.

"If you'll have me, I'll stay, but I need to get back fairly early tomorrow. I have to prepare for a class I teach on Monday."

"Good. I'd like to hear about your teaching and, if you don't mind, about what Mongolia was like. Europe too. You know, I used to think I'd like to take one of those tours of Europe where you see ten countries in twenty days. People make fun of that kind of traveling, but I always thought it's wonderful that Europe is so compact you can get it all in one package."

"You should do it," Liz said.

"Don was never interested. And I guess the time has passed."

"Maybe not, Marjorie. Lots of people your age travel."

"I couldn't leave Mom."

They were already at Marjorie's house. She had hoped Liz would stay and had a pot roast all ready to go into the oven. Liz delayed talking about Mongolia and Randy by asking Marjorie about her son and daughter and grandchildren. They looked at a picture album while dinner cooked. Liz discovered that Marjorie actually knew more about Barbara and about Liz's brothers and their families than she knew. After dinner there was a break in the conversation to watch news and then Jeopardy, to which Marjorie said she was addicted.

Eventually Liz talked about Mongolia, the place, the people, the children and the older people to whom she and Randy taught English. They had a very good conversation about different children's learning methods. Marjorie had loved teaching and had not had teacherly conversations often since she had retired. Liz avoided talking about Randy and Marjorie did not ask direct questions.

U.S. Route 50 was still etched in Liz's mind because Barbara semi-bribed Liz to keep her company at the family gatherings by letting Liz do the driving even a few weeks after she got her learner's permit. Liz had memorized every bend in the road and every sign reducing the speed limit through the barely-there towns.

Now driving was automatic. Last night, while she lay awake in the bed that once was Aunt Alma's, she thought about Geneva and the quilts that might or might not become her thesis. She tried to gather arguments she would give Prof. Simmons.

After a winter of training herself to repress thoughts about Randy, she dreamed of him. She saw him walking in a mountainous landscape, naked, chanting "Om mani padme hum," loudly, making the mountains echo. His voice was the beautiful baritone that she knew in the dream as one knows such things. He was entirely at one with the landscape. She was happy for him but awoke crying. She cried easily; tears had always been an outlet instead of words.

All winter Liz built mental snow forts in her mind each time she wanted to turn to Randy and explain what she was learning about Outsider Art, about how frustrating she found the freshman students who thumbed their smart phones. She hoped some were writing notes about her lectures and the slides she showed. She kept a journal about what she was doing, what her reading told her, and her irritation at the students and feelings of inadequacy as a lecturer. Thanks to Marjorie's understanding and tactful curiosity, the ice had melted, at least in her sleeping mind. As she drove, fueled by bacon and eggs and even a chocolate donut with plenty of coffee, Liz tried to imagine the months ahead.

She did not believe in prayer, but she wished she did. She would ask whatever higher power existed to fill her mind and her life with Geneva Gardiner and her quilts. And because the life of the mind wasn't entirely satisfying, to send her a good man for the lonely times. All she wanted was a consuming subject for her thesis and an occasional, not too casual or meaningless, but not too serious, bit of sex. She did not want to be in love, maybe never again. Well, maybe in the far distant future. Her mother could live without it, or so Liz assumed, and so could she.

Liz drove past the odd little church in Elrod where the entrance was not at the back of the auditorium but right beside the dais with the pulpit, so any latecomer was seen by the entire congregation. Was that some Baptist perversity? Punishment by embarrassment? She had attended a couple of funerals and weddings there with her mother. Marjorie's husband, Don, was buried out back and someday Marjorie would be also. Aunt Alma would go first, taking her place with the deceased grandparents, aunts and uncles buried behind the church. The gravestones stood in neat, close together rows like gray stone sheep waiting patiently for the Shepherd they had believed would gather them to a heavenly pasture.

The road straightened and headed west toward a north-south interstate highway that would take her to Columbus where she'd get another rural road west to Bloomington. On this road, with family and Geneva's quilts behind her and the university life she had settled into more than an hour in the distance, Liz finally let her defenses down. Her mind filled with Randy.

When Liz finished her B.A, at Indiana University in Bloomington, she did her Master's on a fellowship in Rome. She traveled all over Europe.

Art history was her field; and she was determined to see all the important art museums. She succeeded, even getting as far as the Hermitage in St. Petersburg. Finally, her visual memory was so full she became tired, jaded, bored with saints and Impressionist landscapes, portraits of royals and merchants and nudes, tired of Cubism and abstractions. She wished she could have electroshock therapy to erase the images, names and dates related to art history. Why clutter her memory when all those were recoverable with a few strokes on a computer keyboard?

"We need a total change, a physical, emotional, intellectual shock to the system," Randy said. "Art won't go away, but we can." They were in total agreement as they had been for two years. They were sitting at a café near the Trevi Fountain eating spaghetti and sausage with the usual cheap red wine she had finally learned to drink with satisfaction, if not much enjoyment. She remembered the sun sparkling on the splashing water and the late afternoon shadows on the buildings. "Let's go teach English in Mongolia," Randy said.

"Where did that idea come from?" she asked.

"I met a guy near the hostel a couple of days ago—didn't I tell you? He said he had a great couple of years in Mongolia. He was in the north, near Siberia. Forests, he said, not just steppes. Shamans, reindeer herders, throat singers. There's an NGO that sends English teachers to Mongolian villages."

"Do they have art museums there?"

"I doubt it," Randy said.

"Let's go. Europe, arrivaderchi."

Randy made all the contacts; he was good at that kind of thing.

Liz first saw Randy when he was walking around the courtyard of St. Peter's, his head tilted back, enraptured by the Bernini statues. Liz had stopped, also looking up at the statues. He bumped into her. She had only been in Rome a week; it was her first visit to St. Peter's. When she said she was in awe of Bernini, they discovered they were both art history students. Randy took her hand and said, "Come, look at the alter with me." He led her into the basilica. They were silent, equally enthralled by Bernini's golden, twisting columns at the altar. They walked forward as slowly as if it were their wedding procession. Liz felt she had experienced a Shakespearean, "wedding of true minds" minutes after they met.

Randy had a charismatic intensity when describing his enthusiasms. Liz was instantly in love with a young man who could be so open about his reactions to art's beauty. Together, the next two years, they became sated, saturated, boggled, and in danger of becoming addle-brained because of all the art they had seen. They purged their minds of great European art during the stark, frozen winters in the West of Mongolia where the steppes approached the Altai Mountains.

Liz couldn't quite escape art; she fell in love with Mongolia's busy folk paintings, Bruegel-like, erotically high spirited, celebrations of the fertility of early spring. She discovered them during the first month that they spent in Ulaan Baator, and then in a provincial town. She had very little money, but she managed to purchase ten of them. When a third winter loomed, Liz knew she could not face another nine months of sub-zero temperature. She was losing interest in teaching English, even though she enjoyed helping the young people who were eager to learn.

Randy was also losing interest in teaching because he had fallen in love with Buddhism. He talked incessantly about the dharma and the history of Buddhism in Mongolia and Tibet and how it was so strong a religion it thrived underground for the forty years of Russian occupation in Mongolia. Buddhist belief was still alive, if semi-underground, also in Tibet, despite more than fifty years of Chinese repression. Randy could not love something without total immersion. He assumed Liz shared his feelings. She did not. Buddhism seemed baroque, its art was so stylized she could not find beauty or grace in the complex symbolism. If she couldn't love its art, how could she love the religion?

Randy had undertaken an intellectual journey as if he had boarded Trans-Siberia Express one night when she was sleeping. He very quickly traveled away from her into a taiga of Noble Truths. He had asked a friend from college to send him a few American books on Buddhism which was flourishing in the United States. He decided to study at Naropa in Colorado. "Buddhism in America is...I guess it's more American," he said. While Mongolians hid their religion from the Russians, Americans were studying the religion, writing books and building retreat centers. "They've been able to make it modern and under-standable in American ways," he said. "I want to know its past and its present."

"So everything's changing?" Liz said. "Here in Mongolia and in America."

"Of course. Not the original basic beliefs. Sweetheart, come with me, you'll understand."

"I don't understand now, and I don't feel what you feel—only that we don't want to spend another winter here. We belong back home." They did not talk about separating, but Liz decided to go back to Indiana and get a Ph.D. in some area of art. Art was all she knew; but knew she did not have the talent to make painting a career.

Suddenly, as had happened to her mother, when her father left after fifteen years of marriage, Liz had to think about being a woman alone in need of a career that would earn a living. "We" had become "me," although they still reached for each other's hand any time they were side by side.

As they prepared to leave Mongolia, Randy was composed and se-rene. He had a convert's complete trust that his new-found belief would lead him and everyone around him to a state of bliss. "What you chose to do to earn a living is simply incidental to the deeper pur-poses of life. All ego is an illusion," he virtually chanted.

"Your ego may be," she said. "Mine is not."

"All egos are unreal," he said with utter assurance. It was impos-sible to shout her frustration and disagreement in the face of someone so composed. They had never argued, and they did not argue now. She hoped for an epiphany about the perfection of Buddhism that would restore the harmony she had always felt with Randy. No epiph-any struck her, not even in the white-washed ruins at Ereden Zu where Grushi Khan, the Great Khan's grandson, had brought the Fifth Dalai Lama from Tibet to teach Buddhism to the royal scions who would spread it throughout their enormous empire. They stood where those almost mythological men had converted to Buddhism, and Liz felt nothing but unexpected homesickness. They would have to travel separate paths for a while. The time had come to go home.

Randy was among the majority of passengers on the Chicago

bound 747 sleeping, twisted uncomfortably, his head on Liz's shoulder. At O'Hare he would catch a plane to Denver, Liz to Indianapolis. They had truly lived one day at a time and had never talked about a future either together or apart. Together had seemed the most natural thing in the world; now each had an agenda that did not include the other.

Perhaps they were flying over the North Pole when Liz's epiphany struck. She understood that they might never see each other again. She sat frozen for some time, imagining the white expanses below that figure of an airplane on the video monitor. She grasped Randy's hand; he did not wake up. Gradually the moment thawed, the distance numbers had changed, tears were on her cheeks. The plane traversed Canada. Liz knew she would stop her tears, leave the airplane, pull up her socks and live without Randy as long as necessary, even if that was the rest of her life.

Chapter 2

Liz's appointment with Professor Toad was at 11:00. To others he was Prof. Tom Simmons, a recognized authority on American folk art. He had authored half a dozen books and wrote often for the *Journal of the American Folk Art Museum* on whose board he served. Liz respected and liked him, but she couldn't ignore the fact that he looked like a toad. Now in his sixties, soon to retire, life had been both kind and unkind to him. His wife, Cynthia, was a cook of gourmet stature and had published many food related articles in nationally read magazines. Prof. Toad ate well and often. Liz had been a guest at the dinner parties they gave for a potpourri of professors, students, artists, cooks and townspeople.

Tom Simmons was a short man who had become round, not only his body had rounded out but his face now had jowls resting upon a pile of chins. He hadn't always looked amphibian. Liz had once noticed a wedding photo in the Simmons' family room.

She asked, "Oh, is that one of your sons' wedding picture?"

"No," Cynthia laughed. "It's me and Tom. Can you believe?" Cynthia had also ballooned.

"Of course I can believe. It's a beautiful picture." Liz barely managed to keep herself from saying, "How lovely you two were." Instead she added, "It must have been a beautiful wedding."

When Liz arrived, the door to the office was half open. She called, "Hello?"

"Come in, Liz. Let me shut this thing down." He hit a couple of keys on his computer as Liz dropped her backpack on the floor and settled in the chair beside his desk. "So you've been off on a treasure hunt. Did you find the pot of gold?" he asked.

"Maybe."

"Is that a cat-that-ate-the-canary look? Tell me about it."

Liz told Tom-Toad about Geneva and her quilts. "I should have taken a camera so I could show you."

"When you go back, take the best camera you can get your hands on and make sure you know how to use it."

"I've only got a cheap point-and-shoot."

"Can you borrow a better camera from someone?"

"I don't know. Maybe."

"I'd loan you mine, but it's not digital."

This puffball of a man was always kinder than he had to be. He sat back in his chair patting his belly as happily as a pregnant woman rubs her baby bump.

"That's really nice of you. I'd need some lessons. I've never used a camera with all kinds of settings. I don't want to make Geneva self-conscious while I fuss with a camera. She was sweet, but...I don't know. Maybe she thinks I'm prying. People down there can be very private."

"Where exactly?"

"Friendship."

"What a wonderful name. I didn't know there was a Friendship, Indiana," Tom said.

"It's tiny. I'm going back weekend after next to see what's in her cedar closet."

"Boy Scout motto: be prepared. Folk art is usually seat-of-the-pants research. You really don't know what you're going to find. When I drive that annual 500 mile yard sale, I carry two cameras and my tape recorder—do you have a recorder?"

"An old one—not digital."

"Can you afford to buy new equipment?"

Liz took a deep breath. No, she really couldn't afford much. She had a small scholarship, she was teaching and working in the art library. Money was always tight. Next week she was going to the American Quilter's Society annual show in Paducah, Kentucky. She had already purchased her entry ticket, but the trip would add up: gas, parking, lunch, who knows what else? "I'm afraid I really can't."

"You should go to Radio Shack and see if you can get a digital recorder for a price you can manage."

Liz had what she thought of as her emergency Visa card which her mother had insisted she keep and use when necessary. Barbara would pay the bill. Liz appreciated it but was determined to be as independent as possible just as she had done while in Europe. "I'll check it out," she said. "Maybe I can borrow a good camera. I wish I felt confident about whether the quilts are thesis material. But how will I really know?"

"If it's a personal statement by the maker; if you feel the presence of passion. With outsider art, Cynthia says it's a gut feeling. Remember, she doesn't have to be likable. Maybe Anna Moses was a sweet old lady, but a lot of the good outsider artists have been odd balls, recluses, dirty old men, whatever."

Liz laughed. "Dirty old men?"

"What about Henry Darger with all those nubile little girls?"

"All right, all right." Liz thought of the hundreds of drawings of Darger's "Vivian Girls." Most were charming but many of the nudes had disturbed her when she sat in the American Folk Art Museum in New York City and looked through the complete works on the computer file. She had thought about Nabokov's Lolita, although Darger's girls were even younger.

The professor asked, "You say you're going to a big quilt show this coming weekend?"

"Yes. I don't think I'll find anything I can use. It's a competition. I'm sure there'll be a lot of skillful work, but I believe it's a very conventional venue."

"Well, you never know. Don't close your mind just because you found one interesting quilter. Talk to everyone. You have a shy core, Elizabeth, it's not always easy for you to talk to people you don't know. You never know who knows who or what. Believe me, Elizabeth, doing good research in the field is more important than how it gets written up. You can write something twenty different ways, but you've got to get the information. The facts and figures are important, dates and material and everything they remember about how they made their art, which, in my experience, most folks artists are pretty sketchy about. Insight into their personalities is crucial. Read artists' biographies. You've done that, I'm sure."

"I have, and I get so sick of their posturing. That's why I'm—"

"I know. That's why you got me for an advisor. But this is academe, and you're laying the foundation for a career. Unless you're thinking of returning to Mongolia."

"If Geneva isn't the quilt artist I can write about, I may do just that." She had shown Prof. Toad her "day in the life" paintings from Mongolia. He liked them very much.

"I guess worse things could happen," he said. "I'd commission you to buy a few for me."

"I'd love to do that, but I hope to stay right here in Indiana. Thank you, I've gone over my half hour."

Liz was reading and marking student papers. Most students wrote badly. Even when they had original thoughts, the papers were often ruined by haphazard spelling and minimal punctuation. She wondered how students could ignore their spell and grammar check programs so blindly? She wrote notes: *Spell and grammar check EVERYTHING!* Her job was not to teach them to write, but to ingrain a basic view of the history of art. She hated assigning papers and would have preferred giving factual quizzes, but she was required to assign four papers a semester and, of course, to read and mark every one. She did not think she was especially good at writing about art, but she cared about spelling and punctuation and tried to write clear sentences.

Liz had known since grade school that her IQ was high enough to impress her teachers and to inspire her mother to read how-to books about enriching your child's intellectual experiences. Liz had been given music and art lessons as a child. When she started college, she realized she enjoyed the history of art more than drawing and painting. Part of the reason she had gone to Europe to do her master's was because a blunt painting professor had said, "Elizabeth, you are a born academic but you are not in touch with a muse of any sort. You'll break your own heart if you try to make fine art." What a relief! She began to think of herself as a "born academic" but, when teaching, she thought she would prefer a career away from academia, in a museum or editing an art journal.

There was a knock on her door. "Who's there?" she called.

"Sam Goldman. Prof. Simmons sent me. I'm a photographer."

She opened the door. Sam Goldman looked familiar. He was tall and trim and had a stylishly clipped, very short beard-mustache. His dark hair was also clipped short. He was handsome, even hunky like a Calvin Klein ad. He had green eyes that Liz noticed immediately. She always found green eyes disconcerting in a human; they seemed appropriate only for cats. Sam had an ancient, battered leather camera case over his shoulder.

"Come in. I wasn't expecting anyone."

"Prof. Simmons told me you need to learn to take pictures ASAP." He glanced around the messy little living room as if reading her personality by her living space. Liz felt invaded. If she had known someone was coming, she'd have picked up papers and washed her dinner dishes that were on the tiny table. She felt he had found her half-dressed. Why hadn't he telephoned?

"Prof. Simmons sometimes interferes with students' lives, you know," she said.

"You don't need to learn photography?"

"No. I mean, yes, I do. I'm busy. I wish we could have made an appointment at a convenient time." She heard her voice sounding unusually peevish. The green eyes were disconcerting because he had turned his full attention on her as she spoke.

"Okay, I'll leave." He turned to go. He did not sound hurt; he was matter of fact. "Sorry to barge in."

"No, I'm sorry I sound so grumpy. It's a grumpy time for me."

"PMT?"

"No!" Oh, for godsakes, she thought. Why did men jump to the conclusion that women were totally controlled by their hormones? Liz didn't claim to be a feminist, but his response was automatic and stupid. "I'm marking student papers. I loathe it."

"Oh, yeah. I hate that too."

"You teach photography?"

"I did one semester, but it didn't work out. I have a job that takes me away too much. I apologize for the PMT. I'll leave, but I won't be able to come back for a couple of weeks and I thought you needed to do some photography this coming weekend."

"Well, I do. I didn't know Prof. Simmons would—"

"I've got this camera that actually isn't up to my standards anymore. It would probably fit your needs." He started opening the camera case.

"But I really can't afford it. I mean, I know I need something better than my Sure Shot, but I don't expect to have to do really high grade photos in the near future."

"I'm not going to use it. I'd give it to my little brother, but he breaks everything I give him, and if you need it, you know, for a couple months..." He shrugged. "You can use it. Prof. Simmons says you're trustworthy."

"Well, but..." Tom Toad was a steamroller, and this Sam guy was too, she thought.

"Here's the instruction booklet." He pulled the booklet out of the case. "And you can use this old camera case."

"You're being awfully nice but I don't feel right—"

"I'd really like to show you how to use it, just the basics really. But if you don't have time right now, I won't be able to come around again until after the first of May. I've got a job in New York—a sort of auxiliary career."

"I'll make time right now if that's what you want," Liz said. She thought about the quilts in Geneva's bedroom. Good pictures of them would certainly give Prof. Simmons an idea if they were truly extraordinary and worth writing about.

"Okay, good," Sam relaxed. Liz had the feeling he knew he was going to win her over. Well, a man that good looking probably always wins, she thought.

"Do you want some coffee?" Liz asked,

"I'm not a coffee drinker. Got a beer?"

"No, I'm a wine drinker—but I don't drink wine when I'm marking papers."

"Maybe you should. Might make it more bearable."

"It might. Do you want a glass of wine? It's just a cheap Gallo red."

"You gotta be kidding."

"My gourmet days are somewhere in the future, far in the future,

I imagine."

"Except at parties at Prof. Simmon's house." Sam said. "We met there before Christmas, but I don't think you remember."

"No. Sorry."

"That's okay. I kind of blend into the wallpaper," he said with a straight face but a tone of voice that said this was a joke. A man as good looking as Sam Goldman doesn't blend in at parties any more than does a gorgeous woman.

Liz burst into laughter and he laughed too. It was probably one of his favorite jokes, she thought.

Sam settled on her sofa and pulled out a serious looking camera that he put on the coffee table. "Actually, I'd kind of like a glass of that Gallo?"

Liz decided to have a glass of wine also. She put the glasses of wine on the coffee table. "I don't know why I don't remember you, I have a pretty good visual memory," she said.

"I think we just said hello. It was a big party. I remember you 'cause you'd just come back from China and you were wearing a blue satin thingy."

"Mongolia. It was the native costume called a deel," she said. She wore the deel because it was the only thing she had that could be called a party dress.

"You made an impression. Anyway, you're in a hurry so here's the camera."

She was not surprised the deel was memorable; not that she had especially wanted to show off. Art department parties were events for self-expression. People dressed with style and imagination; they were very photogenic. Usually someone was taking pictures. "By the way, did you take pictures at that party?"

"I probably did. I usually do. I think of those parties as gatherings of peacock and quetzals. If I remember, I'll see if I have a picture of you at the party."

"If you do, I'd like to have a copy. My mother gives me a hard time for wearing nothing but jeans."

"I'll look when I get home. Here, let me show you." He spent only ten minutes telling her how to use the camera. He was very business-like and could have been a salesman for a camera store. When his wine was empty, she poured the remainder of the wine into his glass.

"What is it you're going to be shooting?" Sam asked.

"This weekend I'm going to a big quilt show in Paducah."

"Ahh—come again."

"An annual national quilt exhibit in Paducah, Kentucky. It's down in the northwestern corner of Kentucky, about 75 miles from here."

"A quilt show? For beds? You do quilts?" He looked like she might have said she was going to a PTA finger painting party for kindergartners.

"I'm looking for someone who makes quilts in the Outsider Art tradition. Also, there are some really fine artists who do quilts— they're basically fiber artists or painters who choose to do quilts because of the texture and the tradition and the layers of meaning."

"Quilts?"

"Ignorance is rampant about quilts," she said as if he were an ignorant first year art student.

"Mea culpa. I thought they were just things some people's grandmothers make."

"Not anymore, it's a billion dollar industry in the US. I don't expect to find what I'm looking for at this particular show. I may have found my quilter already."

"You mean like a Grandma Moses of quilts?"

"Exactly. But if I can't find one, my back-up plan is to do my thesis on one or more art quilters. Believe me, it's not like the quilt on your grandmother's bed."

"Well, live and learn. So you need to photograph big things on beds?"

"They'll be on walls. I don't know how the lighting is going to be, I assume it should be pretty good."

"Better not assume. Now here's how you can adjust—" He showed her. "Also if you want to do details—will you want to do details?"

"Maybe not this weekend but eventually, I'm sure I will."

"Do you want to learn now or wait?"

"Tell me."

He showed her more about the camera. "I think that's it."

His professionalism was impressive. But a thought had come to her: Prof. Toad was said to enjoy playing matchmaker. Was that what he was up to? Had he thought they might be a match? Little did he know. Men who spent so much time on their appearance were absolutely not her kind. She liked the easy-going sort who tended to forget to get a haircut and never remembered to fold their tee shirts immediately out of the drier and wore them all wrinkled. There was something plastic about Sam Goldman, including his unbelievably green eyes. Could he be wearing green contact lenses? She wanted to ask if others in his family had such eyes, but she felt he would think she was more interested in him than she was. His ignorance and incredulousness about quilts was probably normal, but he might have at least pretended to be interested.

"I'll be going. You can get back to your papers. Thanks for the wine." Sam got up.

"You're welcome and thanks. It's really good of you to bring the camera and explain it all to me. I'll take good care of it."

"I'd love to see how your pictures turn out. Let me write down my email and phone number." He went to her desk and, without asking, wrote on the back of an envelope there.

He wants to see if I learned how to take pictures. Not interested in quilts, that's for damned sure. She did not give him her email or phone number. He didn't ask for them. She closed the door behind him as he left then picked up the empty wine bottle and the glasses. She felt as if a tiny rainstorm had been through, wetting the needy garden but dampening her. He was so handsome in such a self-conscious way, so narrowly focused on the camera and so uninterested in her interests. What a superficial person. He remembered her deel and certainly wouldn't have remembered her if she had not worn something exotic.

Men didn't flock around her; she had always considered herself ordinary looking. She was too serious in high school for boys to pay attention to her, but in college she had found most young men were friendlier. She was not a party girl, but no one was intimidated by her intelligence. Really, Tom-Toad couldn't possibly have misread her so badly; or could he? What did he really know about her, warm as he was? But maybe he wasn't match making, maybe Sam Goldman was the one person the professor knew who had an extra camera.

Liz missed having a man in her life. She had dated Jonathan, a nice painter, a few times during the winter but, after a weekend in Chicago, they had both realized the friendship was never going to be more than casual. It had devolved into occasional Dutch treat movie nights.

She had no women friends who were still on campus but had friendly acquaintances in the art department and at her library job. She was busy; busy enough to let herself say *que sera sera* as far as men were concerned. Certainly she was too busy to think about that tonight. She had a stack of these god-awful papers to mark. Hadn't anyone told these kids the difference between to and too?

Liz was up at 5:00 and out of the apartment a little after 6:00, camera case over her shoulder. She didn't have GPS so had planned her route online. On the outskirts of Paducah the traffic slowed. For the exhibit? Apparently. Soon the cars were barely crawling and when she finally got into town, within what she thought must be only a few blocks of the exhibit hall she realized that parking would be a major problem. She wished she had not come. But how else could she compare Geneva's quilts to what was considered the crème de la crème of quilting today? She had come to train her eye. This was important research. Somehow she had to squeeze into a parking space at least within walking distance of the exhibit. Finally she paid a ridiculous amount to park in a lot that was a nearly bare front yard where the owner was cleverly, and greedily, making a killing from desperate visitors.

At the exhibit hall she stood in line with crowds of sneaker clad women. Several wore jackets they apparently had made themselves with various quilt designs in eye-catching colors. The owners beamed "thank you" when strangers complimented them.

When she got inside the exhibition hall Liz saw the show was divided almost equally between an area for venders and the quilt exhibition space. The crowd was thick; many women were taking photographs, it seemed, of every quilt. Liz decided to take photos only of quilts she wanted to remember and could use for reference. She strolled slowly, trying to block out the excited comments of others around her. She needed to concentrate and look at the hundreds of quilts with a serious, art-trained eye. She began to relax and started to assess what seemed to be going on in the competitive quilting world. She jotted notes as ideas came to her, heeding Prof. Toad's advice and making use of a steno pad Marjorie gave her after their visit with Geneva.

The workmanship was consistently high quality. She overheard comments that told her the complicated, dense quilting was done by industrial size long-arm quilting machines that she briefly looked at in the vendor's area. A category of quilts had been hand quilted, but that was a small number. Most quilts on display were extravagantly quilted, sometimes to very good effect, and sometimes—much too often, she felt—overdone. Done because they could. Craft people were prone to embracing the latest gadget or innovation. What else, she wondered, has technology wrought?

Most quilts, including many with ribbons attached, were in the "pretty" category. Sweet, sentimental, pretty florals, especially the floral appliqués which usually had exquisite hand workmanship. Many geometric quilts also had extravagant appliqué, often floral also. She took a few photos and wrote in the pad, "More is too much," then she added a few question marks in parentheses. Was the craft of quilting entering a rococo period? An interesting contrast to Geneva's quilts. There were many intriguing complex geometrics, she liked them although the color choices were often not as subtle or innovative as she would prefer. Many had a pop feeling, like record covers or advertising designs. She photographed several. The crowd was so thick she gave up trying to get close enough to read the labels and so did not include the quilters' names in her notes as she wrote a little about each quilt she photographed. She hoped this would not prove to be a serious omission. She thought of these as touchstones against which to compare Geneva's work.

Liz watched the women moving like a flock of pigeons milling around crumbs, not on the sidewalk but hung on the divider walls. They were looking and talking to their friends but rarely critically. Some comments were about technique, but mostly she heard admiration and envy. Otherwise she saw utter lack of interest in the ones that were not to their taste. Only a few other women were looking as she was, quietly, alone, often going very close to the quilt to look at stitches. Liz overheard that certain areas of a quilt was "thread painting." Some of it was like pen and ink sketching; but it was done by machine.

Oh, yes, there is another technological advance. In the Middle Ages women spent hours each day stitching by hand, painting pictures in thread. Both high-born women and their maids did the work. Probably, she thought for the first time, the lazy ladies put their servants to work every free minute while the duchess or princess slipped into a little used room for an assignation with a young lover. Now women were thread painting complex birds, animals, romantic heroines in a forest, worn faces of ancestors because some of them could program their expensive machines to do this kind of stitching. Dial "rose," thread the proper color, push a button...was it that simple? She was guessing. She didn't know how some effects were accomplished. She decided to save time for the sewing machine venders who would be able to tell her how much could be done automatically.

Finally Liz found a group of abstract quilts, "art" quilts with interesting surface texture, vivid or subtle dyes and other manipulations of color, resists, overlays. A woman was exclaiming about sashiko stitching. Liz asked her what it was and made a note to research Japanese quilting techniques. She photographed many of the art quilts, some with details. She often had to stand for three or four minutes waiting for the crowd to thin so she could get a clear shot without a sweat-shirted back or a pony tailed head. The inventiveness and surface texture were exciting. Liz thought, I'll write about art quilting if Geneva's quilts were disappointing to Tom. She noted the names of the quilters whose work she especially liked; a few were familiar to her from the reading she had done during the winter.

By one o'clock Liz was tired, her feet hurt even though she was wearing her most comfortable boots. Maybe, like the majority of the viewers, she should have worn sneakers. She had felt a certain professional pride when she was getting dressed. Not that anyone would know she had come to look at the quilts with the eye of an art historian. Surely there was a cafeteria and a restroom—more than one, she hoped, for this crowd. The food area was very crowded, no surprise there. The food, typical fast food, overpriced as it always was in such captive audience venues, exactly what she expected and hated most. She bought a slice of pizza and a coke and eventually had to ask a group at a table with one empty chair if she could sit there.

"Sit right down, Honey," said an older woman with the look of a television sitcom grandmother, but with many extra unphotogenic pounds. "Take a load off your feet."

"Thanks. This is quite a show," Liz said.

"I hope you're not trying to take it all in in one day."

"Actually, I am."

"Not a good idea. You can't see all the quilts and have a good look at the vendors all in one day, not to mention seeing the Museum and the stores in town. Hancocks is a half a day in itself."

"I really only came for the quilts."

"You're not skipping the vendors!"

Liz said as apologetically as possible, "I'm actually not a quilter."

The other women at the table who had been in a conversation among themselves all stopped to look at her. "Oh-oh, a spy among us," one of the women said.

"A potential convert," said another.

"I'm an aficionado," Liz said.

"Come again," said a woman.

"Someone who loves something but is just a looker."

"Oh, well, then you're welcome," said the first woman.

"I know this is not the place to find them, but I'm really looking for someone who makes quilts just because she wants to and doesn't care if they fit in the usual categories. Someone who'd probably never enter a quilt in this show," Liz said. She remembered Prof. Toad had said to talk to people. These women looked like most of the other people at the show, solidly middle-American. But Prof. Toad also warned, "You can't tell by looking." Maybe all these rather plain women had lived very interesting lives. Maybe one among them was a true, even a trained, artist. Liz didn't think so. Yes, she had her preconceived ideas.

"I'm kind of like that," said a woman with salt-and-pepper hair who was wearing a vest she must have made herself because it was made of fabric selvages in chevron patterns. Yes, come to think of it, that was interesting and different.

"Yes, Julie, you are kind of like that. You make some things I'd never think of making," said the woman sitting next to her.

"That's true," said the woman sitting on her other side. "Like this kick you're on using selvages. I'd never have the patience to do that."

"That's okay, Anna, just as long as you keep on giving me your selvages," said Julie.

"How did you get started using selvages?" Liz asked.

"From a book I saw at a fabric store."

"Oh, other people are doing it?" said the woman next to her. "You never told me that."

"YOU never asked," Julie said. "I guess other people are if there's a book. If I used a computer I'd be able to find out." She said to Liz, "You probably use a computer, you could find out."

"Do you remember the name of the book?" Liz asked.

"Not really. I didn't think I needed to buy it. I get a lot of ideas just looking at books. I go home and jot down what grabbed me. I always figure since I've been quilting most of my life, I can make just about anything I see a picture of."

"How many quilts do you think you've made in your life?" Liz asked.

"Oh," she waved her hands in the air, "no telling."

"Do you have a closet full at home?" Liz asked.

"Nope. All I've got at home are the ones on my beds. Three beds, maybe seven or eight quilts on or folded at the foot. I give them away as fast as I make them. There's always a charity looking for donations. Making them is playing solitaire, but I don't need them and I don't have room for them."

"We know at the church if we're going to want a quilt for a raffle, we go Julie to make one," said Anna. "Everybody in church will buy a raffle ticket when they know it's one of hers."

"People love them so they must not be so odd-ball," Liz said.

"Well, I don't think so," Julie said. "I might make a Storm-at-Sea using mostly purples and pinks but then I call it something else like Clouds at Sunset."

"Do you-all know other people like Julie who just like to do their own thing when they quilt?" Liz asked.

The women thought a minute, shrugged their shoulders. "Not really. I mostly do round robins in our guild," one said.

Another said, "We're all doing pretty much the same thing."

"Well, actually, I call some of the quilts here kind of oddball," one of the women said. "I wonder how they got in this show. It's all judged, you know. You can't just enter a quilt. Remember that one up near the entrance with all the swirls and jagged lines on top? That's odd to me."

"It's one of the big prize winners," one of the women said.

"I know it is. But we're just talking. To me it's odd-ball. I'd never put that on a bed."

"'Course not, it's supposed to be put on a wall."

"Well, I wouldn't want it on any of my walls."

"What do you like, Young Lady?" Julie asked Liz.

"Actually, I really liked the one you're talking about. I guess I call it oddball—or just art."

As if the word "art" were a signal the conversation had entered dangerous waters, one woman said, "You know, we're done eating, we should probably stop taking up space here. A lot of people are looking for seats. Anyway, I've got to leave by 3:30 and I've got a lot to see yet. Nice talking to all of you." She got up and so did the woman who had been sitting to her left.

"Nice to meet you," said the second woman. "I'm with her. If I lose sight of her, I won't have a ride home."

Liz got up too. "It was nice talking to all of you," she said.

Liz found a ladies' room. While standing in the long line that she had expected, she jotted notes about the lunchtime conversation. Prof. Toad had said, "Document everything. You never know what you'll wish you had written down." She wondered what Julie's quilts really looked like. Maybe I should get a cup of coffee or something and sit down at a different table, Liz thought. Instead she decided to look at the quilts she had not seen yet and, if she had time, look at the long arm quilting machines and maybe at some of the programmable electronic sewing machines.

By 5:30 Liz's feet ached so much she wished she had aspirin with her. She was also mentally overloaded. She realized everyone was leaving and the traffic would be horrible in this small city that was not laid out for huge crowds. She decided to have dinner and leave a little later. She looked for restaurants on the way to her car. The few she found had lines extending out the door. She came to a bar that had no line. It was not the kind of place many of the quilters would go into. She found a small table and a menu that offered burgers and Buffalo wings. She ordered a beer and a burger with fries. God help me if I ever get too old and middle-aged to feel uncomfortable coming into a place like this, she thought. She pulled out her notebook and began jotting notes about how little art she saw but how much craftsmanship.

"Bet you're here for the quilt show," said the young waiter who looked like a high school junior.

"Do I look like a quilter?" she asked.

"No, but neither does my Uncle Jack."

"Your uncle makes quilts?"

"Not really. He does long arm quilting. Makes good money at it. I might even learn. If he gets enough work, he'll buy another machine and I'll work for him."

"Really? So the cottage industry is about to go sweat-shop."

"Beg pardon, Ma'am?"

"You know what I think? You ought to take my order to the kitchen first 'cause I'm hungry, and then, if you have time, you can tell me more about it."

"Oh, yeah. I'll do that. I'll get myself fired if I don't get that table's orders, too." He nodded at a table nearby.

"Don't want you to get fired. Go do your job."

Liz thought about the financial investment in long arm quilting machines. Of course, in this part of the world where farmers invested tens of thousands in tractors and farm equipment it wouldn't be strange for a woman to invest several thousand for a long arm quilting machine. She noted in her journal: Uncle Jack, not a woman making money at home. Men, she thought, traditionally take over women's work when it becomes truly profitable. Google: who wrote that? How were the machines changing the craft? That could be the subject of an article. Could it be a possible dissertation topic if she came up against a brick wall? But economics would be a drag to research. I've got to get this thesis written so I have time to explore the ideas that pop up, she thought. She was making notes in her notebook when the waiter brought her burger and fries.

"You want ketchup, relish, A1 sauce?"

"Hot sauce. Tabasco."

"Sure. So you don't quilt?" he asked.

"No. I'm going to write about it."

"Oh, a *writer*. Must be a good job."

"Actually, I'm not a writer yet. I'm still in college." He was sizing her up. "I took off a couple years."

"If you want to meet my Uncle Jack I could give him a call. He lives in town."

"You trying to set me up?" she asked.

He went for the Tabasco and came back. "No, no, I'm not setting you up; he's probably not your type. I was thinking more that if you wrote about him, it'd be good for his business."

"I think you'll be good for his business," she said.

The waiter grinned, which made him look about thirteen. "My mom says I got a head on my shoulders. But, a'course she's my mom."

"So why don't you call him? I'm curious about the work he does."

Liz's hamburger was nearly gone. She was sprinkling more Tabasco over the fries when she became aware of a person coming toward her table. "Hi, I'm Jack," he said. He gasped for breath.

"I'm Liz. Sit down and catch your breath. What'd you do? Run here?"

"Yeah, I did." He exhaled with a "Huh!" He waved toward the young waiter and mimed drinking. He took a couple of breaths. "I ran 'cause I figured the streets are jammed and I'd have a hard time finding a parking place, and it's not far."

Liz was surprised to find that "Uncle Jack" was not fifty years old as she had expected. He was about thirty and good-looking in a kid-you-knew-all-your-life kind of way. His brown hair was wavy and a little scraggly where it stuck out from his baseball cap. He had a good solid look and an easy manner. He was comfortable here; it was probably a hangout of his. He was wearing a sweatshirt under another sweatshirt hoodie with jeans. He had a diamond—or cubic zircon—stud in one ear. She thought he probably had a tattoo somewhere, maybe on his shoulder.

He gasped again. "It's not far to drive. It's a longer run than I realized."

Liz said, "Especially dodging ladies hobbling along 'cause their feet hurt."

"And they've all got big bags of stuff they bought. I hate it but I got to love it too," he said. He settled into the chair next to hers, not across the table from her.

"Good for local business. I understand you're a local business."

The boy brought a Corona for Jack. "Hi, Kev. You picked a pretty one this time."

"Your age too," Kev said.

"So he's your procurer?"

"Just for business, not for pretty women."

"Can it, Jack, I'm not Julia Roberts." She knew it was a line, but she was flattered.

"Could-a fooled me."

Liz gave him a cut-the-crap look. He changed the subject. "You're the only person I ever saw eat French fries with Tabasco."

"Everybody in Louisiana does."

"No kidding?"

"Kidding. I've never been to Louisiana. I just like hot sauce. Tell me about your business."

"I do long arm quilting. I've got a Gammill."

"I need to learn things about the quilting business, so you're perfect."

"Mr. Perfect, that's me."

"I'm at I.U. doing a thesis about quilting. I've been taking pictures and writing notes. I want to write about what you might call a folk art quilter. Not Gammill user, an old fashioned kind."

"You've got a fancy camera."

"Borrowed. The owner tried to teach me how to use it and I've been taking photos all day. I hope they'll turn out okay."

Jack took a French fry from her plate and ate it, made a contemplative face as he thought about the taste of Tabasco.

"I think mostly I'll have the back of women's heads."

"Or big butts." He had downed the beer in two long swigs. "Kev," he called to the waiter a couple of tables away. He held up his empty Corona bottle. "So you're going to become a world expert on quilts and write a book?"

"First my thesis and then I'll see if I want to write more."

"About quilting?"

"Maybe about one particular quilter."

"Someone famous? I read the magazines. Who?"

"Not famous, I don't really know if I'll be able to write about her. She's an old lady who's a friend of a great aunt of mine. She lives in Friendship, Indiana."

"Where's that?" He ate another of her French fries.

"You'd better order some of your own," she said.

"I will and I'll pay you back." Jack ate another couple fries. "Sorry. Didn't realize I was hungry."

"Do you know where Madison, Indiana is?" Liz asked.

"Kind of. Somewhere on the way to Cincinnati."

"Yeah, on the river. Friendship's out in the boonies near there."

"And what's so special about her?"

"Hey, Jack. I'm supposed to be interviewing you."

Kevin brought another beer. "Bring the lady an order of fries on me. I might as well have a burger. You got time to stay and watch me eat?"

"I've got time, but I don't like watching people talk with their mouths full."

"Oooo," Jack said. He turned to Kevin. "This lady here, is an in-tee-lectual, and she's got very prissy manners."

"Well, I'm sorry," Kevin said. "She looked nice to me."

Liz smiled; she liked these guys. It was a pleasure to talk to a couple of guys after listening to women all day. "Eat, eat," she said to Jack. "I'm letting the traffic thin out before I start home." She looked at Kevin. "I'll have coffee. You've got coffee here, right?"

"Yeah, yeah." Kevin disappeared.

"So tell me how and why you got into long arm quilting. I thought it was an occupation for women who needed to earn money working at home."

"Men need to earn money too. I got laid off when the Toyota plant closed. My dad's cousin—my second cousin who's dad's age—was one of those women you're thinking about. Always a wife and mother, never had a real job, always made quilts. She bought a second-hand Gammill. She was charging peanuts so she got a lot of business. She wasn't very good, but then it's something you can get better at pretty fast. She worked so much she threw her back out and had all these orders. Last Thanksgiving we were all together and she was complaining she couldn't find anyone dependable. I said I'd learn. You should-a seen my Dad's face. I could tell, in that very minute, for the first time in his life he suddenly thought he'd fathered a gay son."

"But you're not."

"Do you care?" For a moment Liz was confused. His question was so quick it sounded defensive. Jack had been flirting with her but suddenly it seemed entirely possible he was gay.

"Well, being gay doesn't bother me. I just had you pegged for straight, and I'm not wrong very often."

He leaned over and gave her a quick kiss on the mouth. "I'm straight, Lizzie, and I've been planning for five minutes how to get you to come home with me."

"With me honesty is a good policy." She met his eyes. They were nice light brown eyes, not a freaky green like Sam Goldman's eyes. Liz had always trusted her first impressions about people. She had not had such an immediate attraction to a man since she met Randy. Yes, they were going to his house after they finished eating. "I'd like to see your quilting set-up. I watched a demonstration this afternoon."

"So I'll go into your book?"

"Probably not my thesis. Seems to me long arm quilting is changing how quilters work. Seems like a big deal at this show."

"Don't forget the vendors fees, and some buy a lot of ad space in the magazines," Jack said.

"So you really like quilts," Liz said.

Jack shrugged. "Sorta. Some I like, some I don't. I don't see the point of cutting up big pieces of expensive fabric and then sewing them back together. But putting the quilting design on the top, that's interesting. Mostly it isn't flowers and feathers, it's more like doodling on top of a picture or pattern, and I don't have to stay in the lines unless that's what I agree to do. I haven't told anybody this, but I think I make ordinary quilts into something more interesting."

"You're proud of what you do."

"Damned right. I'm pretty good and getting better all the time." He wasn't boasting, he was stating what he believed.

Kevin had put down Jack's hamburger and another plate of fries for Liz along with her coffee. Jack added a lot of ketchup to the burger and half the fries and began to eat. "You don't want me to talk while I eat, so tell me more about this old lady you dug up."

"She's in her eighties but not dead, so I didn't dig her up." Jack chuckled at her and nodded. "I only met her once but I'm going back next weekend. Maybe she's the one I'll write about and maybe not. I hope she is, 'cause I don't want to spend months trying to find someone else. In fact, if she's not, I might not even write about quilting. I've got a backup plan." She told him about the Mongolian day-in-the-life paintings.

"Wow, I never met anybody who's been to Mongolia. Mongolia! My god it must be quite a place," Jack said. "And they're all horny in those paintings. Wow."

"It's like nowhere you've ever been," Liz said. She talked for a while about the diversity of the country: the Gobi in the south, the steppes, vast rolling grasslands with hardly any trees, the northern forests and the western mountains. "All that in one country plus dromedaries and reindeer, and horses, yaks, sheep and throat singers," she said.

"Sounds like a world within a world. What an adventure," he said, eating the last fries. "You must feel like you've got that whole strange experience inside of you just oozing out of your pores."

"I hadn't thought of it that way."

"That's what you look like when you talk about it. Plain old Hoosier on the outside, but on the inside, oh man, very exotic."

Liz smiled happily. This stranger had seen her in a way no one else had. He actually understood her feelings about having lived in Mongolia. Many people at school didn't even know she had had that adventure. Partly she hadn't wanted to think about Randy, so she didn't talk about it to many people. Something about Jack's way of looking at her, listening to her, made her feel comfortable. She even mentioned Randy, but only briefly.

Jack finished his burger and a third Corona. "Where's your car parked?" he asked.

"Close to here. In some guy's front yard. I need to get it out before he decides to charge extra."

"If you'll give me a ride home, I'll show you my machine and a couple quilts that haven't been picked up. And if you want to try your hand at using the machine, there's a quilt that I'm working on."

"I wouldn't want to mess anything up."

"I'll guide you. It doesn't take a genius."

"Kevin said you might teach him."

"Yeah, I might. That kid's been drawing monsters and droids since he was four or five; he's got talent." He waved at Kevin, who nodded.

"How many quilts need monsters on them?" Liz asked.

"If you can draw a good monster, you can do meandering designs. We may become the first two-man long arm quilting team."

"That's what interests me. Once quilting was a communal women's thing, the quilting bees when they got together, and a dozen women spent all day working on one quilt and finished it. Now the top is still made by one woman and quilted by others, but the others are strangers and it's expensive."

"Not for the hours involved and the cost of the machines." Kevin came with a single check. Jack paid it but Liz put a $10 bill in his hand.

"Nobody asked you to treat me," she said. They went out and Liz led the way to her car.

Jack lived in a little ranch style house in a neighborhood that must have been a builder's development. A pickup was in the driveway. "The garage got turned into my workshop," he said. He was about to open the front door. "The house isn't ready for guests," he said. When he opened the door a cat was standing looking up at him with its tail waving almost as happily, if not as frantically, as if it were a dog. He picked the cat up. "Baxter's my guard cat. Let me show you. Here." By the door was a mounted bell with a rope hanging down nearly to the floor. "If there's a stranger at the door, someone Baxter and I don't know, he'll ring the bell to tell me I'd better get out here."

"Really?"

"Oh, yeah. You know they talk about dogs being so smart and cats so standoffish. I'll tell you, this cat is as smart as any dog. All dogs do is bark. There's a different bell by the back door. Plus he's my alarm clock—aren't you, Baxie? 6:30 every morning he hops up on the bed and breathes in my face. If I don't open my eyes right away, he'll start patting me on the forehead just like that." He lifted the cat and held its paw and patted Liz on the forehead.

"Do you do that, Baxter?" she asked. Baxter stared at her as if insulted she would talk to him in a baby-talk voice. He put a paw on her hand.

"He's saying yes," Jack said.

"You're kidding."

"I'm not kidding. He's a genius."

In the living room magazines lay haphazardly on the coffee table along with a crumpled paper napkin and a wadded-up Wendy's paper bag. There were socks on the floor by the overstuffed chair that was clearly the TV watching spot. A handful of unopened mail was scattered on the sofa. The furniture had been purchased to coordinate. The rug and drapes were coordinated also.

"Did you furnish this yourself?"

"My wife and I—"

"You didn't say you were married."

"Were—not presently."

"Oh."

"It was short. A mistake we both made and quickly decided to correct. That's how I work. I try not to make mistakes, but if I do, I try to catch it pretty quick and correct it."

"You're a philosopher, Jack."

"Oh, I'm many, many things, Liz. I think you are too. I think we all are."

Liz smiled as she followed Jack, still carrying the cat, into the kitchen, which was much messier than the living room. There were dishes on the counter, in the sink and an icky looking pot of what she thought was probably oatmeal on the stove. They went through another door. Jack flipped on a light as they entered the former garage. The room was very neat. Cabinets and a large table ran along one wall. The long arm quilting machine was in the center on a big square of carpeting. Industrial fluorescent lights were above. The quilt in the quilting frame was blues and greens in a pattern that was probably original. At least Liz didn't recognize it. Jack put the cat down. Baxter jumped on the table beside the wall and sat like a sentry watching Liz.

"This quilter brought me three jobs over the last year. She likes to do these geometrics, but she always wants curvy quilting." Jack traced some of the finished quilting lines. "Personally, I'd like to do one—not this one, maybe the next one—with outline quilting. She thinks the contrast makes it interesting, but I think with a geometric, basic outline quilting would give it integrity and strength. Now I don't know, it's just something that I kind of think about when I'm here just working away. I wonder if women are sometimes uncomfortable—I guess some women, not all—with strong geometrics and that's why they always want the curvy lines."

"But in the past, wasn't it mostly outline and straight lines?" Liz asked.

"I don't really know. I mean I haven't studied it like you probably have."

"I've been reading quite a bit," Liz said.

"I'm also wondering if women were freer back before television told everybody what they ought to be like. Maybe they were more able to be themselves, at least in things like their favorite quilting patterns. I guess they had to pretty much conform in terms of being housewives and all that. Maybe this is all horse shit. I just have a lot of time to think when I'm working by myself."

"You can play music." She saw a sound system on a shelf with a couple of stacks of CDs.

"Oh, I do. Most of the time. Sometimes I get tired of sound coming at me. It seems to me, men, when they worked alone on a farm, things like that, I don't mean in offices or factories, I mean, you know alone like riding a tractor all day, used to be more individual, more themselves. Now the tractors have cabs and they have sound systems. Maybe I just stew in my own juices when I'm out here alone for hours. Are you bored as a snowman in a blizzard yet?"

"I'm not bored. You can't think too much, Jack. The problem comes when you don't know whether you're thinking something new or if other people have already had those ideas. Every time I think I've come up with something new and brilliant, I find out someone wrote a book about it. I think I read somewhere that there are only six ideas in the world and everything else is a variation."

"Well, that doesn't really sound likely," Jack said. "There's an awful lot of things in the world. I'd like to think I'm the first to have some of these brainstorms."

Jack was trying to impress her—yes, of course he was—and he was succeeding.

"You want to try the machine?"

"You know what? I'd rather sit down and listen to your ideas and find out just what you do, who your clients are, things like that."

They settled in the living room with beers and put a couple CDs on the player, but Jack did not talk about long arm quilting. He told Liz about his marriage, that he'd been totally overcome with Denise's sexiness and thought he wanted to own that for the rest of his life. "After we were married a month or so I realized I didn't own anything. She was just as sexy as ever in the eyes of everyone else too, including herself. She didn't sleep around while we were married—or at least I don't think so. But she was so spoiled and lazy I wound up doing everything. I'll do my share of the stuff around the house but, as you see"—he waved toward the kitchen—"it's not something I'm real crazy about."

"Right."

"But if I planned on bringing someone home, it would look better. I have quilters coming through and, you know, it's like having your mother visit. You get kind of uptight about things looking neat. Anyway, Denise was lazy. So in three minutes that's my failed marriage. You haven't gone down that aisle?"

"Nope. But I spent four years with Randy, so I have a longer track record. Two of those years were in Mongolia. We were in a ger together out west in a small village with no place else to go."

"What's a ger?" Jack asked.

"That's the Mongolian word for yurt. Yurt was the Russian word, and they don't use it. You know Russia controlled Mongolia for over forty years."

"Don't really know anything at all about Mongolia."

"Neither did I before I got there. We had a two-year contract to teach English. Actually, we got along being the only foreigners in the middle of nowhere. It worked because we were in love." Liz said the word because it was the only one that explained their relationship. "Love" felt like an ice cube stuck in her throat; would it melt and let her breathe or would she choke?

"Tell me about Mongolia," Jack said.

Changing the subject, Liz thought. She didn't want to change the subject so soon. She wanted Jack to understand that Mongolia and Randy were indivisible in her mind. She explained that Randy thrived on the hardships; the limited food choices. He managed to eat a bare minimum of mutton, the extreme cold of the winters, the intellectual loneliness. Liz hated the first winter but was inspired by Randy's excitement about braving twenty or thirty degrees below zero, breaking ice in a stream, carrying it in and thawing it for their drinking water as well as their increasingly rare baths. After the too brief, but really glorious summer, she dreaded the second winter but stayed and was sustained by the evenings they sat beside their little kerosene fire zipped into their down sleeping bags talking about the students and their families and reading aloud the fat books they had brought, *Middlemarch, Brothers Karamazov, Moby Dick* and *Auto-biography of Benvenuto Cellini*. Liz was in awe of Randy's idealism; her practical mother never had talked about idealism. To Liz it seemed a mark of superior beings: superior to those who were practical and did not coat their discomfort in the shining robes of spiritual quests.

Randy was sweet and gentle and sometimes wildly funny, sometimes almost manic trying to keep her happy in the deep gray days when it seemed the snow would never stop and the piercing wind would freeze every bone in her face within seconds of stepping out of the ger. She hated that they had to use a chamber pot because she could not manage the semi-open latrines. The ger, of course, was one round room and the curtain she rigged around the chamber pot gave no more actual privacy than if she simply closed her eyes and pretended she couldn't be seen or heard.

Liz loved being with the children, even the sullen teens who could see no point in learning much of anything, let alone English. They would be nomads like their families. But many others wanted to know about the wider world. They wanted to watch television and understand the few programs that were in English. Some families had their own televisions if they were prosperous enough to have generators or a solar panel for electricity to use the satellite dishes.

Because she so hated the living conditions, Liz began to see Randy's dedication as a crazy kind of self-castigation. He had long ago told her that he felt responsible for the death of a younger sister when he was only five and she three. He had climbed an apple tree and would not throw apples down to her but told her she would have to climb up. She climbed and got almost as high as he was when she fell. What seemed a displaced shoulder and broken wrist became a coma.

She died two weeks later. His parents told him she was in heaven and that it had been God's plan and a test for the whole family to endure their pain and loss.

He did not seem to dwell on the role he played but as the winter wore on Liz dwelt on it. She kept trying to tell Randy it was not his fault. He was just a small child who did not understand danger. In fact, the accident had been freakish. She couldn't believe in a God who would have a plan to kill a child to test a family, which seemed to be what his parents believed. Randy's growing interest in Buddhism did not help him. Nothing in Buddhism, as they both understood it, spoke of an all-powerful god who controlled individual destinies. At first Liz thought Randy's Buddhism was a veneer while he still believed in his guilt.

"We come to this world to suffer," Randy said—that was Buddha's great discovery when he left the palace where his parents protected him from the truth of the real world.

"I don't believe that we exist to suffer. We simply exist," Liz said.

"We exist for a reason," Randy said. "Maybe you exist to teach others about art."

"Maybe there's no reason for our existence," she said, partly because she couldn't think of a reason for existence and partly to make Randy stop preaching at her.

"You have to believe something."

"No, I don't. YOU have to believe something."

Their disagreement continued throughout the long cold period from March through May that would have been spring back home. When the question of a renewed teaching contract arose, Liz quickly admitted she didn't have the endurance for another Mongolian winter. She wanted a normal American life. She wanted spring, summer, autumn and a winter she could dress warmly enough to tolerate. She explained only a little of this to Jack.

She didn't mention that during the past winter she had occasionally dated Jonathan. They had gone to Chicago one weekend, to see an exhibit at the Art Institute and had dinner at a jazz club. It was a nasty winter weekend with a discomfort level only wet and windy Chicago can inflict on visitors. They spent a lot of time in the hotel sauna and the big Jacuzzi in their very nice room. She had slipped into the bubbling water and thought of the tin pan of hot water that was all she had to wash with in the ger at the same time the previous winter.

"I guess I'm your opposite too." Jack said. "I don't know anything about art. I've never been to an art museum except the quilt museum here."

Liz shook her head as if in disbelief, but for tonight it didn't matter. She liked him, liked his good sense and his self-assured sexiness.

"I think you're kind of lonely," Jack said. "It's not easy to forget something that didn't work out."

Liz looked away from Jack; she was surprised to find tears in her eyes. Jack was quiet until she said, "Working hard helps."

"I do that too," he said. They sat quietly for longer than either expected. Jack said, "You're not driving home tonight, right?" He pulled her toward him with the arm that had been draped around her shoulders. She leaned into him.

"Not if I have an invitation to stay."

"You have an open invitation for the foreseeable future. Just to show you I'm not a complete slob, I'm going to go change the sheets."

"I'll do a little cleaning in the kitchen," she said.

"No, no, don't do that. It's my mess, I'll clean it up."

"I won't touch that pot on the stove, but I'll do few dishes. I like breakfast soon after I get up in the morning."

"Me too. I think we're going to find we're compatible people."

"Let's not jump to conclusions."

Liz left at seven in the morning. She had a class at eleven. She was relaxed and feeling satisfied. "Well fucked," as a college friend called the sense of well-being she felt. This early in the morning, mist was rising off ponds in cow pastures and in wraithlike pennants above small streams. She liked being in the countryside. She would have two lane highways most of her drive. The houses and barns she passed seemed marvelously prosperous compared to the nomadic encampments in Mongolia. She felt she had not said much about Mongolia and Randy last night, but it was much more than she had said to any one since she had returned home. As she drove a swarm of memories, like the buzzing insects of Pandora's box, filled her mind, filled the car, made her gasp, feeling lightheaded. She pulled off the road onto a gravel lane that probably went to a farm she couldn't see. This is ridiculous, she thought.

She gave herself a "talking to" as her Dillsboro family would say. I have to stop thinking about Randy. I thought I was doing well. I didn't think about him last night after we stopped talking. It was good.

Jack is so different, maybe that's what I need. He's a sincere, honest man who has learned some lessons about life and love, and about the economics of having his own business. He thinks, but not about spirituality and enlightenment. Jack had her phone number and address, but something told her she would never hear from him again. If I want to see him, I'll have to call him. And I probably won't. The farther she drove the more sensible her thoughts became. She had to write a Ph.D. thesis. One thing at a time. She doubted she would drive to Paducah again, and she doubted he would drive to Bloomington.

Chapter 3

Spring came in fits and starts. Friday afternoon, when Liz had finished teaching her class and was ready to leave for Marjorie's, chilly rain fell from a sky the color of old dishwater. The little farms and towns looked empty and as disgruntled as wet cats. Liz was eager to see Geneva Gardiner. She had purchased a yard of a deep red fabric with a print of ebony African masks that she hoped Geneva would like. In spite of the dreary landscape, she smiled at the rhythmic windshield wipers and did not put on the radio. Having a new man in her life reminded her that the sun is shining behind those low clouds. She always thought of that when flying just as she always remembered Georgia O'Keefe's early painting of marshmallow-like clouds seen from above.

Jack had called twice. He wanted to come up to Bloomington this weekend even though he had a ton of work lined up. "This is one hell of a labor-intensive craft," he said to her. "I can't imagine those women quilting queen size quilts on home sewing machines, let alone by hand. They have to be crazy to put so many hours into that kind of drudgery. I think you have to be some kind of Zen master to get pleasure out of it."

"I doubt they know about Zen. Do you?"

"I just read one or two things I didn't understand and don't really remember. But you know all about it, don't you?"

"Only a little bit."

"You're so smart. If I weren't such cocky SOB I'd be totally in awe of you."

"You are, you're just not ready to get down on your knees and kiss my feet," she said.

"Wrong. I'd be very happy to kiss your lovely little feet."

He was less intimidated by her academic life than she had thought. That was part of his charm. Liz hoped next weekend the weather would be good. They had talked about camping somewhere. This trip to Friendship was exciting for what she thought she might find. Camping with Jack would be a complete change from her nose-in-a-book life.

When she looked at her pictures of the bright, pretty show quilts, Liz felt certain Geneva's quilts would be remarkable enough to write about. She hoped Geneva would relate stories behind them that would make her dissertation about one artist's working methods, whether conscious or unconscious, rather than a discussion about Outsider Art. She wanted to write a manuscript that would appeal to ordinary quilt- ers and quilt lovers she had seen in Paducah. She indulged in the fan- tasy of having a small vendor's booth at a show at Paducah where she signed copies of her dissertation, which had become a book with one of Geneva's quilts on the cover.

Ah-ah-ah, she told herself, come back down to earth. Next week- end I'll show Jack the pictures. If Geneva's quilts are interesting enough to capture his interest, that will be a touchstone. He sees a lot of the run of the mill quilts. If Geneva's are truly unusual like the three I saw, they're worth the next year or more of my life. Liz had thought these thoughts before; they recurred during her quiet unfocused mo- ments as if they were mental exercises preparing her for a long period of work just as an athlete's gym exercises prepare him for an im- portant game.

Driving these two-lane roads, with relatively little traffic invited thoughts she had pushed aside when she was busy with her class work and with Jack's flattering phone calls. Liz had Sam's camera. She was pleased with some of the photos she took in Paducah. Since Sam was away she had called Jonathan. He came over Wednesday evening to look at them. He showed her how she could enhance her photos on the computer although she protested that she did not want to distort the actual colors. He understood but lectured her about color percep- tion. She was embarrassed and defensive when Jonathan told her that her eye for color might not be as accurate as she thought it was. He had not seen the quilts. How could he know what colors they were? She thought, that's why he's a friend and not a boyfriend.

Liz had read the camera's instructions carefully, especially the indoor photography information. Geneva's house would be darker than the exhibition hall, especially on this gloomy day. Maybe the sun will come out, she thought. I'll hope and do what I can. She had found a pocket size voice recorder that was inexpensive enough not to use the emergency credit card. She had recorded part of a class she taught, cringing at her own voice just as she often cringed at her early morning face in the mirror.

However, she was nervous about her interviewing skills. She had no idea how to elicit serious thoughts and reasons for a creative act. She wrote a brief list of questions last night; today they seemed silly. Who taught you to sew? How old were you? Where do you get the patterns you use? How do you choose the fabric? She would feel like a total incompetent if she had no list at all.

She was going to stay the night with Marjorie; they would visit Great Aunt Alma after dinner this evening. When she was only a few miles from Versailles, Liz thought she should buy a bunch of flowers for Aunt Alma. Why didn't I think about this in Columbus? Where can I find flowers around here? In Versailles she asked at the gas station at the town's only stop light if there was a big grocery store in town. Yes, just down left. She bought a bouquet of mixed flowers, not beautiful but real. She had driven back to the stop light when she thought that she should have bought some for Marjorie too. Even if your hostess is some kind of cousin, you should give her something. It was getting late, Marjorie expected her by now. Liz drove around a block and went back to the grocery store. I'll show them that Mom raised me with decent manners, she thought. Families. Wouldn't life be much easier if we didn't have families? How nice if we were like, say, sea turtles, little beings equipped at birth to find our way to the ocean after the mother turtle laid the eggs and swam off. What a dumb thought, Liz told herself, I've been driving only an hour and a half and my brain is getting into giddy gear. "Chattering monkeys," Randy called the random thoughts. But Liz liked the random thoughts; if it weren't for them, she would be arriving without the flowers, arriving as if she took family hospitality for granted, as if she had no manners. If she were a sea turtle, she wouldn't have a cousin with a spare room for her to sleep in. As if rousing from restless sleep she noticed the gloomy day had cleared enough to promise a sunny day tomorrow.

"Come in, Liz. Do you have a suitcase?" Marjorie opened the front door just as Liz opened her car door.

"I've got a little bag."

"Well, bring it in. They feed people early over at the nursing home and put them to bed early. If we're going to see Mom before bedtime, we have to get over there right away and then we'll come back and eat supper. I hope that's alright with you."

"Sure," Liz said. She was happy she'd have that visit out of the way. "These flowers are for you."

"Thank you, Sweetheart, but maybe we should take them to Mom. She loves flowers, you know."

"I've got some for her in the car."

"Aren't you the most thoughtful girl in the world? That's just wonderful. Bring in your bag. I'll put these in water, and we'll march right over there for half an hour."

When they went into the nursing home the manager took the flowers to give to Alma. A line of people in wheelchairs sat in the hall waiting for the elevator. Marjorie took time to say hello and introduced Liz to each person. Liz held out her hand, briefly clasping the soft or bony old hands; at the touch each person looked into Liz's eyes, perhaps seeking recognition, perhaps wondering who she was, wondering if she was a forgotten granddaughter, or not wondering at all, just glad to see a different person, happy for a little distraction. She felt her touch was important to these people. We're all the same, Liz thought. We all enjoy having our hands held, even for a moment, even by someone we never saw before and may never see again. Marjorie had lived in or near Dillsboro all her life. She had met most of the patients over the years, sometimes as parents or grandparents of students she taught.

These women, and the few men among them, were alert; they were not tranquilized zombies. One woman was asleep and they had not awakened her, but the others simply had to wait their turn for the elevator and would return to their rooms to watch television and soon to doze off, or perhaps there was an evening washing ritual. Yes, probably. Liz thought, here I am a Ph.D. candidate proud to enter the intellectual elite of the country; and here is a layer of society that surely exists in almost every town and city in America. I am ignorant about—not just ignorant, but misinformed, even frightened of meeting them.

"Thank you for doing that," Marjorie said softly in Liz's ear. In the lounge Aunt Alma sat near an artificial fireplace with artificial logs on which artificial flames flickered. She was stroking the petals of the flowers, one by one. "Hi, Mom," Marjorie said cheerfully. "I brought Little Lizzie back."

Liz bent to kiss Alma's cheek. "Hello, Aunt Alma, it's me again."

"It's real good to see you. You're Elizabeth Jane. That right?"

"That's me. No more Little Lizzie."

"Now whose daughter are you?"

They did not stay long. It was clear that Alma was more focused on the flowers than on their conversation. Her hands slowly stroked the petals between thumb and third finger. She lifted the flowers to her face to sniff their faint, hot-house diminished scent. By the time the last of the wheelchair troops had made it up the elevator, Marjorie pushed Alma into the hall and they went to Alma's room. Liz put the flowers in a vase Marjorie took from the closet. Marjorie helped her mother get out of her sweat suit and into a granny gown. What a bent, skeletal body Aunt Alma had. She had once been a sturdy, upright woman who sometimes frightened Liz with her rigidity, especially, when Liz was very young. Aunt Alma insisted that the children clean their plates at every meal with the usual "Think of the starving children in Africa." Wrinkled skin hung on her upper arms, her breasts were long empty sacks, her stomach another sack, hiding meager contents between sharp hip bones. This is why young people do not visit nursing homes, she thought. Unlike barren trees in the winter, an old human body is ravaged by the weather of their life. What remains is a person who feels and touches beautiful flowers and enjoys the satiny petals, the pretty colors, wishing for a vaguely remembered scent.

The streetlights had come on, the rain had stopped hours ago but a mist hung in the air. It felt like a moist towel against their faces as they strolled the few blocks to Marjorie's house. "Hello means a lot to all those poor old souls," Marjorie said. "You know, sometimes I'm lonely but I have friends my own age I can call or visit. Most of those people are the sole survivors among their contemporaries. Their husbands died a long time ago, they're well over that, but their friends have been dying one by one. Their sons and daughters mostly aren't around."

"Does everyone move away?" Liz asked.

"Oh, some live close enough to visit often, but most are far away and others just don't come. It's a heavy kind of loneliness. They're often confused about who's dead and who's alive." Liz simply nodded, which Marjorie probably didn't see. She went on, "When I'm walking home, like we are now, I tell myself I'll walk my own sadness into the ground between the home and my house and not take it in the door with me. I do what I can when I'm there, but I have my own life to try to enjoy. That's how it's got to be."

"You're very wise."

"I wouldn't call that wisdom, I'd call it saving my sanity."

While they ate dinner Liz asked Marjorie about Geneva. "What's her life story?"

Marjorie chuckled, took a school-teacher posture, and smiled as she declaimed, "Listen, my children, and you shall hear the wonderful story of Paul Revere."

Liz laughed. She and her mother used to drive home from family gatherings mocking Marjorie's habit of quoting lines of poetry. "But what about Geneva Gardiner?" she asked.

"I asked Mom a couple of times this week," Marjorie said seriously. "She said Geneva was a lot of fun when they were young. They went to dances together and shared secrets about the young men they liked. Mom got married first and Geneva worked for a while in Aurora as a housekeeper and cook in a judge's house. He was a widower and didn't have a clue how to do anything for himself. Geneva used to tell Mom how dumb a smart man could be. I think Geneva will tell you about that and about marrying Alfred when he came home during World War II. You're going to take notes, I assume."

"I've got a new recorder," Liz said.

"You don't have a notebook?" Liz shook her head. "You need a notebook. I think I've got a couple steno notepads I used to use for school notes. You'd better take one." She went to her roll top desk and quickly found an unused steno pad.

"It's the 21st century, Marjorie. People don't use those anymore. Stenos are extinct as the stegosaurus."

"So I'm a stegosaurus; I use steno pads. I want you to have one. You can't trust these mechanical things. What if you think you've recorded it all and something malfunctioned? Now, I hope you don't mind watching Jeopardy, it just about kills me to miss it."

The morning was sunny and warm, the trees were turning delicate chartreuse, and the fields were bright green. Yesterday's rain washed the countryside and turned it as green as Ireland is said to be. Geneva opened the door the minute they pulled into the driveway. She came out onto the little porch, looking as perky and eager as the little Scottie dog Liz remembered. It was the only dog she had ever had. Scottie, the uninspired name her mother chose, always greeted her with the same bright eyes and tail wagging eagerness. Geneva was wearing a print dress and a fleece cardigan that looked new. It was white with an embroidered robin on the upper left side.

"I see you're good as your word," Geneva said.

"I try to be," Liz answered. She took Geneva's hand for a moment. "How have you been?"

"You gave me a fit of insomnia. I haven't slept decent since you were here last." She sounded peeved and accusatory.

"I'm sorry. I had no idea." I'm off to a bad start, Liz thought.

"Now, don't take it that way. I'm just saying I'm not used to people paying attention to me, you know. It threw me off kilter just to think anybody was interested in what my quilts look like. I don't make them to please anybody but the African people that'll get them one of these days." She held the door open as they went into the living room.

"I found a piece of African-y fabric," Liz said. She gave Geneva the plastic bag with the red and black fabric in it.

"Well, my goodness, you didn't have to go do that."

"I was curious about what might be available in a fabric shop. There were three or four others, but I liked this best."

Geneva unfolded the fabric and looked at it. She nodded. "I'll find a use for it. Thank you kindly." She folded it as it had been folded and laid it over the arm of a chair.

"You're most welcome. Have you met some African people?" Liz asked.

"Well, I met a couple, a man and a woman, who come over here to visit some churches and stayed with Rev. Redburn, oh, quite a while ago."

"When was that, Geneva?" Marjorie asked. "I don't remember any Africans visiting around here."

"It was 'fore Rev. Wheeler came. Oh, probably 'bout eight or ten years ago."

"Do you remember what country in Africa?" Liz asked.

"One of those countries in the south part where the black people had such a hard time with the whites running the show. I believe they've got it sort of straightened out now, but they're still not doing very well as I understand. I haven't heard anything about it for a while. I'll have to ask Reverend Wheeler about it again one of these days."

"Where's your notebook, Liz? You ought to be writing this down," Marjorie said.

"What do you mean she should write it down?" Geneva asked, quickly suspicious.

"She wants to understand what makes you tick, Geneva."

"I thought you were interested in my quilts."

"I am." Liz said. "But you made them, so I'm interested in you."

"Well, maybe there's nothing to be interested in. Come on in the other room now and I'll show you my quiltin'. Shame to be indoors on a day like this with the warm sunshine. I just lap it up like a turtle that's been in the mud all winter. If you weren't here, I'd be out workin' my garden. The boy come and plowed it a couple days ago."

"Probably too muddy from yesterday's rain," Marjorie said. "I don't have mine turned over yet. We could still get a serious frost, you know."

"I know that, Marjorie. But I just love pokin' seeds into the ground. I could plant my potatoes, but it's a week 'til the dark of the moon."

"You still plant by the moon?" Marjorie asked.

"Root vegetables I do. Potatoes and yams, for sure. Now come into my extra room."

"You should be making notes," Marjorie whispered as they let Geneva go on through the house ahead of them.

"I don't want to be rude."

"Her bark's worse than her bite," Marjorie said into Liz's ear.

In a room behind the kitchen an old sewing machine sat in its console table. There was a cutting table with rulers, scissors, pencils and a cutting mat on it. An ironing board held an iron so old it didn't have a steam function.

I have to take a picture of this, Liz thought. I'll wait until she gets comfortable with me. "I don't see a rotary cutter. Do you use one?" Liz asked.

"I just can't get used to those things. I gave up tryin', they scare me a little with their sharp blades," Geneva said. "I like my scissors. I got half a dozen pairs and I keep them sharp myself with a whetstone."

"A whetstone? Could I see it? I've never seen a whetstone."

"Kids today don't know anything," Marjorie said to Geneva.

Geneva wagged a finger at Marjorie. "Now you be nice to your cousin." Marjorie laughed.

Geneva opened one of two sets of doors in the closet that made up one wall. It had been recently added. The closet was full of fabric in produce baskets and in a stack of shoeboxes. From a basket Geneva took a small smooth stone. "Nothin' to it, it's just the kinda stone it is."

"Flint?" Liz asked.

"No, not a flint, I forget what the name is. I've always just called it my whetstone. Use it on butcher knives too."

"So this is your fabric closet?" Liz asked. "You're all organized."

"I like things neat. People gave me all this material. They give me all kinds of stuff, and some of it I might never get around to usin', some of it I've probably had as much as twenty years." The closet was carefully arranged, larger lengths of fabrics were folded neatly while smaller lengths were divided roughly by color and arranged in the baskets. A clear plastic gallon size baggie held strips and another had odds and ends of fabric. There was a basket of spools of thread and a glass jar with folders of needles in it. Geneva didn't say what was in the shoe boxes. Liz wanted a picture of this closet too. She wanted to go out to the car and bring in the camera, but she didn't feel comfortable interrupting Geneva yet.

"Are those things that are started but not finished?" Liz asked about a pile of what looked like quilts in progress.

"Mostly quilt tops or parts of quilt tops people have given me," Geneva said. "They think I'm like a boa constrictor that'll eat anything. But I won't. If I don't like 'em, I won't work on 'em. I'll leave 'em, and once in a while somebody comes around who likes something, and I'll give a few away."

Marjorie laughed. "Good for you, Geneva. I'm sure you've got enough ideas in your head, you don't need other people's mistakes."

Geneva nodded vigorously. "When I'm makin' a quilt, I want it to be MY quilt, not somebody else's bad idea. I got bad ideas enough in my own head." She chuckled at herself.

"Are you picky about the fabrics people give you too?" Liz asked.

"Not much. I use just 'bout anything that's woven. If people give me those knit things, I just tell them to take them back home. And, a'course, I don't like the loose wove stuff or the slippery stuff. Some people think any kind of junk can go into quilts. They don't realize it's gotta stand up to wear and washin'."

"And so the quilts are over here?" Liz asked, nodding toward the other set of closet doors.

"Yeah. You guessed right. That half's a cedar closet. I had Ben, my boy, line it with good cedar. Told him that was what I wanted for my eightieth birthday, and he come through. He always was a dependable boy." She opened the closet door. The faint scent of cedar had a pleasant spiciness. Most of the shelves were full of neatly folded quilts. A top shelf was empty and part of the next to highest was also empty. The colors were a jumbled rainbow. The patterns were not immediately recognizable.

"Oh, that's wonderful," Liz said. "That's so beautiful. How many? Do you know?"

"No, I don't know. I don't keep count. Whenever there's a fire or tornado around here, I generally give the family a few quilts dependin' on how many's in the family, a-course. Those on the bottom shelf are mostly for people 'round here. Part of them were tops started by other people, kind-a pretty things like I used to mostly make. People like'm better than they like my African ones, so I try to keep half a dozen on hand, then I can use up some-a the material I don't much like for the backings—you know, the kind with funny-paper kind of designs or baby animals, things like that."

"Well, that's real nice of you, Geneva," Marjorie said.

"I know what people think-a my quilts. They think I'm a crazy old lady makin' crazy lookin' quilts. They don't like the colors I like. But I'm not makin' them for people 'round here, so I don't care what they think."

"Could I look at some of your African quilts?" Liz asked.

"Well, I think that's what you come here for, isn't it?" Geneva said, her voice tart. She seemed to be talking to a child who had no common sense. I have to get used to her mannerisms, Liz thought.

"I've got a camera in the car. Can I take pictures of the quilts as we look at them?"

"What fer?"

I didn't know it was going to be this difficult, Liz thought. She explained, "My professor wants to know that I've got something real to write my thesis on."

"He doesn't trust you?"

"It's his job to make sure I'm writing about something that's worthy of my degree. He's only partly sure that quilts are interesting in the first place."

"Men don't pay no 'tention to quilts," Geneva said. "You can go and get your camera, but I don't like pictures of me."

"Oh, I really wanted one—"

"To prove I'm real and not a machine?" Geneva asked, sounding more amused than irritated now.

"Really to prove you're not a whole church full of quilters. If I take a picture of your closet, he might say one person couldn't do all that by herself."

"I haven't had a bit of help," Geneva said proudly.

"I'll tell him exactly that. I'll be right back." Liz went to the car. She took a couple of moments to jot some notes in the steno pad and wondered whether to bring it in. Yes, she thought. I can say I want to write down the names of the quilts as I look at them, in fact that's what I should do.

Liz took a few more breaths and stood a moment with her face up to the sun. She liked being on a farm far from any sizable city. It was very quiet until she heard a rooster crow. Liz saw several chickens near a building beyond some flowering fruit trees at the end of the driveway. A real farm, she thought, the kind that hardly exists now. Geneva must go out at least once a day, rain, shine, snow or sleet and feed the chickens and gather eggs. What a quaint thought. Eggs, she had read, now come from industrial farms—poultry sweat-shops where chickens are forced to live in cramped unhealthy conditions for merciless robber barons, or so some ecology journalist wrote. This farm was as exotic as had been nomadic ger life in Mongolia. Farms like this are the stuff of American nostalgia and sentimentality. She took a picture from where she stood. The flowering trees were beautiful. She walked toward the chickens and took more pictures. She took a picture of the house from an angle where the car could not be seen.

When she walked back to the porch, Geneva was standing there watching her. "Are you one of those city girls never seen real live chickens before?" she asked.

"I've seen them when I was younger and come to visit Aunt Alma. I was thinking about how you have to go out in every kind of weather to take care of the chickens."

"A-course I do," Geneva said. "Somebody's got to take care of them, and I'm the only somebody around here."

"But what about the rest of the farm?"

"My neighbor rents it on shares. It's not a lot, but something."

"It must be a hard life."

"Well, once it was a lot of work, but I wouldn't say 'hard'. Hard sounds like somethin' you hate doin', somethin' that wears you down. It wasn't never like that. It was what I wanted to do, honest work, honest tiredness when I went to bed at night. My own good eggs for breakfast and my own chicken for Sunday dinner. When Alf was alive we had cows and our own milk. Never did pay attention to those that said we should boil all our milk. We drunk it like it was meant to be, tasted a long sight better than any of the store bought milk. Tasted honest, tasted of cow like milk ought to do."

"I'm sure I've never tasted it."

"Don't 'spect you have. You and a lot of others are missing out on more than you'll ever know," Geneva said. "Are you comin' in to take pictures of my quilts or what?"

"I'm coming in. But it's so nice with the sun and the trees and the chickens and the house and...and everything. Thank you for letting me come visit."

"Well, aren't you a sweet young thing? 'Course you got no idea what country life is like."

"I might have more idea than you imagine," Liz said. She was about to mention her time in Mongolia, but it felt defensive, or like bragging. She didn't want to seem different or sound proud of having traveled. She just wanted to be Alma's great-niece who was interested in quilts.

Marjorie came to the door. "What are you doing, dawdling out here?" Liz had forgotten about Marjorie. "I'm getting curious about your quilts," Marjorie said to Geneva.

They went back to the sewing room. Geneva pulled out one quilt after another. The colors were vibrant, the mixtures of prints, florals, stripes, plains, geometrics were eccentric and sometimes clashing. Many patterns were traditional, some of the simplest, many were four- or nine-patch quilts, rail fence, trip around the world, log cabin. Many were just triangles, but the triangles tended to be of mixed sizes often causing a sense of disequilibrium. Marjorie helped Geneva hold up the quilts for Liz to photograph and then refold them. Liz wondered if she was getting the camera's settings right. Sam had assured her she couldn't go too wrong and that the computer programs the pictures would be fed into could adjust some of the mistakes she might make. Liz noted traditional names. Geneva didn't give her quilts individual names. Liz made notes about pattern and color in order to identify them correctly later.

As the quilts were unfolded Liz remembered walking through a museum—where? Rome, the Louvre, the Met—looking at one Roman portrait bust after another, all the same size, every one a true individual. The effect the quilt variations had on her was a similar wonderment and awe. They had looked at only about a quarter of the pile when Geneva began to sound tired of offering information. "I think we should take a break," Marjorie said. "I'm getting worn out. Geneva, would you mind if I put some water on for coffee or tea?"

"Oh, I'll do it. I've been a bad hostess, not offering you-all any-thing." She went into the kitchen.

"You're wearing us all out," Marjorie said quietly to Liz.

"Oh, god. I'm sorry. I'll fold that."

"The prints and colors are so mixed up," Marjorie whispered.

"I LOVE that she does that."

"Is this really what you were looking for?" Marjorie was incredu-lous.

"Exactly. It's not matchy-matchy. There's a gadjillion books for quilters telling them how to match colors, just so. No personal state-ment. I'll try to explain later."

"Well, I think they ought to be pretty, so I guess I just don't get it." Marjorie said. She went into the kitchen to help Geneva.

Liz took pictures of the sewing room, especially of the closet with its stacks of quilts and of the old sewing machine. She quickly jotted more notes in the notebook. All were double bed size. Most were quilted with long stitches, only 3 or 4 stitches to the inch and many were simply tied. All were brilliant combinations of colors with quite a bit of black and red mixed in with orange, green, blue, purple. It wasn't haphazard, Liz thought. Geneva's sense of balance and color were primitive or naïve, yes, but with the élan, the *joie de vivre* that the untutored often had. Geneva had found her style.

Liz was eager to show Prof. Toad the pictures. She wondered what Jack would think of these quilts. He'll probably hate them. What will Sam think? Well, I only care what Tom Simmons thinks. I hope I'm not wrong. No, I can't be wrong. I'll find some choice phrases to de-scribe these quilts. I'll think about what to tell Prof. Toad as I drive home tomorrow.

First things first, Liz thought, I need to interview Geneva. I hope she's not too tired to talk to me. I hope she'll let me record her. And I really need a picture of her. Liz had tried to sneakily take some pic-tures including Geneva as she and Marjorie folded and unfolded the quilts.

"Tea's ready," Marjorie called.

"I'm having a love affair with these quilts. I don't want to take my hands off them," Liz said as she went into the kitchen. "I didn't want to mess up your arrangement, so I left them on the cutting table, but I'll put them on the shelves properly if you tell me where."

"Oh, shoot, they don't have no order. Just so they're folded square." Geneva poured steaming water into cups with Lipton tea bags in them.

They sat around the kitchen table. "Do you have a big family?" Liz asked.

"Not really. I had the three kids, and they weren't too productive, just got five grandchildren and one great-grandson so far. Ben's the only one of mine left. Myra died in a car accident fifteen years ago. Allie died of breast cancer three years ago."

"Oh, that's sad," Liz said.

"A mother never wants to outlive her children," Geneva said. "I'm glad I still got Ben and Robina. They're close by and real good to me."

Marjorie took over the conversation as if to tell Liz to relax and let Geneva relax, too. They talked about local people. Liz was drawn back to sitting around small low tables in a ger with Mongolian families, drinking their strong tea lightened with camel's or horse's or sheep's milk. Yes, she had had unpasteurized milk but never that of cows. Life is funny. She thought about telling this to Marjorie and Geneva, but the experience came from a different world. If I could get along there, I can interview one nice old quilter here in Indiana, Liz told herself. Stop procrastinating and get started.

When there was a slight pause Liz asked, "Geneva, can I ask you about how you learned to sew and all that kind of thing?"

"Thought you'd want to know," Geneva said. "I've been thinkin' back, can't hardly 'member not sewin'."

"Would it be all right if I turned on a recorder?"

"You want to put me on tape?"

"They don't use tape anymore. It's just a little gadget that's electronic. My advisor can be very fussy about things." She thought Prof. Toad could take the blame, everyone understood teachers wanting students to get things right.

"Well, I guess it's okay." Geneva tried to sound resigned, but Liz thought she heard anticipation and pleasure in Geneva's tone.

"You know, it's not a big deal." Geneva said. "I mean there's nothin' special 'bout what I'm doin'." She sounded matter of fact;

there was no false modesty in her voice. She wants to talk about it, Liz was certain.

"So you don't really remember when you started sewing?"

"No, but I know it was my gramma taught me, not my ma. My ma wanted nothing to do with sewin' a-tall. She didn't like housework, cookin' either. I guess she was a tomboy who never grew out of it. Always wanted to be out in the barn with the animals or out in the fields. I had two older sisters and they were doin' most-a the housework an' cookin' by the time they were six or seven. I always had to do my share. My sisters saw to that. Gramma decided I should be the one that learned to sew 'cause there was always stuff needin mendin' or makin'. A-course that left me with the washin' and ironin' too but I never minded. I always liked the feel of cotton in my hands. We didn't have much that was fancy. I mean, I don't even 'member when I first felt silk, an' I wondered what was so special 'bout it. I thought it was too thin to be good for much of anythin'. But they told me it didn't have-ta be thin like what I saw, just like cotton can be woven thin or thick. I used to wonder how people learn all these different things."

"So your mother and father worked the farm and the girls did the housework," Marjorie said.

"There wasn't any boys. Ma said she was allergic to housework. She raised bees for a while, too."

"Do you remember the first quilt you made?" Liz asked.

"Oh, yes. First one was a Christmas present for Evie, my oldest sister. It was for her hope chest 'cause she said she had so much housework she'd never be able to make anythin' for her hope chest. Maybelle was the jealous type, she was the middle sister, so I made one for her after that. Gramma helped me and I even quilted them both by hand. I can still see the one for Evie—it was blue and white squares, really just squares, but I embroidered a blue flower in the middle. Maybelle got a red and white quilt and fussed that she wanted a flower too, so I had to add a rose. She always kind-a bullied me and I kind-a buckled under."

"Is either one of your sisters still alive?" Marjorie asked as if to prove that she was still part of the conversation.

"No, seems like I'm outlivin' just 'bout ever'body," Geneva said.

"Did everyone live near-by?" Liz asked.

"No, I'm the only one stayed around, that was 'cause of Alf a-course. This was his folks' farm, and he took it over when they got poorly. We raised the kids in the old farm house; this here house is new—or it used to be new." She chuckled. "I guess everythin' used to be new. Tornado hit the old house"

Marjorie said, "I don't remember that."

"Big old tree came down right on top-a it. By then only Ben was still at home, so Alf built this house. Used a lot of wood from the old one, in fact. Alf was real handy and a lot of the folks from the church helped."

"Like an old-fashioned barn raising?" Marjorie asked.

"No, they'd just come give him a hand when they could. It's a blessin' livin' in a small place where you have good people around about. I've been blessed all my life that way."

"Was Alf in the Second World War?" Liz asked. She had finished her tea and was taking notes, as she'd been told to do, "just in case."

"Sort-a but not really. He was drafted and went off to boot camp—that was before we were married. He was 'bout to be shipped overseas when he was ridin' in a jeep that overturned. Messed up his left leg and foot and the doctors didn't treat it right. He wound up havin' three toes amputated. That wasn't so bad, but somethin' 'bout his knee and ankle joints was wrong. He never could walk the same as everyone else. So he got sent home after less than a year and we got married and set to farmin' his Dad's place, and havin' children too, a-course."

"I'll bet you had a hope chest full of quilts by then," Marjorie said.

"I did, and I 'spect you can ask if Alma 'members me sittin' and sewin' a lotta times when she came to see me."

"What was it like when you were first married and living here?" Liz asked. "Were you living with your in-laws?"

"Yeah. That wasn't always easy. Alf's father was a narrow-minded man, couldn't ever have much of a conversation with him. Alf was a talker like his mother, thank the Lord. It was like a different world too. Little farm like this, there wasn't any of the machinery people have now. We started out with a team of horses. Work was hard, even though I had my mother-in-law's help—or she had mine's what it came down to."

"You got along with each other?" Marjorie asked.

"Most of the time. She had bad asthma and then she got diabetes. Alf's Dad was poorly by then, too, and, a-course, Alf was partly crippled, though he got around good. He never complained even if I knew sometimes it was hard on him. You know, the Lord gives you hard years, but sometimes He mixes the sweet and bitter, and when it's all over you 'member a lot-a the sweet and forget a lot-a the bitter. When you have a lot-a work to do you just get so dog-tired, you do what you've got-a do and don't have time to feel sorry for yourself—least that's how I 'member it. It was a long time ago. I guess some people 'member good an' some 'member bad." Geneva gazed out the window as if she were watching a parade of memories.

"Oh, I've been talking your ears off," Geneva said. "You must be gettin' real tired of listenin' to me."

"No, I'm not tired at all," Liz said.

"Well, if I don't move my body and tend to my bladder, I'll be real sorry," Marjorie said.

"Bathroom's the door that's closed down there," Geneva said.

"Don't tell her any juicy secrets while I'm gone," Marjorie said to Geneva.

"Now's the time to tell me the secrets about Aunt Alma that she never told Marjorie," Liz said with a smile.

"Oh, Alma's got a secret or two, but she'll have to tell them herself."

"I'm afraid she doesn't remember much these days," Liz said.

"Well, that happens to a lot-a people. Mostly, you know, we 'member those early things. I got a storehouse of memories from the early times of my marriage. They got nothin' to do with quiltin', so I'm not 'bout to bother you with them. I loved my beautiful daughters, least I thought they were beautiful, and I made the prettiest clothes for them I could. There was a time I tried to make them new church dresses once a month. I was a real good dressmaker back then, and I loved dressing them up."

"I'll bet they loved it," Liz said.

"I think most of all I loved seein' them lookin' pretty and hearin' the compliments. Pride—that was the sin I had most of. Good thing we were Methodists and not Catholics, or I'd'a been in confession with the same sin week after week." Geneva gazed out the window and her face became younger with a private smile. Liz felt she was seeing a young Geneva. "Oh, but they looked so pert and pretty dressed up for church.

"Then they grew up and moved away and got jobs and then got married and a-course, got to buyin' their clothes in the city stores. That's when I really got into quilt makin'. Oh, right along I made what was needed for our beds, mostly from the scraps of the dressmakin', a-course. I know it ain't so anymore, but to me quiltin's 'bout usin' up the scraps. That's why I'm never too proud to take what people give me, even the little cuttin's."

Marjorie returned. Before sitting down, she stretched her arms up above her head as if she wanted to touch the ceiling then twisted her body left and right. "If I don't move it, I'll lose it," she said as she sat down at the table.

"What did you use for batting back then?" Liz asked.

"Oh, mostly old sheets and blankets. Then the stores started sellin' proper battin'. I 'member once when I was just a schoolgirl Gramma got a-holt-a some cotton waddin'. Not very nice stuff, had little stems and seeds in it and you had to sort it out and beat it into a batt for the quilt. Wasn't worth the trouble you had to go to."

"Do you have any very old quilts left?" Marjorie asked.

"Oh, no, everythin' got used up. Not a scrap left."

"What kind of patterns did you use?" Liz asked.

"Oh, there was patterns in some of the papers for a while, and the ladies' magazines. Sometimes I used them and made my own patterns out of cereal boxes or whatever was around. Alf made me some nice squared tin patterns. I still got 'em and I use 'em once in a while."

"Templates?" Liz asked, partly because she wasn't entirely sure what the word meant.

"Yeah, that's what you call 'em. Different size squares and triangles. You know the Dresden plate was real popular back then, or fans, you know, half, or just a quarter of a Dresden plate. I had lots of flower prints and they were good for that kind-a quilt. I made a whole bunch and Alf made me tin patterns in a couple-a different sizes."

"Did you sew by hand or on the sewing machine?"

"Oh, on the sewing machine. I never had time for much hand sewin'. I had a lot of work to do, even after the girls were gone away.

Ben stayed with us 'til he got married. Now he lives up between Versailles and Osgood. Been there near fifty years—told me that a week or two ago."

"How's Ben's wife?" Marjorie asked. "I always forget, it is Roberta?"

"Robina. She's partly crippled with the rheumatism. Says she's got pain most of the time, most everything she does. She complains a good bit. Makes Ben feel bad but all he can do is take her round to doctors, and they just give her more kinds-a pain pills. Once you get all crippled up you ain't goin' to ever get uncrippled."

"You've been a lucky woman, Geneva," Marjorie said.

"That I have. I've been blessed with good health. I think I'm goin' to be like that wonderful one-horse shay we had to learn to recite about back in grade school. I'll just keep going until one day ever'thing'll give out at the same time. And that'll be the end of me."

Marjorie stood and took a pose as if she were a school child asked to recite, hands clasped at her waist, her shoulders back, chin up. Liz laughed. Marjorie was undaunted. "I'll only tell you the last lines: It went to pieces all at once/ All at once and nothing first/ Like bubbles do when they burst/ the day of the Lisbon earthquake." Liz applauded, Marjorie did a tiny curtsey.

"Aren't you something?" Geneva said. "You shouldn't laugh at your elders, Liz."

"She and her mother do that to me all the time," Marjorie said. "Now we're going to have to end this visit and let you have some rest."

Liz wanted to ask many more questions. She asked if she could come back tomorrow afternoon after church, but Geneva said between church and going to dinner with one of the families she would be gone most of the day.

"I don't want this young woman to tire you out, Geneva," Marjorie said. "I think you'll just have to make another trip, Liz, or stay over 'til Monday."

But Geneva said it would be fine if Liz wanted to come back about 3:30 tomorrow for an hour or so.

Chapter 4

In the car, pulling out of Geneva's drive, Marjorie said, "You don't know about these old ladies, Liz. They're proud and they don't like to show they're getting tired. Just having company can wear out some-one Geneva's age, anything that changes her usual routine. I imagine she takes a nap most afternoons. I'm sure she spent all of yesterday cleaning that house."

Liz felt like she used to feel when Marjorie corrected her English, embarrassed and irritated that she was expected to live up to a stand-ard she didn't know existed.

They were soon out of town and climbing the winding up-hill road that took them out of the valley that cradled the town of Friendship. Marjorie said, "None of her quilts are what I'd call pretty. I just don't see what you think is special."

"Pretty is good but in fine art it's not as important as originality, the artist's perception." No one in her classes had ever asked that question. "I'm not looking for 'pretty,' I'm looking for what makes these quilts different. To me the colors are more alive and interesting than if they were in combinations that most people would call pretty."

"I guess she thinks African people have different taste than we do," Marjorie mused.

"I'll ask her about that tomorrow. I'm afraid I really don't know how to go about this interviewing job. I need to know everything about her quilting."

"Don't ask everything at once. Let her tell you at her own pace. I guess if you're going to write about her, you'll be coming back."

"My thesis has to be about something original, to me what Geneva does is what's called Outsider Art. It's usually made by someone who has not had academic training. Someone who makes things. Sometimes it's paintings, sometimes they build things, carve thing. They make whatever gives them pleasure even if their neighbors don't think they know what they're doing. Geneva believes that the people she wants to give her quilts to probably have a different idea of pretty than we do. She might be wrong, or she might be right. But she's making these quilts because she wants to do something meaningful. It makes her happy, and her friends respect what she's doing because it's being done out of kindness, even though they don't like her quilts. That's why I think she's a good subject for my thesis. I've looked at articles and books about Outsider Art. Usually the person is a loner, sometimes people think he's nuts. It's usually men. Maybe some of them are nuts, but they aren't hurting anyone. And Geneva truly wants to help people."

"Thanks for telling me that, Liz. I didn't know there was a category like that. So do you think your professor will let you write about Geneva and her quilts?"

"It's my job to convince the committee. If I convince my advisor, I'm almost home free. I think I can, if my pictures turn out decently. I think I told you, his wife collects Outsider Art, mostly paintings made by Caribbean people, especially Haitian. She sells it for those artists because they really need the money. In a way she's being kind like Geneva is."

"Do you think people would buy Geneva's quilts?"

"If I wrote about them, maybe. But she wouldn't sell them. Or I don't think she would."

"Well, if that means you need to come back more times to talk to her or take pictures, you can always stay with me. I've got that room and the only time it's not there for you is when my grandkids are around and even then, they could sleep in the living room. Last summer the oldest two slept out in the yard in a tent just 'cause they wanted to."

"You know what? I would be happy to sleep out in a tent. I love camping."

"Good thing, the strange places you go," Marjorie said.

"I couldn't have done as much traveling as I did in Europe if I hadn't had a sleeping bag." Some summer trips with Randy they camped on hiking trails. She knew remembering some of their nights camping would bring tears to her eyes.

"I sure don't understand the point of writing a whole long thesis about Geneva's quilts even if they are Outsider Art. It's not art you are going to make, is it?

"There's an academic field of quilt study now and quite a few museums show quilts or other needlework. So there's jobs to be had and not much competition yet. That's one thing. Plus I just plain like them."

"But you don't know how to sew."

"I can hem up pants or skirts if I need to."

"That's mending, not sewing. Seems odd to me to study something you don't know how to do."

"Most art historians can't paint a good picture. It's the old thing, if you can't do it, you become a critic or a historian."

"Or a teacher," Marjorie added. "You know, I used think I'd write things, even poetry, maybe. But I found out I wasn't any good at it."

"I thought you just loved teaching."

"I did love it. Loved the kids even though seventh and eighth graders are some of the hardest. And they got harder every year. I'm glad I'm out of it now. You bear right up here."

"Thanks, I thought I should."

"Sorry, I didn't mean to be right-seat driver."

"That's all right. I think I should practice my interviewing on you."

"No, I'm not very interesting. Maybe you should interview Mom. She's losing a lot of her memory, but the right question will get her going about her school days or when she and Dad were seeing each other. Some days she can talk you right into the ground. Sometimes I wished I had a tape recorder. In fact, at times I come home and make notes. Maybe I'll do something with them some day."

"You should write a family history," Liz said.

Marjorie nodded. "It's just an ordinary country family."

"I could go visit her tomorrow morning, or do they have church services?"

"I think some people go to church; someone gives them a ride. But Mom won't go with me, says anyone she'd want to see is already dead. You could come to church with me."

"I don't go to church," Liz said very firmly.

"Didn't think you did. Just thought I'd ask."

The fields on both sides of the road were greening. The scent of barn manure wafted from a field where a tractor was pulling a manure spreader.

"Phew—poor guy," Liz said.

"Not all good honest work smells nice," Marjorie said. "Mom'd be glad to talk to you if you went over tomorrow. She might even be jealous you interviewed Geneva. There was always some kind of competition between them, I thought."

"I noticed something," Liz said.

From Marjorie's house, Liz called Jack as she had promised. He wanted to come up and see her tomorrow.

"I'm here for the day tomorrow. There's so much to talk to her about."

"I've been thinking about you all week," he said. "Look if you don't want to see me again, tell me now, before I get my hopes up."

"I'd really like to see you. But I've got to go back to her house tomorrow."

"If I didn't have a shitload of work backed up, I'd come up to see you, even that late. But I got some new customers from the show."

"That's good."

"Yeah, but you know, all work and no play makes Jack a dull boy."

"Jack, you're not in danger of becoming dull any time soon."

"You're just saying that. You're bored out of your old gourd with a high school educated hick from Kentucky," he said. She couldn't tell if he was serious or just joking.

"Cut it out. I haven't known you long enough to be bored. I wasn't bored last Saturday, which I think I made clear."

"Will you leave some time for me next weekend?"

"I will. Do you like camping?"

"I've got a pop-up camper for my truck."

"Why don't we see if there's a park somewhere halfway between you and me where we could camp?" Liz suggested.

"YOU like camping?"

"Yeah."

"I can't believe it. It's close quarters in the pop-up, but being cozy with you sounds good."

"Do you know a park?" she asked.

"I'll get on the computer as soon as I hang up."

Marjorie didn't have cable or a satellite dish. She only watched Jeopardy and the morning and evening news. Marjorie went to bed and Liz flipped through magazines on the coffee table: TV Guide, Newsweek and the O Magazine, Oprah's vanity publication. Liz slipped into a fantasy: she was talking to Oprah on national television about Geneva's quilts—and incidentally selling hundreds of thousands of copies of the book made from her doctoral thesis with pictures of herself and Geneva sitting in the kitchen or in her sewing room. Liz had never dreamed of being a best-selling author, that was for novelists, self-help writers and the recent denizens of the White House. She was surprised this fantasy crept into her mind. From family odd ball to celebrity, wouldn't that be cool?

If she wanted to make herself and Geneva famous, she would have to spend time here, not only seeing Geneva and finding out all she needed to know about the quilts and Geneva's artistic life, unconscious as it might be. She would have to spend time with Marjorie and Aunt Alma. I've backed myself into a corner with old women. This is the kind of family, mostly uneducated, without any sort of wider worldview, boring Jeopardy watchers, that I have always wanted to escape. She had a moment of chest tightening claustrophobia. No one has the least idea who I am and what I'm doing.

Liz remembered Alma fingering the flower petals yesterday. She seemed to have returned to childhood, as fascinated as if she were discovering flowers for the first time. In a two-year old it would be charming. In an 86-year-old woman it was pathetic. Except she was happy. Everything gone, just the feel of flower petals to make her happy.

Liz went to a window and looked out; she could see little because of the big trees in the yard. She put on her jeans jacket and went out. The town was small; she didn't know anything about it. One main street and a couple of parallel streets, the short cross streets dead ended at fenced in farmland on one side and the US. Rte. 50; on the other, with more farmland beyond. Was it safe to walk the streets at night? What could be dangerous? Maybe a few drunks at a local bar. Was there a local bar? A beer would be good but...not among the local guys who probably hang out there watching pre-season baseball. Not for a woman in her twenties. It was shitty to feel that way, to have to be afraid of small-town men because she was a decent looking young woman. If you're a stranger, you don't even have to be great looking or dress in anything more exciting than jeans and a sweatshirt to turn on a certain type of guy—any guy between 18 and—Jesus!—probably 58, or 68.

The tension passed because of the cool air here in the shadows of the porch. No, damnit, why shouldn't I go for a walk? Why did I trust the men of Mongolia much more than the men of a plain little American town? She walked down the street in the direction of the nursing home. Houses had curtains drawn or dark living rooms with flickering blueish ghosts on television. A couple of dogs barked from back yards. Maybe there was a law that they had to be confined. She hoped so. If she were walking a dog, even, say a little Scotty, even a dachshund, she would feel safer. She met no one and no cars were on this street, but she did not walk very far. She was afraid of her ignorance about the place and its people. She could walk the college campus after leaving the library late at night even though she knew college campuses attracted nut cases. Familiarity breeds comfort.

Liz wished she were going to spend tomorrow with Jack. Yes, he was a small-town guy too, but he knew something about quilts, and he was curious about her. He had been a slow and thoughtful lover. He had a nice body and his longish hair felt wonderful in her hands. He had had the tattoo she expected: an American eagle on his right bicep. "I wanted something I'd never have to apologize for," he said. She had realized how needy she was; she had probably surprised him with how quickly she came. "It's been a while," she said. "I was waiting for the right someone," she added to make him feel good.

He whooped with delight. It was the right thing to say. Or the wrong thing, since it made him think she had immediately fallen for him. Now feeling muddled had replaced her doubts. She wished she still smoked. Standing here in the dark seemed to call for a cigarette. But no, she wouldn't smoke again. She had smoked in Mongolia—all the young people did. Marlboro was big and much advertised. After all, Mongolia is horse country, a country full of flinty faced Marlboro men except their cheekbones were higher, their eyes narrower and more almond shaped than the cowboy of the American big sky country. She liked their faces. And she loved the big sky country, loved to watch even very young children galloping the little Mongolian horses across the grass away from their villages.

What, she thought, am I doing here in Dillsboro, Indiana visiting old women? I got myself into this, I can change my mind and get myself out of it. I can write my thesis on...oh, what the hell, Mongolian folk paintings and compare them to Bruegels, to Grandma Moses, to Norman Rockwell. She couldn't help chuckling at that thought—Norman Rockwell showing a sweet Vermont town in a free-for-all orgy of humans and animals all fucking in a springtime frenzy of fertility. Jesus! I'm losing it, she thought. I'd better go to bed and have a clear head for two old ladies tomorrow. She went in, taking her shoes off so she could tiptoe to the bedroom and not wake Marjorie.

Liz woke to the sound of birds just beyond her window. She did not open her eyes until she remembered where she was. Her apartment in student housing faced a parking lot with no trees close by, she only heard occasional crows on the far side of the parking lot with their clarion caws. Here she seemed to hear half the Audubon birds gathered in the backyard trees. Then she smelled coffee and knew she was at Marjorie's. She didn't have to hurry out of bed, Marjorie wouldn't care. She cuddled against the pillows and listened to the birds. A small town was depressing and even scary at night, but in the morning with the avian choir it was almost Eden. She dozed and awoke when she heard a door close and a car start. Marjorie was going to church to teach her adult Sunday School class. Liz was expected at the nursing home around ten. She looked at her watch and saw it was ten of nine. Perfect. Time for a shower and breakfast.

At the nursing home she greeted the other patients who were in the lounge as Marjorie had taught her by example yesterday. She took time to say, "The sun's beautiful today, isn't it?" or something of the sort to each person. Four people were watching a church service on television and a couple others were fitting pieces of a jigsaw puzzle on a card table near the window that was open just a bit. Aunt Alma watched Liz move around the room. "I know you," she said as Liz came to her.

"Yes, you do, Aunt Alma, I'm Barbara's girl. You used to call me Little Lizzie." Liz pulled a chair closer to Aunt Alma and sat down.

"You're Little Lizzie, all grown up."

"All five foot eight of me."

"How's your mother?"

"She's fine but I don't see much of her. She's an Indianapolis business woman, and I'm in school in Bloomington."

"You're too big to be in school, aren't you?" Aunt Alma was smiling like a little girl who has recently learned how to tease. Liz was delighted that a little sense of humor had surfaced.

"Some of us are kind of slow."

"Not you. I always said, 'There are no dummies in our family.' And you're one of the smartest. Only one in college."

Alma was in good spirits. "I worked for a while and now I'm finishing up my college degree so I'll be a doctor of art."

"How do you doctor art?" Alma asked.

Liz had never noticed Aunt Alma's sense of humor before. Could old people suddenly acquire new traits? Or was Aunt Alma genuinely wondering how one doctors art? Liz answered seriously, "Maybe I'll work in a museum somewhere. Or maybe I'll teach in college."

"Marjorie taught for 35 years. She liked it. Mostly."

"I know, I'm staying at Marjorie's house this weekend. She said she asked you if you'd mind if I interview you."

"Interview me?"

"About family history. You know more than anyone else these days."

"There's things I know that no one else ever did know," Alma whispered. She sounded like a teenager and had the look of a gossipy girl.

"That's exactly what I want to hear. Should we go to your room so you can tell me whatever you want and I can record it?" Marjorie had said she was changeable. Today Aunt Alma seemed a different person than the distracted woman only interested in flower petals that she had been yesterday.

"Good idea. Around here everybody minds everybody else's bees' wax."

Liz pushed Alma's wheelchair to the elevator. During breakfast she had said into the recorder: "Aunt Alma is my grandmother Clara's youngest sister. She's 86 now and in a nursing home. I'm told that sometimes she forgets a lot but sometimes she remembers a lot, especially from her younger years. She is Marjorie's mother and there were three other children, George who lives in Kentucky, Marie who's in Fort Wayne, Indiana, and Wilbur who died of a heart attack three or four years ago. From all those children she has nine grandchildren and four great-grandchildren—I think. I need to check this. Marjorie lives in Dillsboro, only four blocks from the nursing home where Aunt Alma now lives. Marjorie is my mother's cousin; that makes her my second cousin. Marjorie is about five years older than my mother, but they were best friends in grade school even though they lived about twenty miles apart and went to different schools. Marjorie and my mother still talk at least once a month and email often. That's all I remember right now. I'll fill in more about family later."

"Do you want to sit in the armchair?" Liz asked.

"Where would you sit?" There was only one comfortable chair in the small room. Beside it was a small table with a half dozen framed snapshots of family gatherings and the vase of flowers Liz had brought yesterday. A bureau top displayed a forest of framed snapshots. With the hospital-style bed, which had a pastel quilt on it, the room was filled.

"In the wheelchair, I guess," Liz said. "I'll see what it feels like and try to understand what you have to put up with."

Alma chuckled. "I 'spect you don't want to know what I put up with."

"I'm more interested in the juicy secrets you said you were going to tell me."

"When did I tell you that?"

"When we were downstairs. Before we start, would you like me to open the window a little and let in spring air?"

"Is it warm out there?"

"It's nice. So nice I might even do a little sun bathing later on." Liz opened the window. "Tell me if it gets too cool, okay?"

"Are there birds singing?"

"I don't hear any now, but I heard a whole chorus of them before I got out of bed this morning."

"I can't hear them anymore. Wish I could. I always liked birds singing in the spring."

"Tell me something about when you were young. You said something about secrets."

"Well, I guess there's only one big secret and I'm not sure I ought to tell it. I never told it to no one."

"I'll promise not to tell anyone if you want."

"That'd be good if it's going to be on there."

"I'm curious."

"You going to interview Geneva Gardiner and write about her quilts?"

And Marjorie said you might have things to tell.

"I mightn't want to…" They say silently a few minutes.

"She was my best friend in school. We were together all the time; people used to tease us and call us The Siamese twins." Alma's voice was small and far away.

"I visited with Geneva yesterday."

"You did?"

"I took pictures of some of her quilts."

"She's making them lickety-split, trying to pile up a whole closet full 'cause she says anybody can have a bunch of kids and grandkids, but most people don't leave anything behind for others when they die."

"She told you that?" Liz asked.

"She told me that, oh…a while ago. I don't 'member when."

"Where do you think she got that idea?"

"From a preacher at her church. He was a young man—I guess he ain't so young no more, nobody is, are they? But he put the bee in her bonnet." Liz was torn between wanting to find out more about Geneva and wondering about the secret Aunt Alma had never told anyone.

"I guess you've been friends all your life," Liz said.

"That we have. I hardly ever get to see her nowadays."

"Do you remember we went to see her a couple weeks ago?" Liz felt she was starting the conversation from scratch.

"Yeah, I saw her not long ago. Can't remember how that come about. Guess Marjorie took me."

"Marjorie took you and me. Then I saw her again yesterday and she told me how good it was to see you. Says she misses you."

"I miss her. We were best friends. There was a swimming hole, more like a swimming puddle, in a crick at the back of my Daddy's farm that we used to go to in summer time and lay on the bank in our underwear to get a suntan and when we'd go in the water, we'd take the underwear off. We were always afraid some boys might find out but we thought they never did 'til about ten years later when we were both married and setting up house. Cliff from the farm behind ours told us he'd been spying on us all the time. Funny, isn't it, how we think our skinny little girl bodies are something special to hide? We'd've been embarrassed half to death if we knew. When I got married, LeRoy never saw me naked until after the first baby was born and he had to help me get up and get washed. That damned doctor ran off to somebody else almost as soon as the baby came out and he cut the cord—left all the work to LeRoy. Said, 'You're a farmer's son, you know what to do.'"

"Your baby was born at home?"

"Babies were born at home back then and you were lucky if a doctor got there. Most times it was your mother or grandma that was with you, or a neighbor woman."

"Did you have to get up and go back to cooking and cleaning right away?"

"Depended on how hard it was. First one was usually pretty hard, and generally your mother or someone would move in for a week and let you rest. They'd always get a kick out of telling you how loud you screamed and that you'd said words that would make Lucifer blush. I did it myself when Geneva had her two girls. Told her I didn't know she knew those words she'd called Alf for getting her in that pickle. Said she'd learned them from Alf himself when a cow'd kick over the milk bucket. Lordy! I learned them from her and then had a good set of swears for times when things broke down." Alma laughed. Suddenly she was coughing and choking. Liz got a glass of water from the bathroom. Alma had trouble catching her breath.

"Should I call somebody to help you?"

"No. It's just hard to have a decent laugh. Not enough wind any-more."

"That's bad. They say laughing is good for people."

"Depends on how old you are."

"Maybe I'm wearing you out. Maybe I should be going." Liz said. She felt she'd only got a glimpse of Alma's early life. No secrets there.

"Give me a minute or two." She sipped the water. Her hands were shaking. Liz reached for the glass. Alma gasped for breath.

"Maybe you'd like to lie down now?" Liz asked

"No, Sweetheart, I like this chair. I'll be okay."

Liz sat by helplessly for a few more minutes.

"Now what got me off on that?" Alma asked.

"Dirty words."

"Oh, yes. Geneva. I was going to tell you 'bout the only time Geneva and I fell out. Well, it happens all the time on the TV stories, you know, but when it happens for real in your own life...it's a real big surprise all around."

Liz was certain she knew what was coming. She was right. Alma and Alf had an affair, not a very long one, but it seemed possible Marjorie was Alf's child and Geneva knew it because Alf had confessed the whole thing and said he'd go away if she hated him. But she didn't hate him, she forgave him. She didn't forgive Alma for five years. Finally they both got so lonely for their friendship they began to talk on the telephone again. Alf, Alma said, was a very different man from LeRoy. He made love differently, in fact, many different ways that Alma sometimes didn't like, but then when it was over longed for and never dared suggest to LeRoy because he'd wonder where she had ever got such ideas.

"Oh my," Alma said, "it's been a long, long time and I still think what I used to think back then: sometimes I was so happy I said to myself if I died that very minute, I'd die happier than I could ever be again. And I still think 'bout it and think if Jesus Himself stood by my bed and opened his arms to me, I couldn't be the kind of happy I was those times. That's a terrible thing to say, isn't it?"

Liz just nodded a little—she didn't want to stop the flow of talk now that it had started.

"I know Geneva knew that kind of happy. A long time later we talked about it. It just came out. She was saying how happy she felt with her new pastor—the one with the Africa idea—that sometimes the singing and praying just lifted her right up where she thought she could touch heaven. And I said, 'Better than when Alf kissed you down there?'"

Alma's head dropped, her right hand quickly flew up to cover her mouth. Liz said nothing, waiting as Alma took a breath and looked up like a naughty child. Liz hoped the expression on her face hadn't changed.

Then Alma smiled. "Geneva just took my hand and said, 'We've been lucky women, haven't we?' Then she said, 'I'm glad it was you and I hope it wasn't anybody else.' And I said I hoped so too."

Liz waited, surely Aunt Alma would change the subject.

"I think when somebody has the gift Alf had it's a shame not to spread it around."

Alma smiled, her fallen old face lifted like a younger woman's and her eyes became young. She chuckled.

Liz couldn't help laughing. Alma's face had transformed to a much younger woman; it lasted only a few seconds. Liz knew she would never forget and she would not tell Marjorie or Geneva. "Thanks for telling me about that, Aunt Alma. I know what you're talking about and I'm looking for my Alf. But I think I'd be totally selfish and want him all to myself."

"Well, good luck, Sweetheart. They're rare birds, men like that."

They sat for a few moments lost in their own thoughts. "Marjorie made me promise not to wear you out. I think I ought to help you back into this chair or whatever you want to do and be on my way."

"I 'spect I could use a little nap. I do most mornings round about now."

When Marjorie came home from church, she found Liz sitting in the backyard sunbathing. Liz wore the oversized tee-shirt that she slept in; she had found a folding lawn chair in the store room behind the kitchen. She was still thinking how Alma's happy, young face transformed like a video time regression picture. Liz wondered if her own mother had ever known that kind of bliss. Barbara was a child of the hippie era, so maybe she had experimented with sex and discovered how good it could be. On the other hand, maybe not because she was always a straight arrow. Barbara was so prissy and strict Liz couldn't wait to move away to college. And her father? Even though she was no longer a naïve child, she couldn't imagine her parents having sex. She preferred to think of these two old women with the same man. A romance fifty years ago seemed more like fiction than fact. Their world was a different place. But people were the same. They loved, they explored, they discovered, they blazed with delight, and cried with guilt or refused to feel guilt. They knew they would always remember. Alma remembered although she forgot much else.

"Well, aren't you the lazy one?" said Marjorie's voice from the back door.

Liz opened her eyes. "Yes, I'm a lazy lump. Don't change out of your good dress, Marjorie, I'm taking you out for dinner."

Marjorie came out into the sun. "Really you don't have to. I've got plenty in the house."

"I want to. I told you that last night."

"I know, but I thought maybe you were just being polite."

"Would my mother teach me to be an Indian giver like that? —Oops, that's not politically correct, is it?"

"No, you're not supposed to say things like that," Marjorie said seriously in her school teacher voice. "Did you ever think about it? We say 'Indian giver' as if the Indians gave us something and took it back, but we're the ones who reneged after we gave them big reservations. When oil was discovered or people just wanted to farm, we took the land back."

"Once a teacher always a teacher," Liz said.

"Can't help it, and I don't apologize for it either."

As they ate chicken breast cutlets at a restaurant in Aurora, Marjorie asked, "Did you and Mom have a good talk?"

"Better than I would have expected. You're right about asking about the past."

"What'd she talk about?"

"Her deepest secrets."

"Mom has secrets?"

"Everybody has secrets. I'll bet you have."

"Nope, no secrets."

"I don't believe you. No cheating on a test once upon a time? No sleeping around when you were young? No pot parties when you were thirteen?"

"Weeeell..."

"Ha!" Liz grinned.

"Okay, I'll tell you. I shoplifted a pint of vodka once, shared it with a girl friend. We got skunk drunk." She laughed. "I don't know why that's a secret except stealing was such a sin. I thought for a long time I'd go to hell. I still think there's a black mark in my Book of Life."

"Do you really believe there's a Book of Life?"

"I do. I mean not an actual book somewhere at the gate of heaven— or even a gate for that matter."

"Maybe it's all electronic and digital these days," Liz was sorry she had brought the conversation in this direction. She didn't want to talk about religion, or lack of religion. It was a subject she had always been told not to talk about.

"Why the hell not," Randy had often said. A part of his mission in life—or in Liz's life—was to rid her of all the "good girl" rules she had learned as a child. "Don't talk about politics and religion and sex, just because it makes people uncomfortable—what horse shit! We can't know anyone if we don't talk honestly about the most important things." They had had many long, cold nights in the Mongolia village, lying in their sleeping bags on top of the sleeping bench, staring at the tiny fire that oddly enough could keep the ger passably warm even when the wind was howling and temperatures fell to thirty below zero. Randy had been relentless. Sometimes they fought over the concept of privacy—all sorts of privacy, including political or religious beliefs, as well as the lack of physical privacy in the ger.

Those unpartitioned round dwellings made personal privacy almost impossible. She had hung curtains around an area designated "bathroom." But they had to give up all modesty to live together. She liked privacy in both bathroom matters and about her beliefs. She had wanted to erect a curtain around his shrine, but he refused. She felt his half hour a day meditating before his little Buddha statuette and thangka with a mandala in the middle should have been as private as a bowel movement.

Liz resented Randy's increasing prying at her beliefs and ideas, at her self-image and her feelings about him. "They become more complex the longer we're here together," she said.

"Tell me. Put them in words," he said almost like a command.

"It's too inchoate right now. I can't." She meant she wouldn't. She thought that struggle should be inside herself, especially her negative feelings. If she explained he was acting too much like an insecure smart kid always wanting the teacher's attention, he would become defensive and then sulky.

Liz needed privacy to formulate thoughts and sort out feelings; she didn't believe anyone needed to know everything about anyone else. We all need to keep a kernel of quiet selfhood. She pictured selfhood lying just right of her heart, protected by the sternum, warmed and massaged by the pulsing of blood in its myriad arteries and vessels. Randy's constant prying at the kernel eventually convinced her he was not the warm, compassionate person she had thought he was before he decided to be a compassionate Buddhist.

"Come back," Marjorie said.

"Huh?"

"I could see your brain went off on a tangent. Imagining an Internet wired heaven?"

"Oh," Liz said. "I have a lot of trouble with the idea of heaven." She pulled herself back into the conversation. "So you're a thief and a drunkard. And your mother tells me she was a sexy young thing. I've got a lot to live up to in this family."

"You didn't come here for our family history."

"No but now that it's coming out, I don't mind getting two birds with one stone."

"I'm glad for the chance to get to know you, Liz. I never expected I would," Marjorie said.

"Knowing people is what I was just now thinking about. It can get messy."

Marjorie pushed her clean plate away and sat back. Liz was eating more slowly; the food was good if not elegant. "Do you want some dessert?" Liz asked.

"They make a very good lemon meringue pie," Marjorie said.

"I haven't had that for years and years. Have some and I will too," Liz said and caught the waitress's attention with a wave.

Liz had now driven the road between Dillsboro and Friendship often enough for it to seem a very short distance in spite of its many sharp curves. She wanted to get her head clear about what to ask Geneva. She was concerned about what Prof. Toad would ask her, what pieces of information she would need to make a case for the importance of Geneva's quilts.

As she approached Geneva's drive, she saw a navy blue Ford Explorer turn in. She slowed and then followed and parked so that the bigger vehicle could turn around. A man got out of the driver's side and went around to open the door. He helped Geneva out, gallantly, the way men used to treat women. Geneva was in a navy dress and wore a small hat with a bit of veil and small artificial blue flowers. The hat would be labeled "vintage" in thrift stores. It was perfect on Geneva.

Geneva introduced them. "Rev. Wheeler, this is Elizabeth Lissman, the young woman I was tellin' you 'bout who likes my quilts."

He was a plain man with a boyish strong jawed face; he was probably fifty. He had a lot of gray above the ears where his slightly long hair was brushed back into a wing. He had a weak handshake and an automatic smile. "It's nice to meet you. That makes two of us who admire her work. I'm going to go on home now, Geneva. You know Betty is waiting on me to get home and tackle her Honey-Do list." He said to Liz, "I work all week getting the sermon together and tending to my other church duties. Sunday afternoon is the only time I have free to do my husbandly duties."

Liz suppressed a smile at the unconscious double entendre. "It's nice meeting you," she said. "Geneva mentioned you yesterday."

"She didn't complain that my prayers tend to go on quite a while, did she?"

"She said you have a gift for speaking so everyone can understand."

"Well, I thank you sincerely, Geneva. That means a lot to me. I'll see you Wednesday night at prayer meeting." He got back in his Explorer and executed a neat U-turn as Liz and Geneva went into the house.

"I don't mean to hurry you. We can take a little time before we start talking..."

"No, I'm listened out and ready to do some talking. Rev. Wheeler gets so fired up with his sermons that he mostly spends Sunday dinners trying to make sure everyone got his meaning."

Liz asked, "Do you have Sunday dinner there often?"

"No, not more than once in six or eight weeks. I've heard people fight over who'll have the pleasure of my company each week." She laughed a little. "That's what they say. They mean they feel obliged to take care of me. Once it kind of stuck in my craw that they thought I was a helpless old woman who couldn't cook her own Sunday dinner. I was cookin' long before most of them were born. Some days I'd be sewin' and thinkin' 'bout it and I'd feel downright bad and mad about bein'a burden to ever'one. I have a lot of time to think, you know, when I'm here by my lonesome, cuttin' and stitchin'. I said to myself, 'Geneva, you're eighty years old. You know you've done that kind of thing for your neighbors for years; now it's your turn to reap your reward.' I sowed my crop of kindness and now it's comin' back to me. I shouldn't belittle people's good intentions. I should just admit I'm eighty-six and deserve what good is comin' my way."

"I love what you just said. Wouldn't you know I haven't got my recorder runnin' yet."

"Well, you can write that down in your notebook if you want to 'member it. I'm gonna pour me a glass of water. Do you want some?"

"A glass of water would be nice."

Liz wrote notes. "Sunday the 28th of April—talking to Geneva Gardiner at her house in Friendship, Indiana. There, now it's all official."

Geneva put the plastic pitcher back in the refrigerator. "What do you want me to tell you today?" She set the glasses of water on the table.

"How you decided to make the quilts for your African mission and then about meeting the African couple and deciding what kind of quilts to make."

"Before Rev. Wheeler, there was Rev. Redburn. He was a man with a mixed background. His father was a black man who had married a Vietnamese woman. He was light skinned and real good lookin' and a real good preacher. He had been to different parts of Africa because he wanted to find where his father's ancestors were from—except they really didn't have any idea what part. He guessed it was in the part where the most slaves came from back in those times, but couldn't go lookin' for people that looked like him. You know what? He kind-a looked like that man—what's he do? That man named Tiger."

"Tiger Woods? He plays golf."

"Real good lookin' young man."

"Yes, and maybe our very best golfer."

"Well, I don't know nothing 'bout golf but I see-d his picture in magazines and it reminded me of Rev. Redburn. Anyway, there was a couple from South Africa touring around to churches in this part of the country, and down South and I think they'd been in Texas—just all over. They had a slide show 'bout how bad things were there. They got their freedom and vote, but a lot of people were still very, very poor and they were trying to raise money for a church. But when I see-d that slide show with them youngin's so scrawny and with such big white-tooth smiles, I wondered what I could do 'cause I cain't give them much money. We had a big dinner at the church and ever'body got to meet them. And I asked did they know about quilts? And the woman said, yes, she'd seen quilts in the homes they'd stayed in, and she thought they were real nice things.

"I asked her did it get cold at night where she lived. She said it did get pretty cool some parts of the year. And I asked would people like to have quilts for their beds. She said she was sure they would, that they'd probably be so proud they'd cover the bed with them all the time and keep them for best 'cause the designs were so pretty. So I told her I'd like to make some quilts for them, 'cause people had already started givin' me their extra materials and their old blankets to use for stuffing. I was in the habit of makin' quilts and havin' them on hand when there was need, you know, like I said before. The Ohio floods now and then and people have house fires and most ever year there's a tornado around here. And there's quite a few just plain poor people goin' through hard times. I never had no extra money, but that's somethin' I could do 'cause other people helped me by 'memberin' me with their scraps and extras."

She stopped and drank most of her glass of water. "I guess I'm telling you more than you need to know. I kind of got the talkin'-too-much habit from listenin' to Rev. Wheeler."

"You're not talking too much at all. It's just perfect. But the quilts I saw don't look like the usual ones. What made you start making that kind of quilts?"

"Rev. Redburn had a young wife. She was a black woman and real smart and a wonderful singer, too, I have to say. I could-a listened to that woman sing all day long and sometimes I wisht she'd just sing and we'd forget all about the sermon. He wasn't such a good preacher, truth be told. He had all these big words, telling us about the Greek language that part of the Bible was wrote in. I didn't care a hoot-in-a-holler 'bout that. I like to go to church and get a good feelin', get my heart warmed up you might say."

"Sounds like Rev. Wheeler doesn't always do that either," Liz observed.

"Not always but he's better at it. He's a plainer man. Doesn't talk about Greek at all."

"I'm sorry I interrupted. You were going to tell me about Rev. Redburn's wife."

"She's the one got me thinkin' 'bout what kind'a quilts I could make to send to Africa. She gave me a magazine with an article 'bout a quilt show by a bunch of black women in Cincinnati. They were different from what I'd been making, brighter. They looked like they'd be more fun to make. Bigger pieces and none of these fussy little flowers. I never did much like appliqué. I mostly did pieced quilts and these ones the black ladies made were mostly all pieced. I made me one and I had so much fun–not copying 'sactly, doing somethin' different. I think it was the first I learned that you can kind-a ferget 'bout some-a the rules and just make what looks good to you. When Rev. Redburn went to a different church, I give them that quilt as a remembrance. They said they liked it a lot. I hope they really did."

Liz almost said, reassuringly, I'm sure they did, but she stopped herself in order not to interrupt Geneva's flow of words.

"You know, makin' that quilt was like wakin' up one mornin' at the end of winter and seeing the sun shinin' and the grass turnin' green. I decided from now on I'd make quilts that were fun for me. I can't say I'm real sure the African people will like them. But once people at church got to hear of how I was makin' my quilts, that I'd use lots of red and orange and black and brown and bright blue and green and yellow, they stopped bringin' me their scraps from the dresses they made for their grandkids—well, most of them anyway. Sometimes they'd see fabrics in the stores they thought would be good for my quilts and they'd buy some for me, just to see what I'd do with it. Truth is, they gave me some of the ugliest stuff you ever saw."

"Did you use it?"

"Well, sure. You don't turn your nose up at presents. I figured out I could turn those ugly things into strips or triangles that didn't show how really awful they were. And, you know what? That got to be a kind-a fun thing too, like a dare. Use it in plain sight but hide its ugliness. I gotta say, quiltin' got to be more fun when I started in on that. It's still fun, it's like this tap got turned on in my head—you know I never was one to speak up much or put myself forward or anythin' like that. Just found my place and lived a quiet life, never hardly ever broke rules. And I made all those quilts like ever'body else was makin' and they all told me how good I was at it and that made me feel good. Last few years, they just don't know what to say to me 'bout my quilts, so they mostly don't say nothin' a-tall. But they think 'bout it. I know, 'cause ever'so often after church or after Wednesday prayer meetin', someone'll go to the car and bring me a package of fabric and say, 'I thought 'bout you when I saw this, so I thought I'd get you some.'"

Geneva laughed. "Who'd ever think I'd have all this help doin' somethin' they don't like or understand?"

Liz said, "I like hearing you say it's fun. I don't know if people your age think about having fun much."

"You think it's a little kid word?"

"I guess so. I'm not quite sure if I could say the last time I'd say I had fun."

"Well, that's a cryin'-out-loud shame," Geneva chided as if she were correcting a child. Her face turned serious as she was pondering something. "Come to think of it, I guess there's a part of life when we don't think much about fun except for our kids to have fun. I guess I was kind of serious for a while. No, I guess I didn't think much about fun until I stopped followin' the quilt makin' rules and just made what I felt like. That's a funny idea, isn't it?"

"I think that's how everyone who makes art feels, it becomes fun and they get really good at it when they're able to forget about the rules and just do what feels right to them. I'm glad you feel that way," Liz said.

"Well, I didn't say nothin' 'bout makin' art. I'm just makin' quilts."

"To me they look like art," Liz said. "If you don't feel like calling them that, it's okay. I hope you don't mind if that's what I call them."

"It's a new kinda idea to me. You study art in school, but I don't really know what it is except paintin' pictures or makin' statues."

"Art is other things too, things made of glass, or wood and things made of fiber or fabric—and that includes quilts," Liz said.

Geneva shrugged as if this was too much to take in or simply not important. "You're the one makin' a study of art. I won't argue with you."

"I'm not supposed to be doing the talking. So tell me, do you have a plan for sending your quilts to Africa?" Liz asked.

"Well, I tell ever'body I'm makin' a closet full'a quilts. When I die Rev. Wheeler'll find a way to get them to the mission in Africa. He promised and ever'body else promised—includin' Ben. He says, 'Yes, Ma, that's your legacy.'"

"What if," Liz said, "I write about your quilts and some rich person who collects quilts wants to buy a bunch and keep them to show in museums."

"Nope. Can't buy my quilts. They're goin' to Africa, pure and simple." She spoke quickly and firmly.

"I understand. I think they're wonderful and I suspect some other people would think so too. Some people pay quite a bit for quilts to show on their walls," Liz explained.

"You don't say? What kind of good money? Couple hundred dollars?"

"As much as $5000 for some, maybe more if it's by a famous quilter."

"Five thousand? For a quilt?" Geneva was truly surprised. "Well, I guess I just haven't kept up with what's going on in the world."

"Some people have a real taste for special quilts."

"I'll be durned," Geneva muttered.

"Let me ask," Liz said, "if someone really loved some of your quilts, might you be willing to sell them? You'd have money you could send to people in Africa for food or medicine or things that they need besides quilts."

Geneva took a big breath as if she'd just discovered something so amazing she didn't know how to fit it into anything she'd thought before. After a bit she said, "Nope. I want my quilts to go to Africa. That's what they was made for. I don't care what any rich people think of them, and anyway, so far you're the only person I ever met that thinks there's anything special 'bout them. Maybe nobody'd agree with you. Anyway, when I'm makin' them, I'm thinkin' 'bout those skinny African children in the pictures, and those tall beautiful women wearing skirts and wrapping their heads in those African fabrics that I've seen in pictures people give me. That's who they're bein' made for. I want them to know that there's someone in a little bitty place in the middle of America that spent time thinkin' 'bout them, and wishin' them well."

Liz decided she had said enough. "I think that's wonderful. You know, lots of places in the world that used to think America was wonderful don't think we've been so wonderful lately with the wars and all. A person doing something like you're doing will make a difference."

"Not a very big difference, I 'spect," Geneva said, but with no regret. Just a statement of fact.

"But a difference anyway, a difference to some people. We just never know what something we do might mean to other people."

"Well, that's true. That African couple I met, they didn't know they'd change my life. They had no idea I'd learn about a new way of quiltin' and it'd make me so darned happy when I'm settin' here in my little house sewin' away." She waved her hand. "I ain't got much, as you can see. And I've had some real serious sadness in the last dozen years, losing Alf and the two girls. And a'course I cain't take care of things like I used to, don't have half the garden I used to, and couple dozen chickens just for the eggs really. But, you know, I feel so darned good watchin' how those quilts come together. The Lord gave me somethin' to fill my days with usefulness. I don't know what else anybody needs."

"Geneva, I love hearing you say all that. I know I said I wouldn't take up too much of your Sunday afternoon."

"And you got a long drive."

"Couple hours, yeah. You'll let me come back again, won't you?"

"Oh, sure. You're welcome here anytime."

"I don't know when I can come back. It's getting toward the end of the school year and I'm teaching a class and taking a couple classes, and it's test time, you know. But I'll come back."

"I'll look forward to it. You got my phone number?"

"Yeah, I'll call you."

Geneva walked with Liz to the car. "You've got your nice Sunday dress on. Can I take a picture of you here in front of your house?" Liz asked.

Geneva hesitated but then shrugged diffidently. Liz took a couple of pictures and then they walked to the chicken house.

"I think I've had more pictures taken in the last couple-a days than in my whole life up to now," Geneva said.

"I'll send you copies of the good ones," Liz promised.

Chapter 5

Liz pulled her chair beside Prof. Simmons' desk, so they could look at the pictures of Geneva's quilts on a CD she had made. He looked at the whole set silently. When it was finished he said, "I think you're golden."

"Do you? Do you really think she's unique?"

"She's unique and her story's unique." He had read the transcript Liz made of her interview with Geneva, and the two paragraphs of notes she added. "I like those quilts a lot. You've got your subject, Elizabeth."

Liz sighed with relief. "I'm so glad you like them."

"Have you dug up any interviews with other Outsider Artists?"

"No, do you think there are some?"

"It's up to you to find out." He chuckled. "I have to be the teacher, you know."

"Is it okay if I ask Cynthia if her Haitian artist has been interviewed?"

"Sure. Give her a call. He might have been, but, unfortunately for him and for Cynthia, he died a couple months ago. The guy who did the Watts Towers might have been interviewed. For a while he got a lot of publicity."

"I'll check." She wrote a note in a little pad she carried in her purse.

"These are not all?" Prof. Simmons asked.

"No, this was about a third of the stack. She has another little stack of what she calls 'pretty' quilts. More traditional. These are all destined for Africa, she says. The others are to give away when there are local disasters."

"She must work all the time."

"I think she does. She has chickens and a garden and goes to church. The rest of the time she quilts. She has a TV, but she doesn't watch much."

"Let's go through them again. Do you mind? Don't do the slide show, do them one by one," the professor said.

"Do you think I ought to get specific notes on each one?" Liz asked.

"If you can. Probably she won't be able to tell you much, I imagine she works very intuitively."

The professor asked about traditional names for the quilts. Sometimes Liz knew the answer, sometimes she thought they were entirely Geneva's own design. "She says it's fun to put these together," Liz said. "Does that make her a serious artist or something else?"

"Untrained, which is part of the definition of Outsider Artist. Can you imagine Pollock saying he had fun dribbling his paint on the canvases?"

"He might not say it, but I'll bet it was fun."

Tom Simmons chuckled. "I agree. Liz, you've got to spend as much of the summer as you can out there getting all the data you can. You'll want a complete bio and all the notes on quilts she can give you. Can you stay with your cousin?"

"Yes, I have a bed any time. I'm not sure how to get anything but basic biographical information. People are very private in that part of the country. They just don't talk about themselves much. I see my thesis as being about the quilts as spontaneous, naïve art."

"You need as much information as possible on how she works," the professor said.

Liz hesitated. "I sort of practiced on my great aunt who was Geneva's good friend from grade school. She gave me some insights." Liz almost wanted to tell Aunt Alma's story but decided it was not appropriate.

The professor nodded and smiled. "Liz, you're in the best of positions. You're not some unknown person who has to win her confidence. You're not prying, you're serving as a confessor or therapist, in the best sense. Some memories are like the jewels sewn into the hem of a coat like immigrants used to do—at least in books. Old folks' memories come and go, but she was vividly alive at one point in her life. People probably don't ask questions because they think the memories are all gone. But they're in the brain somewhere. You shouldn't feel like you're prying. You were doing exactly what she needs to have you do. My gut feeling is you're really onto something, Liz."

"Maybe more than I want to be."

"It's called education, Elizabeth. Also, if you can talk him into it, it would be good to get Sam to take really professional photos of all the quilts because they could slip right away from us you know. They could disappear into darkest Africa, literally. How's Geneva's health?"

"Really, I have no idea."

"Old people in the country probably don't go to the doctor much. Her blood pressure could be at stroke level or her heart in bad shape. She could even have some kind of cancer and be too naïve to pay attention to the symptoms. You've got to act as fast as you can."

"She looks like she'll last to 100."

"That would be wonderful, 'cause given enough time you might be able to arrange a show of her quilts someplace. Would she object to that, do you think?"

"I don't know." Something else to do, Liz thought. More work.

"You should start working on that," Prof. Simmons said. "She might really enjoy some attention. It's like your payment for her cooperation."

"I doubt she'd feel that way," Liz said. "She knows most local people don't like her quilts."

"Ah! That's more reason to have a show and prove to her that her work is appreciated for what it is, even if her ignorant neighbors don't like it."

Liz was skeptical. Geneva had seemed entirely comfortable making her quilts to please herself. She seemed not to need attention. Liz decided not to argue with Prof. Simmons. He went on, "I'll give you any recommendations you need. But you also need professional photos."

"Well, I hate to impose on Sam. He's got his own work."

Prof. Toad sighed. "Sam... I thought he'd drop out of the program. I had hoped for serious photography from him. But in that milieu—you know all those empty-headed people making tons of money for wearing odd clothes." Prof. Toad made a face.

"What?" Liz asked. "I don't know anything about him. He said he's balancing a couple things."

"You don't know about his modeling?"

"Modeling? Making or doing?"

"With his looks, do I have to tell you?"

"He's a model? Like Vogue and Harper's Bazaar?" she asked.

"He has a career in New York. In fact, a thriving career, I believe. With the kind of money they make and the travel, I thought he'd chuck any kind of serious photography. Maybe there's a real artist under the veneer, but I don't see how he'll manage to get any serious photography done."

Liz was stunned. *So that explains the two-day beard, and maybe the green eyes are contact lenses.*

Prof. Simmons went on, "But he might do Geneva's quilts for you. I don't understand the guy."

"I don't think I want to ask him. I can't pay him."

"I'm sure he doesn't need the money."

"But..." Liz was trying to understand what she was hearing. "I only met him once—or maybe twice. He said he remembered me from your Christmas party because of what I was wearing."

"Liz, you've been around the world, don't be shy about asking for what you need and want. He does have photographic talent and you need good photos. Have you thought that this project could become a book?"

"No...no I haven't thought that far."

"Art needs to be seen. And if this is going to fly away to some African village, you should think of documenting it, at least. I take it you are thinking ahead to a career when you get over this hump."

"Of course. I'm just floored."

"Okay, I'm supposed to be a bit of a mentor so here's my suggestion: ask Sam about taking photos, say you want to publish a book from your thesis work. You'll need good photos, so you can offer a potential contract. Some percentage of sales of a book. Don't look so surprised. A book could be very appealing if what you've said about the explosion of the quilting world is correct. These are very accessible as works of art, more so than a lot of what's being done at the big international art shows. The story that goes with them could have a special appeal."

Liz thought the professor was jumping to conclusions about how much the quilts would appeal. As Marjorie had said, "They're not really pretty." But, she thought, they're as accessible as the work of some of the serious quilt artists, except they don't come with a record of exhibitions and prizes. She sighed.

"What's that sigh for?"

"All the hurdles I can see on the track ahead of me."

"Getting a Ph.D. is not supposed to be easy. If it didn't require real work, it wouldn't mean anything."

"Yes, Sir," Liz said. She smiled and stood up. She shook Prof. Toad's hand. She felt overwhelmed by all the new information. The idea of Sam as a fashion model! Otherwise, she had a topic. It would be the train that would take her into the unknown territory of the rest of her life. This was an example of what unexpected territory might be ahead.

Liz had agreed to meet Jack on Saturday. Not a minute too soon to get out of Bloomington, into the countryside. The roads were new to her, but they were country two lane highways, south to the Wabash and into Illinois to a state park Jack had found. He emailed a map with the route marked clearly. She grew up in Indianapolis but felt peaceful in the farmland just as she had been peaceful and happy on the steppes of Mongolia. If Jack had a family farm, she might find herself happy to be a farmer's wife. Maybe a little career working with—well, why not the American Quilters Society in Paducah, Kentucky. At least I know about how Jack earns a living and where he lives. Is there anything wrong with being a country girl? Jack's being a little pushy.

I'm out of practice with men. It was so comfortable with Randy. Liz realized that after a winter of study and teaching, thoughts about a man in her future ping-ponged with what she knew was limited experience with serious men. Randy was more complicated than she thought.

It's all too complicated, Liz had decided. I'll concentrate on Geneva. Tom Toad doesn't understand what it's like out there on that little farm so far from a university, hidden away in a nook in the hills. I wouldn't understand if it weren't a familiar part of my family background. If Mom and Marjorie weren't close friends...if, if, if... She glanced at the map and notes Jack had sent. It's not far. This could be what I need or a wasted couple of days.

The day began gray and damp. As she got into her car she felt it was probably a terrible mistake. By the time she found the entrance to the park the sun had come out strong and bright. Driving just sixty miles south made a big difference. The hillsides were washes of rosy clumps of redbuds and spatterings of shy white dogwoods among the bare limbs of the larger trees, many with the yellow-green promise on leaves fattening in the brilliance. She found the entrance to the state park a little before 11:00. She wondered how she would find Jack. When she approached the toll booth, which was not open so early in the season, she saw Jack leaning against his truck.

They found a parking lot near a clearing at what was a campground in season with picnic tables, simple grills and an unlocked bathhouse with working toilets. The facilities were surprisingly tidy. Jack had a thermos of coffee and she had picked up a box of donut holes. They sat at a table in the sun and talked. She told him about her visit with Geneva. Then remembering Prof. Toad's analysis, she couldn't resist telling Jack about her visit with Aunt Alma—how talking about her excitement about sex had momentarily turned her into a young woman, much prettier than Liz had ever imagined she might have been. "I thought I was seeing things. Maybe I was."

"Do you believe in ghosts?" Jack asked.

"No. Do you?"

"Yeah, I do. I think people can project visions, and see visions and that energy remains in some places. I read a lot about that kind of thing."

"You're like a box of Cracker Jacks, packed with a surprise."

Jack laughed and kissed her. "That's me, Babe."

"So what kind of vision was I seeing?"

"You were seeing her like she actually looked—whatever, fifty?— years ago. Her memories were so strong, you could read that vision."

"So you're a mystic," Liz teased.

"I think everybody can be. There's a ghost hunter show on TV, and they find ghosts. They do." But now his voice told her he knew she would be skeptical and he needed to draw her into his conviction.

"TV can make all kinds of things happen," Liz protested.

"No, not this show. I may not have a college degree, but I can tell truth from lies."

"Jack," Liz said. "You've got to cut this out. I don't care if you've been to college or not."

"I care."

"Then you should go to college."

"I don't want to go to college. I just care about it when someone like you says, 'No,' and that's the end of something. Like anyone who disagrees is a dummy."

"I didn't mean that," she protested. She was deeply skeptical of anything on television.

"You did. In a way."

"Okay, I did. In a way. We're not here to fight. Let's find a trail and see where it goes." Liz didn't want to have spent an hour driving here, which would mean an hour driving back, and a day blown unless they did something together that they both enjoyed.

Jack screwed the top on his thermos. "I mean there are things you don't learn in college and, anyway, I've got a good business going which is better than a few college guys I know who don't have jobs."

Defensive, Liz thought. Men are like that. Stop generalizing and concentrate on Jack.

They left Liz's car in the parking lot and soon found a "loop trail" sign with a weathered map. The trail followed a creek into a ravine and came to a waterfall that cascaded noisily over boulders. They saw several kinds of birds; Jack knew their names. They saw the white scoots of a pair of deer crashing in panic through the underbrush. The sun was so warm and the air so still that they got sweaty and took off their jackets as they climbed the hill out of the ravine.

"You ordered a perfect day. I could walk in the woods all day," Liz said.

"Could be all day," Jack said. "This might be a ten-mile trail."

"We can handle it. Even if we run into a bear."

"Me Tarzan." He pounded on his chest and gave an ape-man cry.

"Oh, God, Jack, you'll have all the apes in the county coming after us."

"Just the female ones." Jack held her hand until the path narrowed and they had to walk one behind the other. "I'll go first in case of snakes."

"Now you think about snakes."

"I've been thinking about them all along. Mostly thinking it's too early. Too cool for them to be out," Jack said. "I figure if we clomp as we walk, they'll make themselves scarce anyway."

"You know one reason Australia is low on the list of places I want to go?" Liz asked.

"Snakes?"

"They've got a lot and ninety percent of them are poisonous. And there's one nasty bastard in the jungles in the northern part that actually chases people."

"No."

"That's what I read. And its poison kills you in fifteen horrible minutes."

"How come you like to travel so much?" Jack asked.

"I like to see things. I mean, for real, not just photographs—they're always different than you think they're going to be. I learned that when I saw the pyramids. You think they'll just be these piles of stones in the dessert. You've seen pictures a thousand times. But, oh, my god! You stand there by them and they're so big."

"But so what? Is it better than being here in the woods?"

"No, it's not better. It's different."

When they had stopped beside a little waterfall and sat on a rock to rest Jack asked, "You know what I'd like to do sometime?"

"What?"

"The Appalachian Trail. The WHOLE thing. Did you ever read *A Walk in the Woods*?"

"I fell off the sofa laughing." Liz said. "That guy who threw away the coffee filters..." They both laughed.

"You want to do the Appalachian Trail?"

"I might if I ever had the free time," Liz had thought about it when she read the Bryson book, but she discarded the idea. "Maybe someday

I'll have the freedom to spend a summer walking the trail. I don't know..."

"You can't think that way," Jack said very seriously. "You gotta say, I want to do it and I am going to do it and then make the time and do it. That's the only way to do something big like a whole summer of hiking."

"You know what? You're totally right."

"Let's do it." He sounded as if he was ready to start making plans.

"Jack, we don't know each other. You don't have a clue how bitchy I can get when I'm tired and my feet hurt. And the truth is, I really hate carrying a big pack. I like walking like we're doing today. I RE-ALLY like this kind of walking."

"So you don't want to do a big trail with me?" His voice was sincerely disappointed. It didn't seem to matter to him that he had a business or that she was finishing a college degree. Just do it.

"If anybody could talk me into it, it'd be you, I think. To tell you the truth, I'm really scared I'd wimp out."

"You getting tired?"

"A little, but not grumpy tired yet."

When they got back to the truck the sun was sinking toward the treetops. "There's a town a couple of miles back the way I came," Jack said. "I've got my little gas grill. How does a steak sound?"

"Fantastic."

They found a supermarket and shopped and decided to park the truck with her car in the camping area. The restrooms even had electricity. They set up Jack's grill. They ate the deli potato salad and pickles they brought. "I've got something for you," Jack said. He dug around behind the driver's seat and came back with a bottle of Tabasco sauce. "For your steak."

"How'd you know?"

"You had it on your hamburger and fries, remember?"

"Oh, yeah."

"I never saw a woman do that before."

"You're a very observant guy."

"Oh, I got lots of special qualities you haven't found out about yet."

By the time they finished eating the mini pies they had bought for dessert, Liz was feeling very satisfied. Evening was falling. The lights of a car approached. It was a state trooper. The moment Jack saw car lights he tucked his bottle of Wild Turkey under his arm inside his jacket.

The trooper stopped very close-by and rolled down his widow. "You-all camping here tonight?"

"We thought we would. I know it's not properly open," Jack said.

"You from Kentucky?" The trooper had noted the truck's license plate.

"Yea-ah." Jack's accent immediately grew thicker. "My girlfriend's from Indiana and this is kind-a half way."

"Well, it's alright to be here but I gotta tell you, sometimes kids come around later on. Mostly just parkin', but you never know what they'll be up to."

"Drugs, you mean? If you're telling us it can get dangerous, we don't want to be here. We're too old for that shit, you know?"

"They know I come around pretty regular, and they prefer a place on the highway where they can take off ahead of me," the trooper said. "You're probably all right here. If I come by later on and see that camper shaking up and down, I'll just give you a blast of the siren so you know things are all A-OK. Oh, by the way, you know there's a law against booze in the park."

"I hear you, Officer," Jack said. The trooper went on around the circular road of the camping area and out.

"Where's the whiskey, Jack?" Liz asked.

"Here." He took it out from under his arm. "I don't think he saw it. He just knows human nature."

"You thought it was going to be a trooper?" Liz asked.

"I didn't want to share with anybody but you. Do you feel safe here?"

"I felt safe in gers in the middle of Mongolia. Didn't bar the door. But I'm not sure about small town teens. Do you feel safe?"

"Well, if he says so, I think it's probably okay. But if you want to get up in the middle of the night to go to the jon, I want to walk you there, you know, just in case. Is your car locked?"

"Yeah, but I want to get the pictures of Geneva's quilts." She had had the quilt pictures printed to give to Geneva when she visited again.

"Yeah, I'd like to have a look."

When everything was cleaned up around the camper they climbed in. The floor had only a thin mattress with blankets. There really wasn't room for anything else but it provided the coziness they both had been looking forward to all day. Jack lit votive candles up on the shelf above the truck cab. He stashed the Wild Turkey there with the glasses and the bag of groceries for breakfast.

Liz started stripping to get into the bed, it was cool in the camper but would be just fine under the blankets beside a warm body. Jack made a playful lunge at her. They kissed and tumbled about for a while, removing Jack's clothes in the process.

"Do you want to see my pictures or not?" Liz asked.

"Yeah, before we get otherwise occupied."

Liz took the packet of pictures out of her jacket pocket and showed them to Jack. "They're unusual quilts, not the kind people bring for you to quilt."

"Yeah, I'll say," Jack said, glancing at them, quickly, one after the other, as if he were quickly assessing a hand of cards just dealt to him. "You wouldn't call them pretty, would you?"

"Yes and no. Not pretty the way most people think of pretty. But pretty interesting. They have a special character and style—her style."

"Yeah. That they do. How come you're going to write about this kind-a quilt when there are so many good ones people are making?"

"Because these are different."

"You're right about that. I don't really see what you're going to be able to write about."

"You don't have to like them." Liz took the pictures from Jack.

"Hey wait a minute. Don't get in a huff. Let me really look at them." He stood up and pulled a toolbox from the shelf above and dug out a big flashlight. "I don't want to diss something that's important to you." Jack spread the pictures out on the blanket over his lap and shone the flashlight on them. He studied each picture one by one. "So she's making these to send to people in Africa."

"This is her idea of what they'll like. She doesn't have any real African fabrics, so she uses what she has. And what she has is what people in her church give her."

"Yeah, I see some Disney stuff here, and that one has some Spider-Man prints." Jack's finger found the spots on the photos.

Liz knew if he were looking at the pictures, full screen on her laptop, the novelty designs would be even more obvious. Incorporating them, even though Geneva was not familiar with most Disney characters or with Spider-Man, seemed a distinguishing feature of Geneva's naiveté and outsider status. "Right," she said. "But she cuts them up into pieces so you don't immediately recognize the original pattern."

"Well, I recognize them. The colors are all—I don't know what the word is, but they don't go together. It's like noise, you know? Noise is not music and the colors in these patterns are not pretty together like this."

"Not everyone thinks the same things are pretty," Liz said. "You don't turn down jobs, do you, just 'cause you think the quilt's not very pretty?"

"No, but I don't think I'd much like working on some of these. You know, I've got to sit there and look at the thing, four, five, six hours and you don't want to look at something that just bothers you for the best part of a day." He held a few up closer to the light. "I see she tied quite a few of them. Didn't quilt them."

"Right. It's quicker to tie a quilt. She's 86 and she wants to have over a hundred to give away and she's not sure if she'll have enough time to make that many." Liz felt that in defending Geneva, she was also defending herself, defending her idea that these were important quilts.

"How many has she finished?"

"I don't know, and she doesn't either. She knows it's over fifty."

"They're good clear pictures. You're pretty good."

"Sam showed me how to adjust the settings. It wasn't as complicated as I expected. But Marjorie got tired of holding them up and refolding them. So I've got to go back and photograph the rest."

"Who's Sam?"

"A photographer in the art department. My advisor asked him to teach me about handling a good camera."

"Not a boyfriend?"

"A colleague. Not my type of guy, too pretty-pretty."

"Gay?"

Liz shrugged. "Doesn't matter. He's got money and cameras coming out his ears."

"I hope he's gay."

"Jack..." It was time to define some parameters. She didn't want to get into a sticky situation with serious expectations too soon. "I'm not at a stage to get serious. Been there, done that, gotta get up my nerve again."

"In the meantime—?" Jack sounded like a school boy whose hand has been slapped for a mistake he understood but couldn't resist making.

"We're here and I've had a great day so far." She gathered up the photos and put them back in their envelope.

Jack affixed the flashlight by its magnetic patch to the side of the camper. "I want this handy in case we need it in the middle of the night."

"Are you worried about being here alone?" Liz asked. She was a little bit uneasy since the trooper had stopped.

"I got no idea how often that trooper comes around. I usually travel with my deer rifle, probably should have brought it."

"If you're that worried, maybe we should find some place in town. Like across the street from the police station," Liz said.

"I'm not that kind of worried. I'd just feel a little safer."

"Do you actually hunt Bambi?"

"Are you one of those 'Bambi' people?"

"In a kind of knee-jerk way, I guess."

"I like venison. Do you?"

"I've only had it once. It was okay."

"I'll cook it for you sometime. I promise it'll be better than okay, even without Tabasco."

"Let's not get in any kind of an argument, at least until daylight."

They heard the state trooper's brief blast of siren at some point in the night. Jack chuckled and Liz mumbled, "All's well." They curled closer together in the nest of their blankets and went back to sleep.

Liz started home Sunday around ten, after they'd had a camp breakfast and fast paced hike in the very crisp morning. She felt peaceful and satisfied. Jack was easy to be with. His insecurity about her higher education came up now and then, but she thought he was becoming more relaxed. He was comfortable in the woods. He knew trees and animals and he made good coffee. He didn't understand eggs "over easy" and broke the yolks, but he could learn. She liked his looks, plain but not dull. Just a "good guy" kind of good looks.

Jack didn't understand Geneva's quilts, but he had tried. He had really looked at the pictures trying to see what she saw. He simply didn't have the background. She hoped he had understood that she really liked being with him but wasn't ready for a serious relationship. What a fantasy. It never turned out that way. Her relationships had always become too complicated or too serious too soon. Certainly Randy took for granted that she would always be in sync with what he wanted to do.

Problems, problems, Liz thought as she drove past a prosperous look-ing farm with three silos standing like helmeted soldiers protecting the barn. She hadn't thought of asking Sam to do the photography. She couldn't imagine Sam in that part of Indiana, really out in the boonies. Among the small farms Sam would look as odd as a tourist in hot pants in Ridyah, Saudi Arabia. Prof. Toad was right. She needed really good photographs and she needed them as soon as possible. Ge-neva seemed healthy and hearty. Perhaps she would live to be 100. It could happen; more and more people were becoming centenarians. However, Geneva was 86 and living alone on a farm with only a son and some church people who came by to keep an eye on her. Geneva was alone most of the time—sitting at her sewing machine quilting. I hope she's well enough to last until I get my thesis written, Liz thought. I can't waste time

She really didn't want to ask Sam to photograph the quilts. If only she could get permission to take the quilts with her and bring them to a studio in the art department where they could be well lighted and easily photographed. Talking Geneva into parting with them briefly would be easier—well, maybe not easier—to accomplish, but easier to attempt than asking Sam to go to Geneva's. Yes, that's what she'd try to do.

Next weekend Jack wanted to see her again. Well, maybe, or maybe not. She didn't want to let him think she would always be available. But...she thought of how warm and satisfying the night had been. He was a sweet, if not very adventurous lover, thoughtful and...well, just sweet. Sweet did not appeal to her in quilts, but it certainly did in men.

Chapter 6

Liz found a note under the door when she got home. It was written on a grocery receipt that had apparently been crammed into a pocket and then smoothed. "Came by to talk about a far out idea. Pls call. Sam." A phone number was scribbled on the bottom. She put the note on the table. Why did he like dropping by? She didn't know anybody who actually went to see someone without a call or an email first. She emptied the dirty clothes from her backpack into the laundry basket and sat down to check her email. Nothing from Sam, he had just dropped by. What a strange guy. She needed to do half a dozen things. No time to see Sam—well, she'd call and say so. After she had a proper shower. The shower in the park bathroom had only cold water.

She was blowing her hair dry when the doorbell rang. "Jesus!" she muttered. She knew it was Sam. As soon as she opened the door she said, "I don't believe you."

"It's me in the flesh. What don't you believe?"

"I was going to call and say I have a thousand things to do and maybe we can talk later tomorrow."

"Well, I'll go away if you're really too busy. But I saw a light in the window, and I thought we could go to the Italian place on the corner for pizza or spaghetti or something and I could run my idea past you."

Liz pursed her lips and visualized the inside of her refrigerator. It was nearly empty. She had been thinking about scrambled eggs, but she had had eggs for breakfast. The only other possibility at the moment was canned soup. Pizza sounded better. "You talked me into it."

"Good. You ready?"

"Give me a sec to put on some lipstick. I can't go anywhere with you—all things considered—without at least some lipstick."

"Do the evening gown and diamond tiara and I'll buy a bottle of Chianti."

Liz put on earrings. She was not ordinarily self-conscious, and it was not that she wanted to impress Sam. His movie star looks made everybody stare at him. She didn't want people thinking, why is a guy like that having pizza with a dog like her? As she put on lipstick she looked at herself critically for a moment—a well-fucked look was still on her face, everything seemed to lift up into a smile of satisfaction. She added a little gel to keep to her hair in place. What a drag it would be to be Sam's girlfriend. The models he probably dates during his weeks in New York were into that kind of primping and perfecting. They can have him; I don't want to feel that every time I go out for a slice of pizza I have to worry whether my eyebrows need plucking.

When she came into the living room Sam asked, "Did you get prints made of the pictures you took of Geneva's quilts?"

"Actually they're in my pocketbook. I showed them to someone this weekend." She quickly considered explaining she'd been away with a man but then thought, no, it's none of his business.

Sam seemed shy about coming to his point. He talked about pizza for a while and asked whether she wanted regular chianti or chianti classico. "I'm afraid I don't know the difference. I usually have a Diet Coke."

"Classico is fuller bodied. You'll like it better."

"I'll take your word for it. Do you know a lot about wine? You know, like saying it has a woody taste with overtones of wild dock weed and a vague hint of groundhog?"

Sam laughed. "I'm trying to learn, but I don't have your imagination. I actually come from a family that never has so much as a beer in the fridge."

"Are you the black sheep?"

"In some ways, I guess I am. My older brother was the first in the whole family to go to college. He's a lawyer. Everyone's very proud of him. When I said I was studying art they thought I'd learn to draw nudes or else paint canvases all white or all black and call them Composition Number Twelve."

"They must be glad you're a photographer."

"Yes, they understand that."

The waitress came and flirted with Sam for a few minutes before she asked for the order.

"And what do they think of your New York career?" Liz asked when the waitress left.

"They don't understand really. They suspect I'm lying and that I'm really into drug dealing or something illegal. If I were doing TV ads, they'd tell the whole neighborhood to watch."

He talked about his family until the pizza came. They lived in Gary and were second generation from Lithuania. His grandparents had managed to get out of a displaced persons camp after WWII and emigrate to stay with their cousins in New Jersey until his father got a job that moved them to Gary. "In a nutshell, Dad hated the job and Gary. Mom was seeing the guy who's my step-father. Dad left. It was rocky but settled down"

"Now I feel like I should have my recorder and practice my interview technique on you," Liz said.

"I'd like to read your interview with Geneva," Sam said.

"Really?"

"Yeah, what I wanted to talk about is her quilts."

"What do you think of them?" She had emailed the photos to him.

"I keep thinking about them. Did you bring the prints?"

Liz pulled the packet of prints from her shoulder bag. She was surprised by Sam's interest. Was this what he had been so eager to talk about?

"Light's terrible but I can see the design this way." He went through the pictures slowly. The waitress brought the pizza and stood hoping he'd notice her at least long enough to say thank you. Liz's thank you was far from sufficient for the girl. "I'd really like to see the quilts for real."

"You would?"

"Yeah, I really would. And I'd like to meet this little lady." He held the picture of Geneva opening a quilt and one of her with her chickens. "She looks like she could chop a chicken's head off, cut it up and cook it for dinner all in an hour's time."

"I imagine she can. And probably has. But she's small, smaller than she looks in this picture, probably no more than five-three."

Sam took a very big bite of pizza and chewed it slowly, shuffling the photographs. "Liz, I don't know how you'd feel about this, but I wonder if you'd let me come with you to her place. I'd love to rig up a line to display the quilts on, set up the camera on a tripod and get some professional quality photos. I'd really like to photograph every quilt she's got, whether it's in the bunch she did for Africa or the others. It'd be fascinating to have the contrast and comparison."

"You want to photograph them?" Liz could hardly believe what he had just said.

"Is that insane?" He looked worried.

"No. I can't believe it. I've been wondering if I had the nerve to ask you to do that. It might take a couple of days."

"That's okay."

"We'd have a place to stay—my cousin Marjorie's house is always available," Liz said.

"That's not important, I'm sure there are motels too."

"Not many and I doubt they'd be up to your standards. It's truly Outer Nowhere."

"I can stay anywhere. Would Geneve let me do that, do you think?"

"Geneva, like in Switzerland. I don't know how she'd feel. I hope she'd agree 'cause Prof. Simmons thinks I need really good photos."

"And you know what I thought," Sam said. "I hope this isn't impinging or—I don't want to be pushy or anything—but, you see I need something unique for my master's portfolio." Sam spoke diffidently as if he expected Liz to be appalled by the idea. He hurried on, explaining, "I've shot a load of people in the New York streets, but everybody and his brother-in-law has done that kind of picture at least since the '70s. I can't compete with Robert Frank, et al."

"I can't believe you're saying this," Liz said. "What I kind of dreamed was maybe it could turn into a coffee table book, your photos, my thesis. There might be a market for a book like that."

"You think it's possible?"

"I don't know what's involved. I guess it could be just excerpts from my thesis so as not to scare off people who just want eye candy." Liz felt she was blurting out all the extravagant daydreams that had swarmed like gnats as she drove back from Illinois. Oh-oh, she shouldn't have suggested his photos would merely be eye candy.

Sam ignored the implied slur. "If you're willing to go for it, I am."

A folded slice of pizza was frozen in his hand midway between his plate and his mouth. "What a great challenge. The color, the design and the texture. Some of them have these tuft-y things on the surface..."

"They're tied instead of being quilted."

"What do you mean, tied?"

Liz explained about the ways the three layers of the quilt could be held together. Sam didn't even know that quilts had to have three layers to be called quilts. He listened to her as he ate most of the pizza and she talked. "So I need to shoot details too, to show the quilting or the tying and the stitches, right?"

"Yeah, that would be perfect."

"Hey, great minds running on the same track. You and me, can you believe?" Sam's face became more real as his excitement animated it.

"I'm stunned you like these quilts."

"Maybe it's best to be a know-nothing. I look at them with fresh eyes."

"I guess I do too," Liz said. They shared an excitement that totally surprised her.

"A couple of fools rushing in where angels would fear to tread," Sam said and laughed. "We're a team, Lizzie. This is fantastic."

"Professor Toad tells me *tempus fugit*. He says I have to hurry up and document these quilts. When are you free to go photograph them?"

Sam sighed. "I've got an exam this week and Friday afternoon I'm headed to New York. I'm booked solid for two more weeks—they have to get fall print ready by the first of June. After that I'll be back most of June."

"That'll probably work for me. I've got a lot of loose ends to tie up and I want to do a draft outline to run by Tom so I have a firm idea what direction to go when I get to interview her again. Let me tell you, this interview stuff is...well, I'm learning secrets. Wow." Liz felt that Sam had just become a partner.

"Like?"

"Like hanky-panky."

Sam laughed. "Hanky-panky?"

"An old fashioned word for old fashioned people."

"Some things weren't discovered yesterday," he said.

"Sam, you don't know these country people. They're straight arrows."

"Sorry, I don't believe it. People are people." Sam tapped the envelope of photographs. "Here's a country person I'd like to get to know. Is your Aunt Marjorie like her?"

"Cousin," Liz corrected and then explained about Marjorie and Aunt Alma. "I was raised in Indianapolis. I thought it was a big city, but it's hardly the Big Apple," Liz said.

"Gary isn't exactly sophisticated either," Sam said. "But you've traveled a lot."

"And you're not a country bumpkin either," Liz said.

"Partners?" Sam asked.

Liz held up a wine glass. "Partners," she said as they clinked glasses. Liz saw the waitress who had been fixated on Sam turn away and walk into the kitchen.

Liz made an appointment to talk to the director of the campus art museum. She did not expect to be able to arrange a show of Geneva's quilts there. But she had met Ilona Robinson at an art department function and thought Ilona would have some suggestions. Best of all possible daydreams, maybe Ilona would help make some contacts. As she was walking through the center of the campus toward the museum, she saw Prof. Simmons approaching from a cross street. "Hello! Elizabeth!" he called out.

They talked about the fine weather and the flowers that were struggling up around town. "Did Sam get in touch with you?" he asked.

"Was that your idea?"

"Was what my idea?"

"That sounds like a guilty answer," Liz teased.

"No, I really don't know what. He called and said he's seen your pictures and thought he'd done a pretty good job tutoring you. He said he liked the quilts, and I told him they were first rate from the point of view of Outsider Art."

"Can I quote you? I'm about to talk to Ilona Robinson for some leads about where to go to try to get a show of them."

"Sure, quote me all you want. Tell her to call me if she feels like it. So Sam told you he liked the pictures."

"No, Sam said he likes the quilts. But he thinks he should take the pictures," Liz corrected.

"Sounds like a good idea." Liz was about to ask if he suggested that to Sam, but Tom read her mind and answered, "I didn't say he should take the pictures for you. I wouldn't insult you."

"Sam wants to work with me on a book about the quilts," Liz said. "Thanks for the hint."

"I didn't mention any such thing. He thought of it on his own." He saw the skeptical look on her face. "Really, we only talked four or five minutes on the phone."

"Why don't I believe you?"

"You should believe me. You're underestimating Sam."

"It's hard to believe there's a thinking brain northward of that beard," Liz said.

Prof. Simmons shook his head. "Don't jump to conclusions. He's not all surface, I assure you."

"You know what I find weird about him?" Liz asked.

"Weird? I don't think he's weird at all."

"He comes by to talk. He doesn't call or email or text. He shows up at my door."

"He must like you."

"I'm not his kind of woman." She made a brief gesture to include her unglamorous self: her jeans, Levi jacket, unmade-up face.

"I think you're more attractive than you think you are," Prof. Simmons said.

"No, really, Tom. It's like he's uncertain of his ideas and has to watch people's reactions just to say what's on his mind," Liz said, realizing as she said it that she had discovered a truth about Sam.

"Hmm," Tom pursed his lips and rocked on the balls of his feet for a minute. "That may be true. He's probably been a really good-looking kid all his life and discovered that he could get his way if people could watch the look on his face. I think you're onto something. He trusts his face more than his mind."

"He probably knows it's more perfect than his mind," Liz said.

"No, no, Elizabeth." The professor actually wagged his index finger at Liz. "He's not dumb; he's a smart guy."

"I think we just unlocked his secret."

"You did, which shows how smart you are," the professor chuckled.

"I don't know about that. I can't make fine art, I can't make wonderful quilts, I take fuzzy photos and I haven't learned to interview very well yet."

"But you will. You'll come out with a first-rate thesis—and probably a book that'll sell, if you find the right publisher."

"Thanks. That's music to my ears. Thanks a lot."

"I really believe that, Liz. I like this project of yours more all the time."

Liz knew she was beaming with happiness. "I'll be late if I don't get moving."

He glanced at his watch. "Me too. Nice running into you."

Liz gave him a quick hug. "Thanks for setting things up with Sam."

"I swear I didn't."

"You're my favorite advisor anyway."

Ilona was friendly and easy to talk to. She looked at the quilt photos and clearly did not understand what was exciting about them; she said firmly it was not her area of expertise. She had no interest in showing them but quickly came up with four contacts. "The American Quilters Society Museum in Paducah is a possibility, but I suspect you need a publication first," she said. "In fact, getting a show before a publication is putting the cart before the horse."

Liz explained Geneva's intention of giving the quilts away before or immediately after her death. "If she lives another maybe five years, I think when her closet is full—especially if she's slowing down physically—she'll find a way to get them shipped to some church group in Africa. And if she dies before she fills her cedar closet, they'll be lost to us forever."

"She's truly determined?"

Liz explained her brief attempt to talk about selling them and sending the money to a charity. "She hesitated only a moment. Her desire to pass on the work of her hands is much stronger than the simple desire to donate to—well, I think who she is giving them to is kind of amorphous in her mind. She met a couple from South Africa once and they are the picture in her mind."

"What a fascinating psychological discussion you can put into your thesis," Ilona said. "There are overtones of feminism as well as moral issues and the making of art based on beliefs that are individual in both areas. Her ideas may be erroneous but nevertheless she's sincere and produces true works of art. I'm taking your word for that."

"You can talk to Prof. Simmons for confirmation."

"If I were going to display them, of course, I'd get his commentary. But your enthusiasm is very convincing. Do you think she'd be willing to display them someplace local? You know, a library or a bank? Just to begin to get a resume together?"

Liz smiled thinking of Geneva having an artist's resume. "It's extremely rural there. I suppose Madison, which is a bit of a historic Ohio River town, might have a library or—I think there's a historic mansion. They probably would only want authentic period quilts. But that's an idea I'll explore."

"She may have more pride of ownership than she's let on so far. You know, when people spend a lot of time making something with all their heart and soul, it's not generally just to hide away in a closet."

Ilona apologized for being unable to be more helpful, but she had given Liz some web sites and names. Liz assumed Geneva wouldn't want to travel any further than, say, Indianapolis which was about a hundred miles. Maybe the state fair, Liz thought. She hurried home to get on the Internet and begin trying to find names of people to contact.

Jack called at eight o'clock. "I just had a brainstorm," he said.

"I know what you're going to tell me," Liz said.

"No, you don't. I've been thinking about training Kevin to use the machine, you know. And I'm going to be loaded with work as of about ten days from now. So I'm going to spend Saturday afternoon showing Kev how to quilt. It would be easy to show you at the same time."

"Two birds, one stone," Liz said.

"Right. Of course, you'd stay over. Would you be willing to drive all the way down?"

"Well..."

"Needless to say, Baxter and I would make you VERY welcome."

"You're tempting me. Could I manage a look at their museum? And do you know the name of the museum director?"

"I've heard her name, but I don't remember and I don't know her. I'll find out. You want to meet her?" He sounded eager to do whatever would entice her to come.

"Well, it's premature but I've been exploring the idea of a show of Geneva's quilts," Liz explained.

"I'll find out what I can for you. I think they plan their shows way ahead."

"I'm sure they do."

"You're gonna come, right? Say yes. Say yes."

"Yes."

"Great. How are things going with you?" She told him only a little about Sam. He told her a great deal about the clients who had been contacting him since the show. Apparently he was getting a good reputation and it seemed likely he'd be able to buy a second machine, a newer more computerized one. It would be a big investment, but he had a track record and his father told him he was in a good position to get a business loan. He was feeling very happy, and all the better at the thought of Liz being there overnight on Saturday.

When Liz walked into Jack's house it was obvious he had been cleaning and polishing. The floors were shiny, the kitchen was spotless. Baxter was not yet very friendly, but he seemed to remember she had been there and was tolerant. In Jack's garage/workroom was a stack of quilts to be quilted and one in the machine. Liz was able to look at all the quilts very closely and to touch them, which had been forbidden at the quilt show. She studied their construction as well as their designs, the choices of color and fabric. She didn't know how some were made and usually Jack didn't know either. The patterns were very different, yet, of the stipple, meander, and other quilting designs Jack offered, most had chosen either stipple or meander. "Which is great,"

Jack said. "That gives me all the freedom I need. I've done both so much I can watch TV with one eye while I work."

Jack called Kevin who arrived twenty minutes later looking hot and sweaty. "What were you doing?" Jack asked.

"Playing softball. But I told them I'd have to leave when you called." Kevin went to the kitchen and got a Coke. He started into the garage. "Oh, no you don't." Jack grabbed him by the back of the shirt. "Nothing but water in here."

"You take this very seriously," Liz said.

"I'm a professional," Jack said. "I won't have anybody working with me who isn't professional either—got that, Kev?"

"Yes, Sir." Kevin saluted.

Jack explained the machine, mostly to Liz because Kevin had been around enough that he knew the names of parts and processes. Liz watched as Kevin grasped the machine's guide bar tensely and slowly, very slowly, guided the needle in the design. "Relax, Kev, relax," Jack said. He put a hand on Kevin's and helped him guide the machine. "Like doodling," he said. After about half an hour Kevin relaxed enough to finish a section of the quilt.

"Your turn," Jack said to Liz. If anything, she was more tense than Kevin had been. But Jack stood behind her, embracing her and holding both her hands on the bar as he guided her. They all worked together, taking turns, until Kevin had to leave to go to work at the bar.

"You're getting it, Buddy," Jack said.

"I feel like I'm watching the start of something important," Liz said.

"I predict that in ten years almost no one will be quilting at home on a regular machine. All the quilts will be sent to people like me and Kev. The quilts will be stronger and last longer—not that anybody really cares about that. It's a throw away society."

"Not if you designed and made it. The makers want the quilts for their grandchildren to take to college with them," Liz said.

"Maybe, but maybe not. They'll have learned all kinds of new techniques by then and the fabric designers will be pushing something new and different, and they'll find the ones they made ten or fifteen years ago uninteresting and plain."

"You've been thinking a lot, Jack."

"I have."

"And I'm going to write it down."

Jack grinned as Liz pulled the steno pad Marjorie gave her out of her backpack. "You can quote me in anything you write. That's the way business works. Nothing stays the same. This machine is already five years old, it'll soon be outdated. I'll need a new one."

"And a nice big debt to the bank," Liz said. "That's the American way."

"Yeah, well...I guess that's right," Jack said. "You get kind of worked up about these things, don't you?"

"I never used to until I was in Mongolia and realized how people can live much more simply. The American way isn't the only way."

"Write your book and tell the world," Jack said. "Go, Liz Baby. Go!"

"Can it," she said.

Liz quilted about a quarter of what remained to be done. Then Jack took over and finished the top. Liz sat on a high stool nearby and was almost hypnotized by the needle moving over the surface of the quilt, a kind of simple dance, like the work of a master puppeteer. Jack didn't seem to be rushing, but the top was soon finished. "What happens to the edges?" Liz asked.

"The quilter binds it however she wants. There's a couple inches of batting and backing so she has some choices." He took the quilt from the frame, folded it neatly according to his note on the bag and then zipped it up. "I'll email her tomorrow that it's done and she can pick it up. When Kevin starts working for me, I'll have him do the email stuff. I don't like being my own secretary."

"Okay, so now I know this part of the quilting world. I suppose I ought to find a shop owner to interview and find out about the fabric sales and the whole part that comes before. But for Geneva it's people giving her fabrics and batting so she doesn't go into the shops."

"It depends on whether you want to understand the whole quilting business or just her."

"Right now mostly her. This was very interesting, but I probably won't use it."

"Well, damn, I don't like being useless."

Liz knew he was teasing but she answered seriously, "I didn't say YOU, did I?"

"I can be useful enough to take you to dinner. We've got reservations at a nice place."

"I didn't bring fancy clothes."

"Don't need them, just your fancy self."

Jack changed to clean clothes. Liz put on a different top and a silk scarf she'd thrown into her bag knowing they might go out somewhere. Most people in the restaurant were in jeans and sneakers as they were. He asked if she wanted to go some place that had music, but she said no. It had already been a long day. Jack was happy to go back to his house where they watched half a DVD. They agreed it wasn't very interesting, so they talked about their families while they sipped shots of bourbon. They went to bed early because that's what they really wanted to do. Just before she fell asleep, Liz breathed deeply, lying with her head on Jack's shoulder. "I'm comfortable here," she said. "You're easy to be with."

Jack's arm tightened around her, pulling her a little closer, although they were already skin-to-skin. "That's what I was thinking if not in those exact words. Thanks for driving all the way down here." She fell asleep.

They went to the quilt museum the next day and were standing at the door when it opened. Jack had handed her a list of names, phone numbers, post office and email addresses of people associated with the museum. Looking at the very professionally done exhibits, one group show, one one-person show, and an historical show, Liz knew this was not a venue for Geneva's quilts until they had a reputation. Someday they might work very well as a one-woman show.

Liz left soon after they returned to Jack's house. She had a long drive and wanted to get to her computer and make notes about all she had seen. As she drove the two-lane highways, sometimes getting stuck behind a slow old Sunday driver in a car older than hers, she began dreaming of a show at the Whitney in New York like the Gees Bend show. She constructed a complicated daydream of making Geneva famous and, incidentally, herself well known in the quilt world as the discoverer. That would surely lead to lectures and panel discussions, possible curatorships in one of the several quilt museums in the country. Jack had no role in the daydream. She wanted to accomplish something on her own and she wanted to be free to live and work anywhere that she was offered an interesting job.

I don't even have an introductory chapter written, she thought, and here I am making a reputation for myself. Get real, Liz! You've got to start writing. She began to think how the notes on the exhibits could fit into her discussion about Geneva's quilts. She began working up an outline for her thesis. She would have to ask Prof. Toad's opinion. Was she leaving out anything important, a discussion of Outsider Art? That might need more examples than she had studied so far. She wanted to talk about it only as a historical background, find some elegantly succinct way to describe the phenomenon and mention the great variety of outsiders, give some examples, very briefly but with such pithy details anyone would know she knew much, much more. And footnotes, of course, a dissertation must have footnotes. But she only knew of the Gees Bend women and had read a mention of another black woman whose name she hadn't been thoughtful enough to note as an outsider quilter. Surely there must be others. But maybe they hadn't been discovered, maybe that would be part of her future work.

Oh, my god, she thought. Cut the crap, Lizzie. I'll do the necessary reading. If I don't, I'll get stumped by some random question in the oral exam. What have I got myself into? She was suddenly caught up feeling like a child wading into the ocean. She would love to swim far out, easily propelling herself along, but she was very small and hadn't learned how to swim yet.

Liz let the feeling of panic grip her for a few miles. It subsided as she remembered her peaceful evening with Jack. What a stroke of luck that she had eaten in that bar where Kevin was waiting tables. She smiled as she remembered her first sight of Jack standing in front of her table, out of breath from running nearly half a mile to meet her. A story worth remembering to tell grandchildren someday... Oh, no, I won't go there. I'm not ready; it's not time.

———

Sam loved the drive to Friendship. He had never been to any part of Southern Indiana except Bloomington. Only a few miles east of the university, Sam said, "I didn't know it looked like this out here."

"You should explore Brown County State Park, it's beautiful," Liz said. She explained that hills were formed by deposits from the most recent glacier during the ice age that ended about 15,000 years ago. "We must have had the same Indiana history book in junior high school. I loved learning all that stuff."

"Obviously I didn't learn it. I remember two school field trips to Indianapolis. Once a cool friend's dad took us to see the trials for the Indy 500." He only remembered miles and miles of flat, flat farmland.

"So tell me how you got into modeling?"

Sam explained that he had spent high school summers at the New Jersey shore with cousins. An older neighbor was into body building and did some modeling in New York City. Eric was gay and had a crush on Sam. Sam was uncomfortable with Eric's attention but flattered and excited about the possibility of making money when Eric said he would pay for head shots and take them to the agency president. Eric encouraged Sam to grow a two-day beard and to cut his hair shorter. He had even insisted on plucking Sam's eyebrows. "That was the weirdest thing that had ever happened to me," Sam told Liz. She laughed.

Eric's agent liked Sam's looks; he was surprised Sam wasn't gay, but after a video test he announced that Sam brought a truly masculine attitude to photographs that Eric and his colleagues lacked. Sam was given a summer contract. His mother and stepfather insisted he go to college instead of staying in New York. Sam wasn't comfortable with the modeling and fashion milieu after such a short time and had dreamed of being a serious video artist, so he went to college. But the agency president liked his looks and gave him summer jobs that, once he graduated and thought about getting a master's, turned into to current routine of occasional work all during the year. The money was irresistible, and Sam was now comfortable with his double life.

"So I'm a chameleon. This is my fourth or fifth look," Sam said. "The way I look is not me, it's my income."

Sam watched the fashion photographers to learn their techniques. The top photographers could be creative and inventive; they were sent all over the world. Some were celebrities. It was an enticing world, but lately he had thought he didn't have the ambition to compete in that world. He had talked to some of his professors and had begun to feel that he needed a niche of his own. "So," he said. "I'm exploring this niche—photographing quilts and maybe other kinds of contemporary art. It's more technical than creative. I'm glad you're willing to let me have a go at these quilts."

"It's pretty clear I don't have the technical know-how. I need you."

"I've been looking at the countryside too," Sam said. "Tell me about this town we're going to."

"Friendship is a little town in a valley beside a creek. I didn't find it especially picturesque, but maybe you'll see it with different eyes. The only fly in the ointment, and we won't have to deal with it this time of year, is that there is an annual skeet shooting contest in town."

"Are skeet some kind of birds?" Sam asked.

"Clay pigeons—I think someone said they aren't shaped like birds, they're really disks. A machine automatically fires them into the air."

"That's a sport?"

"Yeah. I think it's better than shooting live ducks and geese."

"Bet they do that too," Sam said.

"I suppose they do. I think skeet's an organized sport with trophies and all. Did you ever shoot a gun?"

"No. But I had a cowboy outfit with a cap pistol when I was little. There's a picture of me looking fierce when I was three or four."

Liz laughed. "I'll bet you looked about as fierce as the Lone Ranger."

"Fiercer than Tonto. My mom has it in one of those frames with about twenty pictures, you know? Tacky, tacky."

"What's she think of your modeling career?"

"She's proud as a possum."

Liz laughed, she had never heard that expression.

"My stepdad's not so proud. He thinks I'm turning gay, he thinks it's a disease you can catch. I tell him I'm learning about photography from the other side of the camera and watching all the tricks of the guys who make really big bucks. When I tell him how much the top fashion photographers make, he shuts up."

"It would only be okay to be gay if you were making big bucks?" Liz asked.

"I'm not, so it's not really important if he's a bit of a bigot about it."

"You don't think we have a responsibility to educate our parents?"

"They had a responsibility to educate us," he said.

"But don't you think we ought to try to teach them—"

"No, Liz. Do you always get these heavy, serious ideas?" Sam asked. "Just cause you're a couple years ahead of me doesn't mean I'm a kid to lecture at."

"Oh, god, I'm sorry." She reviewed her conversation, geology, state history, bigotry. She had become more serious than she used to be, mostly thanks to Randy and their long ethical conversations in Mongolia.

They drove past fields where farmers were plowing with wide ploughs turning twelve or fifteen furrows at a time. "It must be boring as all hell to drive around and around a field all day like that," Sam said.

"They have radios and iPods and cell phones with them. I don't suppose they have TV."

Sam pondered a bit and then said, "We're lucky, aren't we?"

"Who? You and me?" Liz asked.

"Yeah, being able to do interesting things. I'm totally curious to meet this woman and see her quilts. I couldn't be bored if someone ordered me to be."

"I'm going to have to check in briefly, just for a few minutes, with my cousin, Marjorie. She said Aunt Alma had a stroke and she refuses to do any of the physical therapy. We don't have to go see her." Liz felt apologetic because she knew she would hate having to meet someone else's relatives when she really wanted to get on with a project. She had no picture in her mind of Sam's family but certainly they weren't from a small town like Dillsboro. They certainly didn't speak with remnants of a southern or even a hillbilly accent.

"Listen, I think we should go to Madison and check out that B&B. If it's crummy we can find a motel. Better to have that all taken care of so we don't have anything to worry about later in the day. It's only ten after eight."

They had started early so they could have a whole day of photographing the quilts. Okay, Liz thought, we'll go to Madison first and photograph all day and then I can call Marjorie and tell her I'm beat. Then there's tomorrow. But Sam will have met Geneva and heard her accent and Marjorie sounds highly educated compared to Geneva. Sam made her feel self-conscious in every possible way. He wasn't doing or saying anything even slightly judgmental, it was his looks, his perfect clothes, comfort and curiosity.

The B&B was a large white house with a view from the upstairs bedroom window of the river and the green banks of Kentucky beyond. They were the only guests, there was only a king-sized bed. "Shall I ask for a room with two beds, or for a second room?" Sam asked. "I didn't plan this—I swear to you. I'm not trying to lure you into anything, really." He was blushing.

Liz laughed, glad that he was the one who was uncomfortable. "I expected two beds, but this is the room with the view. How do you feel about sharing the bed?"

"Liz, how I feel isn't the important thing here. How do you feel? I can promise to keep my hands to myself. But if you entice me..." He raised his eyebrows, trying to do a Groucho Marx leer.

"We're grownups and it's a big bed." She believed him. She couldn't imagine that he was actually interested in sleeping with her anyway. Her sense of privacy and proximity had changed enormously after two years in a ger in Mongolia. She didn't want him to go to the expense of renting an extra room for her. She was so accustomed to being thrifty the extra expense embarrassed her, the $85 for this room in the pre-season springtime seemed extravagant.

"I feel...I'm embarrassed, I really didn't plan—"

"I totally believe you, Sam. I'm cool if you are."

"If you're cool, really—?"

"I am. Later on I'll tell you about the joys of visiting families in a ger in Mongolia. We've got a long day of work, so let's just take the room and see if I can find my way to Friendship from here."

"You have the Google map, don't you?"

"Yeah, of course."

"Let's go. I want to meet this woman."

Liz had never approached Friendship from the southwesterly direction, but Sam was a good navigator. "It's like being in another country and it's not even a different state," Sam said. They followed a two-lane road between old-fashioned small farms where farmers were working in fields.

"That guy's plowing, right?" Sam asked as they drove beside a field with newly turned earth. The man on the tractor was on the other side of the field.

"Right. Probably going to plant corn or soybeans."

"How do you know that?"

"That's what people grow around here."

Sam was quiet a moment and then asked, "What about alfalfa? Don't they grow alfalfa?"

"Yeah, I guess, but that's hay."

"What do you mean it's hay?"

"That's what they grow it for. I don't know how they plant it. I'm not a farm girl." Liz had been enjoying sounding knowledgeable. Where did Sam come up with alfalfa?

"I thought you were."

"Are you serious?"

"Yeah, I'm serious. I thought you knew all about all the country things."

"I just happen to have relatives down here. Marjorie is a school teacher and her husband worked for the highway department. Aunt Alma's husband was a farmer, and I think he was also a school bus driver. We didn't come visit all that often."

They turned onto another road and passed a hilly pasture with cows in it. "What kind of cows are those? Are they the kind that give milk?" Sam asked.

"If they're cows, they're female and they give milk." Liz was able to gain back some of her superiority.

"I thought they were all cows."

"Sam, you are a college graduate and you've never heard of bulls?"

"Oh bulls. Yeah. Male cows."

Liz laughed and turned to see if he was insulted. "Cattle. I think we Americans are getting more ignorant all the time."

"Don't call me ignorant."

Liz glanced at him. He was joking, not angry. "Those 'cattle' back there were kind of blond. I thought the milk kind were black and white." Liz laughed. "Hey! Watch where you're going, you nearly clipped the mailbox," Sam said seriously.

Liz slowed to about ten miles an hour. "Sam, I don't believe you said that. Don't you know anything about animal biology? Females give milk, black, brown, blond or purple."

"Oh, female! I get it." He laughed. "I never saw a purple cow—do you know that poem?"

"And I never hope to see one. But this I'll tell you now, I'd rather see than be one!"

"Brilliant. You're good company. No wonder that guy wanted you around in Mongolia with him."

"That is not a subject we're talking about, okay?"

"Kind of an ouch subject, huh?" Liz didn't answer. She was comfortable being with a guy who was not coming on to her.

Liz recognized the road she was on now because it was the way she had left the last time she was here. "We're almost in Friendship, now the trick is to find the little street that leads to the little road that goes up a little hill to her little house."

"Is it big enough to see with the naked eye?"

"If you have good eyesight. I think the street starts at the pizza place."

They found the road. "It's a mile or so. A shingled house with a dark green door and the mailbox by the road has a picture of a chicken on it, I think. Some kind of bird."

Geneva was out at the chicken house when they pulled into the driveway. As she came toward the car she walked briskly, not at all like an old woman. "I'll introduce you and then you can get your gear out."

Sam was formal. He shook Geneva's hand, saying, "It's nice to meet you, Mrs. Gardiner. I saw the pictures Liz took last time she was here."

"My pictures were not very good," Liz said. "But Sam's a professional."

"I'll get my stuff out of the trunk."

"Well, it don't make no difference whether you got a good picture of me or not," Geneva said.

"Oh, yes it does," Liz said. "How are your chickens?"

"I got a problem."

"With the chickens?" Sam asked.

"With something that come and got one last night or this morning. Found a few feathers and a foot out behind the hen house."

"Like a fox?" Liz asked.

"Could be. Or a weasel. Sometimes there's stray dogs. That chicken might-a been out all night. I don't count'em when I lock'em in at sundown. I'll be more careful now."

"Something killed it and ate it right there?" Sam asked. "Were there tracks?"

"It's all weedy back there."

Liz asked, "Can you do anything about it?"

"Just be careful to lock'em up. Sometimes a weasel'll burrow into a hen house, but I haven't seen a weasel around for quite a while. I 'magine it was a fox or a stray dog. I've heard people say they've seen coyotes around, too."

"Coyotes in Indiana?" Sam said.

"I've heard," Geneva nodded vigorously. "Haven't seen none."

"I thought they were only out West," Sam said.

"I've read they're in most states now," Liz said

"So you're going to take pictures of the rest of my quilts?" Geneva asked.

"I hope to take pictures of all of them, unless you've got too many."

"I got a goodly number, you know," Geneva said.

"How long have you been making them?" Sam asked.

"These ones, I guess maybe ten years. I give some away ever now and then—when there's a need, like a house fire or a tornado come through."

"Don't you get tired of sewing?" Sam asked.

"No, it's my favorite thing to do."

Sam had hauled out a tripod and a couple of camera cases. "I see you've got a clothesline back there, maybe we could use that."

"Won't you have a lot of light and shadows?" Liz asked.

Sam walked to the back of the house to look at the trees and think about the outdoor light. "Let's see what kind of space we've got inside. I've got to be far enough back to get the whole quilt."

"It's a little house with little rooms," Geneva said.

"Well, we'll find an answer. Mrs. Gardiner, I'm eager to see the quilts."

"Are you one of the lovers or haters of my kind-a quilt?" Geneva asked in an almost flirtatious way. My god, Liz thought, all he has to do is be himself and he charms the panties off women of all ages.

"I'm a lover of what I saw in Liz's pictures. I suspect they're a lot better in reality."

Geneva took them into her sewing room and opened the closet.

"Look at that." Sam sounded truly amazed.

"Why don't we start where I left off and then if there's time retake the ones I took pictures of," Liz suggested.

"First let me take a picture of that closet." Sam took several pictures of the closet with its stack of quilts, several with Geneva opening or closing the door. She insisted on re-combing her hair and Liz was sure she had added some blush to her cheeks, or she was naturally blushing to be photographed by this charmer who was treating her as if she were a duchess showing him her manor house.

Sam went out to walk around the house and the barn to look for the best place to display the quilts.

"You've got a good-looking boyfriend," Geneva said. "Polite too."

"He's not a boyfriend, he's just a photographer who I'm working with. How would you feel about having a book about you and your quilts, with pictures Sam takes and things I write?"

"I...I think it would...why would you want to do that?"

"Well, first of all, I have to write about you and your quilts for my thesis to get my degree, like I explained."

"But that's not a book, is it?" Geneva asked.

"Sam is working on an MFA in photography so he needs to have a collection of photographs to show what he can do. Sometimes it happens that people spend a lot of time writing their papers and come up with things that make pretty good books. Sometimes the university publishes them. I think, and Sam thinks, that if we did a book with pictures of the quilts, people would want to see it and read it and be willing to spend good money to buy it." Geneva frowned a little and grunted as if this was an amazing, possibly ridiculous, idea. Liz added, "And if that happened, you'd get part of the money too. It would be only right. I'm not talking about a lot of money. I mean hardly any books make much money, not unless you're a movie star or a politician."

"Well, that's a new thought to me," Geneva said slowly.

"If it should happen, it wouldn't be for quite a while. I haven't written anything yet except notes and a transcription of our talk that I recorded. I meant to bring you a copy, but I forgot. I'll mail you one."

"Oh, I don't need to know what I said. I didn't tell you no lies."

"I didn't think you did."

Sam knocked briefly before he came in the door.

"You can just come in," Geneva said.

"Well, I don't like to interrupt. Do you mind if we take your quilts outside, Mrs. Gardiner?"

"Everybody calls me Geneva."

"I have a very strict mother who says you always call older ladies Mrs. I don't think I can get out of that habit."

"I didn't know anybody raised their children that way these days."

"Not many, but my grandparents are that way too. It's a habit I don't really want to break. So if you don't mind..." Geneva smiled and nodded. So, Liz thought, his family would surprise me as much as my family will surprise him.

Sam said, "I think the barn door would be a good spot. I brought nails and a rope we can hang the quilts on with clips, we won't let them touch the ground."

"You thought of everything," Geneva said.

"That's part of being a photographer. The really good ones have two or three assistants to do that kind of stuff. I've just got Liz, and this isn't her kind of work."

"Well, I can help," Geneva said.

"Okay, we're a team. We'll see how much we can get done," Liz said. She felt like a Girl Scout.

Sam asked, "You don't mind some nail holes in your barn door, do you?"

"Shoot no. Nail all you want."

"Thanks. Liz, will you spread the tarp I put in the trunk of the car on the ground out by the barn? Then you can bring out a half dozen quilts for starters. And I'll rig up my rope."

Liz went into the house with Geneva. She asked, "Would you mind if we record some more later on, today or tomorrow?"

"Tomorrow? You're going to be here tomorrow?"

"Yeah, we came on Friday so that we could work on the photography tomorrow too. I didn't want to make it Sunday 'cause of church."

"Too bad you're not staying. I'd like to take your young man to church with me," Geneva said, a cheerful smile crinkling her face.

Liz laughed. "He's a nice guy. You know there's different tastes. His kind of good looks doesn't especially appeal to me."

"Takes all kinds," Geneva said. "Just as well I can't take him to church. Pride goes before a fall."

"I don't think you're in danger."

"At this age, it's all in the heart," Geneva said.

They gathered an armful of quilts. As they went out the door Geneva looked toward her chicken house. "I think I'll keep my shotgun handy," she said.

"What for?"

"Whatever's after my chickens. I don't like losin' them. I'm not in the business of feeding the varmints in the neighborhood. Let 'em catch rabbits, there's plenty of rabbits 'round. Though they run a lot faster than a chicken."

"Could you hit a fox?"

"Probably not a fox, probably wouldn't even see a fox. They come at night or real early in the morning. But if it's a stray dog, I could probably pepper it a bit with buckshot. Teach him a lesson."

"We've got an Annie Oakley here," Liz announced to Sam as they reached the barn. Sam was using a rock from the driveway to hammer long nails into the door.

Geneva smiled like a shy schoolgirl as Sam turned to give her a look. "What do you shoot?"

"Nothin', really. I just said I'd keep my shotgun ready in case a dog come round after my chickens."

"I'd like to be here if that happened," Sam said.

"I'd let you shoot him."

"Me? No, I couldn't shoot a dog even if it was MY chickens it was after. Besides, I've never had a gun in my hands," Sam said. "I'm not much of an all-American hero."

"You'll do," Geneva said. Liz remembered that Marjorie had reported from Aunt Alma that Geneva had always been full of high spirits and fun. She could imagine Geneva as a much younger woman from the sound of her voice.

They worked for a couple of hours bringing quilts out and standing back while Sam took pictures of the whole quilt and then used a smaller camera to take close ups of details. Liz made a list and wrote notes about the colors and patterns and everything else Geneva told her. Usually she mentioned a traditional pattern but often said, "But I kind-a changed it around some." Sometimes Geneva remembered that a certain friend had brought a particular fabric. Once in a while she mentioned that the pattern was like something from an African picture in a National Geographic magazine.

"People have been so good to me. They give me all these things," she said. "I'm blessed with good friends, and they tell their friends, and sometimes it seems like there's a real river of people passing down their sewing scraps and even giving me whole big pieces of fabric they don't want any more, or stopped liking, or forgot why they bought it in the first place. You'd be surprised how many people buy things and then forget what they bought it for. It comes through two or three hands and lands up here in my house and gets put into a quilt sooner or later. Isn't that a downright amazing thing?"

"It's kind of them," Liz said.

"There's more kind people in the world than you might 'magine from all the bad things on TV," Geneva said.

By noon they had photographed the quilts Liz had not photographed before. Sam had insisted on re-photographing all of them. Assuming the weather stayed this nice, which was predicted, they could finish tomorrow. Liz remembered Marjorie's warning about tiring Geneva.

Sam wiped his forehead. He was getting sweaty from standing in the sun. He said, "I don't know about you two, but I'm tired and I have a serious craving for pizza. Do you eat pizza Mrs. Gardiner?"

"Not much, I don't. Haven't developed the taste for it," Geneva said.

"Sam, are you saying you want pizza for lunch?" Liz asked.

"Yeah, it would hit the spot."

Liz asked, "Do you both want to come with me to town or shall I bring it back?"

"I could make you lunch. I got sandwich fixings," Geneva said.

Sam said, "The truth is I'm addicted to pizza. I'll go if Liz will trust me with her car. I'll get pizza for me and anything either of you might want or need. Do you need anything in town, Mrs. Gardiner?"

"Nope. Betty Wheeler took me to the grocery store yesterday," Geneva said. "You like coffee with your pizza? I could make you coffee."

"That would be good," Liz agreed, although, in fact, she preferred Coke. Maybe Geneva had bought things for sandwiches for lunch. But her income was limited, and Liz didn't want to take anything. "Sam, it's not that I don't trust my ten-year-old chariot in your hands, but I know where the pizza place is. Maybe you and Geneva can get acquainted."

"My pleasure," Sam said; he almost did a bow to Geneva. "Do you want to leave your recorder?"

"Now I got to answer your questions too?" Geneva asked. She attempted to sound peeved, but she looked as if she could hardly wait to be left alone with Sam.

"No, I'm no interviewer, but you may say something we want to remember. Like telling me when this house was built."

"Well, shoot, I know that like I know my own name. Alf built it in 1959 right after the old house got ruin't in a tornado."

"I'd like to hear what it was like to be young and building your own house. We'll take these quilts in and put them away." He picked up the quilts from the tarp and started to the house with them.

———

As Liz drove into the little town, she tried to plan an agenda for the rest of the day and tomorrow. Geneva did not seem to be tiring, but she was 86 and this was an exciting and probably stressful day. The weather was perfect for photography, but it was hot. Didn't older people suffer more from heat? Maybe she and Sam could photograph more of the quilts in the afternoon and suggest Geneva have a nap while they worked. Then they could drive up through Dillsboro and see Marjorie for just a little while. If Geneva seemed tired after lunch, they could finish tomorrow.

Sam seemed agreeable to anything she suggested. Liz had no idea he would turn on his charm for an old lady like Geneva, but it seemed to be his natural way of dealing with people.

She was impressed by how professional he had been and how well thought out his preparations were. He had brought everything he might need. He had a tape measure and insisted they get the dimensions correct to the quarter inch. Geneva was embarrassed when a quilt was not perfectly square but both of them told her that wasn't important.

The quilts were aesthetically exciting, one bold pattern and color combination after another hung on the weathered barn door. She had sewn unlikely, clashing prints side by side and it made a complex whole that was surprisingly satisfying. The quilts had the sophistication they had studied in modern art but did not expect in a quilt. Sam would sometimes ask about the unusual piece of fabric, "Is there a story about this red print?"

"Oh, somebody just give it to me and I thought it'd go nice. I kinda like somethin' a little surprising. Makes me smile even if others might think it's a mistake and I 'spect they do," Geneva explained.

When Liz returned with the pizza, Geneva said, "Marjorie called. She said to wait to come see her. Alma had another little stroke this morning and Marjorie just got back from the hospital."

"How bad was it?" Liz asked.

"She said 'little.' It happened as she was going to breakfast, and the attendant called the doctor right away."

"She doesn't want us to come today?" Liz asked.

"She just said to wait. I guess you should call her." Liz nodded. Maybe I won't have to take Sam to meet family. Geneva sighed and said, "Poor Alma—you know when things start to go bad, they just kind of snowball at her age."

Liz put a hand on Geneva's arm and said, "But her age is your age."

"Nope. I'm fifteen months older." Geneva laughed like a child telling a joke. "Let's have some lunch." She poured the coffee she had made and then made herself a sandwich of white bread and baloney and lettuce.

After lunch they insisted Geneva lie down for a nap. She said she'd just have a quick rest in her recliner. They went into the sewing room for another armload of quilts to photograph. Geneva had fallen asleep almost immediately and was snoring softly, so they tiptoed out the kitchen door.

Hanging the first quilt on the barn door, Sam said, "I got all kinds of stuff on tape for you. When you ask her a question it's like the tap opens up full force. I don't think she talks to people much, and she's got a whole lifetime of memories bottled up inside."

"Thanks, Sam. You may be worth your weight in gold."

"Don't I wish? With her asleep, how are we going to get the names and facts?" he asked.

"I photographed these before, remember? I've got notes. What I haven't got are dimensions."

"Or clear pictures. Or details."

"Don't rub it in."

They worked for a while; Liz made notes to help her match the information she already had. When they had completed the pile of quilts, Sam wiped sweat off his forehead. He lay down in the shade and sighed. "I love it here. Listen...you can't hear a thing." A hen cackled. "What kind of bird is that?"

"I think it's a hen that just laid an egg."

"Really? I'm feeling schizophrenic. I can't believe this skin contains the same human being who was in New York three days ago going up and down the subway, in and out of taxis, talking about shoots and clothes and designers with people, like me, who had never heard a hen cackle because she laid an egg. Do they always do that?"

"Actually, I don't know. I remember gathering eggs at Aunt Alma's when I was little."

"Don't you feel schizophrenic?" Sam turned his head to look at Liz.

"Why?" She shrugged.

Sam closed his eyes. "Being here and having this kind of thing as memories but also having been in Mongolia for two years? Isn't it just amazing that we can be in such different places and feel comfortable? We are so adaptable. How do we fit the pieces together? Did you ever think about that?"

"No, not really. You know lots of people are like Geneva who's never been more than a couple hundred miles from home and never had to be anything but what they grew up expecting to be." Liz looked at the aged barn door and wondered how many times Geneva had opened and closed that door. She wondered suddenly if Geneva had ever come out to the barn to, maybe, tell her husband dinner was ready, and then they embraced, suddenly feeling romantic, and made love on the hay in the loft. She couldn't ask Geneva that. They had three children and children put an end to spontaneous love making.

After a thoughtful pause, opening his eyes and shading them against the sun stippling through the leaves, Sam said, "What a wild thing life is. Modern life. It's amazing."

"You're in a philosophical mood."

"I get them once in a while—this schizophrenic feeling—I guess that's not the right word. It's not like I'm hearing voices that aren't mine. I think I'm a bunch of different people. Geneva came to this farm with her husband to live with his family in a house that was crushed by a tree in a tornado."

"Yes, she told me that."

"She's one whole person in one place. I feel like—I don't know— two, three, four different people. Today I'm someone I never was before. Isn't that odd? Do you think I'm crazy?"

"No, I think you're curious—in two senses."

"What two?" Sam rolled to his side

"Curious because you want to know things, and curious like different than a lot of people." Liz thought, yes, that's true. She remembered *Alice in Wonderland*, "curiouser and curiouser..." So far this had been a curious day and, as she thought of the B&B with one big bed, the day promised to get curiouser.

"I know. You're kind of curious too," Sam said.

"No, I'm flat out plain."

"Elizabeth, you are not plain in any way. You picked a curious subject for your thesis. It could have been Berthe Marisol or Van Dyke or Lucien Freud or—"

"I'm tired up to here of all those old masters—well, not tired of Lucien Freud, but there are people working on a biography and no room for me." She changed the subject. "If we could find a place to show some of Geneva's quilts, do you think she'd let them out of the house? I've been emailing museums, but I wonder if it's a waste of time."

"I think she might—if it's not too far away and they gave her a nice legal contract promising their return at a certain time."

"Yoo-hoo!"

Liz looked toward the house. Geneva was at the backdoor. "We're taking a break too. You weren't the only one a little tired," Liz answered.

"I just made some of that Crystal Light," Geneva called.

Liz turned her recorder on while they drank the cold lemonade substitute. Geneva seemed delighted to tell Sam the story of her life on the farm, the three children, how she adored her girls and Ben, the boy who was his father's helper from the time he was very small. Liz thought of questions to interject but decided to let Sam handle the conversation. "There must have been artistic people in your family," he said.

"Well, the girls were, especially Myra. She could draw an animal that looked like it could walk and talk by the time she was eight or nine. Not many kids could do that."

"Did you save her drawings?" Liz asked.

"Well, I did for a while, but things pile up and I have spells of cleaning out."

"What about your parents and your aunts and uncles. Were any of them artistic?" Sam asked.

"Well, Dad could whittle. He whittled and fished at the same time. And what he whittled was fish. Ma said he done it so he'd have somethin' to bring home when they weren't bitin'. But he was good at it;

you could tell what kind-a fish they were. He'd even put the whiskers on a catfish. He used to go down to Rising Sun and go out on the Ohio with his cousin who lived down there and had a motorboat."

"Did your mother make quilts?" Liz asked.

"Ma didn't quilt, but she made clothes, aprons especially. Sold them at a store in Aurora. She'd do all kinds of fancy things, ruffles and rick-rack and what not. Some were so pretty women'd buy them and just wear when they had company. Never wear them when they were really cookin', just when they were bringin' the dishes to the table."

"So it runs in the family," Sam said.

"What? Makin' things?" Geneva asked. Sam nodded. "Yeah, sure. We were all handy. My oldest sister, Wilma, she taught art in school before she got married and started havin' kids."

Sam looked at his watch. It was after 4:00. "It's getting late. You don't mind if we come back tomorrow and finish up photographing the last twenty or twenty-five quilts?"

"No, you're quite welcome."

"And I want more pictures of you, you know?" Sam said, definitely flirting now.

"Can't really see what fer," Geneva said, suddenly shy. "'sides, you took all those pictures of me opening the closet door."

From both Geneva's voice and the downward tilt of her head Liz was sure Geneva felt the same need to look her best that Sam always inspired. She couldn't repress a smile.

"What are you laughing at?" Geneva asked.

"I'm not laughing," Liz quickly came up with an answer. "I'm just smiling because we want pictures of you. They're your quilts. Quilts don't hatch by themselves like baby turtles, you know."

"What time is good for you tomorrow?" Sam asked.

"Ever'time's good for me. I'm not goin' nowhere."

"Well, then we'll be pretty early, maybe 8:30," Liz said. "You don't have to put on your false eyelashes for the pictures."

"Huh?" Geneva said.

"Just teasing you," Liz said.

Sam said, "You don't have to put on a good dress or anything special. We just want you like you really are."

———

Maryann, the owner of the B&B, invited them to have glasses of sherry with her and offered to give them some history of the town. Sherry? Liz thought, it's like being in an English novel, is high tea next? Maryann brought out a pretty cut-glass decanter with matching glasses for the sherry and then talked for more than an hour about the settlement of this pretty river town and its history here on the north side of the Mason-Dixon line—which the Ohio River marks. As she talked, Liz watched Sam listening attentively and thought, he's leading another life now, and so am I, I guess. She felt as if she should be wearing a cashmere sweater with pearls, a tartan skirt. She had never had sherry before; she liked it.

Maryann recommended two restaurants that were within walking distance. The streets were quiet, almost deserted. "Small city or large town?" Sam asked.

"Yes," Liz answered.

"You said that like a New Yorker," Sam said. "Middle-sized town."

Madison was built below the higher hills that showed how the river had cut a course in the fifteen thousand years since the last glaciation. Liz was reminded how the nomads of Mongolia liked to camp in such protected areas to avoid the murderous gales of the winter. At the first restaurant a large crowd could be heard half a block away. A banner over the door proclaimed, "Girl Scouts Award Banquet." They walked three blocks further and found the second restaurant quiet and nearly empty.

"I'm buying dinner tonight," Sam said.

"You don't have to."

"It's your car and your gas and your discovery—anyway, we don't have an official agreement about our book expenses..."

My god, his New York business sense is kicking in, Liz thought. Is this going to become a formal, difficult business? "Don't look so upset," Sam said. "But we do need to talk about how we're going to handle the accounting. I've got a manager and an accountant—I'm sorry to sound like such a hard-ass, but for me taxes are something to think about. If there are going to be expenses I can write off, the accountant will want receipts and all that shit. You ought to think in those terms too, you know. I'm planning on this book being a success."

"So you really think the quilts are that interesting?"

"That interesting and that important. If they're really going to disappear into darkest Africa, what we do with a book is going to be historical and documentary. In fact, I just had a thought."

Liz knew exactly what had come into Sam's mind when he said "documentary."

"A film?"

"A film," Sam said at the same time. "I'll bet we could find a film maker, if not here, certainly at the NYU film department. I probably know people who know people—"

"YOU probably do," Liz said. What had she done by getting mixed up with Sam Goldman? Her simple little thesis—rather, her somewhat difficult thesis—was HER idea, her problem. Now her excitement was being co-opted by this man who knew people who knew people.

"I do," Sam said. "I'm sorry but that's the schizophrenic part that I was talking about."

"If I had already written the thesis...but I don't have a word, really. It's putting the cart before the horse."

"It's Mrs. Gardiner. If she was just Anna Moses, painting her pictures and living to be 101, and selling them as she painted them. But you found this woman who's a time bomb. However long she lives—she looks pretty spry and healthy to me—the quilts are going to disappear."

"I'd like vodka on the rocks with twist of lemon," Liz said to the waitress.

"I'm sorry, I have to see your ID," said the waitress, a middle-aged woman who was almost as broad as she was tall.

"Oh, sure." Liz reached into her bag for her wallet. She said to the waitress, "But he's only seventeen and a half."

"Actually it doesn't look like me. It's four years old," Sam said, opening his wallet to his driver's license.

"He's not your little brother, is he?" the waitress asked as if telling her not to lie. "I can see that."

The waitress looked at Sam's license for a long time, trying to see if it were counterfeit. He was clean shaven in the picture with longer hair. "It's real, I swear. She's just being mean to me."

"Who's the designated driver?" the waitress asked.

"We're walking," Liz said.

"Nobody walks," the waitress said.

"We're staying that the Riverview B&B and we walked here from there and we're walking back," Sam said.

"If we can find the way when the street lights get turned off," Liz said.

"They stay on all night," the waitress said. Her sense of humor was buried so far inside her corpulence she had no idea when people were joking. The waitress, who was slow and inattentive, finally brought their food. "She's only getting ten percent," Sam muttered when she plunked a basket of bread on the table halfway through the meal and ignored their nearly empty water glasses.

They took turns in the bathroom and settled, leaving a wide margin in the middle of the bed. Sam set his cell phone alarm for 6:30.

"Mind if we forget the TV and talk about quilts?" Sam asked. "I need to get up to speed."

"Fine with me."

"I'll tell you the ones that stand out in my memory. You tell me about them."

They talked nearly until midnight. "You've got to get cracking on the thesis," Sam said seriously. "I'm going to become a total noodge until I can start trying to sell the idea."

"Noodge? What kind of language is that?"

"You haven't heard 'noodge'?"

"I don't think so."

"I'm half Jewish and noodge is Yiddish for a nag, a pushy nag."

"Oh, which half?"

"My Dad. He's not observant except on the High Holy days. Did I tell you my grandparents are from Lithuania? That was before the Nazis, turn of the century—former century. It was my parents who came from POW camp."

"There happens to be a lot of Jewish people in Indianapolis," Liz said. "But I don't think they speak Yiddish."

"What do you really think about the idea of a documentery?" Sam asked. "I'm thinking probably a short one, maybe half an hour, mostly interview and Geneva making her quilts. Maybe follow her to church."

"Before you talk to the people who know people, we'd better talk to Geneva."

"Tomorrow. Okay?"

"You'll do the talking?" Liz asked.

"Yeah. I think she likes me."

"Damnit, Sam, she's got a school girl crush on you."

"Do you really think Geneva likes me? I was afraid I'd be too strange. I almost bought a Red Sox baseball cap to wear."

Liz cracked up. When she stopped laughing, Sam said, "I mean, really? Does she like me?"

"I saw her patting her hair, straightening her dress, twinkling her eyes at you."

"She did not twinkle her eyes at me." Sam laughed. "I'll try to find a film maker; probably a woman would be best. Anybody I might find, you'd have to educate about quilts. That would be easy enough, I'm sure."

"I'm not sure Geneva will say yes. There is such a thing as true modesty and actually being unimpressed with the media," Liz said. She felt Geneva was too sensible to be awed by any documentary idea.

"No! Modesty, yes. But everybody's impressed with film," Sam said. "We'll get the best interview we can, even if we don't manage to get the rest of the quilts photographed. The interview will be the main agenda item tomorrow morning. All about how the idea came—"

"I've got that," Liz said.

"Let's see if we can fill it out more. The spiritual side."

"Sam, I will not let you commercialize her religiousness."

Liz had to protect Geneva from Steam Roller Sam. Sam knew nothing about the seriousness with which elderly ladies like Geneva take their lifelong connection to their churches. He had never been to an actual church service; if he went to High Holy Day services it had been a long time ago.

"Not commercialize, just talk about it."

"Sounds like you want to play to the new-agers." Liz was not only protective of Geneva, she did not want her picture of Geneva cheapened with easy jargon.

"No. I swear. I want an honest story about the impulse to make these quilts with all the time and work involved, all the creativity that she pours into them. It is, you know, very artistic."

"I seem to recollect that yours truly was the one who had that thought first."

"Right, right, I know that. That's why we need your serious discussion of how naive art is created, the comparisons, the theories, the traditions that they don't even know they fall into. We'll interview you in the film—no, you'll be the narrator. You'll have a well-written script so you sound like a major authority."

Oh, God, Liz thought, I would have to write that script. She had no doubt he would find a way to do this documentary now that it was taking over his imagination. "I have so much research to do." She threw in one of the few Yiddish expressions she knew. "Oy vey!"

Sam laughed. "We gotta get crackin'. Aren't you excited?"

"Yes. But I'm more afraid we'll lose the quilts just when we need to have them around. I wish we could talk her into selling them to a collector."

"Do you know any collectors?"

"No, but I know they exist, and I could try to find them—except there's no point. She wouldn't even talk to anyone. It's smarter to work on getting an exhibit somewhere."

"What about here?" Sam asked, gesturing broadly.

"What do you mean here?"

"This B&B. They've got beds, they've got walls, they're in the middle of town, they'd probably like to attract attention."

"I was thinking of a serious venue."

"Any venue is serious if you get the right kind of coverage."

They talked on and on, thinking of the famous riverboat, the Delta Queen, that cruised from Cincinnati to New Orleans, thinking about state fairs and office buildings. Eventually Liz began to yawn and soon Sam had caught the yawning contagion. They agreed tomorrow morning's first order of business was to get Geneva to talk about her process and her reasons for making the quilts and how the gift to needy Africans would be arranged. Liz turned her back to Sam and fell asleep almost as soon as she turned off the light on her side of the bed.

Chapter 7

❦

Liz awoke when she heard the shower running at a quarter of six. She was surprised she had slept through the night. When she had so many new ideas, she tended to mull them over all night long. She rarely had someone to share them with. Against her will, Sam had infected Liz with his excitement about a documentary. The rural setting could not be more perfect. Liz lay in bed thinking these thoughts while she listened to the water running and then the buzz of an electric shaver. His "beauty routine" was surely much more complex than hers. By 6:45 they were downstairs asking Maryann for coffee. She was drowsy and a little grumpy. "Breakfast is 7:30 to 9:00—it's on the card on the dresser."

"Yes, we read it," Sam said. "But we've made a fascinating discovery and we can't wait to get back to work." He told her briefly about Geneva's quilts.

Maryann was not enthusiastic. "People don't care about those things anymore," she said.

"Don't you ever watch Antiques Road Show?" Sam asked.

"Yeah, but when they have quilts they're old ones."

Sam launched into a sales pitch about how people would flock to see quilts created by "another Gramma Moses." While Maryann made coffee Sam talked and talked. He said Liz was an expert in American folk art and was writing her thesis on her discovery of an amazing artistic talent. Once the word was out people would flock to see the quilts. He paused to suggest that since the menu on the dining table offered waffles or pancakes, he would prefer waffles. "It's a mix you keep on hand, I presume," he said.

"No, no, I make my waffles from scratch."

"That's incredible, that's fantastic. That's why we're paying you twice what we would pay at a motel. Because you're worth every extra cent."

Liz went to the window to turn her back and not reveal her grin at Sam's sales pitch.

"Well, since you're the only guests at the moment..."

"We'd love it. It would be the perfect start to a wonderful day." Sam's magic was working.

Maryann set up the waffle iron and pulled the real maple syrup from the back of the refrigerator. "I'll warm this a bit," she said as she poured syrup into a glass cream server, then put it into the microwave.

"You know what? Would you mind if I photograph you mixing the batter from scratch?"

"Oh, my hair isn't even properly combed."

"You can comb your hair while I get my camera."

"I'll walk around the block," Liz said. She went out after giving Sam a thumbs up gesture. She thought, he's laying it on like birthday cake icing and Maryann fell for it with a slurp. He'd have her excited about showing off Geneva's quilts by the time she had the waffles cooked. Slick Sam the Seducer, she thought. He did a number on me last night—documentary, Sundance, PBS...for Sam the sky was the limit. I fell for it last night; does it still make sense in the light of morning? To tell the truth she would love it—a film would reach more people than a book even if both had limited audiences. But Geneva had to agree. She probably would say no. What, after all, would a film have to do with her desire to help needy people?

They were at Geneva's driveway a little before 8:30. When they knocked on the door she did not answer. Sam tried the door; it wasn't locked. "Hello! Mrs. Gardiner!" There was no answer.

"Maybe she's feeding the chickens," Liz suggested. "She was worried about whatever killed that one yesterday, remember? She said she'd load her shotgun."

"I'd love to see that," Sam said.

They walked back toward the chicken house. Chickens were wandering about, pecking at the grass. "There's her shotgun," Liz said. She was not familiar with guns, but from some distant memory, or perhaps from movies, she knew it was a double-barreled shotgun that she saw leaning against the chicken house.

Then they saw Geneva coming through the field behind the chicken house. She was walking slowly holding up the front of her skirt as if she were carrying something in it.

"Mrs. Gardiner, good morning," Sam called.

Geneva stopped. She looked confused for a moment. She was breathing so heavily they could hear her catch her breath before she said, "Oh, is it that late?"

"We're a little early," Liz said.

"Are you okay?" Sam asked

"Sorta. I...I...look what I've got." She gasped in a breath. "Poor little things." Tears started from her eyes.

She held her skirt as if opening a package. Three puppies were there, they were very young, maybe two weeks old, brown with white spots and one with black spots.

"What's wrong?" Liz asked. "Where's their mother?"

"I kilt her. I'm sorry now. I wish I hadn't kilt her." She began to sob, gasping for breath. Swaying as if she might fall.

Sam caught her with his arm around her shoulders. "You need to rest. Let Liz carry those puppies and I'll help you to the house," he said.

Liz took the puppies out of Geneva's skirt. Two were easy enough but she had difficulty finding a way to hold three. Finally she did as Geneva had done. She made a pouch in the front of her tee shirt and carried the wiggling little pups against her diaphragm. Geneva had collapsed against Sam, still sobbing. He picked her up in his arms and carried her to the house. Liz hurried to open the kitchen door. Sam helped Geneva to sit in her recliner.

"I have to take care-a them, they're orphans now and it's my doin'."

"You killed their mother?" Sam said.

"Geneva, do you want to lie down and catch your breath?" Liz asked.

Geneva did not seem to hear Liz. She was talking to Sam. "I heared a lot-a squawking and I took my shot gun out to the chicken house. There was a yeller dog with a chicken in its mouth. Chicken was putting up a fight and the dog didn't see me coming. I shot it." She paused and gasped, coughed, put her hands on her chest as if the gasps and coughs were painful.

What if she's having a heart attack, Liz wondered.

"Does anything hurt?" she asked.

"You shot the dog stealing your chicken; you were protecting your property," Sam said very gently.

"I wounded it, got its side and stomach and it howled and ran around, then it run towards me and I shot the other barrel right into it and kilt it. That's when I see-d it was a nursin' mother. I wouldn't'a kilt it if I'd'a knowed."

Liz got a glass of water. Geneva could barely talk, she seemed to have almost no breath.

"You didn't know, and it was killing your chickens," Sam said. He was holding her hands together in his.

"I had-a get it away from the chicken house. It'd attract vultures, you know. So I drug it down to the holler back by the woods, just feeling so bad, thinkin' 'bout the babies out there somewhere with no mama to come feed them. They'd get et by the vultures probably. So I walked back, tired as I was, along the fence line where there's lots-a bushes and weeds. And I see-d one-a the pups. And when I got close a couple more come out. I think that's all there was. I looked and didn't see no more. But they're hungry and got no mama's milk 'cause I kilt her," she gasped, unable to sob for lack of breath.

"I'll give them some milk." Liz put the puppies on the floor. They went in three different directions, more crawling than walking on their unsteady legs, looking for a place to hide.

"I'll take you to the bedroom so you can rest," Sam said.

"Geneva, does anything hurt?" Liz asked, still thinking about a heart attack.

"I'm tired all over, and I cain't hardly catch my breath."

"I think we should take you to a hospital," Liz said.

Sam looked at her. He finally read her thoughts. "Do you have pain when you breathe?" he asked.

"Kind-a. Like a fist sort-a in my chest."

"We'll take you to a hospital," Liz said very definitely.

"Just put me on my bed. If my time is come, I just want to go quietly," Geneva whispered.

"No," Sam said. "No, Mrs. Gardiner, you've got more living to do. You've just had too much effort and excitement this morning. We're here at just the right time to help you. You need to take your pocket book with identification."

"It's on the dresser," Geneva whispered.

"If we leave a bowl of milk on the floor, do you think they'll manage to drink a little?" Liz said, thinking out loud, not expecting an answer from either Geneva or Sam.

"Try it," Geneva said. "Ought'n'ta be any deeper than a saucer or they might drown."

Liz went into the bedroom and found Geneva's purse. She grabbed a quilt that was folded on a chair near the bed. Then she remembered Marjorie saying that aspirin should be given to people having strokes or heart attacks. She had said that the attendant at the nursing home had emphasized that she gave Alma two aspirins immediately after she had her little stroke. It might have prevented further strokes. Liz went into the bathroom and looked in the medicine cabinet. Yes, there was a bottle of St. Joseph's aspirin. She shook out two.

Sam was pouring milk into a saucer. He put the milk away and grabbed a puppy and put its face in the milk. It struggled to get away.

"Geneva, please take these two aspirins," Liz said. "They might help." She handed Geneva the glass of water. "Can you swallow?"

Geneva took the aspirins and wiped her mouth and wet cheeks on the fabric from the shoulder of her dress. "Meant to change my dress 'fore you-all got here."

"Maybe they'll figure out how to drink," Sam said. "Let's go." Liz took the quilt, Geneva's purse and her own shoulder bag. Liz opened the door for Sam, who had scooped Geneva up in his arms again. "There's a hospital in Madison. Remember the sign on the highway?" Sam said to Liz.

"No. But if you say so."

"I saw it. Open the back door for us, please." He maneuvered Geneva into the car.

"Here." Liz put the quilt partially over Geneva. "Cover her so she won't get chilled."

Liz started the car and found her hands were shaking. She took a deep breath.

"My doctor's Dr. Helleran up to Versailles," Geneva said.

"I think the hospital ER is the best place," Sam said. "Are you comfortable?" He spread the quilt over Geneva and arranged her as comfortably as he could manage, holding her as if she were a baby. Geneva was still gasping for breath.

"We should call your son," Liz said as she carefully turned the car around in the driveway. "What did you say his name is?"

"Ben," Geneva gasped.

"My cell's in my camera case," Sam said to Liz. "Is yours handy?" Liz's purse was on the floor in the front.

"I have to stop a second to get it," she said. "I hate to stop."

"So stop. I'll call him," Sam said. "Do you know his number?"

"Yeah," Geneva whispered.

Liz stopped to get the phone. She was breathing fast and her stomach was tied in knots. She fumbled with her purse and finally found the cell phone in the bottom, handed it to Sam and pulled onto the road spewing gravel.

"Stay cool, Liz," Sam said. "Tell me the number, Mrs. Gardiner."

She gave him the number.

"I need the area code too."

She told him.

"What's his name?"

"Ben," Liz and Geneva said at the same time. Sam punched numbers.

Geneva said, "Hate to bother him, he was gonna come down this afternoon and look around to see if it was a dog or fox or what—"

Sam talked to Ben's wife, who answered the phone. He explained who he was and what was happening. After a very brief conversation Sam said, "They'll be there as fast as they can." Geneva had closed her eyes as if too tired to stay awake.

Liz wanted to race the car through the town, but she made herself drive reasonably. Please, don't die, she thought, please, Geneva don't die now.

Geneva was not asleep. She said, "They won't want those pups if I can't take care of them."

"But they'll take them," Sam said.

"Don't know. Ben's stubborn 'bout things like that. I don't want him to kill'em."

"If he won't take care of them, we will," Sam said.

Geneva's breath was coming in gasps again. "I wisht you'd a laid me on my bed. Feels like I'm 'bout to die. I want to die all quiet at home in Jesus's arms."

"Well, this isn't the day you're going to die," Sam said. "'Cause you're in my arms and I know for a fact I'm not Jesus. You'll have to make an appointment with Jesus another time."

Geneva tried to laugh a little, but she didn't have enough breath. Liz wanted to floor the gas pedal but forced herself to near thirty miles an hour on this narrow, winding road. As soon as she reached State Road 428, a straight asphalt two lane highway, not very busy this Saturday morning, she pushed the car up to 80 and still felt they were barely moving. She told herself, people don't die suddenly like they do in the movies. We have time to get to the emergency room. We'll make it. Lucky EMS drivers with sirens so they can go as fast as the ambulance will go.

In the rear view mirror she could see part of Sam's face. He looked like a teenager, frightened and confused. But his voice was going on, talking about how he hoped the puppies weren't making a mess in the kitchen but if they were he and Liz would clean it up and find a box to put them in. There just hadn't been enough time before they left. If they dumped the bowl of milk on the floor, they'd get all wet and lick it off and get some food that way. He thought of one thing after another to say about the puppies, that if there was a problem he and Liz would take them home and feed them with bottles if necessary. He was speaking softly and slowly as if he were telling a child a bedtime story, but he was glancing every now and then at the speedometer. Liz knew he was thinking some of the same thoughts she was: would they make it, people don't really die so fast, he hoped he could help her find the hospital.

"There's the sign. Next right."

She had seen the sign. From the turn it seemed a long way, houses, gas stations, diners, churches...there. Hospital. Emergency entrance. Arrow. Around the corner. The emergency room was quiet. Sam carried Geneva, Liz carried Geneva's purse. "Could be a heart attack," Sam said to the nurse behind the counter. He heard a bell beyond the swinging door and knew the admitting secretary had pushed a bell to signal help. In only a few seconds a man and a woman in white coats came through pushing a gurney. "How are you feeling?" the man asked Geneva as she opened her eyes when she felt herself being lain on the gurney.

"Better but..." she gasped.

"Do you have pain?" the woman asked.

"Some. Here." Geneva put a fist on her sternum. The doctor and nurse nodded at each other.

"Wait here," the nurse said to Liz and Sam. They took Geneva through the swinging doors.

"I need some information," said the woman behind the counter.

Liz went to answer questions. She dug into Geneva's purse to find her Medicare card. When she was asked questions, like date of birth, that she could not answer she said, "Her son is on the way. He'll be able to tell you."

Remarkably soon a large, sturdy man in overalls and a Cincinnati Red Sox cap came in followed by a woman almost as tall as he, also sturdy looking. The woman was walking slowly with a cane, limping. "I'm Ben Gardiner. I believe my mother's here," he said to the woman at the counter.

"I need some information from you," the secretary said.

"How is she?"

"The doctor will be out when he has information for you. Now, I need to know her date of birth."

Ben gave the information she needed.

"I'm Robina. You must be the quilt woman," said Ben's wife to Liz. Robina sat heavily on one of the plastic chairs.

"Yes. I'm Elizabeth Lissmann and this is Sam Goldman. You must have driven very fast."

"We were not much further away than you were when we got your call. And Ben passed everything on the road. How did you find her?"

"Wait a minute," Ben said to them. "I want to hear this too." He turned back to the woman at the counter.

Liz and Sam explained about the dog and the chickens. "Where's the shotgun now?" Ben asked.

Liz and Sam looked at each other. "I saw it leaning against the chicken house," Liz said. "We didn't move it."

"We were looking at Mrs. Gardiner; she had her skirt up in front, making a pouch for the puppies," Sam said.

"Puppies?" Ben said.

"She said she had to save them because she killed their mother," Liz said firmly.

"Just like her. She should'a hit them on the head with the butt of the gun," he said.

"Where are they now?" Robina asked.

"In the kitchen—well, in the house."

"That'll be a fine how-do-you-do," Ben said.

"How many?" Robina asked.

"Three. I told her I was sure you'd take care of them," Sam said. He touched Robina's arm lightly, Liz noticed.

"I wisht you hadn't said that," Ben said.

"Our good old dog died just last February and Ben said that was the end of it. No more dogs," Robina said. "We loved that dog a lot."

"And he loved us," Ben said.

"Well," Liz said, "I'm not supposed to have pets where I live. And Sam travels a lot."

Ben sighed. "I'll take care of them. For Mom, not 'cause I want any dogs."

"Don't kill them," Liz said. "We promised Geneva. We could give them to a shelter."

"Then they're all yours," Ben said.

"Well, I don't know, Ben," Robina said. "These young people might of saved Mom's life and it's not right for us to saddle them with the puppies. And it's not right to kill them if they promised Mom..."

Ben took a deep breath. "We could give them to that preacher. He's always putting ideas into her head."

The doctor came through the swinging doors. "Are you Ben?" he asked.

"I am. How's she doing?"

"We're stabilizing her. We've only done an EKG so far. It's not normal but not too bad either. Seems like you-all," he nodded to Liz and Sam, "got there just when things were starting to go bad. You did the right thing coming straight here."

"I gave her a couple of aspirins," Liz said.

"You did? Good. How'd you think of that?"

"I've got an aunt her age and I was told to give aspirins."

"Good. That helps. And bringing her in right away. Lot of people her age start having chest pain and shortness of breath like that, if they're alone, they just lie down and think it'll go away or decide it's time to die. She told me you said she couldn't die yet 'cause she wanted to die in the arms of Jesus and you said you weren't Jesus."

Sam laughed. "She remembered I said that?"

"Yeah. Good thinking."

"Thanks." Sam stood up. "If no one minds, I need to go out and have a cigarette."

Liz was about to say, but you don't smoke. She nodded.

"There's a cafeteria," the doctor said. "If you want to get some coffee."

"Later, maybe." Sam went out.

Geneva had talked to Robina and Ben about Liz, but they had many questions. Liz answered them as they waited for the doctor to come back with more information. Ben was wary about Geneva's intense involvement with her church. He and Robina went to church but not the one Geneva attended. "We go when we can make it," but apparently not very regularly. Ben explained he had tried to get Geneva to move in with them since their children had married. But she insisted she could live alone and would let them know if she had any problems. They called her at least once a day and dropped by two or three times a week. They said that Geneva's church friends also came by and telephoned often. "A stubborn old lady is just going to be a stubborn old lady 'til she can't move no more, and then she has to go to the nursing home like your Aunt Alma," Ben said.

"I can understand that," Liz said. "And I understand how you worry. I think you were right, she would have just laid down in bed and probably died, or if it's not so bad, after a while she'd get up and go on about her life."

"And probably never tell anyone about it," Robina said. Ben nodded and sighed in agreement. They sat in contemplation for a minute or two. "Feeding those pups," Robina mused. "Can't believe, we got two problems instead of one this morning."

"We should have put them in the bathroom," Liz said. "I wasn't thinking very clearly. I was scared. I never held a steering wheel as tightly as I held that one coming down here."

"You couldn't think of everything," Robina said. She patted Liz's knee.

"We're real grateful," Ben said. After a pause he said, "Mom said you said something about a collector might want to buy her quilts."

"I told her that there are quilt collectors, and if I could write about her quilts and they got to know about them—or maybe in an exhibit in a museum—they might be interested in buying them. But she said no. She was making them to go to Africa and that's that."

"Well, that's what she always says," Ben said.

"And we promised that's what would happen to them," Robina said. Much as Ben might like the idea of selling the quilts, his wife would oppose him. Not only were the two well matched in size and shape, they were equally determined about their intentions.

"I told her I respected that and all I really want is to write about them and about her. We had planned to do a long interview this morning."

"What's your boyfriend get out of this? Or did he just come along?" Ben asked.

"Sam's a photographer. We photographed most of the quilts yesterday. I think there's maybe twenty, thirty more to photograph."

"Thought you already photographed them," Ben said.

"I took pictures but, you know, taking pictures when you have only a borrowed camera and a real photographer are two different things. Sam tells me my pictures are all lousy. If my thesis turns out to be publishable, then Sam and I will collaborate on a book with his photographs using some of my writing. Photography is his field in college. He needs a photo portfolio. He thinks it could be the quilts."

"You think it'll be a book?" Robina asked.

"I'm hoping it will and my advisor thinks there's a possibility. By the way, Sam is a friend, but not a boyfriend. We were even talking last night about a documentary film. We thought we'd mention that to Geneva today."

"He does film?"

"No. But he knows people—he spends a lot of time in New York."

"So you want to make my mom famous?" Ben said.

"The quilts are wonderful and she's truly an artist." Liz looked at Ben, challenging him to disagree.

"You think so?" Robina asked.

"Yes, I really think so. Sam thinks so too. And my advisor who's a professor at Indiana University agrees."

"I don't think they're very pretty," Robina said.

"Nobody thinks they're pretty," Ben added.

"I don't use the word pretty. I think they're wonderful art," Liz said.

"I expect you know more about art than we do," Robina said.

"I hope I know something. I've spent six years studying, and I saw just about everything I could see in Europe and most of America," Liz said. "But different people have different tastes. I got to the point I didn't like a lot of the famous paintings I was studying, and I wanted to see some art that was different. So I started looking at Outsider Art."

"Is that something new?" Robina asked.

Liz explained, "It's art made by people who didn't go to art school. There are a lot of people making what are called art quilts who actually studied art; that's a different kind of quilting—"

The swinging doors opened. The nurse came toward them.

"Mrs. Gardiner is resting. She has some blockage but there was no infarction. We think the quick trip to the hospital prevented that. We think a catheterization can unblock it. The cardiologist is on his way and will be able to explain the procedure. If you're the next of kin—"

"I am and I have her power-of-attorney, too," Ben said.

"Are you her health proxy?" the nurse asked.

"No, we never talked about that. I'm sure she ain't got one."

The nurse nodded and said, "You can see her now before the doctor gets here."

Ben and Robina were on their feet.

"Coming?" Robina asked Liz.

"I think she'd prefer to see you two. In fact, I think maybe Sam and I ought to go make sure the puppies aren't tearing up the place."

"Or pooping everywhere," Ben interjected.

Liz continued, "If you don't mind our going in there when she's not home. The door's not locked."

"It's all right," Ben said. "Listen, we're real grateful you were there when she needed you."

"If you give me your phone number, I'll call you later when you can tell me more about how she is," Liz said.

"You tell her," Ben said to Robina, "I'm going ahead with the nurse."

"I'll come right along," Robina told him. Ben left the room in a few quick strides. Robina gave Liz the phone number. "Mom said last night she likes you—she likes Sam too. Said he was the best-looking young man she'd seen in a long time."

"I told Sam she was flirting with him," Liz said.

"I think her flirting days are past," Robina said.

"Sam expects every woman he meets to flirt with him and they do."

Robina shook her head; the idea that Geneva could still flirt was too odd to imagine.

"If we leave the puppies in her house, will you and Ben take care of them?"

"We will. They're a nuisance and I wish she hadn't found them," Robina said. "Puppies are hard to give away, you know."

"I'd feel terrible if Geneva came home and the puppies had been killed," Liz said. She did not trust these two sensible people in the down to earth matter of unwanted puppies. She had heard in her growing up years casual mention of drowning kittens and puppies. Farm animals had to be useful; dogs and cats were not house pets. She was very small when she learned the difference between city and country pets.

"I won't let Ben kill them. If Mom's going to pull through this, it'd be a good thing if she had a couple dogs around the place. I worry that everybody knows she's an old woman alone out there. Listen, we thank you for all you done and tell Sam the same." She hugged Liz. Then she said as she was about to leave, "I'm kind of sorry Sam's outdoors, I'd enjoy giving him a hug too." Robina laughed and Liz laughed with her.

"I'll give him a hug for you." Liz went out to the parking lot. Sam was sitting on the guardrail that ran along a side of the lot.

"How is she?"

"They said we were in the right place at the right time and saved her from a bigger, more serious attack."

"She'll live?"

"Yeah...probably."

"Then I can stop mumbling shit under my breath. I thought all our great ideas were gurgling down the drain."

Liz drove more slowly and with far less tension on the way back to Geneva's house. Entering the driveway, they saw the minister's Ford Explorer. As they got out of their car Rev. Wheeler and a woman came out of the house.

"Good morning," Liz called.

"Afternoon," said the man pointedly.

"I'm Elizabeth, we met a couple weeks ago. You're the minister."

He was now in dark chinos and a plaid shirt. The woman was wearing a bright blue leisure set in velour. Her hair was long and wavy; she had on dangling earrings that were far dressier than the sneakers she was wearing.

"This here is my wife, Betty."

"Nice to meet you," Liz said, offering her hand. She found the preacher's limp handshake disgusting. She had taken an immediate dislike to him, and the touch of his hand confirmed her feelings.

"Hi, I'm Sam Goldman. I'm a photographer; I'm working with Liz."

"Josh Wheeler. We look in on Geneva when we pass by her house."

Betty did not offer her hand. "Something seems to be wrong," she said. "I never knew Geneva to have puppies and give them the run of the house."

"She's in the hospital at Madison," Liz said. She quickly outlined the morning's events, emphasizing that they had called Ben immediately and he had reached the hospital less than five minutes after they did. "We're here to see that the puppies are all right and to lock them in the bathroom where they can't do much damage until Ben and Robina can come take them to their house."

"I imagine he'll want to put them in a sack and throw them in the first pond he comes to," Josh Wheeler said.

"They're God's creatures too," Sam said as if he were making a pronouncement from the top of Mt. Sinai.

"In this part of the world, we have too many stray dogs and they're a menace to livestock and poultry," Josh Wheeler said to Sam. "There's no room for bleeding heart sorts among the farmers 'round here."

"Geneva wanted to save them. Robina said she'd like for Geneva to have a dog or two, for safety's sake," Liz said.

"Dogs are good companions to older people," Betty said quietly.

"We didn't have time to pay proper attention to them when Geneva seemed to be having a heart attack," Liz said.

"I'm going to go in and see if they've done any damage," Sam said.

"I'll go in with you," the minister said.

"Good," Sam said, "You can help me look for puddles of puppy pee."

Josh glanced at his wife as if to say, I am only doing this because I am a good man who turns the other cheek when necessary.

They went into the house.

"There were some puddles of pee on the kitchen floor," Betty said, raising her voice slightly, as if calling to her husband.

"I don't know anything about puppies. Are these big enough to drink milk from a bowl?" Liz asked.

"I'd say they ought to have milk in a baby bottle," Betty said. "You could go down to the general store in Friendship and get one."

"I'm afraid they'll have to manage on their own until Ben and Robina get here," Liz said. "Unless you want to take care of them."

"Josh is not a lover of dogs," Betty said. "Maybe you gathered that. We have two cats."

"They're cute." The few minutes she held them against her chest the puppies had cuddled together making a single warm lump. She thought she would really like to have one of them—except she wasn't supposed to have pets in student housing.

"So you're the woman who wants to write about Geneva's quilts?"

"Yes. I don't know if you know Marjorie Emmett in Dillsboro."

"I've met her a time or two, I think," Betty said, frowning as if she should remember such things.

"She's my cousin and her mother, Alma Harrison, was a school friend of Geneva's. When I mentioned I was going to look for an unusual kind of quilter to write about they told me about Geneva." Liz thought the minister's wife, and her husband, ought to know that she had local connections, that she was not some "city slicker" who wanted to take advantage of a poor old lady.

"Oh, I see. I know Geneva said she'd been real happy to visit with Alma a while ago."

"Yes, I drove Aunt Alma and Marjorie down here. I just remembered, Ben asked about the shotgun and I said I thought it was out by the chicken house. Would you like to come with me to see if it's there? It ought to be back in the house."

Liz would have loved to go directly in the house and see how Sam and the minister were getting along puppy wrangling, but she went back toward the chicken house. Betty tagged along. "So what do you think of her quilts?" Betty asked.

"I think they're works of art. That's why I thought it was important to have Sam photograph them before they get shipped off to another continent."

"'Works of art'? You really think that?" Betty was incredulous.

"I do. I'm sorry they'll be leaving the country. They're part of a great American tradition."

"I'd never have thought of it that way," Betty said. "There's the shotgun. I'll get it."

"Thanks," Liz said.

Betty picked up the gun, looked at it and then held it so the barrels pointed at the ground. "I think this is the right way to carry it. Is that right?"

"I've never touched a gun," Liz said.

"Me either," Betty said. "I thought I was about the only person in this part of the world that never held a gun. You know about the skeet shooting event down here, don't you?"

"I've heard about it most of my life. But my Mom and I were never here for it."

As they approached the house, Sam and Josh came out, closing the door firmly behind them.

"We'd better be going, Liz," Sam said as she approached. "We're supposed to see your cousin before we start back home."

Betty said to Josh, "You should take this shotgun in and put it away."

"I don't know where she keeps it."

"Well, just put it somewhere safe," Betty said.

"I'll let you take care of that," her husband said.

Betty started into the house but turned back to Liz and Sam. "It was a pleasure meeting you two. Maybe you'll be back and we'll meet again."

"My pleasure," Liz said.

"You're always welcome to come to church services if you're here on a Sunday," Josh said, looking only at Liz.

"Thank you," Liz said.

In the car Liz said, "I don't think you're invited to his church."

Sam chuckled, "I told him I'm Lebanese and my family is Muslim."

Liz laughed and glanced at the grin on his face. "Did you give him a hard time?"

"I tried. He's afraid of dogs. Said a Rottweiler mauled him when he was a little kid and he's never cared for dogs. I think the puppies actually terrified him."

Liz laughed so hard she had to slow the car almost to a standstill before she recovered.

They were nearly in the center of Friendship. Liz told Sam, "I can call Marjorie and tell her we've had a rough morning and can't make it. You don't have to go through meeting more locals." She thought Sam had been through a lot this trip. She was suddenly very tired and wanted to go home and have a long hot bath and do nothing else the rest of the day.

"No. You said your Aunt's had a stroke and probably Marjorie needs someone to lean on."

"That's sweet of you," Liz said. "You're a real good guy, Sam, even if you do lie to men of the cloth." Sam laughed happily. "And I meant to tell you," Liz said, "I was very impressed with the way you scooped Geneva up and carried her so easily."

Sam laughed again, sounding as happy as if none of the morning's drama had happened. "All the working out I do so I'll have perfect pecs means I'm not only pretty to look at, I'm strong enough to lift and carry when the need arises."

"You've got impressive pecs. I noticed that last night."

"You were paying attention?"

"Oh, stop flirting with me. I've got a guy."

"So you said. Two it seems."

"One. Randy and I are too far apart. Not just geographically."

Sam was quiet for the next couple of miles. "I like this landscape. It feels like America once upon a time."

"I feel that way too. I think it's a hard life for farmers."

"I guess that's the American way," Sam said.

"It was only a minor stroke," Marjorie said. "The doctor says the nursing home is the best place for her." Then Liz and Sam told her about their morning. "I don't like that preacher," Marjorie said. "The wife seems okay, but he's just too sure about everything and loves to hear himself talk. I've been to a wedding and a funeral in his church, and I never heard longer prayers. The man actually thinks he needs to tell God what chapter and verse he's referring to while he prays." Sam laughed very hard at this. "It's getting late, you two have almost a hundred miles ahead of you. I imagine you want to be getting on."

"I was looking forward to meeting Aunt Alma," Sam said.

"You're just being nice," Marjorie said.

"No, I'm serious."

"She might still slur her words a little, but she seemed pretty normal when we got back to the nursing home last night. Do you really want to meet her?" Marjorie asked Sam.

"I'd like to," Sam said. "Truly."

"Well, she's been asking when Little Lizzie's coming back. But we'll get there and she'll ask who you are," she said to Liz.

"I don't mind. If Sam really wants to come."

"Why don't you two believe me? I'd really like to meet her."

"We won't stay long," Marjorie promised.

As they walked the few blocks, Liz told Sam that it was good to say hello to any of the other patients they might see. Everybody craves a visitor. "I'm good at that," Sam said.

"You should go into politics," Marjorie said.

"Nobody ever said that to me before. I really don't pay any attention to politics."

"Who's the Vice President?" Liz asked.

"Hillary Clinton?" Sam guessed.

"Stop!" Liz said.

"What is she if she's not Vice President?" Sam asked.

"You're a funny guy," Marjorie said. "Or are you serious?"

"Seriously, I'm serious," Sam said.

Marjorie shook her head in disbelief. Liz explained the most recent election to Sam. "If you weren't from Lebanon, you'd pay more attention to American politics," Liz said.

"You're from Lebanon? You don't have an accent," Marjorie said.

Liz explained about the Lebanon reference. Marjorie loved it but said in a serious, teacherly voice, "Everyone really ought to know who's the Vice President and who's the Secretary of State. You're getting an advanced degree after all."

"Marjorie, you can't expect too much of someone who thinks only black and white cows give milk," Liz said.

Marjorie laughed.

They turned off the sidewalk and went toward the entrance of the nursing home.

"You need some education, Mr. Photographer," Marjorie said. Sam shrugged charmingly and reached for the door handle. He stood aside in gentlemanly courtesy to let them enter first.

"Wow, that was amazing," Sam said as they walked back toward Marjorie's house. "You read all this stuff and you imagine terrible things about nursing homes, like people looking like mummies or wandering around like shell shocked refugees. I mean, you think it's going to be hell."

"Is that why you wanted to go?" Marjorie asked.

"Liz said it was much nicer than she expected, so I wanted to see."

Aunt Alma had once again asked whose child Liz was and thought

Sam was one of Liz's brothers. The signs of her recent stroke were minor. Her speech was slurred, her head tilted right. She complained that she couldn't hold anything in her right hand. However, she was in a cheerful mood. When she was told about Geneva's trip to the hospital in Sam's arms she didn't seem to understand. But she very lucidly told Sam about Geneva. "She was always a spunky girl," Alma said. "I liked bein' her friend 'cause she had all kinds of ideas and included me in the fun. One Halloween we turned over three different outhouses, and my brothers got all the blame. We never ever told them we did it; they'd probably've thought up something mean to pay us back. I don't know if Geneva ever told anyone, don't think I ever did 'til just now," Alma said. "People never thought to blame a couple of girls for that kind of mischief." She laughed happily.

"Did you do other things that people thought girls shouldn't do in those days?" Marjorie asked.

Alma seemed not to hear the question. She said, "You only have one or two good friends like that in your life. Your husband's never as good a friend as your best girl friend."

Marjorie glanced at her watch and decided the visit had been long enough. Alma said to Liz and Sam, "Now you tell your mother I said hello and I hope she'll come see me one of these days. You grew up to be real nice kids. I'm proud to have you in my family, you can tell her that too."

As they walked home, Marjorie said, "I thought she'd be upset about Geneva."

Liz said, "I wasn't sure you should tell her. But it didn't seem to bother her."

"She only listens part of the time, her mind wanders," Marjorie said.

Marjorie phoned Robina who said Geneva was resting and would have angioplasty tomorrow and might be able to go home with Ben and Robina the following day. They would take care of the chickens and the puppies. The doctor had said the quick trip to the hospital was the best thing they could have done and that part of her breathlessness had probably been anxiety about shooting the dog.

As they were about to leave, Liz asked, "Sam, would you mind driving? I'm feeling really overloaded." Liz put a CD in the player and they listened to music the first half of the trip. Near Columbus Sam said, "We didn't have any lunch. Let's get something to eat."

"Oh, I totally forgot lunch. I could handle a Big Mac unless you want to find some real food." She had glimpsed the golden arches ahead.

"Sure," he said and pulled into the parking lot. Sam looked at Liz. "You look kind of shell shocked," he said.

"That's what I've been feeling, just riding along seeing random moments from this weekend like CNN repeating the same story over and over in my head. I had no idea what I was getting into. And no idea what I was getting you into."

"I got myself into it and—don't take this as being perverse—but I'm loving all of it."

"How can you?"

"This is the realest thing that's happened to me in quite a while. I was scared and I got overwhelmed there in the hospital for a while—"

"You said you were going out for a cigarette. I thought that was kind of odd."

"I don't remember saying that."

As they met in front of the car Sam reached for Liz. "You handled everything great." He hugged her. She hugged back. They stood hugging a long moment. "We're fantastic. We're going to have a fantastic book and maybe a documentary," Sam said. "I think maybe I'm about to become a grown up person."

While they waited for their food, Sam explained he had a week to work on the photographs he'd taken. "I'll see if anything needs to be reshot. I'm sure there will be, you never get things all right the first time. And I'll start thinking about a presentation order."

"We'll need to talk about whether it should be chronological or somehow thematic. If you see a theme," Liz said. "I didn't, but I think there may be an artistic progression. Geneva might not remember the order in which she made them. I wish she'd written the dates on the back."

"I didn't see any," Sam said. He explained that he had booked three weeks of work in New York. "I scheduled it that way 'cause I was thinking of going to L.A. with some friends for the month of July. But

I think I'll chuck L.A. and get back here so we can photograph the last few quilts and do the interview with Geneva. She should be well in a month, don't you think?"

"I really don't have any idea what's involved with this heart stuff. I wonder if this is going to make her think about moving in with Ben and Robina."

"What if it makes her decide to get the Africa quilts on their way before something else happens to her?"

"I wish you hadn't thought of that," Liz said. "I guess we just have to wait and see."

"In any case, you've got your work cut out for you for the next month," Sam said. "The more writing—or at least outlining—you can do, the better."

"I was planning to take a year to write my thesis."

"If it turns out you have a year or more with Geneva, that's great, but…"

"We can't count on it. I know. You're being a nudge—"

"Noodge," Sam corrected.

"You're really half Jewish—true or false?"

"True."

"Lithuanian? Not Lebanese?"

"Lithuanian. I saw some old espionage movie set in Beirut and it looked like a great city. Which I guess it isn't any more. Do you realize we last ate Maryann's waffles at 7:00 a.m.?"

Chapter 8

Liz had two messages on her landline from Jack. "Didn't want to bother you with the cell," he said. "I just wanted to say I'm thinking about you. Don't like you running around with that photographer. Call me when you get home."

She called and told him the whole story. Everything she said about Sam made Jack jealous. She reassured him that Sam was a colleague, a partner, not a boyfriend. "End of discussion. Cool it, just cool it."

"Okay, okay."

She liked being with him. He centered her in the world of people who were doing physical work, trying hard to make a living and contributing something by their artistic—or semi-artistic—work.

Liz listened to the recordings of Geneva talking about her quilting and her life. Geneva felt good making useful objects that no one needed a specialized education to appreciate. The quilts, whatever their artistic worth, were real, warm, comfortable bed covers, not an article in some magazine that few people would read. Quilting—which maybe she could even learn to do. Maybe, Liz thought, it could become my art...someday. Not now, I've got to get this work done. A "maybe" to bury deep in the future. Someday it could be more satisfying than a job involving all kinds of interpersonal politics and various financial problems, fund raising, grant writing, PR, news releases. The kind of life she could expect if she worked in a museum, possibly more satisfying than making other people's work available. I've got to stop thinking about this. Nagging at the back of her mind, for the first time, now that she had discovered the joy Geneva felt in her work was the question who she truly wanted to share that life with. She had been so sure she and Randy would always be together, in sync. A tightness in her throat choked her so she couldn't breathe belief into the thoughts.

Jack? A settled, small city life? Jack's jealousy added a sharp negative bite. He did not understand her tension about Geneva's illness.

It was nearly ten; she needed to have a relaxing bath and a good night's sleep...if she could turn off her thoughts. She needed to tell someone the story including, not leaving out, Sam. She did not often call her mother. Barbara had never cared for any sort of art. When her parents divorced the two boys, who were older, went to live with their Dad. Liz, only ten, remained with Barbara. Needing an income to supplement alimony, Barbara began planning birthday parties for neighbors. For the first year or two Liz thought it was fun to help her mother with balloons, flowers, piñatas and decorations. But she hated the times Barbara made her wear a maid's dress and apron and serve the ice cream and cake.

After taking a series of business seminars, Barbara managed to turn party planning for suburban moms into event planning for businesses. In the last four or five years Barbara had become very successful arranging retirement events for company executives or awards ceremonies for outstanding insurance or drug company salesmen. Since Liz had been out of the country for over four years, their relationship had become less maternal and more like high school friends whose lives had gone in different directions.

During the winter Barbara had mentioned dating a man she thought she might get serious about. She had said, "Don't tell your brothers about this yet. They're the ones who might be censorious." Censorious? Liz had thought. Where did that word come from? Why censorious of a possible romance? Their father was no longer alive, he had died in an auto accident almost five years ago. Anyway, she certainly wouldn't discuss the hinted-at romance with her brothers. Liz had never been close to her two brothers, who were seven and five years older. She corresponded with them, or most often, their wives, only at Christmas and birthdays. How odd to think of her mother confiding about a romance.

Barbara had been curious about Liz's romance with Randy and about the break up. Liz had simply told her mother last fall, "We didn't fight, we just realized after two years of living in very close quarters that our interests were going in different directions. He's a more spiritual and socially conscious person than I am. He wants to help the world; I want to get a Ph.D. and a decent job." Barbara understood very well the importance of having the skills for a job. She didn't pry into the philosophical differences between Liz and Randy. Liz had been surprised when Barbara said, "But Sweetheart, there are many kinds of art, not just painting pictures, but don't give up on making art if that's what you really want to do."

"I did but I don't any longer. I don't have that kind of talent. I'll find a different kind of life in the art world. You're a good role model, Mother."

"Really? Am I a good role model for you?" Barbara seemed touched and genuinely surprised. Liz felt their relationship shifting. During the dull winter months when Liz was readjusting to an academic life and too busy to think about Randy's absence and her own aloneness, she rarely thought about her mother. Barbara called in December to say she and her new man were going to the Barbados for the holiday. She sent Liz money to go to New York and go to museums and visit with a couple of women artist friends who had an apartment in Red Hook.

Thinking in a vague way about her mother, Liz went into the bathroom to pour a bath, but then she did not turn the water on. She went back to her living room and called Barbara. "Is something wrong, Sweetheart?" Barbara said immediately when she heard Liz's voice.

"Nothing's wrong, Mom, I'm just a little tensed up. I need to talk to someone. Are you in the middle of something?"

"I'm just watching TV which I am turning off right now. What happened?" Barbara sounded glad to find she was still needed. Liz told her mother about the whole weekend except, as when she talked to Jack, she did not mention sharing both a room and a bed with Sam.

"You were fated to be there at just the right time," Barbara said. "Sweetheart, just like Geneva is responsible for those puppies' lives, you and Sam are responsible for Geneva's now."

"What?"

"Well, that's what they say about people who save someone's life.

You are forever tied to that person."

"Do you believe that?" Liz was astonished to hear her mother say something that was either superstitious or moralistic. Barbara had always been entirely practical and down to earth.

"I sort of do. I mean, you know, that's not the kind of thing I think about much. But as you were talking just now, that came into my mind just like..." She laughed. "This is funny, just like I was reading a tablet from Mount Sinai."

Liz was even more surprised. The mother she knew did not talk like that. An ethical pronouncement?

"I'm sorry if I shocked you," Barbara said.

"That's almost like something Randy would say. I don't know if you sound Buddhist or Jewish. You're neither."

"It just came out of my mouth. I'm as surprised as you are." There was a moment of silence between them. Then Barbara laughed and Liz laughed with her. As they quieted, Barbara said, "Don't you think it's remarkable that Sam wanted to meet Aunt Alma?"

"Yes. I really was surprised and so was Marjorie."

"I'll bet Aunt Alma was too. Or was she sort of out of it?"

"She thought he was my brother. Mom, Sam turns on a 500 megawatt light every time he's around a woman, even if she's 86 and has had a stroke. He can't help himself. I'm sure he needs therapy, but that's how he behaves and they all eat it up."

"I'd like to meet that guy. And what about this Jack?"

"He was jealous when I told him about Sam."

"Sounds like he should be."

"Not really. Sam was wonderful with Geneva. I don't know why but his charm just doesn't work on me. I think he's too pretty-pretty."

Barbara laughed. "Is that possible?"

"There's an ad in the latest Vanity Fair. You can see what he looks like." Liz explained what to look for. She didn't want to go on about Sam. She felt calmer now; in fact she felt a warmth toward her mother that was new.

Sunday morning, a week later, Sam called from New York. "Jesus, Sam, it's only 6:30," Liz complained when she heard his wide awake and cheerful, "Good morning, Little Lizzie."

"Oh," he said. "It's 7:30 here."

"Well, I'm in a different time zone."

"I suppose your long haired friend is there in bed with you," he said.

"No, I'm quite alone and was planning to sleep until 9:00 and then have brunch with Tom and Cynthia Simmons."

"Listen, I've got to tell you—" He explained that he'd talked to a friend who was in the NYU Film School. The friend could not come out to Indiana this summer but had promised to teach Sam how to handle a small video camera. They had gone shopping for the newest and smallest available. "He says that if worst comes to worst, we can use your recordings of Geneva talking about her work as voice over when we show the quilts, the closet full of them, the house, the farm. So don't you think you ought to get out there as soon as possible and do a very long interview?"

"I haven't heard you ask how she is," Liz said. She wanted to close her eyes and pull the cover over her head to block out the sun that was coming in around the edges of the blind. She did not want to let the "what ifs" take over her mind so early this morning when they were going to be the subject of nearly all her thoughts all day.

"How is she?" Sam asked.

"She's doing fine. Ben's going to take her back home today. He's going to see that someone from church drops in every day, or even twice, and he or Robina will call her twice a day."

"Poor woman, she's going to feel like a prisoner on parole," Sam said.

"She's being taken care of by people who love her."

"Who are treating her like an inmate or an infant." Sam sounded unusually irritated. "Maybe they should install a web cam in her house."

Liz had never heard him in that kind of mood. She was shocked that he could be sarcastic about the care and attention people were giving Geneva. "What the hell has got into you?" she asked.

"I've caught your case of the grumps."

"Sam, I was sound asleep."

"I'm sorry, really. I'm at my gym, there's a ton of people and I didn't think about the time difference."

"What do you mean, Geneva will feel like a prisoner? People care about her."

"I was talking to my manager at the agency. She's been taking care of her seventy-nine-year-old mother who refuses to move out of her apartment even though money's no issue. Apparently the old lady was a serious feminist back in the sixties and doesn't put up with being either pushed around or pampered. She loves her independence. I think Geneva does too."

"Is all of New York City in on our project now?" Liz asked.

"I'm getting all the info I can gather. This is my project too, you know."

His project? Yes, he was doing the photography and they'd share credits if a book could be printed, but she discovered Geneva, her Ph.D. rested on it. Sam had his other life, a storybook life she could only imagine since she didn't read the fashion magazines or the gossip columns about the kind of people he met in New York. Sam didn't know who was Vice President of the United States, and she didn't know the names of fashion designers. It was 6:30 in the morning, for crying out loud.

"Do you mind? I just want to go back to sleep for a couple of hours."

"Go ahead. But maybe you ought to get out to Friendship this week."

"I've got a million things to do this week." Liz knew that after talking to Prof. Simmons she would add a few million more items to her research agenda.

"Are they as important as that frail old genius out there who's been delivered from death's door?"

"Come off it." She knew she sounded bitchy, but she didn't need melodrama.

"Sorry. It just seems so important. The bug's in your ear. Go back to sleep."

The bug was in her ear, and she could not go back to sleep. If Geneva would allow her to come for two or three days, they could have some quiet talks. She could be a kind of home care person, feed the chickens and the puppies and Geneva. The idea seemed both ridiculous and sensible. Maybe she should call Marjorie and explore the possibility. She wasn't going back to sleep. Her eyes were open watching the buttery yellow strip of sunlight on the wall. Her body wanted to relax, but her mind would not stop. Even if she just went out to talk to Geneva and stay with Marjorie as usual, she'd have to call Jack and postpone his visit next weekend. Some trade off: puppies and chickens and an old lady instead of going out on the river with him in a friend's boat, sleeping in Jack's arms, getting up to make bacon and eggs and pancakes.

The only sensible thing to do was get up. Damn, Sam was a pain. He barged in without calling. When he called it was 6:30 in the morning! And he thought this was his project. Jeez! Barbara had asked, "Can a man be too perfect?" Huh! Sam was definitely not perfect.

Liz turned the noisy hair dryer on and watched herself blowing and brushing and wondered, What am I doing with my life? I'd be happy just quietly living in Paducah, working at something interesting, maybe for the museum, maybe for the magazine, even sitting on a high stool in Jack's garage guiding a quilting machine. No, no. Jack is easy to be with, relaxed, but he understands art about as much as Sam understands politics. At least Jack tries. Sam is happy in his ignorance. Isn't there such a thing as a man who a woman can really talk to as an equal? Is it all half a loaf? If Tom Simmons weren't such an ugly old toad and so happily married, he'd be the man I could fall in love with.

Liz turned the hair dryer off and brushed her hair back into a loose, low ponytail. I'm not getting any younger. It's time something happened in my life. No, that's not right. At the moment too much is happening. If I went out to stay with Geneva—or to stay with Marjorie and visit Geneva every day for maybe a week—I'd have to put up with the Wheelers. I'd have to find out how Ben really feels about that pile of quilts. Yes, he promised his mother they'd go to Africa, but the idea of money made his face light up. I have to talk to Tom about all of this. But it's not part of his job. I've got the research outline to talk about. He's not a shrink specializing in aging farmer's widows. And what does Sam know, for heaven sakes?

Liz sat down on the edge of her bed, then let herself curl up as if she might go back to sleep. But it was getting late now. She needed the very good coffee she knew would be waiting for her at the Simmons' comfortable, art-filled house on the east side of town.

"You must go," Cynthia Simmons said. "The first interview showed she trusts you. She probably has never had a sympathetic, understanding person to talk to. It will be wonderful for her to be able to talk to you. You have no idea what it feels like to be alone off in the boonies with not a single soul around who even begins to appreciate what you're doing." Cynthia was not just Tom's wife; she was an active supporter of a group of Haitian artists whose work she purchased and then sold at semi-annual soirees at their home. They too were producing Outsider Art. She also marketed the Haitian art to galleries in New York, Chicago and Houston. Not an academic like her husband, she was actively involved in the lives of the artists who were struggling to support themselves and, usually, an extended family. "And I think it's especially good for women artists to have at least one person who cares what they're doing," she added.

"How do you know about that, Darling?" Tom asked. "Your Haitians are men."

"I'm a woman and I have friends," Cynthia said. She was serving frittata onto plates that had been warmed in the oven. Liz was tossing a salad and Tom was mixing V-8 Bloody Marys.

"If Sam goes charging full speed ahead with the book and the film idea, it doesn't mean you have to have your thesis finished. You can write something much more reader friendly and do the serious work afterward," Tom said.

"Well, it's hard to believe he knows enough people who know people to really push the idea along very fast," Liz said.

"He just might," Tom said. "Even in very big cities there are overlapping cliques, the multiplier effect can be considerable."

"He's a charming guy," Cynthia said. "If I were younger, I'd have a serious crush on him."

"You DO have, Darling. And I'm jealous as all hell that one young man can be so beautiful," Tom said. "Don't tell me you're impervious, Liz."

"The chemistry is not there," Liz said. "But I was very impressed how real and sensible he was during the whole rush to the hospital. He even wanted to see Aunt Alma in the nursing home."

"He did?" Cynthia sounded incredulous. "My god, he really is perfect."

"I was amazed. He was great at the nursing home."

Tom sipped his Bloody Mary and smiled. "You women don't give us men enough credit. We can be mensches when we need to."

"Another Yiddish word," Liz said.

"What do you mean another? That's the only one I've heard all day."

"Sam used one. Nudge—no, that's not right."

"Noodge?" Cynthia asked.

"Right. How come everybody knows these words but me?" Liz buttered some toast that had just popped up.

"We lived in Brooklyn when we were in graduate school," Cynthia said.

"So what exactly does mensch mean?" Liz asked.

"It's more than just saying 'man,'" Tom explained. "It's being a real man, but not the great American macho male. More like a real human being with layers of feeling."

"Tom's a mensch," Cynthia said. She kissed him on the forehead before she put the plate of buttered toast on the table. She sat and they began to eat.

"I think Sam's a mensch under all the glamour and barbering," Tom said.

"I'll tell you one thing that bothers me. It's embarrassing going into a restaurant with him," Liz said. "He looks so damned good. His clothes never stop being perfect. I think they make expensive men's clothes out of special fabrics that never wrinkle."

"That's the secret of expensive clothes for men or women," Cynthia said.

"This is a totally perfect brunch," Liz said. "I'd rather have a delicious frittata than clothes that never wrinkle."

"You didn't bring your handsome boyfriend," Marjorie said when Liz arrived Friday evening.

"Handsome, yes. Boyfriend, no. Sam's working in New York for the next couple of weeks," Liz explained. "How are you and Aunt Alma?"

"I'm okay. She's hanging in but kind of fading," Marjorie said.

"Fading?"

"Just a feeling I have. Come, sit down, have some iced tea. Have you heard how Geneva's doing?"

"I phoned her this morning. She sounds like everything is back to normal. Do you think I should believe her?"

"She probably thinks it's true." Marjorie took a pitcher of iced tea out of the refrigerator and then got a handful of ice cubes from a container in the freezer compartment. "Do you want lemon, sugar, Equal?"

"Equal and lemon if it's no trouble."

"I wouldn't offer it if it was trouble," Marjorie said.

"I'm counting on you to tell me how to treat her. I want to do a long interview and maybe take a few pictures of her sewing. But I don't want to tire her out or be a nuisance. Do you want to come with me so you can signal when I should shut up and leave her alone?"

"I don't think that's necessary. It's probably even a bad idea. She knows what you want to talk about, and she's probably feeling grateful to you and Sam for being there and getting her to the hospital."

"Or maybe she resents it. I think she partly was hoping to die."

"I doubt it. At least not really, even if she does believe she's ready to go stand on Christ's right hand with all the other righteous." Marjorie gave Liz the iced tea and spooned sugar into her own iced tea and stirred it, making the ice cubes clink and tinkle. Then she laughed. "I keep thinking of Sam saying the time for her to die in Jesus's arms had not arrived because she was in his arms. I think I've told everybody I know that story."

The day was very warm and humid. Liz drank nearly half the glass of iced tea all at once. "Tell me more about Aunt Alma?"

"I think the stroke scared her and she's depressed. But I imagine she's just going to hang in there for a while. She'll be 87 in September. I expect she wants to have that birthday and a party. Old people do that kind of thing, you know. I wouldn't be surprised if Geneva has set her mind to finishing her stack of quilts, right up to the ceiling of her closet and will manage to stay alive and working steadily until she gets it all done."

———

Geneva looked as well as she had looked the first time Liz met her.

"I'm real sorry Sam's away for a while," Geneva said.

"He has to earn a living," Liz said. "He called last night and said to give you his best wishes."

"Well, thank you very much." When Liz arrived, Geneva had been washing dishes. The three puppies were in the kitchen. One was asleep on a bath towel crumpled up in a corner and the other two were tumbling over one another at Liz's feet. She picked them up, one in each hand, and put them in her lap. "Is the other one all right?"

"Yeah, she's all right. She's the lazy one. They've got personalities already just like human kids. The black and brown one's all energy and curiosity. See, he doesn't want to stay in your lap. But the mostly brown one will settle down if you pet him and just stay there like a cat. You expect him to start purring." Liz put the spotted one on the floor where it scurried over to a bowl of water. Liz stroked the brown one; he closed his eyes with a look that was almost a smirk as if he had conned her into doing exactly what he wanted.

"So have you got back to quilting since you've been home? Or are you resting?"

"They told me I could only set up at the sewing machine a couple of hours a day for the first couple-a weeks. But since last Thursday I've been back to normal."

"That was only one week," Liz said.

"Well, let's say I lost count," Geneva said with a look like a naughty schoolgirl. "Rev. Wheeler like to took a fit. I'm sorry to cause him trouble, but that man don't have no idea how satisfying making something is. Does me good to sew and does me no good to sit around readin' the Bible or watchin' the serials or takin' a nap. If I'm not makin' good use of my time, it's a sin, you know. Not that the Bible says so, but then I don't think it was writ by anybody in their eighties who knew their life was windin' down."

"Oh, Geneva, I should be recording this. Does it bother you if I have the recorder on?"

"No, put it on and I'll say it all over again."

She's getting to be a pro, Liz thought. She put the contented puppy on the floor where he went in two little bounds to jump on his brother who was now under the kitchen table. She pulled the recorder from her backpack "Could you say it again, about making use of your time?"

Geneva repeated her comment and paused. This time she did not include Bible reading as a useless activity. "I'll tell you something—I'll tell you a couple things, in fact," Geneva said. She reached down to the floor and scooped up the brown pup who liked to be petted. "First off, I ain't ever had anybody sit here and talk quilts to me. Not that people don't sometimes ask how I'm doin' with them. But no one's been interested in what they look like. It's real strange to try to talk 'bout that, 'cause when I'm workin', cuttin' and sewin', I kind'a don't think 'bout much. I don't say to myself, well, now I need to use more green or maybe I should put stripping between these blocks. I mean, those things I just kind of do. Sometimes it's 'cause I only got so much of one material and I know it won't be enough to use everywhere. Make do or don't do is somethin' I've heard and done all my life. I know some people figure out how much they need of somethin' before they even start and then they go out and buy that exact amount. But I've always been in the habit of makin' do."

"I'd love to be a fly on the wall when you're making a quilt," Liz said.

"What I'm sayin' is, there's not much of anything that goes through my mind," Geneva said. "It's kind of just what I been doin' for so long it's almost second nature."

"I understand what you're saying. I think maybe there are two kinds of people: the planners and the seat-of-the-pants-ers."

"That's probably right. I'm not a planner, that's for sure." The puppy that had been sleeping on the blanket had begun wandering around the room. Geneva watched it. "I think I got one too many pups here. Ben swears he doesn't want one, but I'm working on Robina." Liz picked up the black and brown pup which was jumping at his newly awake brother. The pup was a bundle of wiggles and squirms. "He's got enough energy for all three," Liz said.

"Yeah, just like babies. They're all people soon as they're born."

"Are they a problem in your sewing room?"

"Oh, yeah. I keep the door closed when I'm not in there. If they pee on something I can wash it but if they chew it up, it's ruint."

"You got yourself a handful of trouble when you rescued these pups," Liz said.

"But I had to. If I hadn't found them, I guess they'd'a died pretty quick, got caught by a hawk or somethin'. And I'd'a never knowed 'bout them. That's the way the wild world works, you know."

"Do you think about that kind of thing a lot?"

"I think 'bout how things're changin'. Lots'a farms going back to wild, fields too little or too hilly round here for the big tractors ever'body's got these days. So the trees are growin' up and the deers are comin' in. Use'ta never had no deers, now they're ever'where."

"Life's all about change," Liz said.

"But I was goin' to tell you what I was thinkin' 'bout 'cause of a nurse down-ta that hospital. She must-a been assigned to me special. She was around a lot. Got a pretty name, CherryLee. She asked me what I did with myself all day long. Wanted to know what serials and shows I watch on TV, things like that. And I told 'bout makin' my quilts and said I got a closet almost full of them. I told her I wanted them to go to a mission in Africa. And when my closet was all full it'd be time to stop and get rid of them and go to my eternal rest."

Liz smiled.

"What're you smiling 'bout there?" Geneva asked.

"I'm smiling 'cause Marjorie said you'd be sure to stay alive until you got that closet full of quilts."

"I 'spect I will."

"I'm sorry, I interrupted about CherryLee," Liz said

"Oh, I was 'bout to tell you, she looked at me like I was completely cuckoo. Then she said, 'You know, Mrs. Gardiner, there's an awful lotta African people in need 'round here.'

"She said she lives in a trailer park and just 'bout nobody had any jobs and there aren't any jobs to be had and people had gone on food stamps and couldn't drive nowhere 'cause they didn't have money for gas and she didn't believe there were any people off in Africa who could be hurting more than her neighbors. She said, 'I don't understand why people want to help people they don't even know when there are people right under their nose don't have enough of anything."

"I guess I just gaped at her, 'cause I didn't have any answer. No point in tellin' her I do give away my prettier quilts to those in times of need but that the ones I'm makin' for Africa are not the ones people think are pretty. They might think it's kind of insultin' to get a quilt they think is ugly."

"You did or didn't tell her that?" Liz asked.

"I didn't tell her, 'cause, you know, CherryLee is a Negro person too and it seemed like I was goin' to dig myself a hole I wouldn't be able to climb out of."

"You mean because she wouldn't know what you mean about pretty ones and African ones?" Liz asked.

"Yeah, and I thought 'bout that a lot when I was in the hospital with nothin' to do but watch television. Anyway, CherryLee apologized for lecturin' me 'bout what to do. Said she was just worked up 'cause she had been at somebody's house and the kids were sleepin' under the thinnest old holey blankets she had ever seen and it made her want to cry. So I told Ben right away after we got home I wanted to take three or four of the pretty quilts down to her. 'Course it was Robina that drove me down there. On the way home Robina said, 'You know, Mom, her friends are probably all black people, and they might appreciate your other quilts as much as people in Africa would.' 'Til Robina said that, I never gave that idea a thought. What do you think?" Geneva asked.

"Do you mean would American Black people like your quilts?"

"I think ever'body 'round here probably has the same kind of idea what's pretty. Ever'body pretty much dresses the same way, not in those wrap around skirts like the African women in the pictures I seed. I think Americans are different than Africans. You think that's right?"

"Probably." Liz said. "On the other hand, people like me and Sam think your Africa quilts are wonderful and there are other people like us. We'd like for the people that would appreciate them to have a chance to see your quilts before they get sent away. I mean before they get sent to a trailer park or to Africa."

"Well, he took all them pictures," Geneva said.

"Yes, he did. But we'd really love to be able to have a show of your quilts. Someone at my college gave me the name of someone in Cincinnati to call. It's a person who puts together shows of quilts by African-American women." Liz had not meant to mention this possible connection because she had misgivings about the premise: a white woman who thinks she's making African type quilts when there are many black women who are truly inspired by the quilts of their ancestors or by trips they've made to Africa. The idea was politically complicated. So far Liz had been unable to think how to formulate a letter to the Cincinnati organization.

They heard the crunch of tires on the gravel driveway. "I 'magine that'll be Robina," Geneva said.

It was Betty Wheeler. "Yoo-hoo, Mrs. Gardiner! Geneva! You in there?"

"I'm here. Come on in," Geneva called without moving to get up.

Betty came in. She was in a bright pink tee-shirt and pedal pushers with pink peonies printed all over them, she wore dangling heart earrings. She was carrying a grocery bag in each hand. "Hello, Elizabeth. Geneva said you'd be here today, so I thought I'd bring you all some lunch."

"Now you didn't need to do that. You know I got food in the 'frigerator," Geneva said.

"Well, YOU know I just love to do this kind of thing. There's baked beans and corn bread that I just made this morning."

"You shouldn't'a gone to all that trouble. You should'a been making breakfast for your husband."

"Oh, I did that too. But, you know, corn bread's one of my favorite things to make and I made a big pot of baked beans yesterday for us and have plenty to share with you. And I put in some carrot cake, 'cause I had that too. So how are you feeling today?"

"Fine. I'm feeling as fine as ever. How are you feeling?"

"Couldn't be better...well, that's not true if you want me to be honest. I got a little headache 'cause we're going to Versailles to an ecumenical prayer meeting later on this morning and I'm supposed to do the prayer at the end of the women's meeting. I just always get a headache when I have to do any kind of talking in public. Keeps me awake half the night and gives me either a headache or a stomach ache before-hand."

"You shouldn't agree to do it," Liz said.

"But it's one of the things a minister's wife's got-ta do now and then. Like they say, it comes with the territory. You teach at college, don't you?" she asked Liz.

"Yes, I teach a class."

"Don't it make you nervous?" Betty asked.

Geneva got up and took things out of the grocery bags, then she folded the bags neatly.

"No, I wouldn't say nervous, but sometimes I have to spend more time than I'd like either preparing or marking papers. Really what I do is get up and talk about things I know and it's easy enough. It's assembling the slides and references I don't like. That's why proper professors have assistants."

"Well, I guess it's different when you know what it is you have to say. I can pray all day when Josh is saying the words."

Liz wanted to say, I hear he goes on just about all day. She bit her tongue.

"It'll help if you take a couple of quiet long breaths before you start praying," Liz said.

"I guess it would. I just about forget to breathe at all while I'm waiting to be called on," Betty sighed and made a face like a pouty teen.

"Well, here's what you can do," Liz said. "When they call on you, bow your head and close your eyes and everybody else will probably do the same. Then, don't hurry. Take one deep breath and hold it a little while and let it out slowly. Then do that all over again. It'll make everyone else feel good and help you too."

"You really think so?" Betty asked.

"I think so." Liz wondered if Betty would be upset if she were told this is a yoga technique. Were they afraid of Eastern philosophy?

"But won't they think I'm never going to start?"

"Maybe, or maybe they'll be glad for a little quiet time."

"I could say, let us have a moment of silence."

"Yes, you could do that."

"I never knowed you were shy 'bout prayin'," Geneva said.

"Thank you. I pretend I'm not shy. Coming from a college professor that gives me a little bit of confidence I didn't have before," Betty said. "Josh just don't understand that speaking in public could make anybody nervous. He's been doing it since he was six years old. He's a natural-born preacher."

Geneva handed the folded bags to Betty. "Here, you can probably use these another time."

Betty took the bags. "Now Geneva, have you got enough of your medicine?"

"Got plenty."

"And you're not forgetting when to take what?"

"They're all in that pill box Ben gave me a while ago."

"Well, thank you. I gotta go. You take care of yourself, and you know you can call us anytime. It was good seeing you again, Elizabeth. I'll try to take your advice this very afternoon."

They heard her car start. "That girl's got a real calling to be a preacher's wife," Geneva said.

"You're right about that," Liz agreed.

"Poor little thing," Geneva said.

Liz laughed. "Why did you say that?"

"I guess I shouldn't'a. Somebody's got to be a preacher's wife and do the errands and the cookin' and all. Don't guess she'd have any purpose in life if she hadn't'a married him."

"I don't know, maybe she could have been a teacher or a nurse or a doctor or—a lot of things."

"But girls like her think they gotta have a man. Get your man and then get your life, that's how it is for them."

"Was it different for you?"

"No. Back then it was hard enough to finish high school before you got married and started having babies, for sure in this part of the world. But I wasn't boy crazy. I liked the work there was to do. I had a housekeepin' job for a couple-a years workin' for a judge down to Aurora. I liked having a job and a pay day. Lots-a people nowadays don't seem to like any kind of work. But I liked it. Then when I was married I liked the work. The chickens and the gardenin', even the cookin' and washin' and ironin' and sewin'. I liked all that, and polishin' furniture to make it shine and pushin' the lawn mower and makin' the front of the house look good. I guess I just got born with satisfaction in my personality. And then Alf was a good lookin' boy and a good man." She paused and played with the puppies a while.

Liz waited for Geneva to go on with her thoughts.

Geneva put the dog down and sat with her elbows on the table, her head resting in her uplifted palms. She looked out the window for a moment. As if she were reading Liz's mind, she said, "Would you be shocked or upset if you knew your Aunt Alma and my Alf were adulterers for a couple of years?" Geneva did not look at Liz.

The Biblical word surprised Liz. This is how Geneva remembered it. Did she remember the time Alma said they had laughed together? "Aunt Alma doesn't remember a lot of things."

"I'm sorry she forgot that."

"She didn't forget it," Liz said.

Geneva looked at her, surprised. "She told you and Marjorie?"

"Just me. I'm sure she never told Marjorie. I was interviewing her, by myself. And she told me. I didn't tell Marjorie."

"So you are the keeper of secrets," Geneva said.

"I suppose I am. I didn't expect that kind of secret."

"People here in the countryside got the same kinds of secrets ever'body else has," Geneva said. "We're not simpler. People think we're simpler, dumber, sometimes more religious. Well, some of us are some of that and some of us ain't."

"I don't think you're simpler or dumber or...well, I guess I do think you're more religious. More than most people I know."

"Right now, my mind's pretty confused about what I'm doin'. CherryLee got me to thinkin' 'bout what charity means. And 'bout what kind of person I am. How come I keep my mind on someplace half-way 'round the world that I ain't never seen, instead of twenty miles away that I also ain't never seen because I just didn't look, just didn't think? I been just pure ignorant about people, not quite my neighbors, but not so far away."

"But if you hadn't been thinking about Africa and the people you met from there, you wouldn't have decided to make quilts that are different from the usual ones," Liz suggested.

"I don't know if that's true. It might be. But it might not. I think I'd'a got bored with the usual quilts. I know I was getting bored with Dresden plates. That's why there ain't none round here."

"So you're the kind of person that gets bored doing the same kind of thing. Is that how you feel about cooking or other work?"

"When it comes to cooking, I like to mix different things together. Yeah, I guess that's how I am. Never put it in words a-fore. When I'm gardenin', I like to try different kind of beans or squash or whatever

I'm plantin'. Not much you can do with chickens, but I've raised banty hens and I raised some geese once. Might'a kept on, but I didn't like the taste of goose eggs. They were stronger flavored than hen eggs and I just didn't like them much. And banty eggs are too little to be much use. And the banties are too little to make much of a meal. I'd say I'm kind of restless. And that's why I like makin' quilts that are different and when I found out 'bout the kinds of colors and patterns they have in Africa I got real excited. Sometimes I'd go to sleep dreaming 'bout the colors I'd put together, 'specially when someone'd just give me a new batch of materials."

"What do you do when you get a new bunch of materials now?"

"Well, it's kind-a like Christmas time. Always is. I'm like a kid; I just love presents. Somebody gives me a grocery bag or a shoebox full of materials, they might be cuttin's, they might be pieces of old shirts or dresses and nowadays, there's times when they're a bunch of new materials, 'cause it seems like people buy a lot'a it and then change their minds. They don't have the make-do feelin' I always had. They buy and throw away or give away. So when somebody brings me a bunch-a stuff, I go right to the ironin' board and I take it out piece by piece and iron each one and then fold them neat and lay them out on the table and arrange them by color. Some patterns I kind-a hate and some I like a lot. And I'll fold the ones I don't like kind-a small and the others bigger and they'll be layin' on the table for a while, maybe an hour or even half the day 'fore I put them away in the color boxes or bags I got all sorted out. Makes me feel like a kid with new toys. Sometimes if there's something I like a lot I'll cut it into squares or strips or triangles then and there and put it out where I'll use it right away or use it for a new quilt as soon as I finish up with the one I'm sewin'." Geneva was smiling, looking a bit like that child with new Christmas presents. Liz thought it would be lovely if Sam were here videotaping Geneva as her face was so animated. She would be beautiful in a documentary.

"Do you always finish one before you start another?"

Geneva got up and put some water on the stove and took some milk in a baby bottle out of the refrigerator.

"I been feeding the babies with the bottle," she said. "Robina says they'll drink if they're hungry enough. But I had this here baby bottle for a long time and a lot-a animals've drunk from it. I think it makes them feel good. 'Sides, it makes me feel good. I used to love feedin' my babies. There's somethin' 'bout watchin' a helpless little thing bein' fed."

"Could I feed one?" Liz asked.

"I like to let the milk warm up by setting out for a while," Geneva said.

"Okay. I asked about finishing one quilt before you start another."

"Oh. No. I don't finish the whole thing necessarily. Sometimes I have a pile of tops made that need to have backs. Sometimes I don't have any batting or old blankets to use for stuffing and the tops kind of pile up."

"Is getting batting a problem?" Liz asked.

"Well, it is, kind of. People don't think of giving it to me like they do their scraps, and it's sort-a expensive even in Wal-Mart. I just don't have any extra money, you know. Robina gets it for me mostly. Sometimes she'll bring me two or three bags."

The puppy Geneva called Speedy jumped hard against the kitchen cabinet and fell to the floor.

"Look at that. He thinks he can jump all the way up there and get that milk. He seen me put it out," Geneva said.

"That's a smart dog."

Liz's cell phone rang. "Excuse me."

Geneva got up and got the bottle of milk, although it was still cold. The puppy jumped against her legs. She scooped him up and settled with him in her lap. He grabbed the nipple of the bottle and began greedily slurping. The other two were playing in a corner with a leather bone and didn't notice.

"Are you at Geneva's?" Marjorie asked.

"Yes."

"You're coming up when you're done there, aren't you?"

"Yes, if it's still convenient."

"I'll be glad to have you here, I just want you to know I'm not sure where I'll be. Mom died this morning and there's a lot to attend to."

"I'll come right there," Liz said.

"No. No, there isn't anything I need you to do. It's just legal things I have to do and talk to the funeral home."

"If I can do anything—"

"No. You've got your work. I just wanted you to know. I showed you where the key is, do you remember?"

"Yes, I remember. Are you sure you don't want me to come, make phone calls or something?"

"No, really. I've been thinking about it a lot the last couple of weeks, I've got a list in my head of things to do."

"All right then. I'm sorry and sad." Liz closed the phone.

"Alma must-a passed away," Geneva said.

"Yes, this morning. Marjorie says she doesn't need any help."

"I 'spect that's what she thinks but you ought-a go on up there anyway. You can make coffee. You can cook, can't you?"

"I can get things at the store and make something."

"Just get a ham or a good size chicken and bake it," Geneva said.

"You think I should go? She insisted she could handle everything." Liz didn't know what to do. She wanted to continue the interview since Geneva was relaxed and talking easily.

She had never been present just after someone died. She had no idea what sort of things had to be done. She knew phone calls would have to be made to relatives. She didn't know what kinds of decisions Marjorie had to make. Marjorie had said that Alma had some kind of funeral insurance policy and had made choices of caskets and plots in the cemetery.

"You should go," Geneva said again. "People will be droppin' in. If you're there you can make coffee or tea and do dishes. Marjorie knows how to do things, but she's never lost her mother before. That's not easy even if she's got it all planned out."

"Okay, I don't know anything about what to do."

"I think there'll be more to take care of than either of you 'magine."

Liz gathered her things and said good-bye to Geneva who dumped the puppy out of her lap and went to the door with her. She glanced down her drive. "There comes Robina," she said. "This here is a real busy place lately."

As Liz was opening her car door the other car pulled up beside her. It was Ben, not Robina. "Mornin'," he said. "How you doin'?"

"Fine, how are you?"

"I'm good. You're not leaving so soon, are you?"

"My Aunt Alma died this morning and Geneva says I've got to go help Marjorie even though Marjorie said not to. I decided Geneva knows best."

"I'm sorry to hear that. She was in the nursing home, wasn't she?"

"Yes. She had a stroke a month ago and was failing, you know."

"I was hoping to have a talk with you while you're here."

"I guess I'm going to be here longer than I thought. I'll probably stay through the funeral and maybe a day or so after. I'll give you my cell number and we can find a time to talk."

"Maybe you can come to our place."

Liz wrote her phone number on a page in her notebook, tore it off and gave it to Ben.

"I'll talk to Robina and give you a call. I 'magine the viewing will be tomorrow evening or maybe Sunday and probably the funeral'll be Monday morning," Ben said.

"Is that how things work?" Liz realized that she needed everyone's advice. She was reminded of how she and Randy learned about community events in the Mongolian town, picking up information from everyone; even the children understood more than they did.

Chapter 9

Liz's phone rang as she was driving to Dillsboro.

"Where are you, Liz?" Barbara asked.

"Between Friendship and Dillsboro."

"Driving? You shouldn't drive and talk on the phone."

"There's nobody on the road except me."

"One death in the family is enough. You know, don't you?"

"Yes. Marjorie called. I'm pulling over and stopping. When are you coming down?"

"I'll have to see which is better, the funeral or the viewing. I hate viewings but I've got a lot of things going on at work so if I can be there on Sunday, that'll be best."

Barbara outlined how funerals there usually were done. She said, "You'll be sitting around mostly. Do you have anything decent to wear?"

"I only brought jeans." Liz knew what her mother was going to say.

"Well, take yourself to the nearest Target or Sears or whatever they've got around there and get at least some slacks or a skirt or one of each and something other than sneakers. There'll be people in sneakers but not you. Use the Visa, that's what it's for. Buy something you can wear later on."

"Like when?"

"Like if you ever come visit me."

"Jeez, Mom."

"I'm serious; don't wear jeans tomorrow. We have a role to play in this family. I've got a nice navy blazer that you can wear. It's a 10, that's what you wear, isn't it?"

They had had a version of this conversation before. Liz had insisted that family accepted you like you were. Barbara insisted they were the city mice come to visit the country mice. Liz had said that was disgusting. "I did not raise you and your brothers to be country mice," Barbara insisted. "I don't want to be embarrassed by seeing you in jeans with holes in the knees."

"I don't have—"

"I know. Just do some shopping."

"All right. I didn't know things were going to get so complicated."

"You're about to get a Ph.D. in Family," Barbara said. "Higher education."

"Oh God," Liz muttered. A large truck passed noisily, blowing its horn.

"I thought you were off the road."

"I am but it's only two lanes."

"Let me know when the plans are firm, and I'll decide when I'm coming. If it's tomorrow, I'll make it early so I can be of some help. I'd like to meet Geneva, too."

"I'm sure you can. I don't know about seeing her quilts, you might have to wait for an exhibit."

"There's going to be an exhibit?" Barbara sounded excited by the idea.

"If I can arrange one. It could take a year...or more."

"A year! These old ladies die."

"I know, Mom. We're trying to do some filming while Geneva's still around."

"What do you mean 'we'? Is Sam there too?"

"No. He's in New York. I think I should get on up to Dillsboro."

As Liz drove she sighed, accepting her mother's orders. It was the usual tug of war, and Liz always lost. Today she decided to lose gracefully.

She had usually pouted all the way to Dillsboro when she was younger, wearing a skirt or a dress she hated. She would stare sullenly out the side window, not talking to her mother. Her brothers usually spent weekends with Dad. But Liz—Little Lizzie, Elizabeth Jane—had to come along feeling like a doll Barbara dressed for the occasion. Liz preferred the family gatherings at state parks because she was allowed wear jeans or shorts and escape the adult chatter by hiking the trails. She loved being in the woods alone. The trails were not very long; sometimes she seemed to have the park to herself. She would pretend she was an Indian scout. When other people came talking noisily down the trail she sometimes moved off and hid behind a big tree or a patch of brambles, hating how ordinary and uninteresting they were. She was afraid she was also ordinary and uninteresting in much the same way, except in her own mind. There she had nothing in common with either her family or the strangers who shared the state park.

Marjorie was not home, but a neighbor, a rotund woman in stretch jeans and a sweatshirt, was in the kitchen unloading the dishwasher. "Hi, I'm Eileen. I live across the street in that yellow house," she said. "Marjorie said you'd be coming and said to settle in your room."

"I hope I can make myself useful," Liz said.

"There's not much to do. I put coffee on—you want a cup?"

"Not now. Making coffee was about all I could think to do to help."

"You don't really have to DO anything, you just have to be around. Talk to people."

"What do I talk about?"

"Oh, the weather, I guess. Or talk about Alma if you feel like it. It's nice you're here. Marjorie's been glad you're doing this study of Geneva Gardiner's quilts. She thinks that's pretty special. I don't know Geneva and never heard of her quilting 'til Marjorie told me you was the one visiting lately. In a town like this, you notice strange cars in a neighbor's drive. When I first saw your car a couple of different times, I told her I was wishing she had a boyfriend."

"Marjorie?" Liz asked, astonished anyone would suggest Marjorie might have or want a boyfriend.

"Why not? She's not too old," Eileen challenged.

"I just never thought of it."

"I can't help thinking about things like that. I've had three husbands and I'd have a fourth if I could find the right man."

Liz thought the stretch jeans were an unmistakable advertisement of Eileen's availability. "I imagine there's not a lot of choice around here."

"Don't I know it? Still, I don't look forward to sleeping by myself the rest of my life. Summer's okay, but come winter, I want a warm man in bed with me. I've got a little kitty cat, but he only keeps my feet warm. It's not my feet that want to cuddle, you know what I mean?"

Liz nodded. "Isn't there anything I can do to help?"

"Not really. Just sit around, talk a little bit. You know, people don't wail and cry like in some movies. We're kind of quiet people. Well some are. I'm kind of loud myself." She laughed cheerfully. "I'm on my good behavior right now. But if we need a few good jokes to perk people up, I've got a few to tell."

Liz talked to a variety of people who dropped in, mostly women, a few with husbands who, after a few minutes, stepped out to the yard to smoke a cigarette. The women all hugged Marjorie and said, "I'm real sorry." Liz would like to have been the designated coffee pourer and cup washer, but everybody was at ease in the kitchen as if they were at home. People talked a little about Alma, although none of them were her contemporaries. They knew her because she had lived with Marjorie for three years before she moved to the nursing home. A little before ten o'clock, the last woman left and Marjorie said, "Soon as she's out of the driveway, I'm turning off the porch light and the lights in the living room."

They went into the kitchen where there were several washed coffee cups in the dish rack to put away, a plate of cookies and part of a sheet cake to cover with plastic wrap. The refrigerator was full of casseroles in a variety of containers, all covered in foil or plastic wrap. "Sugar and caffeine, the worst possible combination in a situation like this," Marjorie said. "Do you want some real food?"

"No, I'm stuffed. I think the sugar and caffeine will keep me up half the night," Liz said.

"You can watch TV, it won't bother me."

"I've got a couple of books to read."

"I'm sorry your interview with Geneva got interrupted. It would have been all right if you'd stayed there all afternoon."

"She ordered me to get up here. Then Mom called and told me the same thing. I'm just obeying my elders."

"You always were a good little girl, Lizzie." Marjorie smiled. Liz laughed and Marjorie laughed with her but only for a moment. Marjorie's face was tired; her shoulders drooped. She straightened a pile of paper napkins that lay in the middle of the table, an automatic, keep-busy habit. They sat silently for a few moments. Marjorie got up and opened a kitchen cabinet where dishes were stacked. She began rearranging dishes. "People've made a hodgepodge of where I keep things," she said. "I just need to straighten it up." Liz watched and thought about going into the spare room, settling with her book, or just turning out the light and letting her mind play over the day.

"So how is the handsome Sam?" Marjorie asked as she sank into her chair like a cat finding its usual place to settle on a cushion.

"He's in the big city making big bucks and even bigger plans for making a film about Geneva."

"A film?" Marjorie's voice had more energy; she smiled at the idea.

"A documentary," Liz said. "Short, maybe half an hour."

"I thought he was a regular photographer."

"He is, but he's so excited about Geneva he's bought himself a video camera and is learning how to use it."

"What's Geneva think about it?" Marjorie frowned.

"I didn't get a chance to talk to her about it, but I think he can talk her into just about anything."

"That's not necessarily a good thing. Some people don't want to be on film or on TV." Marjorie's tired face became lighter as she thought about a different kind of problem.

"That would be news to Sam. Almost everybody he knows wants to be in film—or in print or something. I'm surprised he's not taking acting lessons."

"You know what I don't like?" Marjorie asked.

"What?"

"All this reality stuff that's taking over TV. I just don't like it even though I watch a little now and then. It's like nobody knows what privacy means any more. Sometimes I feel like high school girls don't think they're anybody unless they're like somebody on TV. They can't get dressed in the morning without trying to look like some actress or singer. I may be retired but I can't help paying attention to the kids I see around here."

"What about boys?" Liz asked.

"Oh, they haven't changed that much, not around here. Boys don't think they're anything if they're not on some ball team or have a loud, hot car. Been that way for a long time; it's the girls that've changed. Girls pick up on things a lot faster than boys. What bothers me is the clothes they wear. I know I'm old fashioned, but I just hate looking at a gang of girls with their fat tummies hanging over their low-cut jeans. They don't have a clue how ugly it looks. And their make-up and the awful shoes. Guess I sound like a grumpy old lady. Well, I am. I didn't retire a day too soon."

Liz laughed a little. "Mom insists I go shopping and get some decent slacks. I'll have to take myself to the nearest Walmart tomorrow morning, if you don't mind. I'll have to do it before she gets here. Plus she's bringing me a navy blazer so I'll look like a real estate saleswoman."

"Barbara worked hard at being a good mother," Marjorie said.

"I'm 26 years old," Liz said.

"I'm 64 years old, but I never stopped being my mother's daughter. Now I'm an orphan." Marjorie's face aged as she shook her head. "Silly to say orphan at this age, isn't it?"

"Not if that's how you feel." Liz hesitated a moment but then she put her hand on top of Marjorie's and squeezed a little bit.

"How I feel is done in. Unless you need to use the bathroom right away, I'm going to go take a hot bath."

Marjorie gave Liz specific directions to Walmart ten miles away and then how to take a different road that would be an easy way to find Ben and Robina's house. Robina had called and suggested Liz come around 11 o'clock. A gray sky was drizzly and a little chilly. As she drove over rolling hills where a few cows were grazing, Liz thought how lovely this countryside would be on a sunny day. Marjorie's directions were excellent. Liz found the white farmhouse with a screened in porch and a row of tulips coming up but still tightly furled along the short walk.

Ben opened the door. He was not in bib-overalls, but in what Liz thought were probably Sunday clothes, slacks and striped shirt. Robina came in from the kitchen, she wore a sneaker on one foot and a fuzzy house slipper on the other. She limped, favoring the foot with the slipper. The two of them made Liz think of the Grant Wood painting, although they were a very different physical type, both large people who looked like they had worked hard, eaten well and grown to resemble each other due to weathering by the same elements. Robina offered coffee and cake. "I appreciate your offer, but you have no idea how much coffee and cake there is in Marjorie's house right now. I just can't look at either one," Liz said. "I was awake 'til after 2:30 last night because of all the coffee."

They settled in the overstuffed suite of furniture in the living room. The picture window had a fussy arrangement of printed drapes and a valance in the same pattern as the upholstery on the furniture; sheer curtains made the dim day even darker. The room was decorated with Robina's crafty touches, embroidered pillows, a milk can painted with a scene of bluebirds on a nest, which was a stand for a lamp with an owl painted on its ceramic base. Liz asked Robina, "Are you the crafter?" She couldn't bring herself to say "artist." Robina admitted that she couldn't resist various craft classes at a senior center. She liked painting birds best of all. She explained she used pattern outlines and painted according to directions. But she would never stoop to using a decal, that was outright cheating.

After a little talk about Alma and the plans for a viewing and funeral, Ben said, "I don't think we rightly understand why it is you're taking pictures of Mom's quilts and interviewing her. And I don't think she understands either. So I thought I'd ask you." Liz was not sure how to read his tone of voice. He was curious, concerned, protective. Was he pleased too, or did he think she had ulterior motives, some scam?

Liz explained her study of art and that she felt the great art of the past was being studied by people smarter than she was. She said "smarter," but she meant more academic, more comfortable in a world of specialty. She explained that she was drawn to the kind of art that often isn't thought of as serious art and that her mentor at the university was a specialist in American folk art. She tried to give a simple definition. Ben and Robina did not ask her questions. Liz felt like both a defendant and an expert witness.

"Do you think Mom's some kind of artist?" Robina asked.

"Yes. First of all, she loves the work of making the quilts and designing them gives her the kind of satisfaction all artists get when they have a new idea."

"Her quilts are different, that's for sure," Ben said. "Does that make them art?"

"I think it does. I've had all kinds of art and design classes; I think I know talent in whatever form. I took the pictures at first to ask my advisor if I was right. You know if I'm going to get a degree, I have to write a thesis about something that really is art."

"And he thinks they're art?" Ben asked

"He does. He's excited that I discovered Geneva's quilts. My big job is to do a lot of writing to explain how they fit the definition. You know I keep telling people around here that it's not so different from Grandma Moses. She didn't paint like the fancy city people who ran the art schools. But art critics agree that she had a special way of seeing things. I think it will be that way with Geneva's quilts. They're not like the arty ones that well-known art quilters are making, but they're not the ones people are making who use all the modern techniques with their expensive sewing machines."

"I never would'a called Mom an artist." Ben sounded surprised and proud. "She never used-ta make quilts in those colors and with the pieces not all square and straight."

"So you're going to be a specialist in outside quilts?" Robina asked.

"Outsider," Ben corrected. Robina just glanced at him to acknowledge his correction.

"I think I'd like to work in a museum and arrange shows and maybe even work on films about outsider artists," Liz said. She was pleased at herself for having broached the subject in a roundabout way.

"If they're in museums and get famous like Grandma Moses, they're not still Outside Artists, are they?" Ben asked, surprising Liz.

"They still are. There are some outsider painters who just go on doing what they do even though their work has been shown in galleries and people have written articles about them. The thing is they have a natural ability, but they didn't study art in school so what they're doing is not considered fine art. You know a lot of people in colleges can be stuffy. I'm lucky to have an advisor who likes this kind of art."

"So that's what Mom's doing when she makes her quilts," Ben said.

"I think so. Like most outsider artists, she's making do with what she's got. Most are people who can't afford expensive materials. She told me yesterday that she has trouble getting enough batting, so when I was at Walmart this morning I bought a couple of rolls of batting for her."

"That was nice of you," Robina said.

"Well, thank you very much," Ben said.

"I'm not here just to take advantage of her," Liz said, looking directly at Ben. "I'm very excited by her quilts. And since she wants to give them away, the only way to document what she's done is with photographs and interviews...and maybe some film."

"And you said you might want to show some in a museum?" Robina asked.

"I've called some people at museums. So far they've mostly given me names of other people to call. Quilts aren't understood by regular museum people, and that's one of the things I hope I'll be able to change a little bit with what I write, not just about Geneva's quilts but about art quilts in general."

Ben asked, "When you talk about value—you said someone might want to buy Mom's quilts."

"I think that would be possible, but it wouldn't happen all of a sudden. I probably shouldn't have said anything because she doesn't want to sell them."

"What would they be worth, do you think?" This was the real reason they had asked her to come talk to them. She wished she had never mentioned that there are collectors who buy quilts.

"I'm just learning about these things. I know that art quilters who work with interior decorators and with architects get several thousand dollars for a commission. You know, when they make a big quilt to hang in corporate office buildings, or sometimes in a church or a hospital. I know that fine quality old Amish quilts go for up to $10,000 at auctions. But those are special cases. I really can't answer you. It's not important since these quilts will never be for sale."

"Mom's real set in her ways, but sometimes she changes her mind," Ben said. "Did she tell you about that nurse who spouted off about poor people down at a trailer park?"

"Yes. She said it was making her think about charity."

"That woman was upset that day because someone got kicked out of her home and didn't have a place to go," Robina said. "She apologized and said she shouldn't'a said anything."

"Once something's said, you can't unsay it," Ben said. "And maybe it was a good thing she did say something. She's right about how we can be blind to what's going on with our neighbors. When Mom gets that kind of bee in her bonnet, she chews on it like those pups are trying to chew her furniture all to pieces."

"Did you see that leather bone we bought for them?" Robina asked.

Liz was happy to change the subject. "They were fighting over it," she said. "Are you going to take one of the puppies?"

"No," Ben said.

"We might," Robina said at the same time. "I like the lazy one. I like an animal that lets me pet him."

"Her—that's an animal that'll give you more animals," Ben said.

"That can be fixed," Robina answered.

"I'm sorry I really can't stay much longer," Liz said. "My mom is coming, and she insists I get dressed properly for the rest of the day. If there's anything else you want to ask me about—"

"You think this here work you're doing is going to make Mom famous?" Ben asked.

"I'm just a student writing a paper. I'm nobody important, you know. But I want to do a lot of writing and Geneva's quilts are something I want to write a lot about. I hope that people will pay attention. I can't say she'd become famous but—" She shrugged.

"But if you become famous, she'll become famous," Robina said.

"You know, not many writers become famous for this kind of writing. And there are dealers." Liz decided she might as well throw that idea into the mix. If Geneva should change her mind, and if Ben and

Robina were interested in money, a lot of things could change. If she weren't completely honest, they would not trust her no matter what happened. She didn't want the quilts to be scattered piecemeal, at least not until she and Sam had finished a book.

"Like antique dealers?" Robina asked.

"Right. Some deal mainly in quilts, and quite a few antique dealers keep an eye open for quilts—mainly old ones, of course."

"Well, I'd say you came here and opened some can of worms," Ben said.

"I didn't mean to upset anything. I really just wanted to write my thesis. When I first came down here I had no idea I'd find quilts like hers."

"No, I 'spect you didn't," Robina said. "Funny how you can get waist deep into things before you know what's happening."

"You're so right. The last thing I wanted to do was rock everybody's boats."

"Seems like some good could come of it," Ben said.

"Already has," Robina said. "Mom's as cheerful as a jay-bird about it. She's not letting on to everybody, but she talks to me different now about her quilts."

"What's different?" Liz asked.

"She's prouder. Sometimes she used to not want to show me what she was sewing," Robina said. "Sometimes I'd kind of nag her and she'd tell me it wasn't anything important."

"It's good to know what's what. It's like the *Antiques Road Show* where people don't know the value of some old thing that's been around the house forever," Ben agreed.

"It's a little like that," Liz said. She moved forward on her chair. "I really ought to be going. But I want to answer whatever questions I can."

"I think we got the idea now," Ben said.

"We hope you'll let us know whatever's going on. You know getting upset about things is bad for her heart, like killing that dog," Robina said. "She's there by her lonesome and her brain just keeps gnawing at ideas like those pups with that leather bone."

"I guess most of us are like that," Liz said. She stood up. The others stood up too.

"We don't mean to keep you from your family. It's a sad time for you-all," Robina said.

"We'll be at the viewing," Ben said. "I told Mom I'd take her up there."

"I hope Geneva will recognize me with lipstick on," Liz said.

The drizzle had stopped and the clouds were thinning. The sky was undecided; perhaps the day would clear up or perhaps more rain clouds would blow in. When Liz reached the junction of 421 and Rte. 50, she saw a red Prius on Rte. 50. That must be Mom; people down here don't drive Priuses. Liz looked at her watch. It was noon, the viewing didn't begin until 2:30. If Barbara was there for Marjorie, Liz felt she wouldn't be needed. Her mother could do the meeting and greeting, the hand shaking and hugging and self-introductions. Liz drove slowly through Versailles and lost sight of the red car. Down the hill from Versailles, she turned in at the entrance to the state park. No one was in the gatehouse, she drove along the narrow road, up to the artificial lake. A familiar trail began across the road from the parking lot.

She would have to put on the new pants and the print blouse she had purchased as well as the blazer her mother was bringing. Worse still, she would have to put on the new low-heeled shoes and stockings she had also found at Walmart. She parked near the beginning of the trail. She would remember the trail if twenty years had passed. She walked along, side-stepping muddy puddles. She thought of Ben and Robina and how her simple interest in Geneva's quilts was changing their perception of who Geneva was. She had become more than the aging parent for whom they felt responsible

Mom was right, she felt responsible for Geneva in the same way Geneva felt responsible for the puppies whose mother she had killed. She had never imagined she would affect a stranger's life and then be responsible, worst of all responsible for bringing up the idea of money. That dirty word, that magical, powerful word, that definition of an artificial idea. Money. Liz had to admit she was doing this for money. Not that she expected money, not even from a book. She knew enough about the publishing world to know that only best sellers make much money. Most picture books were produced for the same reason art was produced: because someone needed to express something and share the discovery.

Liz wanted a niche in which she could find satisfying work. Some of the satisfaction would, of course, be reasonably good pay. Connect the dots, Liz said to herself. What I'm doing is changing lives here, what Sam dreams up changes my attitude, what Jack teaches me changes...what? Maybe my ambition. I let Randy change my life for four years. I thought I'd never let a man's enthusiasm carry me off onto some sidetrack again.

Liz remembered a discussion in the dim light of a ger when Randy's intense face became startled by his own thoughts. He was talking about how they were changing the lives of the young people they were teaching. Suddenly he realized they were changing the community too, not necessarily for the better. The English-speaking young people wanted to go to the city; they would leave their parents and less ambitious siblings in a diminished community to carry on the difficult nomadic life. Would the steppes eventually be deserted? Randy talked and talked that night trying to balance his discovery of guilt against his pride in how successfully they were teaching teens to speak English and understand both the relatively new concept of democracy and capitalism that seemed to be the future of Mongolia. She loved him for caring and struggling to see both their worth and the harm they were doing. He seemed to Liz much older and more thoughtful than anyone else she knew. At least some of his questioning and concern had become a part of her. In moments like this when she was thinking about Randy she was torn between sadness for the loss of those conversations and anger for his detour into Buddhism which seemed to Liz entirely selfish, entirely about Randy's need for something he would call enlightenment.

I hope I've learned that lesson. No more thinking a man has all the answers. I don't want to play God the way Randy did. I don't want to push Geneva to do anything she doesn't want to do.

When she reached a place where the trail crossed the creek that had been on her right, there were stepping stones nicely spaced across the six or seven feet of shallow water. As she started to cross a sudden noise to her left startled her. A great dark shape lifted from the edge of the creek with a flap of wings and a gust of displaced air that ruffled the hair on the top of her head. The bird flapped along the creek in the direction she had come. The sound, the rush had been so sudden, such an interruption of her thoughts she barely had time to realize it was a bird and not an apparition. Heron, she thought. She wished she had looked up the creek and been able to observe it standing still as a statue watching the water for frogs or tiny fish. Walking in the woods should include looking, not burying herself in thought. When Liz stepped on the second stone in the creek it tipped. Be careful, she told herself. You don't need to get soaking wet falling into the creek. She looked at her watch. I'll give myself another ten minutes and then I'll turn around and go back.

"You may have to represent your generation," Marjorie had said. Liz knew her brothers would not be there and would barely give Aunt Alma a thought. Of Alma's grandchildren, one lived in Colorado and had called Marjorie to ask about how to send flowers, another was in the Air Force stationed in Iraq. Of the two granddaughters, Kate was married and the mother of five-year-old twins. She lived in Cincinnati and would come to the funeral. Louise was, when last heard from, with a boyfriend in Florida and, according to Marjorie, probably dealing drugs. Marjorie said sadly, "Gone to hell in that proverbial handbasket."

My Ph.D. in Family, as Mom said. I did not sign up for this. Liz wished she could get in her car and drive back to Bloomington right now.

When she came to another spot with stepping stones across another creek that would join the first, Liz turned around. When she reached the parking lot it was a little after one o'clock.

Lipstick was not enough. Barbara had a complete make-up kit in her overnight bag. What joy, Liz though. We'll have to sleep here in the same bed tonight. No! I won't. I'll sleep on the sofa even though it's too short to be a proper bed. I'll curl up. She passed her mother's inspection just in time to have a few bites of a chicken noodle casserole before reapplying lipstick and going to the funeral home. The town was so small they walked only three or four minutes to the funeral home and arrived ten minutes before the official viewing time.

Mrs. Bushnell, the undertaker's wife, greeted them at the door. She wore a Hillary Clinton-ish black pant suit and had Barbara Bush hair already snowy white although she and Marjorie had been only a couple years apart in grade school.

"We always give the family some private time before the public is invited. Are there others in the family expected?" Marjorie gave the names of her brother and sister and their children, who were on the way. Mrs. Bushnell nodded, jotting notes in tiny handwriting in a small notebook that fit in her jacket pocket. She opened a door to a room with four rows of folding chairs slip-covered in ecru damask. At the end of the room was the casket with the lid open. Wreaths of flowers with ribbons were on either side.

Barbara took Marjorie's right hand. She gave Liz a look telling her to take Marjorie's left hand. Liz did not, although she walked close enough for Marjorie to take her hand if she wanted. They walked to the coffin; Mrs. Bushnell followed a couple of steps behind them. "She looks good," Barbara murmured. Aunt Alma's face seemed fuller than Liz remembered. Probably her cheeks were padded with cotton.

"She always wore her hair pushed off her forehead," Marjorie said.

"Oh, I didn't know." Mrs. Bushnell pulled a small comb from a pocket and combed the hair back.

"No, to the right," Marjorie said. "Here." She took the comb and fixed the hair.

"Should I get a bit of hairspray?" Mrs. Bushnell asked.

"Probably," Barbara said.

Mrs. Bushnell went out a different door than they had used.

"The Bushnells are famous for getting things wrong," Marjorie said quietly to Barbara. She fixed the way the collar of Aunt Alma's dress lay.

Liz watched the cosmetic corrections. If she had expected anything, it was that Marjorie would want to touch her mother, perhaps kiss her forehead. She was surprised to see Marjorie treating her mother's corpse the way Barbara had treated Liz's unmade-up face.

She tried to find her feelings about Aunt Alma, a woman she had known almost nothing personal about until a few weeks ago when they had their one actual talk and she had had the moment of enlightenment as Aunt Alma briefly relived some of her life's happiest moments.

Oh, God, it's going to be a long afternoon, a long day, Liz thought.

Marjorie took Liz's hand a moment. She said, as if reading her mind, "Are you tired of all this already?" Before Liz could answer she said, "If you go out that door," she pointed to the one Mrs. Bushnell was coming through with the hair spray, "there's a small pantry with coffee and tea and probably cookies. You can get away from everybody else. It's just for family, but I won't tell the others about it. You're the only one who spent any time at all with Mom in the last couple of months."

"Thanks," Liz said.

"I told her she's getting a Ph.D. in Family," Barbara said.

"It's more than she bargained for," Marjorie said.

"We don't bargain for life, it dumps loads of tar to fix the potholes," Barbara said.

"Is business bad?" Liz asked.

"A recession is not a time when corporations give lavish parties."

Mrs. Bushnell asked Marjorie if she wanted to stand by the door to welcome people. As if it were an order, Marjorie went to the door. Barbara motioned for Liz to sit down in the front row of chairs next to her.

"You work hard, Mom, you can take a little vacation," she said.

"I may spend part of the summer on Cape Cod."

"Cape Cod?" Liz asked. As far as she knew her mother had never been there.

"There's a man... This is not the time to talk about it. I'll tell you later." Liz saw her mother quickly suppress a smile. Her slight blush was as incriminating as feathers stuck to a cat's whiskers. Barbara had forgotten she had mentioned "a man" on the phone.

"I won't let you forget." That would be nice, Liz thought. She won't have time to fuss about me.

"I saw the Paul Stuart ad—that was your Sam, wasn't it, with the sophisticated three-day beard?"

"The ad in Vanity Fair?" Liz asked.

"He's very handsome. I'd never have thought—"

"He's a colleague, not a boyfriend. He's photographing the quilts."

"Asking to meet Aunt Alma doesn't sound purely collegial."

Marjorie's brother and sister-in-law were the first ones in. They hugged Marjorie and came to say hello to Barbara and Liz before going to Aunt Alma's coffin. The afternoon was underway.

Robina and Ben came in with Geneva between them. Geneva wore a church dress, a print with tiny yellow flowers on a light gray background. The dress seemed timeless; she wore a crocheted sweater over it. After hellos, Liz introduced Barbara to them, then retreated to the back of the room. She watched as Geneva went to the coffin and stood for a while completely still until she reached up and wiped tears off each cheek. Ben put an arm around his mother and whispered to her. She nodded. Geneva looked around until she saw Liz. Liz went to them. "Are you all right?" Liz asked Geneva.

"I've been losing friends, like ever'body does at this age. But I mind losing Alma 'bout the most. I been thinking of lots-a things we did together. I'm real grateful to you for bringing her down to see me last month. We had a nice talk."

"I'm glad too," Liz said. "Perhaps if you feel like it you can tell me about some of the things you've been thinking about."

"Think maybe you could come tomorrow mornin' early, 'fore church?"

"Yes, I could, how early?"

"Maybe 'round 8:30. I don't go to church 'til a little 'fore 10."

"I'll be there," Liz promised.

"You can bring your recorder if you feel like it."

"I always bring my recorder," Liz said. "Except when I forget."

They were quiet a minute or two. Ben seemed to have something to say, but he didn't say it. Liz wondered if he were at all jealous that his mother might have a new confidante.

"She looks real good. They do a nice job here," Geneva said. "I hope they're as good to me when my time comes."

"We'll make sure they do," Robina said. Liz smiled; she knew Robina would be as conscientious as Marjorie had been.

Liz leaned close and said to Geneva, "I think you look very pretty today."

Geneva gave a little chuckle and smoothed the lap of her dress.

After the Gardiners left, Liz felt she had put in enough time to have earned a respite in the private pantry. She had been pacing her coffee consumption but now she needed some. She had just sat down when Barbara came in. "I'm telling you now and I'm going to put it in a legal document: I do not want a viewing."

"Good, 'cause I wouldn't fix your hair," Liz said.

"I know, that's why I said that." They laughed quietly. "Really, I think this is a barbaric ritual. Furthermore, I don't want to be buried out in Elrod with that part of the family. You can have a simple memorial gathering after a quick cremation. Seriously, Elizabeth Jane, I want you to remember that."

"I'll remember."

"I'll put it in writing and I'm going to make sure your brothers know in case you happen to be in Timbuktu or Katmandu when I die."

"I assume your new friend will know too. Is there going to be a wedding?" Liz asked. She was happy to have a new topic to talk about.

"I should be asking you that."

"No wedding in sight."

"Not the handsome Sam?"

"I told you Sam's a colleague. That's the absolute truth. Jack is definitely only a boyfriend, end of story."

"So far."

"Mom, I'm writing a dissertation and time is of the essence."

"She looks pretty healthy—Geneva, I mean."

"She had a heart attack."

"I know. Marjorie says Sam was a hero. He sounds very promising."

"I would rather hear about your boyfriend." Liz thought, Good heavens, Mom only has to see a picture of Sam to go into fantasies about having him for a son-in-law.

"Tonight, I'll tell you." Barbara looked smug. Liz laughed.

"Mom, you blush when you mention him. You must be up to some hanky-panky."

"At my age anything that happens is definitely between consenting adults." She blushed even redder. "I'd better get back out there." Barbara got up, leaving her coffee cup half full. "You take your time."

Liz sat staring out the window at a flowering tree in the backyard. Her mother had occasionally mentioned men she had dinner with or went to events with, but she had never suggested she was seriously interested in any of them. After so many years, Liz assumed Barbara would never remarry. She was not far from sixty. At that age, why would she want to get married? Well, perhaps if the man were financially better off. Barbara would always consider the financial side, although Liz knew her mother had been investing seriously for several years. Liz found it hard to believe in marriage except if people were dedicated to having children and staying together to give them a solid home. She had read that Margaret Mead had once suggested that was the only kind of marriage that should require legal sanction.

The weekend motto played in her head: "A Ph.D. in Family." Her family in particular, and Geneva's family as well. About two dozen people in the other room were related to her. They had names she had heard since childhood; she had played with some of them on swings and slides in state parks during family gatherings. They were going their way, she hers. Even Katie—who happily had left the twins at home in Cincinnati—was a little wary of her. "You're the adventurous one," Katie said when they sat side by side for a few minutes. "You went off someplace I hardly believed existed. How did you have the nerve?"

"My boyfriend said it would be exciting. And it was," she replied.

"I'd say scary," Kate said.

"I think having twins is scary," Liz said.

"I'll tell you a secret." Katie whispered in Liz's ear, "It's a fucking nuthouse."

"You're definitely the brave one," Liz said.

"I didn't plan it," Katie said. "An act of God, none of that fertility stuff." She laughed.

The relatives of Marjorie's generation did not know how to act toward Liz. They felt correctly that they had nothing to talk to her about. One cousin had asked if Mongolia was close to India. "It's close to India like Alaska is close to the Panama Canal," Liz said. Then she felt like a pretentious ass.

"Oh," the cousin said, trying to save face and show he knew at least a little about geography. "Was it Inner or Outer Mongolia?" Liz gave a quick history lesson on the political struggles of Mongolia. "Outer, if you must give it an old fashioned name," she explained. She sounded snobbish and knew she must have been equally snobbish back in childhood. Of course no one wanted to talk to her. She thought about apologizing but didn't.

Before she could say anything the cousin, without sounding angry or hurt, changed the subject. "You know I never got to know Alma very much." He glanced at the coffin. "I don't think I would have recognized her if I met her on the street. You don't come to this kind of thing because of who died. It's for the living. I've always liked Marjorie. Did you get dragged here too?"

"Basically," Liz said. She didn't want to get into a long conversation. She thought she was unlikely to see this man again, at least not until Marjorie's funeral, surely many years away.

"Just be there," Geneva had said. Here in the pantry, Liz was physically here but doing nothing vaguely useful. She could go out into the public viewing room and just be there for Marjorie, and for her mother too. I might as well get whatever mileage I can out of being all decked out to look like my mother's daughter, she thought. She went back to the viewing room and sat down beside Barbara.

Liz awoke when she heard Marjorie walk very softly through the living room into the kitchen. Her watch said 7:35. She got up. She stretched up and then bent to touch her toes. She was stiff from sleeping curled up on the sofa. She went to the kitchen and said, "Good morning." The coffee pot had been on automatic and the carafe was full.

"Was it awful sleeping on the sofa?" Marjorie asked, keeping her voice soft not to wake Barbara.

"It was okay. Geneva asked me to come down at 8:30. I'll just take a quick shower and have some coffee."

"And cake or pie," Marjorie said. "Unless you'd like bacon and eggs. I could make it for you."

"No, I'll have some of the apple pie if there's any left."

By the time Liz was ready to leave, her mother was up and show-ered with her hair wrapped in a towel.

Last night, before bed, Barbara had told Liz about Phillip Baker, who owned a real estate management company. The family had been Hoosiers for generations, but his mother had a Mayflower pedigree. One branch of the family lived in Chatham on Cape Cod. "He's not as handsome as your Sam," Barbara said, "but a very good-looking man, I must say. And he likes to dance. I've gone to too many parties with men who can't or won't dance. For a serious and successful business-man, he has a wonderfully light spirit. He's fun to be with."

"A light spirit," Liz had repeated.

"Men get so stodgy as they get older," Barbara said. "They might have been great at the Watusi and the Frug when they were young, but they put on an armor of their own importance and forget how to move their bodies unless they're playing golf or tennis."

Liz laughed; she had never heard her mother talk like that. Bar-bara had also produced a pint bottle of Johnny Walker from her over-night bag which she and Liz partly drank after Marjorie went to bed. Barbara drank with a single ice cube, Liz added a lot of water, she did not like scotch very much. "I've had a lot of experience," her mother said. "I decided not to compromise. I've saved and invested and been pretty conservative so I'm not going to need a man to support me ten years from now. I assumed I'd be alone. But Phil's different."

"Are you talking about marriage?"

"Not in so many words. Not yet. I'm hoping he's the kind who'll actually surprise me some day with a bottle of champagne and a pro-posal under romantic circumstances—watching the sun set over the golf course or something of the sort." She laughed.

"If it's what you want, I hope it's sooner rather than later." Liz finished her drink. She got up and washed out the glass.

"You don't want any more?"

"No, that'll put me to sleep. More might give me a headache to-morrow."

"I'd love to have a double wedding," Barbara said. For a moment Barbara seemed like a high school friend planning what they would wear to the prom. Liz always felt her mother was so much older, that age, as much as being mother and daughter, put them on completely different plains. Barbara was that most difficult to deal with species of human: parent.

Liz shook her head. "I'll dance with Phillip at your wedding. I'm going to bed."

"Good night, Lizzie. If that sofa's too uncomfortable you can crawl into bed with me."

The morning was fresh and beautiful. Apparently there had been a brief shower during the night. There were small puddles beside the road as Liz drove to Friendship. She opened the car window. The sky was truly robin's egg blue with streaks of clouds at the horizon; the fields were paint-by-number green. They would surely put a grazing cow into a state of ecstasy. The recently plowed fields were a deep brown that glistened wetly. As she passed one of the houses that was near the road, and not set back down a drive or lane as most were, a sleek, short haired dog ran out and chased her car, barking, for a few seconds. She thought of the busy puppy that Geneva especially liked.

Geneva called, "Come in," when Liz knocked. "Come in the kitchen."

Puppies ran to meet her, and she stooped to pet them. "They need names," she said as she went into the kitchen.

"I been thinkin' 'bout that. You want some bacon and eggs? I got up late and I'm making breakfast. Went out and took care of the chickens so I'd not be out there while you were here."

"I ate a piece of apple pie a little while ago."

"Have some real food. I guarantee the eggs're fresher than any you've et in a long while."

"That's an offer I can't refuse. I don't know if I've ever had fresh-from-the-hen eggs."

Geneva cracked a couple of eggs into the skillet. "People don't know what food's 'sposed to taste like these days," she said.

Liz thought that Sam would love to have Geneva's fresh eggs. She decided not to say anything about him. "I got the impression you've got something on your mind," she said.

"I been thinking." She laughed at her own joke. "You know, some-times I think I don't do much thinking for maybe hours at a time, I mean, not really. I just go through the day doing what I do. Not that I turn my mind off, but I don't ponder things much, 'cept my daily Bible reading. And sometimes that not so much, 'cause there's nothing in the Bible I haven't read and thought about some time or other, so even that thinking is kind of an old habit. You know what I'm talking 'bout?" She took a couple of pieces of white bread from the plastic package and put them in the toaster. She laughed at herself and Liz chuckled.

A plate of crisp bacon sat beside the stove. Geneva had planned to give Liz breakfast whether she wanted it or not. "I think I know what you mean. I had a boyfriend who talked about things like that." Geneva nodded. Liz thought about Randy's long monologues as he was discovering Buddhism, especially his amazement that an ancient religion had studied the way the mind works. When he talked about dharma and boddichita she had let her own mind wander. She was not drawn to a different vocabulary for familiar concepts. The turning of prayer barrels at monasteries and the chanting monks were exotic but did not draw her into their incense scented miasmas as they had captured Randy from the first time they entered a monastery together.

After a half hour of a lecture about his new knowledge Randy would stop talking and say, "You're not listening." She would agree and he would be quiet and she would go back to whatever book she was reading. Soon he started talking again. He was convincing himself and only wished to convince her to solidify his own sense of correctness. He had written her an email a couple of weeks ago saying he had enrolled at the Naropa Institute for the summer sessions; his winter classes had been challenging and he did not want to lose the momentum of continued understanding by taking a summer break. Liz had let herself wonder if they might spend part of the summer together. Clearly she would not see him unless she went to Colorado.

Liz was quiet while Geneva watched the eggs and the toast and got out another plate.

A percolator of coffee was on the stove. "Should I pour us both some coffee?" Liz asked.

"That's a good idea."

When they were sitting at the table with their breakfast after Liz had time to taste the eggs and realize that, yes, they were more flavorful than any she could remember eating, nodding, saying, "Ummm, good," she sipped coffee and asked, "But what are you thinking about when you decide to think?"

"That I don't know what's going on. What's going to happen—I mean about the quilts and Sam's pictures and all?"

"Ben asked me the same thing yesterday," Liz said.

"Thought he would," Geneva said.

"I told him, I don't really know what's going to happen. Here's what I do know: I will write about you and your quilts for my dissertation. I want to compare them to other groups of special quilts. I could give you a whole bunch of names you never heard of. I need to sound like I really did my homework—and I'll tell you, that's what I've been doing the whole winter. Almost no one knows about quilt artists. I have to write a thesis so I can get my degree. I'm a pretty slow writer."

"And what about the pictures?"

"Well, at first I needed pictures to prove I'm not making it all up. I had to show my advisor and the committee who'll read my thesis that the quilts exist and are different and interesting. They won't know much about it, so I have to be able to compare what you're doing to other people who they also don't know, so I'll have to get permission to use some of their pictures too. I've done the studying; I've got to start doing the writing."

"What 'bout Sam?" Geneva had finished eating but left scraps of food on her plate, which she put on the floor. The puppies rushed to lick the plate.

"Sam is also trying to get a degree. He's not much of a writer as far as I can tell but his degree will be in photography. What he'd really like is to produce a beautiful book with pictures of your quilts and then use what I write in his book."

"Kind-a lazy of him," Geneva said She chuckled like an indulgent mother talking about a spoiled son.

"I told him that."

"I 'spect he can talk most women into most anything," Geneva said.

"Most. But not me."

"Not you?" Geneva smiled.

"Actually, I'd like to have my writing in his book because people love beautiful pictures and they probably won't read what I write any other way."

"Yeah, people like pretty pictures," Geneva said. "But my quilts ain't pretty."

"I think they are, and Sam's pictures make them look like modern art."

"I don't know nothin' 'bout modern art."

"That's okay—you won't have to buy the book." Liz laughed. "We'll give it to you." Geneva laughed with her. They were quiet a moment, then Liz said, "Now, honestly, I have to tell you, they are your quilts and you can ask for a contract and for a percentage of whatever money the book might make."

"Ben said there could be money in it."

"Could be. But probably not very much. And it's not going to happen very soon. A good art photography book takes quite a while to be published. It could be a couple of years."

"So I gotta live to be 90 to enjoy it."

"I think that would be a good idea," Liz said. "I've had enough with this death thing and the funeral isn't even until tomorrow morning." She had finished her breakfast. "Sorry I didn't leave anything for the puppies. It was too good to share."

"Glad you liked it."

"If you had a contract with Sam, he'd have to give your heirs whatever you would have earned. Honestly, I don't think it would be much. Books are exciting to the writers, but it's hard to sell enough to make any money. Can I wash the dishes for you?"

"No, I'll do it."

"No, you did the cooking. I can wash dishes."

"I'll wash," Geneva said, picking up her plate. "You can dry."

"Okay." Liz took her plate to the sink. "I don't want to make you late for church."

"I got plenty-a time. The Koeneke boy comes by 'bout quarter-a ten and I just have to take off my apron." She filled the sink with hot water and detergent. "What about Sam's idea of a movie?"

Liz had hoped she was done explaining. Sam certainly complicated her life. "I don't know. He thinks it's a good idea. There are short films about true things, they're called documentaries. One person with a little camera can make a documentary. They can be very short, say fifteen minutes, or they can be longer, an hour or more. Sam wants to do one. He thinks if he can do that, it will be almost as good as if he wrote a paper about his photographs."

"He is kind-a lazy, isn't he?" Geneva shook her head indulgently.

"You've lived longer than I have," Liz said. "I imagine you know men better than I do."

"It's a different world," Geneva said. "You can put the plates up there when they're dry." She nodded toward a cabinet.

"I agree it's a different world. My mother tells me this weekend is teaching me things I'd never have learned otherwise."

"She's a good-looking woman," Geneva said. "And you looked real good yesterday all dressed up."

Liz laughed. "I'll tell her you said that. She made me buy some clothes and she actually put make-up on my face."

"I could tell she's a little bit bossy," Geneva said.

"A lot bossy. She was only beginning to learn to be bossy when I left home for college. Now she's in business, she even has a secretary to boss around."

"That's okay. Tell me, what happens if Sam makes a movie or—what did you call it?"

"Documentary. As I understand there are places he could send it to have it shown, and if people liked it, maybe it could be shown on television. I don't know. He'll have to explain that to both of us."

"When's he coming back?"

"Two or three weeks."

"He's not your boyfriend?"

"No. My advisor is also his teacher, and he knew I couldn't afford a good camera, so he asked Sam to loan me a camera. Sam's making a lot of money at his New York job. When he saw the pictures I took, he liked your quilts but thought he could take better pictures and he wanted to come here with me. That's the whole story."

"None of my business anyway," Geneva said. "But I appreciate how well he took care of me. Saying he wasn't Jesus so I couldn't die yet." She laughed her affectionate grandmotherly laugh. "I was ready to die, you know. I am, anytime. You think about that at my age."

"I guess you do if your mind's working right. It's sad when people's minds are muddled and they can't think clearly." Suddenly Liz realized the puppies weren't around. "Geneva, where are the dogs?"

"They're lazy too, you know. They're probably all sleeping in a heap in the other room. Most days there's a puddle or two but they're learnin'. Still hurts my heart that I shot their mother. I'm glad I found 'em, gives me something to smile at ever'day. I forgot 'bout havin' younguns around. It's good for the old heart."

"Maybe even for the real heart, the one that got its arteries cleaned out when you were in the hospital," Liz said.

"I 'spect so. You wouldn't want to come to church with me, would you? You'd be welcome."

"I really don't go to church, but thank you for the invitation. You know, my mother would be mortified if she thought I went to a church in these jeans."

"Mothers get mortified by their kids all the time. Part-a bein' a mother."

They heard a horn honk in the driveway. "That's the boy come to take me to church."

In Dillsboro Liz declined to go to church with Marjorie. Barbara seemed relieved that Liz was firm; it gave her the excuse of staying at Marjorie's so they could work together to get the kitchen in order. They put the remains of casseroles in plastic containers and individually wrapped single pieces of pie or cake for the freezer. They vacuumed and dusted the downstairs. They finally sat down with tea at the kitchen table.

"Is a good job going to come from all this quilt research?" Barbara asked.

"I don't have a clue," Liz said.

"Well, what do you want to have happen?"

"A good job. Any good job. Don't grill me, Mom, it's been grill Liz weekend and I don't have answers. Geneva wants to know what's going to happen, so do Ben and Robina. I don't know. Sam stirs them up about fame and fortune. That's how his brain works. I don't believe it for a minute. But I can't help dreaming about it. I'd love writing and researching...or maybe I wouldn't."

"What do you do next?"

"Bring Sam out again so he can take videos of Geneva working and going about her life."

"And then?"

"More research, writing. I'm trying to find a venue for a show of Geneva's quilts. It would make a book more appealing to a publisher. Or if the book was in print it would help sell the book."

"And maybe Geneva would sell some of her quilts, right?" Barbara asked.

"I don't think she'd ever want to. But Ben might put some pressure. I wouldn't like that."

"Money hungry men," Barbara said off-handedly.

Liz couldn't help saying, "Some women too."

"Some women have to earn their living and save for their old age. You're one of those women unless you snag Sam."

"Mother!"

"He's just a friend," Barbara mimicked. She got up and, rinsed her teacup and put it in the drainer. "I've got to make myself presentable. So do you, you know? I suppose people will stop in here all day long."

"Well, I hope so, I'd hate to have cleaned the house for no good reason," Liz said.

Chapter 10

Jack and Liz met at Evansville. He had borrowed a small cabin cruiser so they could spend the weekend on the Ohio River. It was Kentucky Derby weekend—exactly the beautiful spring weekend Derby people prayed for. They went ashore to a sports bar because "watching the race was a tradition, since before I was born," Jack said. He was in a betting pool and made no money on the race. "As usual" he sighed. The rest of the weekend was quiet, easy and lazy. Jack had stocked the tiny refrigerator and picnic cooler with food and beer. Liz had bought chips, pickles and an apple pie.

Liz told Jack about the viewings and funeral. "Marjorie actually combed her mother's hair. I couldn't believe..."

"Yeah, that's how it's done in my family too," Jack said. "When my cousin Harry died in a motorcycle accident, his wife made a big deal about how he didn't look like himself without his glasses. He always looked like a nerd who didn't belong on a cycle, but that's who he was. Nobody knew where his glasses were, apparently he wasn't wearing them when the medics picked him up. So the funeral home people didn't know. During the viewing Wendi stalked out, drove out to the accident site, searched the weeds in the ditch and found his glasses. She brought them back, cleaned them with someone's Wet Wipes and put them on him. I was right in the room when she did it. 'Now it's Harry. First thing he did in the morning was put his glasses on and last thing he did at night was take them off. I want him to see how beautiful heaven is.'"

"She believed he needed glasses in heaven?"

"Yeah. Don't you?"

Liz looked at Jack for most of a minute, his serious face, his eyes

225

not blinking, challenging her. She thought she knew him, but he had never spoken about religion before. Was he, underneath the guy she thought she knew, a serious believer? He had said he truly believes in ghosts. Then he broke into guffaws. She shook her head and caught the contagion. They laughed until they fell weakly against each other. "I've got to get to know you better," Liz said.

"That's why we have our elegant yacht for the weekend. It's been so long since I last saw you, I was beginning to wonder if you really are as cool and fun as I thought you were."

"Am I?"

"So far." He kissed her.

"Are we going to sleep in those bunks?" She had seen the narrow two-bunk area just behind the tiny galley kitchen.

"We're going to bring the mattresses on deck and sleep under the stars. Tonight we'll have stars and the moon too. I asked The Man Upstairs to give us a great night."

"In the middle of the river?"

"We're going up-stream twenty miles to this baby's home, up a little creek to my friend's place where this boat docks. They'll leave us alone."

The lazy weekend was the change of pace Liz needed. She did not feel self-conscious about her somewhat skinny body. After lunch, she fell asleep to the gentle rocking of the boat and awoke when Jack put a sheet over her.

"Hey! How am I going to get tan?"

"You've had enough sun. I don't want you burned so that I can't touch you tonight. Just looking out for my own selfish designs on your body."

"Meanwhile, did you catch some fish for dinner?"

"Didn't try."

Liz said, "I was counting on a catfish fry."

"Sorry. Some of us are a tiny bit imperfect," Jack said.

Liz put more sunscreen on her face.

"You've never made a quilt, right?" Jack asked.

"As you know, I'm imperfect too. Maybe someday I'll learn. Actually, I don't even know what to do with a sewing machine."

"Maybe someday we'll take some classes together," Jack said.

"I thought you never wanted to sew little pieces of cut-up fabric together."

"I might have said that, but I've been known to change my mind."

"You're getting a creative urge?"

"I just keep thinking, it can't be that hard. Plus, when it's done it's yours, you're not sending it back to its owner," he said. "I like that quilts are useful—like for cool nights on the deck of a boat with some-one who needs to be warm and cozy. I've got a borrowed quilt for tonight, one from Kevin's mother."

Liz smiled, looking at the big solid guy with a tattoo of an eagle on his left shoulder and lengthening brown hair that was starting to curl into a silly looking flip. He was thinking about learning to quilt.

"If I told anyone in my family, even Kevin, about that idea, they'd razz me until I couldn't do it no matter how much I wanted to. With you I could do it comfortably. That's the point of working for your-self."

"There are some very well-known men quilters," Liz said.

"Not well known to my family."

"If you want to, you ought to. You, too, could become an outsider artist. Maybe."

"I really don't have time. I work twelve-hour days, sometimes seven days a week."

"You don't have to. You can be very businesslike and only take as many jobs as you can handle."

"I try, but some five-hour jobs become seven or eight."

"Then you build in a fudge factor."

"Fudge factor? Where do you learn these things?"

"I read it somewhere."

"Maybe I should take up reading," Jack said.

"You know what, Jack? You really should. You need to think of yourself as a small business owner." He had the urge magazines called "entrepreneurial," but he didn't know it. "If I get you a couple of books about running a small business, will you at least look through them to see what ideas you can use?"

"I guess I'm kind of lazy about learning all that business stuff. I just don't feel like, you know, one of those gung-ho business types. I just like what I'm doing and it brings in enough money, at least for now. If you're looking for a high-powered guy, the kind that gets a heart attack at forty-five but he's made his first million, it ain't me."

"I'm not looking for that. I was suggesting you could do what you're doing and not have to work such long hours and maybe even make more money."

"Maybe I'm not the business type."

"My mother has turned into a business person. She can be boring when she talks about business. Doesn't seem like my mother but I gotta give her credit. She's enjoying it. She took the courses and read the books."

"Tell me about her."

Liz talked about her mother, but she stopped short of suggesting she would introduce them.

The next day they had breakfast with Jack's friends, Bill and Brenda. Then they went back out on the river for another quiet couple of hours and a bit of cramped sex on the floor of the cabin. After a long satisfied lull Jack asked, "Do you think you could see yourself living in Paducah? Maybe working for the museum or the magazine. Or even working with me?"

Liz's stomach clenched. Jack wanted to replace Denise.

Jack had said, "I really wanted to be married, but when it came to choosing a girl I just didn't have my head screwed on right." Another time he said, "I guess I just didn't have any idea what being married was all about." This, Liz thought, was the way he approached things, whether marriage or his business. Weren't most decisions made by the seat of the pants? Liz knew what Jack was going to say and that he had waited until the end of the weekend out of nervousness or so they would both have time to think about it. She didn't want to hear his questions and didn't want to answer.

Barbara had said during the funeral weekend, "There comes a time for most people in their late twenties or early thirties when they're ready to get married. It happened to me and it happened to your brothers and it'll probably happen to you. I thought you'd come back from Mongolia and have a wedding."

"I'm nowhere near ready. The Ph.D. comes first."

She said to Jack, "I can only see as far ahead as the Ph.D."

"It's only a could-you-imagine kind of question," he said. She knew it was much more serious but pretended to believe him.

"I could imagine...but I'm afraid to imagine anything beyond this summer. People have been asking me so many questions I don't have answers for. Geneva and her son want to know what's going to happen. I don't know. I don't think I know anything." She felt like a wimp, whining about her confusion. She felt worse for never having told him much about Sam. Not that Sam mattered in her feelings about Jack, but she felt uneasy and dishonest. This was the wrong time, the literal eleventh hour of this weekend. "I've loved being here with you this weekend. It's been a perfect oasis—well, I guess an oasis can't be a river, can it?"

Jack chuckled. "You're always trying to find the right words. You really ought to be a writer. You can write anywhere, you know."

"I know, except for me it's really hard work. I don't think that's the way I want to make a living."

"It depends on how big a living you want or need to make, don't you think?"

"That's another question I can't answer."

"When two pool their income it goes farther."

"Jack, stop. Please. Please—please. I'm not ready to have that conversation." Jack leaned back and looked at her very seriously. She couldn't tell what he was thinking, she only knew that her stomach felt knotty and her chest was tight. If she felt a flush of happiness, it would have been easy; but this was a helpless feeling between wanting to run away and wanting to have him hold her. The moment extended, she had to meet his eyes, but she could not hide the fear she knew was all over her face.

"No rush," Jack said. "I'm happy when I'm with you. And I think Paducah might be a good place for you."

"It might...I just don't know."

"You are the absolute opposite of every woman I ever met," Jack said. "This subject is going to come up again, you know."

She knew but right now she wanted to get in her car and drive the quiet two-lane roads home to Bloomington.

———

Too much driving time: Liz was on her way to Dillsboro late Thursday afternoon, planning to get to Marjorie's about 7:00. She was still thinking about Jack's near proposal, as she had thought about it all the way home from Evansville on Sunday. She immersed herself in work most of the week, but her mind kept going back to the feeling of queasiness in her stomach. He hadn't said "marriage." Some words don't have to be said, they make the air vibrate without being spoken. Liz imagined married life in a small house, say the one Jack now lived in. House cleaning, furniture and cooking, laundry. No! No, no. She didn't want to think about it at all. Children! No. If that was the package, no and no and no.

Liz had never had a babysitting job, her two nieces and one nephew had been born far away, she had received announcements and sent gift certificates and had actually only seen the nephew on one visit to her mother when Brian had come to show off the grandson. She held the drooling little bundle of wiggles all wrong. "You're so awkward," Barbara had said. "You hold a baby like this."

Liz had enjoyed some of the Mongolian children, but they were older, little bundles of clothing with bright dark eyes and bow shaped red mouths that laughed easily. She couldn't help smiling at the older children, five or six years old, who stared at her American face, light eyes and light hair, nose like a tea kettle spout (as all foreigners had). They chattered to her about their toys and their horses and took her by the hand to come look at the goats and sheep. They eagerly repeated back to her the English names she gave them as if she had not called their goat "Goat" but a name like "Billy." No, she did not think she lacked feeling for children, as long as they could walk and talk and were not her responsibility day in and day out.

Good heavens, maybe I'm turning into Aunt Alma—except Aunt Alma liked the babies and the smallest children that she called "little people." She didn't like them when they reached "the sassy age," which was often six or seven and on into the teenage years.

Jack had emphasized that marriage to Denise had been a simple mistake they both wanted out of immediately. Liz knew, but hadn't tried to explain to Jack, that she had not made a mistake when she adopted Randy's dream of teaching in a distant country. Randy had brought heart racing joy the first day she spent with him in Rome. She often thought of how he showed her the Bernini altar, almost a rehearsal for a wedding march. Only after three years did she realize she could not follow his journey, which she understood when he began to define it as a "Journey." When it took on a capital J, it meant a life path for Randy and antsy jitters for Liz. She did not want Randy to define her life journey; he was becoming too serious about big questions.

How had Buddhism shaped the Mongols from the murderous war machine Genghis Khan created with his warriors on their study little horses? What changed them into a wise and gentle people, stoically and peacefully living in a landscape of endless grassland with a vast dome of sky overhead that brought the terrible challenge of winter and occasional devastating summer drought? Randy admired the Mongols who had maintained who they were, and, in many cases, maintained their religious practices secretly for forty years under the iron atheistic rule of Communism.

Randy had a breadth of view that she had loved and wanted to learn by the osmosis of being with him day in and day out. But his way of seeing the world could not be transferred. She was in Mongolia to escape the given wisdom of the art world and, in fact, the whole world. She wasn't sure what she wanted, but it wasn't a Buddhist spiritual journey. She wanted to live a life of her own that did not have rituals and rules, she wasn't drawn to wise teachers who had the answers, who could guide the student toward their personal insights. She wanted to find her own answers in the usual hit or miss, good and bad, happy and sad way.

All these thoughts had played a loop in her mind driving back to Bloomington last Sunday afternoon. Her memories had been more comfortable than thinking about Jack and the warmth of waking beside Randy during the depth of winter. They zipped their sleeping bags together and piled their blankets over them. They needed all the body warmth they shared.

During her busy week she concentrated on her work, but during the eighty-mile drive today she remembered the comfort of waking in

Jack's arms. He was bigger than Randy, not in a he-man way, just naturally a size or two larger. She briefly thought of sleeping in the same bed as Sam and not touching; she was grateful that he kept his promise. But the memory of sleeping skin to skin, made her breathe more deeply. Don't all animals seek to sleep skin to skin or fur to fur?

After nearly twenty years of being single, had her mother now rediscovered that pleasure? Oh! What did she know? Perhaps Mom had had a series of men in her life Liz knew nothing about. Marjorie said she missed Don. Surely Geneva remembered sleeping with her Alf. I need to think about something else. She turned on the radio but could not find a music station she liked. As if Jack weren't enough of a briar patch in the thicket of her recent concerns, Sam had called Tuesday night very excited, full of ideas about a documentary. He had talked to a woman named Melanie in the NYU film department whose mother was a highly paid consultant for investment companies.

Carla was also a feminist looking for an outlet that had nothing to do with her work, that would, in no way, threaten her male colleagues. Carla would foot a bill up to $50,000 for a documentary. With that they could make a very simple 30-minute film, edit it, try to get it into the competitions. They needed footage of Geneva and some really good writing from Liz—something exciting and punchy, but condensed, about the good Christian woman who lives in Friendship, Indiana.

"What a great name!" Carla had exclaimed when Sam had dinner at her Tribeca apartment. "The Friendship Quilts." She would foot additional cost to send Sam and Melanie to South Africa with a pile of quilts. Friendship across the continents. Maybe Geneva could be persuaded to go too.

"Yo, Sam, cool it," Liz had said. "You know she won't."

"I don't know. And you don't know either. You assume. We haven't asked. It might be the thing she'd most like to do. The high point of her new-found artistic life."

True. Liz had assumed Geneva wouldn't want to venture farther from home than Indianapolis or Cincinnati. If Sam presented the idea to her in his charismatic way... No! Liz would not allow that kind of coercion. No. Period. Forget it. She had upset Geneva's peaceful life enough already.

How do I know? She asked herself last night, lying awake, unable to fall asleep. She hoped for a good interview with more insight into how Geneva felt when making the quilts, how she chose the patterns and colors from her stash. Such information could be used voice over when Sam was back next month and shot video of Geneva actually working on a quilt. For a few hours, she was caught up wondering how to give Geneva the freedom of choice. How could she protect Geneva from Sam's enthusiasm?

Was she underestimating Geneva's strength of character by thinking she, the sophisticated college student, knew what would be good for Geneva? As Liz questioned herself, she realized, too, that she wouldn't be asking these questions if she had not had long conversations with Randy. Nights when Randy agonized over how their opinions, which were asked by Mongolians who wanted to understand how life worked in America, affected people in a changing culture, a young democracy with the literacy rate only lately beginning to climb. The Mongolians were people of strong traditions but with no understanding of modern politics, no notion how the power of the first world, and of ever more powerful China nearby, was altering the way they would live and even the way they would think in the future.

I think too much, Liz said to herself. And still the loop of fear of making bad decisions filled her mind. The chattering monkeys as Randy called her thoughts. Liz felt it was necessary to go over and over her feelings and the new thoughts. Finally the question became: Am I in love with Jack? What does "in love" mean? Not just the original happiness of being caught up in Randy's enthusiasm. She wanted something that could last longer, mutuality, sharing, a desire to live a life with that person. Maybe she wasn't the sort of person who could do that. Maybe she was too selfish, too afraid of finding herself swept into a whirlpool of someone else's needs.

The loop had become denser, like a fugue that had started as one theme but began to weave other strands of thought, other themes. How did I get three men in my life? Liz wondered. Randy, Jack, Sam—and I should add Professor Simmons too. I've never even specifically sought out a boyfriend, not since high school when it seemed so important to have a boyfriend. Back then she never stayed with one long enough to call it going steady.

Marjorie had a casserole that she insisted on heating in the microwave for Liz when she admitted, "I forgot to stop at a restaurant to get a sandwich." She had been caught up in the looping dilemmas as she passed all the fast food places in Columbus. She wasn't very hungry until she smelled the casserole and started eating.

"Has it been a hard couple of weeks for you?" she asked Marjorie.

"No...sort of yes, I guess. It was time and I was prepared and I'm not sad about Mom's death like people are when they feel someone died too soon. I watched her failing for the past three years. I keep thinking about that word, you know?"

"Failing?" Marjorie nodded, yes. "You would, you're a teacher."

"Yes, failing everything, failing to live safely, failing at the civilized essentials, like cleanliness. She gave up shampooing her hair. Why? she asked. She knew but couldn't remember—like a kid who can read okay, but can't remember the facts of history, just can't grasp that history is a story. Thoughts like that keep going through my mind. I don't understand how someone can fail at life after being successful for eighty years."

Marjorie has a mental loop playing too, Liz thought. "You're adjusting," Liz said.

"Yes. We get into habits, you know. I had cataract operations about this time last year and for months I'd reach for my glasses as soon as I sat up in bed, even though I no longer needed them. It'll be like that with Mom, I guess it was like that when Don died—only worse because he wasn't sick very long. He died too soon."

"Thoughts pile up," Liz said.

Marjorie patted Liz's hand. "Thanks, Elizabeth Jane. I'm glad you're doing this work with Geneva and come stay with me once in a while. You're good company. Barbara did a good job with you."

"I'll tell her you said that."

"I told her on the phone a few days ago. She was proud of you at the funeral."

"She still likes dressing me up."

"You're still her little girl." Liz made a face, but she knew Marjorie meant it in the broadest way and that she was feeling like Alma's little girl, suddenly left on her own. After a pause, Marjorie asked, "Are you going to bring Sam again one of these times?"

"For sure." She told Marjorie about Sam's film ideas.

"Oh, my goodness, a documentary. Do you think he'll really do it?"

"I'm afraid I think Sam can do just about anything he wants to. He's living a charmed life right now. If it ever goes up in smoke, he won't know what happened."

"You care a lot about Sam," Marjorie said.

Liz shook her head. Marjorie gave her a look that said don't try to fool me. So Liz answered, "A book was his idea, a documentary is his idea. But first, it was MY idea. I just wanted to write about Geneva and her work."

"It's a good idea, the book. I don't know about a documentary."

"Sometimes I'm sorry I ever got involved with him. And it's Professor Simmons' fault. I just...sometimes I'm overwhelmed."

Marjorie asked, almost shyly, "Are you involved with him?"

"He's doing the pictures for a book. It's hard to believe it could happen. But I also know he'll make it happen."

"I mean, are you *involved* with him?" Marjorie asked.

Liz smiled at herself for missing the question the first time Marjorie asked. She shook her head. "No, it seems strange, but we're not that kind of involved. I'm not his type and vice versa. I'm glad of that."

"Maybe you're wrong."

"I don't want to be wrong. But I want, I guess, to make Geneva famous. I like her so much, I want something good to come of this for her, not just for me. And not necessarily for Sam. Why should he have a magic touch?"

Marjorie was playing with the cutlery. "Young people today have very complicated lives. It's different today."

"Okay, I'll tell you about my complicated life," Liz said. Marjorie was no longer worrying about her mother; perhaps the distraction of Liz's love life would be good for her. She told Marjorie about Jack. She spun it into a long story; they got up and did the dishes while she was still talking. "I don't think I'm ready to spend my life with one person. I'm not sure what marriage is about," she said.

"Some things have flipped," Marjorie said. "Women don't want anything to bollix up their careers. Young men, I mean men like your

Jack, understand that they need women, need something solid and they're ready to get married and settle down before the women are. Maybe Sam is that way too."

"Oh, I don't think so. Anyway, I'm sure he has girlfriends in New York, beautiful girls."

"Seems like he likes you."

"Seems like he wants to get his degree on my coat-tails."

"Do you really think that?"

"Sometimes. And sometimes not. Okay, I'll tell you—and don't you tell Mom—when he was here before we stayed at a B&B in Madison. There was one king size bed. I didn't want him to touch me and he didn't. I'm not his type, and I don't want to be."

"Is that true? You don't think he's pretty wonderful?" Marjorie met Liz's eyes, challenging as only a mother or an aunt would.

"Jack is not going to be the one. I enjoy being with him but... He's..." She didn't know what to say. "He's just not the one. Maybe Randy was the one and no one will replace him. But that's over."

"Is it?"

Liz felt tears fill her eyes. She had not told herself, definitively "it's over." But yes, it's over. Jack could never take Randy's place. She sat down at the kitchen table, picked up a paper napkin and wiped her face, blew her nose. "Sam is just using me, my discovery."

Marjorie sat beside Liz, took her free hand. "Things are so much more complicated today than when I started teaching in 1971. Women want more. But I think love is still love."

"How did you stay in love with one guy thirty-five years?"

"Really forty-seven years. We were sweethearts in school, and then when I graduated from college we got married."

"Were you really in love all that time?"

"There was nobody else I wanted to be with. He was a very fine human being. He had his quirks, everybody does—you know that. We were right for each other. I guess you feel it or you don't."

"I don't. Not for any of them. But...right now, I need Jack, I think. It's good to be wanted and to be with him."

"Well, don't hurt Jack by pretending to feel what you don't."

"I'm not pretending and it's hurting him—it's going to when I can tell him. Right now, I can't. I like having him with me, wanting me. I want to be honest, but I don't want to be alone. I was alone all winter.

He's good; he's just not...not complicated enough. I'm being selfish."

"I think you are, Sweetheart... Do you want to watch Jeopardy with me?"

"Sure."

When Liz got to Geneva's house at 8:30, Rev. Wheeler's Ford Explorer was there. Liz knew she should recognize it, but she didn't until she followed Geneva into the living room and saw Joshua Wheeler sitting in the La-Z-Boy with a cup of coffee in his hand. He pushed the button to retract the leg rest and stood to shake her hand—limply. "I came to visit Geneva early so that I'd have a chance to visit with you too," he said.

He was in a bright green polo shirt and tight jeans that surely were purchased before he gained the donut of fat bulging above the belt.

"How are you?" she asked.

"Fit as a fiddle and strung just as tight."

Liz had never heard the expression. She stared at the minister; he was not a good-looking man. He had a long jaw and big ears and crooked nose that must have been broken in some kind of fight. Was he strung tight? He seemed to be. "I waited until you came to tell Geneva my news," he said.

"Why, what news?" Geneva asked.

Liz didn't want to hear whatever he was going to say. She wanted him to disappear here and now. She wanted nothing to do with anything he had on his mind.

"I've got a long email, with some very touching pictures, about the plight of the people in Zimbabwe. Starvation is looming for thousands." The minister seemed to be mimicking a newscaster. "They desperately need all the help the outside world can give them, but the dictator and corrupt government officials intercept the aid other countries send. Food goes to black markets and not to the needy. But there's a bit of light in this dreadful situation." He had shifted into a preacher mode. "Our network of missionaries, many who are next door in Botswana, can take in supplies, only a carload at a time, but every little bit helps. We, here in the prosperous United States, have been called to send whatever we can."

"They need quilts?" Geneva asked.

"They need everything," Joshua Wheeler said. "Most of all they need money for food. I believe Liz talked to you about selling your quilts..."

Geneva looked confused. "She doesn't want to buy my quilts."

Liz felt the chill of an icicle between her shoulder blades. "I mentioned there are collectors. I haven't attempted to follow up because I know Geneva doesn't want to sell her quilts."

"That's right," Geneva said strongly. The minister pursed his lips as if thinking what to say. He rubbed the bump on his nose. Geneva added, "But I want to help if I can."

"Yes, I know that. That's why an idea came to mind." The minister leaned back into the chair and pushed the button that let him recline again.

"What idea?" Geneva asked.

"The possibility of an auction. Perhaps an electronic auction of selected quilts."

"Who would handle it and who would collect the money?" Liz asked quickly.

"The church, of course. We have a strong mission network." He had a plan.

Liz wondered, why did he wait for me to talk about this? He might have twisted Geneva around his little finger.

"You want to sell my quilts at an auction so you can send money to Africa?" Geneva repeated.

"I prayed for guidance in this matter. I woke up this morning and it was right there in my mind like a heavenly voice had whispered to me. Food and medicine are more urgently needed than quilts. A serious famine is looming."

"That's the kind of thing we generally take up special offerings for," Geneva said.

"Yes, it is. When the need is great we do all we can, each and every one of us."

"I am making my quilts for families, to cover small children, mothers and their babies on cold nights." Geneva's immediate reaction surprised Liz. She was so delighted she wanted to cheer.

As if he hadn't heard Geneva, Joshua said, "With your endorsement of the importance of these quilts, Elizabeth, they will be especially attractive. They will bring much higher prices than ordinary quilts even though many people are not familiar with Geneva's quilting style."

Liz quickly said, "My work will not be done for at least a year. You should think of other ways to raise money since there is an urgent need right now."

"We would only need a few words from you, perhaps saying something about the Grandma Moses of quilting," Joshua said.

Grandma Moses? I've never mentioned the name to anyone around here. Liz shook her head no as she was trying to think of what to say. He had planned his pitch.

"I'm not selling my quilts for anything," Geneva said. "I have a plan and it's the same plan I've had for a long time now. When I have a closet full, I will be ready to send them to needy people in whatever part of Africa the church missions tell me needs them most."

The minister looked away from Liz and directly at Geneva. "But you told Betty you were giving thought to selling them." Joshua Wheeler leaned forward toward Geneva.

"I didn't say no such thing. I said ever'one else thinks money's important. My quilts aren't money, they're just the work of my hands."

Liz moved near Geneva and put an arm around her shoulders. "That's right, Geneva. That's absolutely right."

"Well...perhaps Betty misunderstood." The minister leaned back into the chair with a thoughtful look.

"I 'magine you're right," Geneva said. "I'm sorry I can't help you. It hurts my heart to think of people going hungry. I never give it much thought really until the nurse, CherryLee, at the hospital told me about people at the trailer park where she lives who are hungry. They been weighing on my mind, so I asked Robina to give me a ride down there and I give them five of my quilts. How can there be people 'round here without enough to eat?"

Joshua's mouth actually fell open. Liz squeezed Geneva's shoulders and let her arm drop. "You gave away some of your quilts?" Joshua asked.

"The prettier ones. I always aim to have some around for times of need."

"What trailer park? The one off the Cross Plains road?"

"Down b'tween Madison and Rising Sun. Down in the river bottom there."

For a moment the minister frowned, trying to remember the place. "That trailer park? The one with the long row of mailboxes out by the road?"

"Yeah, there was a lotta mailboxes. CherryLee lives there with her daughter and so does her sister. Her husband ain't had no work since the start of the year," Geneva said.

"They're all ni—black people, aren't they?"

"The ones I seen were. Since CherryLee is a black person, I took a couple of my prettier ones and also a couple brighter quilts because Liz said American black people might like my colors. And they did. That made me feel real good."

Joshua sat up straight on the edge of the chair, leaning toward Geneva. "That place is a hornet's nest of drug dealers and parolees from prisons in three states," he said. "The paper's always running articles about shootings and stabbings down there. You're lucky you got out alive."

"Oh, I don't know 'bout that. Ever'body was real nice. Robina and me went in and had iced tea with MerryLee who's CherryLee's sister. Kids were in need of a bath, but in summer time most kids are in need of a bath."

"You're lucky you got out of there. I know the minister down at Rising Sun and he tells me the police are at that trailer park every weekend. There's all kinds of riff-raff living there—jail birds, drug dealers and users. It's a good thing you had Robina with you. Not too many of them would mess with two white women at the same time."

"Reverend Wheeler, you are probably exaggerating. Geneva was helping someone who helped her in the hospital. That's what I'd call Christian charity," Liz said.

The minister looked at her quickly, then looked down. "I call a spade a spade, that's who lives in that there trailer park, from what I hear."

"Spade is not a very good word these days" Liz said. "Reverend

Wheeler, Mrs. Gardiner invited me here to talk with her about her quilts this morning. I really think you should leave now."

"I've got Geneva's health and welfare in mind. I'm warning her about dangers she is unaware of."

"Thank you for your concern, but I don't think this house is big enough for both of us this morning." Liz spoke firmly; she was tense all over.

"I don't wish to be where I'm not welcome." The recliner clunked loudly as he stood up. He took a long, deep breath and opened his mouth, hesitated and then said, "I'll be going."

"You know you're welcome here." Geneva said to the minister. "But, you know that Alma Mason was Liz's aunt. She cut short our last visit because of Alma's death, and we have a lot to talk about today."

"The Lord bless you and keep you, Geneva." He turned away but then turned back. "You too, Elizabeth." He left quickly, letting the door bang shut.

"Oh, dear," Geneva said. "I'm sorry you two had words."

"I'm sorry, too. I'm very sorry. It wasn't my place to tell him to leave."

They heard the SUV start, turn around and roar down the drive.

"It was all right. I couldn't'a done it but it's all right that you did. I've got hot coffee. You want some?"

"Please." They went into the kitchen. "I hope the quilts you gave away are ones that Sam photographed."

"I think they were except for a Split Rail and a Shoo-Fly from the other side of the closet. I think maybe you took pictures of them, too, the day you come with just Marjorie." Geneva poured coffee and put the cups on the table. "You know, it's funny how he wants to send money to Africa but he sure don't like the African people 'round here."

"It's easier to like people far away," Liz said. "May I turn my recorder on while we talk?"

"Sure, that's part of what you're here for, ain't it?"

Geneva talked about her visit to the trailer park, the family she visited and their friends who came in to say hello. "I asked them if they liked the couple of bright colored quilts best—the ones I think are in Africa colors. But I didn't tell them why they were different," Geneva said.

"Which did they like best?"

"They couldn't make up their minds. Even the kids had different ideas. So I guess it don't make much difference to them."

"Does it make you think differently about what you're doing?"

"Not really. The bright quilts're what I mostly do nowadays. They look best to me, and if other people don't like 'em, well, they're not going to have them anyway." She sipped her coffee then stirred in a half teaspoon more sugar. "You didn't like Rev. Wheeler's idea about an auction."

"I thought he had no right to decide that. He wasn't even asking you. It was like he thought they were his to do with what he wanted."

"Some people are like that."

"I hope he won't come back and keep talking about it. You stood up for yourself but...never mind." He was not only Geneva's minister but he and his wife, along with a few other people in the church, saw that Geneva had a ride to the store when she needed something, took her to church, dropped in to see how she was doing.

"You don't trust him when it comes to money, do you?" Geneva asked.

"No. I've read too many things about ministers who managed to get rich, some even got sent to jail."

"Money is temptation," Geneva said. "Ben can't help thinking 'bout your saying sometimes people buy quilts like mine. I been thinking I probably ought to see that they're given away before I die... Not that I don't trust my own son but times are hard, you know. Most people can't live as plain and simple as I can."

"You can put in your will that they must go to Africa," Liz said.

"I ain't got a will. I don't like lawyering."

Liz knew lawyers were expensive and Geneva couldn't afford it. "Wills can be very simple. In fact, I think it's possible to print a form from the Internet and then write in a few important things and just have it witnessed by a notary public. No lawyers involved. I could print one out for you, if you'd like."

"Sure. I'd give it a look and see what Ben thinks."

"Next time I come I'll bring the form," Liz said.

"You won't forget?"

"It's here." Liz tapped her recorder. "I'll hear you telling me not to forget."

"I never thought of that." Geneva smiled. She leaned toward the tape recorder as she spoke. "I can say, now, Liz, you be a good girl and don't get in any trouble." Geneva chuckled and leaned back in her chair.

"Do you have any new quilts to show me?" Liz asked.

"I finished one yesterday and I'm 'bout to start a new one today. You want to see how I pick out fabrics for a new quilt?"

"I'd like that." Liz took the cups to the sink, rinsed them as Geneva put away the milk and sugar.

"Geneva, here's a brand new thought. Sam wanted me to ask you this."

"Sam's thinking 'bout me?"

"Sam thinks a lot about you. He wonders what you would think if he could arrange for the quilts to be taken to the mission or the small towns or whatever's going to eventually happen to them, would you like to go and actually give them to the people?"

Geneva stopped at the refrigerator door and looked at Liz as if she had heard a question in a foreign language and was trying to decipher it. "Sam could do that?"

"Sam has big ideas. I don't know if he could do that. I said I didn't even want to ask you. But he said I really should ask you so if he ever was able to do it, you wouldn't have a heart attack right then and there."

Geneva laughed, almost giggling like a girl being told a naughty joke. "I never met anybody like Sam," she said. "That would be a wonderful thing. A very wonderful thing. I'd feel like Santy Claus."

"Really? You'd be willing to get on an airplane and fly for hours and hours to do that?"

"Well, I don't suppose it'd ever happen."

"I don't know." Liz thought how wonderful it would be to see Geneva in an African village with a big stack of quilts to give away—like Santa Claus. Would people want them? Sure, people always want freebees. Liz changed the subject. "When you've given away quilts before, did you go give them to people? I mean before the trip to the trailer park."

"No, when there was a tornado a couple years ago the church was collecting things and I just gave them to Betty Wheeler. That's usually what happens. There's at least one tornado somewhere around here most years. And there's floods some years, you know."

"Did it feel good, giving them away to CherryLee's friends?"

"Well, yeah. I was glad, even though it's getting to be summer and they won't need them much 'til fall. You should'a seen those kids' bright eyes, getting'a present. They decided right away who got what and they didn't fight over it neither."

"You said one was a Split Rail Fence. Let me show you the pictures I've got and you can tell me which ones you gave away and I can make a note."

"You got the pictures with you?"

"On my computer. My Mom gave me a new laptop computer for my birthday—"

"You had a birthday?"

"Last week."

"So you're getting older just like me."

"I'm trying to catch up with you."

"I got a head start and you ain't never going to catch up with me. That there's the computer?"

"Yeah, it's little so I can carry it around with me. Mom came down from Indianapolis with it and a printer too. She's starting to take this project seriously. I've got the pictures of the quilts all on here."

Geneva watched Liz turn on the computer and bring up the photo file. "Well, ain't that just like magic? And they look so good."

"These are Sam's photos." She scrolled through the photos. "This is a good time to tell me if I have anything labeled wrong," she said. Geneva pulled her chair beside Liz's at the kitchen table. She corrected some quilt names. They talked about ones Liz especially liked.

The morning went by quickly. When they finished the photos Liz asked if she could help Geneva do any errands in town or anywhere. "I need to go to the hardware store in town and get some bug spray for my potato plants," she said. "Next week's soon enough. Thank you kindly for asking, but I don't need nothin' else in town," Geneva said.

"I hope it'll be alright between you and the Wheelers," Liz said. "I'm sorry if I insulted him."

"He needed to hear that." After a pause Geneva said, "I didn't care much for the way he talked about my quilts."

"I didn't either," Liz said and nodded her head. "Some people need a little insulting, if you know what I mean."

Geneva chuckled. Then she asked, like a school girl asking about a boy she has a crush on, "Ain't it 'bout time you brought Sam back?"

"He's due back in Bloomington next week. I know he wants to come out here as soon as possible."

"Good. He can tell me about his idea 'bout Africa."

"But Geneva, I want you to know something. Sam's a dangerous person."

"What do you mean dangerous?" Geneva looked truly alarmed.

"He's dangerous 'cause he's got this trick of talking almost anybody into doing anything. You've got to watch out for that. He could have you doing cartwheels out on the lawn."

"Cartwheels!" Geneva laughed so hard she made Liz laugh too. When she stopped laughing she said, "I think I'm too old to be taken in by a good-looking young man."

"I'm not really making a joke. Sam's got a head full of ideas—not always so different from Rev. Wheeler. He thinks everybody will like his ideas. I don't want him to steam-roller you."

"How 'bout you being steam-rollered?"

"Well, my secret is that Sam isn't the only man in my life. He's not the romantic part. He's just my photographer."

"No, he's not. He's a lot more than a photographer." Geneva sounded truly defensive. "He's a good man. He saved my life. And so did you. I think 'bout that a lot. I'd-a been dead and buried before Alma if it weren't for you two bein' here that day."

"Maybe," Liz said. "Or maybe you would have called Ben and it would have been okay anyway."

"No, I wouldn't'a called nobody, I'd-a lied down and died."

Even though Geneva was entirely serious, Liz said, "You might have caught your breath and gone on about your work."

"Well, it's over and done with and there's always something new to think 'bout. I got a lot on my mind 'cause'a today," Geneva said.

"What I'm saying," Liz tried to explain, "is just don't let anybody, including Rev. Wheeler and Sam—or me—talk you into anything you don't want to do."

"I been takin' care of myself a long time, I'll keep right on doing it," Geneva said firmly.

Jack came to Bloomington, for the first time, Saturday afternoon. Liz had tried to discourage him. She did not want to be pushed to answer his unasked question, but he had said on the phone, "We'll just have a relaxed Saturday evening and Sunday. I just want to be with you." Liz thought about Saturday dinner. She could barely cook, and she did not want to give the impression of trying to impress him with her kitchen skills. She went to the grocery store and bought a pre-roasted chicken, vegetables, salad and a frozen peach pie. She also got a couple of bottles of Reisling and a six-pack of Corona beer. Fine, that's it. The apartment was clean although she didn't touch the piles of papers on the desk or the piles of books on the coffee table, the bedside table and on the floor beside the chair where she usually sat when working on her laptop. She actually ironed the clean sheets and folded the towels in thirds. She didn't want him to think she was a slob. After all, tit-for-tat, Jack had obviously cleaned and straightened his house when she visited him.

He arrived with wine and a coffee cake he had bought at a farmer's market the day before. They went to an Almadovar movie. He said he had only seen one other movie in a foreign language. He wasn't sure he liked this one. And he thought he missed a lot because he wasn't used to reading subtitles. Liz wasn't sure he understood Almadovar's quirky story. Sunday morning she gave him a walking tour of the campus. "My god, it's big," he said. "Are all the Big Ten colleges this big?"

"I haven't been to the others, but I think they are."

"Don't you feel lost with so many people?"

"Not really. It's like living in a city. You know a few people, those in your dorm and some of the ones in your classes. Lots of people you just don't pay any attention to."

"I'd feel like a needle in a haystack," Jack said.

"I never thought much about it. I went to a big high school."

———

The day was hot so they drove out to Lake Lemon to swim. Jack was true to his word, no pressure. In the afternoon they went back to Liz's apartment and she pulled up Sam's pictures of Geneva's quilts on her laptop. "Oh, my god, there's so many," Jack said after about half of them. He was obviously getting tired of trying to appreciate so many unfamiliar patterns.

"Seventy-four here. She's gave five away last week to a nurse she met in the hospital."

"I guess what women bring me you'd call mostly contemporary," Jack said.

"Yeah, or contemporary hyphen traditional."

"Is it possible to enlarge some of those details?" Jack asked.

Liz enlarged some of the details of Geneva's quilts. "Looks like she didn't have much patience doing the quilting," he said.

"You'd notice that, wouldn't you?"

"Well, it's the only thing I really know about. I mean, the women tell me good quilting is four or five stitches an inch by hand. I don't know how long that takes but it must be a hell of a lot of work for a good sized quilt."

"It is and Geneva doesn't have that much patience or time. There's only a few she hand-quilted, most are machine quilted and mostly just straight or outline stitching. Here's one she tied. I think about a quarter of them are tied."

"I don't really know if what I'm looking at is actual size—" Jack said.

"It's not. And you're right, she enjoys making the tops and just wants to get done. She says she usually has one to hand stitch at night when she's watching TV."

"She needs someone like me," Jack said.

"She can't afford you. Your clients are comfortable women in nice houses who shop for eight- or ten-dollar fabric."

"A lot of them are kits," Jack said. "They tell me."

"You're kidding," Liz said.

"They're proud of it; they don't try to say it was their own idea."

"Really?" Liz was astonished people would let someone else choose the fabric and then follow intricate directions how to cut all the pieces and sew them together and then pay Jack to quilt the quilts.

"They think that's quilting?"

Jack nodded. "There's a lot of kits for sale. You ought to look at the catalogs from fabric stores. I don't think it's so odd, you can get kits to make all kinds and sizes of quilts. It's the American way, isn't it? I built a lot of model dinosaurs when I was a little kid. And, hey, don't cakes all come from boxes?"

"Give me some names to research the kits," Liz said.

"Hancocks of Paducah, Keepsake. Just Google quilt kits, you'll get a batch."

"Thanks, Jack. I didn't know that. It's like paint by number."

Jack shrugged. "Glad to be of use. They're prettier than most people make on their own. The colors are all well matched and the fabric's top quality. I'd say at least half of what I quilt are kits. Women ask me to turn their quilts into something to make it really theirs."

"Really 'theirs'—jeez. You're doing the work. I suppose she puts it on her bed and tells her neighbors she made it."

"I guess she does. Or she gives it to her daughter for a wedding present or something like that."

"Do they enter them in contests as if it were their own?"

"I don't think they're supposed to, but I imagine some do. Come to think of it, they could kind of lie about even the long-arm quilting. Some long-armers teach people and let them do their own."

"I didn't know any of that," Liz said. "I'm so glad I know you. Maybe you don't understand Geneva's quilts but there's a ton of things you know about. What kind of woman would pass off those quilts as her own?"

"The ones that can most afford it. You know a kit, depending on how big the quilt is, can be fifty, seventy-five dollars. Then throw in my charge on top and add the cost of batting and backing and you're pushing two hundred dollars."

"They could buy a Chinese cheapie for fifty dollars," Liz said.

"But it wouldn't be the colors they wanted, and it wouldn't be such good fabric and good stitching," Jack said. "I never thought much about it. You're making a kind of a federal case. It's bad enough the billionaire bankers are frauds, the sweet lady next door making a quilt is a fraud too." He laughed at his own joke.

Liz shook her head. "Like dinner."

"What about it?"

"I didn't cook it, I just heated it."

"You made the mashed potatoes."

"I didn't peel potatoes and boil them and mash them. They were from a little bag; I just added hot water and milk and butter."

"Nobody has to do these things," Jack said. "If it's important to you to cook, you can do it. If not, you made a perfectly good dinner spending fifteen minutes heating and stirring."

"But the point is I didn't cook."

Jack ignored her.

"I guess there's a bunch of chemicals involved," Liz added.

"And they all cause cancer, right?"

"Oh, Jack, I'm so sorry!" Liz said melodramatically. "I was poisoning you."

"Poisoning yourself too. It's like the Titanic, all us Americans will go down together from the crud we're eating." Jack waggled a finger at her. "Betty Crocker is a mass murderer."

They both laughed.

"Geneva made me eggs one morning when I was there. They tasted different than the eggs I buy in the supermarket. Her chickens live in a little stinking house and wander around the barnyard all day eating bugs and stuff. I'm sure if I roast one of her chickens it'd taste better than the chicken we had."

"Probably be tougher too," Jack said. "Seriously, you know what? I don't care. I like sticking stuff in the microwave."

"Me too. The world's a shitty mess, isn't it?" Liz said.

"Yeah," Jack said off-handedly, tired of the subject. "Okay if I scroll through these?"

"Sure."

"That guy's a pretty good photographer. Of course a quilt isn't going to wiggle around and make faces at you, and you can control the light."

"Those were taken outdoors on a bright sunny day."

"I can tell." He seemed impressed but was not going to say anything very positive about Sam's work. Liz decided not to be defensive for Sam. She didn't want to argue this weekend.

———

As Jack was getting ready to drive back to Paducah, there was a knock at the door. Liz opened it and didn't even have a chance to say hello. Sam started talking the minute he saw her. "Lizzie, it's all working like a charm. I'm putting together the greatest team. We're going big time, you and me!" He was about to grab her and literally twirl her around when Jack walked into the living room from the bedroom with his gym bag all packed.

"Hello," Jack said loudly.

Sam looked at him for a couple of breaths and Jack stared back. Liz said nothing because all she could think was, Oh, shit! Finally she managed, "Sam, Jack."

"Hello," Sam said, putting on a George Clooney suaveness. "I'm working with Liz on the quilt project. I've just had great news and I wanted her to know all about it. Since we're partners."

"I've seen your pictures," Jack said.

"That's me. The photographer."

"So you're going to make a video?" Jack said. Liz took in immediately that Jack would not use the word documentary or film, very much on purpose. He was also proving that Liz had talked about Sam to him. Sam was not as much a surprise to Jack and Jack was a surprise to Sam.

"A documentary," Sam said. Then he turned to Liz as if Jack weren't there. "I've found a backer. I had dinner with her Friday night, and everything is falling in place. She's going to have a lawyer start working on a contract tomorrow."

"That's kind of rushing things, don't you think?" Liz said. "We have to get Geneva's consent first."

"I have a pretty long drive, so I'll leave you working out the details. Okay, Hon?"

Hon? Liz thought.

"Thanks for coming up. It's been a good weekend." Liz heard herself sounding stiff and uncomfortable.

Jack gave her a serious kiss. "That it has."

"Drive safely," Liz said.

Sam said, "Good meeting you, Jack. Take care." He sounded as if he meant have a head on collision with a semi-trailer. Liz was as surprised by Sam's belligerence as she was by Jack's cool.

"So that's the Kentuckian?" Sam said, going to the sofa and collapsing into it.

"I didn't think I needed to tell you he was coming."

"Does he come up here often?"

"He's never been here before. We usually meet halfway."

Sam raised his eyebrows and made a face. "A handy motel?"

"No, never." Liz would be damned if she would be defensive. Sam had come in all excited about something and now they were sidetracked. "Sam, it's really my private life."

"Yeah. But you've been a big part of my everyday thoughts so I sort of...never mind."

"Tell me about this woman."

Sam turned the telling of his meeting with Melanie, the film school graduate, as of a couple of weeks ago, and her mother, the Wall Street honcho consultant, into a drama. He described Melanie as wild haired, white framed sunglasses, and funky platform shoes. She called herself a Neo-feminist and was excited about working on an "iconic woman's subject like quilting." Her mother was an understated string-of-pearls wearer who had rediscovered Sassoon asymmetrical haircuts. "Quite a team. Seeing them together you'd think they were a Lesbian couple," Sam said. "You'd never think mother and daughter."

"Carla took some persuasion. She thought quilting was too old fashioned and rural. But I used some of your tutoring to convince her it was a good subject and that Geneva is a fascinating woman. Carla's got a brain like a computer and a secretary who's a whiz at Internet research. Once Melanie explained the whole picture and how Mom could help her get started in a career, she was ready to go gang-busters."

As Sam talked about mother and daughter Liz began to picture Sam's New York life. She thought of him as the guy Prof. Toad suggested was so insecure he needed to talk to people face to face in order to work his persuasive magic. "Let me ask you this—" she began when he paused a moment.

He was on such a roll he responded with, "What? Would I like a beer, a glass of wine, something to relax with?"

"Would you? There's half a bottle of Reisling."

"Left over from your romantic dinner?"

"As a matter of fact, yes."

"Sure. Why not?" He got up and followed her to the kitchen where dishes were in the sink soaking in water that was losing its bubbles. "I wish you'd told me you were seeing a lot of that guy."

"Would it make a difference?"

"I don't know. Breaking into your good-byes like I guess I did was kind of awkward."

"If you called ahead like most people do—?"

"That's not my M.O."

"I know." She was glad she had a couple of clean wine glasses. She poured the wine, being more generous to Sam than to herself.

"I like Reisling. Did he bring it?"

"No. I bought it because I like Reisling, especially with Grand Union roasted chicken." Liz wanted to get away from Jack and back to Sam's plans. "Sam, forget about the wine. I was going to ask whether you slept with the mother or the daughter."

"Would I do that?"

"I don't know anything about Sam the Male Model in the Big Apple." Liz was sorry she had said it the moment it was out of her mouth.

"We don't know each other at all, do we?" He sat down at the kitchen table as if he were floored by the discovery.

"I didn't think we needed to. You're running away with your plans, and I don't think I like the way you operate."

"She came on to me, Liz. Women do that."

"Of course. Which one?"

"Well, Melanie weeks ago, but I'm not her type. I think she wants to come out as a lesbian but can't because she likes being seen with men like me." Sam sounded a little more self-reflective than Liz had assumed he was.

"So you didn't sleep with her?"

"Not Melanie."

"Oh... Her mother?" Sam nodded and made a face like a little boy confessing to pushing the other kid first. "You're a whore, Sam."

"No. I see your point but...it was one-time thing. But I'm not a gigolo. She's not in need of one."

"Are you being funny?"

"You've got to understand business. It's that kind of thing."

"I'm just a country girl. I don't think I want to understand." Liz was having trouble understanding Sam's attitude this evening. It seemed to change with every response.

"And you've got your redneck boyfriend."

"Stop it. I'm not getting into that kind of conversation." She got up. "I'm going to wash the dishes, if you don't mind. I wanted to tell you about Geneva giving away some of the quilts and my run-in with the preacher." She turned her back and ran hot water into the sink.

Sam sipped his wine for a couple of minutes while Liz washed and rinsed dishes noisily as she tried to calm herself and figure out what was going on. Sam had slept with a woman probably old enough to be his mother. No matter how chic the woman was, the idea was sickening. But why was it bothering her? If they were to be partners in any kind of work, she needed to believe in his trustworthiness. Was everything about Sam a facade? He certainly did not seem like the hero who scooped Geneva up in his arms when she was having a heart attack.

Sam got up and took the dish towel off the bar on the oven door. He began drying the dishes. After another minute or two he said, "Tell me the whole thing, Geneva giving away quilts, the preacher, whatever."

Liz talked about her visit and finally told Sam that Geneva had said she would love to go to Africa. "I was so surprised. I guess I took it for granted that everyone in that part of the country is content to stay put and sort of xenophobic."

"Geneva's more complicated than we thought. Is she all right? I mean does she seem like her heart's strong? She's not gasping for breath?"

"She seems fine."

"Good. It would be wonderful to take her to Africa. I'm the one who would feel like Santa Claus."

Liz almost said, Along with Carla Claus footing the bill. She caught herself. Was she as jealous of Carla as Sam was of Jack? Both were ridiculous. Totally ridiculous.

When the dishes were washed, dried and put away, the table and countertops wiped clean, Sam said, "You're probably tired and I came straight here from the airport shuttle. I probably have a pile of mail. When can we go to Friendship? Next week's the Fourth, of course, does that matter?"

They decided to go to Geneva's the weekend after the Fourth, which fell on a Wednesday—therefore it would be next weekend. "We can stay at Marjorie's. I slept on the sofa when Mom was there for the funeral so it's okay."

"I'd rather go back to the B&B and sleep with you again," Sam said.

Liz was about to say, we didn't SLEEP together, but of course he knew that and was pushing her buttons. Her silence was enough of an answer.

"It's up to you. We'll talk about it." He started to pick up his bag but changed his mind. He kissed her, neither deeply romantic nor brotherly. A little tentatively, fondly. "Night, Elizabeth Jane." He looked at her; he caressed her face between his hands. He went out.

Liz did not breathe for what seemed a long time. She could not think; too much had happened. She felt some of the breathlessness she had felt long ago in the Vatican courtyard when Randy took her hand and led her into St. Peter's to look at the golden Bernini altar.

Oh, no, she thought. No, no. She walked slowly into the bedroom where the sheets were rumpled and the quilt Geneva had given her that she used as a bedspread, was folded, as she and Jack had folded it. She pulled the sheets off and put them in the laundry basket and remade the bed. She opened the window even wider for the cool breeze that was slightly billowing the curtain.

"Oh shit." She fell across the bed and began to cry.

Chapter 11

Barbara called to ask Liz to come home for the Fourth of July. "I want you to meet Phil. We've set a date."

"Congratulations, Mother. Are you inviting the boys?"

"Of course."

"I mean for Fourth of July."

"I did but David says he only has the one day off. I left a message for Brian but he won't come. They'd both better come for the wedding. It's not 'til October. I suppose they'll disapprove."

"Why should they? You deserve to be happy. You are happy, right?"

"I'm very happy. We're house hunting. I feel like I'm twenty-five again."

"Great, Mom. I'll be there by—what?"

"Tuesday evening, five-ish. We'll have dinner. Just us, so we can talk."

"I don't want to go to any parades."

"No parades. Wednesday a backyard barbecue, three other couples."

"Okay. And if I bring a draft of my introductory pages, will you read it?" Liz was uncertain how to start the thesis: she could be academic but that wouldn't be good for a picture book. She could sound like she was writing about the greatest discovery since toothpaste but that wasn't academic, or she could be factual, but that was boring. She had three tentative opening sections. She wasn't sure her mother's opinion would be helpful, but she had to show someone before she showed Sam or Jack or Prof. Toad.

"Of course. Do you want Phil to read it too? He's very literate."

"What do you mean by literate?"

"He reads books. Serious books."

"Like?"

"Let me think what he's read lately...oh, that Gladwell guy. Oh, and Pinker, too. And Jamie Diamond. He cares about ideas."

Liz had no idea who her mother was talking about. They could be the latest spy thriller writers for all she knew. She jotted the names down and thought she'd Google them.

"If he wants to. I've got three sets of first pages, five or six pages each. I can't decide which way to start. Maybe I'll have to chuck them. I wish I were more of a writer."

"I'm curious to see it, Sweetheart."

"By the way, Mom, was the proposal romantic like you wanted?" Liz asked.

"Oh my god! I called you but you didn't answer so I didn't leave a message. Phil was here making breakfast for me. I thought you were probably sleeping in on a Sunday morning."

"So—?" Liz asked. "Tell me."

"So—ta-da!" She laughed; Liz laughed with her. "Last Saturday night we went to a pops concert, you know like they do the Boston Pops, with tables and waiters serving wine and snacks. At the end they played "The Champagne Polka." The conductor invited audience members to come on stage to dance with some dancers from the ballet. Phil said, "'Come on, let's dance.'

"I don't really know how to polka, and I didn't think he did either. There was three other couples from the audience who were brave enough, you know. Who knows how to polka? Phil had taken a couple of lessons. We kind of whirled across the stage. At the end, the concertmaster stood up with a champagne bottle and announced he was going to pop the cork but there was a question to be popped first. Phil pulled me to the microphone. Then, honest to God, he got down on one knee and asked if I'd marry him. And I said yes, and kind of jerked him up. Everyone applauded. Can you believe?"

"I wish I could have seen it."

"I'll never forget. Isn't that fantastic?" She laughed.

"How'd he arrange that?"

"One of his golf friends is the President of the Symphony Board of

Directors."

"Now I've got to meet this guy." When Liz hung up she was smiling. Barbara sounded like Cinderella telling the Prince the crystal slipper was hers.

Liz arrived a little after 5:00 at the house she grew up in. Keeping it was an important part of Barbara's divorce settlement. Liz's few visits since returning to Indiana had been both comforting and confusing. Barbara had done some redecorating, but her tastes had not changed. It still felt like home even though all the kitchen appliances had been upgraded and the downstairs walls were different colors, but still quietly pastel. A few pieces of furniture had been replaced but the arrangement was almost the same. Barbara's life was not centered around her home so much as the office she had opened near downtown's commercial area.

Liz's brothers' rooms had changed very little although one contained a baby crib and changing table and the twin bed had been replaced by a double, which was all the room could hold. Liz's room too had the same furniture but the teen-age posters, Van Gogh's Starry Night, Vermeer's Girl with a Ferret, Picasso's Blue Guitar Player, had been replaced by a wall of framed enlargements of photos Liz had sent from cities in Europe and from Mongolia. Randy was in one from Venice. Liz had thought of asking Barbara to take it down and put something else up. But she couldn't. When she stepped close to the picture, she remembered the sun sparkling on the Grand Canal and the pigeons pecking Randy's shoes in search of crumbs. It was well before selfies; a new-found friend had offered to take the photo. Liz spent so long looking at the photos Barbara had to come, take her by the arm and lead her down to the dining room.

They sat down to a dinner of Caesar salad with the addition of an avocado, and ice filled glasses of sangria Barbara said Phil had taught her to make. "I'm watching my weight," Barbara said. But she had a baguette from a French bakery and butter to put on it. "There's lots I want to hear," she said as they settled at the table.

"Me too," Liz said. "Your life's getting exciting all of a sudden."

"Not so sudden, I've actually known Phil six or seven years. I was a friend of Selina, his wife, before she discovered the cancer. I miss her. We both miss her. We like the same movies: Bergman, Almadovar, Spike Lee, and the Brits. Phil and I didn't start dating until about a year ago. He had to live through some serious grieving. When he cares, he cares a lot. That's the most special thing about him." She smiled and looked so happy Liz couldn't remember ever seeing her mother with such a satisfied expression.

"So tomorrow—?" Liz asked.

"We're having three couples over. They're interesting people— maybe I should say, by Indiana standards. They're the kind of friends who like to meet their friends' kids. They're not the kind who brag about their kids—but I guess I am. I've been telling them about you and Mongolia and Friendship, and they are really curious to meet you."

"Oh, oh, am I going to hate tomorrow? I didn't bring a dress. I don't even own a dress."

"I don't care what you wear. You're going to like these people and you're going to really like Phil. But you're the star attraction. I promise it'll be a good afternoon. You'd look great in a sundress. We could run out to Macy's quickly before they close and get you something."

"Oh, no."

Barbara shrugged; of course, she knew that would be Liz's reaction. "What's going on with Geneva and with the men in your life?"

"A lot. Too much. But Geneva first. Maybe I should be ashamed, but I'm not. I kind of kicked the preacher out of her house."

"Why? Are you getting possessive?"

"It's the quilts. I got ticked off and told that preacher to get lost. He had plans for selling some of her quilts. And he was being a bigot about the black nurse she gave some quilts to. I apologized to Geneva but, really, I just wanted him away from there."

They talked, made another pitcher of sangria and Barbara made popcorn like she did when she had serious talks with the boys or with Liz. Then Liz talked about Jack and how she was both comfortable with him and then uncomfortable with his near proposal. She explained Sam's ambitious ideas and her resentment that he was taking over her idea. She almost blushed telling her mother that Sam was so eager to make his documentary become reality he slept with Mrs.

Moneybags.

"He gets what he wants. I told Geneva he's a dangerous person. I believe that. But it would be just wonderful if we could take Geneva to Africa with her quilts even though I don't want to see them disappear. It's such a mess, Mom. He is dangerous."

"Well...he's not just thinking of himself."

"Maybe he is."

"Your voice does different things when you talk about him. No way will I try to tell you what you should do. I thought Randy was the perfect one; he was certainly different than these two. You have no idea what an attractive woman you are."

"Oh, Mother—"

"Elizabeth, you are very special, and these men see that. Don't stop talking to me about them, okay? Now here's something else: you won't be coming back to this house much longer. We've found a house we love and this will go on the market, maybe the end of summer, maybe not until after the wedding. So you should start thinking about what you want to save—your books, the paintings you did in high school that you stashed in the attic, furniture..."

"No paintings, that's for sure."

"I might want one or two."

"Books I'll think about."

"I don't want you or the boys to be sorry I sold something that matters to you. You don't have to think about it now, but pretty soon. And it's almost eleven and we've got a party planned for tomorrow."

"Always a party planned," Liz said.

"That's my talent, you know."

Phillip Baker was not a surprise. He looked like many other men Liz saw when she went to Indianapolis—or anywhere else in the country. He was tall enough to have played basketball in high school and college as Barbara said he had. He had put on a comfortable, but not unattractive, amount of weight. He was tan from playing golf and tennis, had a receding hairline, a face that reflected approximately sixty years of living and outdoor sports. His handshake was firm and his voice had a baritone timbre like a radio announcer's. He had the easy manner of people who are successful at what they do.

Phillip managed commercial real estate. He had offices in one of central Indianapolis's tallest buildings. For the Fourth of July barbecue Phillip presided with easy assurance over a fancy propane grill. Barbara and he had invited three couples, their contemporaries. Liz was the only person under fifty, her brothers couldn't make it. "Sorry, Mom." Since she couldn't join in conversations about golf or tennis, Liz fell into step as Phillip's gofer, fetching and carrying food, drinks and condiments from the kitchen to the patio.

"I told Barbara you might be bored with this crowd," Phillip said as they went into the kitchen together to get steaks and chicken breasts that were marinating in the refrigerator.

"Mom wanted me to meet you."

"Did you want to meet me?"

"Of course. But my opinion doesn't count, you know."

"It counts a lot—at least with me," he said, looking at her very seriously.

On his best behavior, Liz thought. "Mom's not going to change her mind about you."

"I hope not."

"Maybe she's a little afraid you'll change your mind about her after you get to know me. She's self-conscious about her unconventional daughter."

"Getting a Ph.D. is not unconventional, it's impressive."

"I'm sure that's not all she's told you about me."

"I've had the full biography."

"As she knows it," Liz said.

Phillip smiled. "Of course. Barbara and I have been parents long enough to know our kids aren't telling us the truth, the whole truth and nothing but the truth. By the way, you're not here to play maid-for-the-day. If I understand right, cooking is not a big interest of yours."

"I'm a disappointment in the culinary area."

"My information is that you are not a disappointment at all. She cares what you think. We're going to show you the house we're buying later on. I told Barbara you'd be bored by our friends. But they won't be bored by you."

"She warned me. Meanwhile, I need to observe you up close and personal."

"I think I'm also supposed to impress you with my congeniality and good looks. She wants you to like me and to pass the word on to your brothers."

"Actually," Liz said, "I haven't talked to either of them for months."

"She didn't tell me you were on bad terms with them."

"I'm not. We just don't have anything in common. I try to email or phone on their birthdays, but they mostly don't remember mine."

"You weren't close when you were small?"

"They were close to each other. They're almost Irish twins, you know? Thirteen months apart. And I was five years younger. I was an afterthought, or accident, and kind of a loner in the family. It made me an outlier—sort of like Malcolm Gladwell writes about." She had done some homework as she told Barbara she would.

Phillip did not pick up on the reference. "I've got two sons too. They're only a little younger than your brothers." Liz decided that Phillip was a serious man who would not slip into any kind of banter. Maybe he relaxes with his cronies, she thought. He seems like the kind of businessman who would have cronies, maybe one or both the men out on the patio drinking beers. Phillip continued about his sons. "One's in Fort Wayne, an industrial chemist with the Water Department, and the other is in Sausalito, California, trying to be an artist, running a gallery. You might like him since art's your thing. If you're ever going to be in the San Francisco area, I'll arrange for you to meet."

"I've never been to San Francisco."

"Well, actually you'll meet at the wedding."

"You're sounding just a little like my mother."

"Oh, I don't mean any match making. He's gay. But you're both into art."

"Do you mind that he's gay?" Liz asked.

Phillip looked at her with a surprised expression. Liz wondered if anyone had ever asked him that before. It wasn't a subject the typical Republican business world of Indianapolis would talk about freely. In a pause she imagined gears turning in his mind. Maybe her mother had warned him that Liz could be blunt. Phillip reached a decision and said, "Yes, I do mind. I can't imagine why; but he says there is no why. It just is. I like things to have reasons."

"Sometimes that just seems to be how it is for gay guys."

"So he says." He paused a moment and changed the subject. "Let's put the chicken breasts on first. Some people will want their steaks rare." He moved the chicken breasts from the pan where they were marinating to a foil-covered platter. "I had the impression from Barbara that you were all a very close family."

"She's close to David and Brian. I'm just not the call-and-chat type. There's no negative feeling. I have my life and kind of peculiar interests as far as the rest of the family is concerned."

"But you and Barbara are pretty close, aren't you?"

"She was having a rough time starting her career when I was a kid and she talked to me a lot about her problems."

"She's done a great job consulting. But you know, and she knows, that being a party planner is a career lots of people don't take very seriously. She probably should have chosen a different field; she's got a lot of organizational skills. She could have done other things."

"But she loves parties, everything from first birthdays to big charity galas."

"I met her at an IPO party a client was throwing. I like parties too—I'm kind of a party person under the Polo shirt."

"She's glad you like to dance."

"I love to dance. We're taking tango lessons and we might go to Argentina next winter," Phillip said.

"Let's take these out to the grill. Mom will get jealous if I monopolize you here too long."

"I think she trusts me. And I'm sure she trusts you."

"Why are you sure?"

"She let you go halfway around the world for two years with a guy she never even met."

"I just said, 'I'm going.' She didn't have a voice in the matter."

While Phillip was taking orders for rare or medium steaks, Liz went into the kitchen again, this time to help her mother. "After they all leave, we'll show you the house we're going to buy," Barbara said.

"It's not one of those things they call McMansions, is it?" Liz asked.

Barbara looked for a moment as if she'd been caught in telling a fib, but she said, "It's not brand new and really not very big. It's in a nice wooded section and it's got history and dignity, and mature plantings. We're not young show-offs. It's probably more modest than you expect." Liz was mixing frozen lemonade in one pitcher and her mother was stirring Mai Tais from a bottled mix in another. "He's pretty wonderful, don't you think?" Barbara asked.

"There can't be many like him available."

"Don't I know it? The ones like him are under lock and key by women they've been in love with for thirty years—and I mean 'in love.' There are more rock solid marriages, at least in Indianapolis, than the magazines and TV shows try to tell us. You have to catch a widower quick before some sexy young secretary grabs him." She laughed. "You know, I'd given up. It's like those women who want to get pregnant and simply can't and when they give up and decide to adopt, bingo! They get pregnant. We were friends first. He's really special, Liz. I mean it."

"Being happy makes you look lovely," Liz said. Barbara looked much younger and prettier than she had at Aunt Alma's funeral. "That's a good haircut."

"I've lost seven pounds, too," Barbara said. "I'm going to Curves faithfully. I'm shopping for just the right dress for the wedding. You'll be my maid of honor and I'll get you a dress too, of course."

"Not frou-frou," Liz said firmly.

"Liz, you are really full of dos and don'ts and opinions," Barbara said. "Of course it won't be frou-frou. I'm not twenty-five. If you were getting married, you could be frou-frou."

"Well, I'm not, and if I was, I wouldn't."

"You didn't mention Randy last night. Is he still important?"

"No... Not really. Well, in a way, he'll always be important."

"Four years is a long time. And you shared so much."

Liz had thought about that in the bedroom with the photos last night, not falling asleep until after midnight. "Do we have to take more glasses out?"

"If you can carry a pitcher in each hand, I'll bring a tray with glasses. I'll open the door."

As soon as the guests left, even before Liz and Barbara put all the dishes in the dishwasher, they drove across the city to the house Phil and Barbara were buying. "I like it," Liz said. It was more modest than she expected. A remodeled kitchen and new bathrooms only needed tile work. "I have a house full of things," Phil said. "Barbara has a house full of things. It's going to be a total amalgam—"

"We'll have two big tag sales," Barbara said. "You saw, I still have the crib in Brian's room. I offered it to both of them."

"Give it to a family shelter."

"She's going to start the grandchild thing, you know," Phillip warned in a voice that was actually teasing Barbara.

"She's got grandchildren and doesn't need any from me."

"She said you'd say that." He put his arm around Liz. "You're giving her a hard time."

"That's why she needs you. To get her mind off me."

"I try," he said. "I take her dancing."

"I want to see a tango at your wedding," Liz said.

"Did you tell her about that?" Barbara asked. Phillip nodded. Barbara said seriously to Liz, "Just don't forget the facts of biology."

"Jesus, Mom, cut it out. Show me the back yard. With all these trees around, you'll need some bird feeders."

Phillip said, "I've got four feeders in my backyard; they'll all come here. Barbara doesn't know anything about birds, but I guarantee that a year from now she'll be able to name every bird she sees."

The next morning Liz slept later than usual. The bed in her room, where she had often slept until noon as a teenager, embraced her as if she had never left for college. The songs of birds outside and soft classical music from downstairs took her back ten years. Barbara had used Liz's all-time favorite sheets with the word "sleep" printed all over them. Liz let herself fall back asleep twice until she woke up and thought about following the scent of coffee downstairs. When she finally went into the kitchen her mother was sitting at the table in the breakfast nook reading Liz's papers.

"I'm almost done, just one more page then I'll make you some breakfast."

Liz poured herself coffee and stood at the back door looking at the familiar backyard, now empty of everything except the grill and a few folding chairs. Visiting her mother and Phillip in their new house would commence a new part of her relationship with her mother. Odd. She was just beginning to feel at ease with their adult-to-adult camaraderie. Well, it was time.

After Phillip went home last night, Barbara asked Liz as she was yawning and heading for the stairs, "Do you like him?"

"Yes, I like him. I think he's real."

"He looks like—and he usually sounds like—all the other guys," Barbara said. "But he has a heart. I mean he doesn't bury it behind cigars and golf even if he likes cigars and golf. There's a real, good heart in him."

This morning, Barbara had once again become Mom reading Liz's schoolwork. Liz waited for the verdict. She wasn't thinking about it, but she knew she would never stop being her mother's daughter, hoping to excel.

Barbara said, "There!" She laid the papers on the table. "I wish I had had time to go down to Friendship and see those quilts. They've got to look better than in the pictures."

"Those are the pictures I took and Sam says they suck."

"I hope his are better." She put a cast iron skillet on the stove and went to the refrigerator for sausage and eggs.

"So what about my opening?" Didn't Barbara realize that was more important than breakfast?

"I like your second approach. The first one was all just..." Barbara paused. "Just flat facts. It felt like you didn't know what you wanted to talk about so you piled up the information. The second one made a lot of sense. The third one wasn't that different except you used a lot more big words and examples and it got kind of muddled. So I liked the second."

Liz was happily surprised by her mother's judgment. She knew all the assessments were accurate, but she needed to hear it from someone else. "Yeah, I think you're right. What else?"

"Well, I need some pictures of your other examples of outsider art."

"Of course."

"And I think you shouldn't introduce Geneva until you do more about Outsider Art. Then don't simply tell us she's just an innocent old quilter out in the boonies. She's got a goal. You told me she can't be a missionary to Africa herself, so she wants to send her quilts as her proxy. She's not the kind of missionary who wants to convert people, she simply wants to comfort them. I think it's important to know why she's making those quilts."

"That's a good phrase. I'll make a note—" Liz opened the drawer where she knew her mother kept notepads and pencils for grocery lists.

"Do you think it's good?" Barbara asked, now eager and glowing with delight. "Good enough to go into a Ph.D. thesis?"

"It might be. I'll see how to fit it in."

"So your high school graduate mother is not so dumb." Barbara pretended to be bantering as she turned the sausage patties.

"Did I ever say you were dumb?" Liz asked.

"No—well, I think maybe there were times you told me I had really dumb taste in clothes. I seem to remember a certain pinstripe gray pants suit you said might work on Hilary Clinton but not on me."

That was an old argument. Liz ignored it. "Tell me more about what you think of the introductions. Did you look at my outline for the rest?"

On her drive back to Bloomington, Liz sang along with the radio, left the windows rolled down and the A/C off. She felt that things were moving along nicely, even if Sam's ambitions made her nervous, even if she could sense the summer already flying by and a new school year looming in six weeks. She would be teaching two introductory art classes and have less time for writing and rewriting. And a wedding. Oh, yes, and shopping with her mother for a dress. Well, one thing at a time, the journey of a thousand miles... I've taken a good many of those steps, she thought. She pushed buttons until she found a radio station she liked better than the one that was beginning to crackle.

——

The next evening Sam actually called Liz instead of appearing at her door. "Are you on your computer?"

"Yes, I'm working."

"Here's a website to go to right now."

"I'm not interested in breaking news." Liz felt grumpy. When friends called to say to watch a certain TV show or go to a website it was always something she did not want to see.

"It's not, it's what we have to do after we see Geneva—or before."

"Okay, tell me." Liz found the website of Quilt National, a biannual show of art quilts.

Sam explained, "It's the other side of Ohio, about 125 miles due east of Cincinnati."

"Jesus, Sam, that's a long drive from here."

"I'll rent a car; you're stacking up miles on yours. It would be good to drive something newer."

"It's not the mileage, it's the time."

"This is THE quilt show to see. These are the best art quilts in the world."

"Says who?" Liz asked.

"That's the show's reputation. It's juried, it's prestigious. It's international."

"It says a dairy barn in Ohio, for Christsake. It's not what we're interested in."

"Liz! I'm disappointed in you. This is your subject and you want to miss the most enlightening show of art quilts in the country that happens only every two years?"

"I went to a big show in the spring."

"This is a different caliber."

"It's got nothing to do with Geneva's kind of quilts." She closed the website. Why was Sam bothering her?

"How can you know what makes an outsider quilt artist if you don't know what the serious insiders are doing?" he demanded. All of a sudden he was going to be a quilt expert too? He's taking over the project and taking over my life.

"I don't have time."

"We have to have time. We're two bumps on a log in this world of quilting. We don't know anything. I've ordered their catalog."

"Good, then we won't need to drive an extra four hundred miles—"

"Why are you being so resistant? I can have good ideas too, you know."

"It just seems like—" Liz sighed. "Everything is getting so complicated. I've got so much to do and I'm not a good writer. I write every paragraph twenty-five times. I'm sweating blood over this damned thing."

"I should have come over. But I just never know who I'll run into over there."

"Jesus, Sam!"

"I can't talk about ideas on the phone. I'm having the catalog overnighted. I'll show it to you tomorrow—assuming it really does come overnight."

"All right."

"Think about this, we can drive out there from Friendship or Madison, leave in the morning, get there, see the show. Stay overnight. If the show is really interesting, we can go back the next morning and then back to Friendship. It's not THAT far. It looks like a straight shot on good highways, the only heavy traffic will be Cincinnati and we don't have to go through the city, there's a ring road that should be easier. I really want to see what art quilts are."

"Show me the catalog when you get it," Liz said.

"Definitely."

"Do me a favor—call me when you're coming."

"Are you expecting company?"

"No! I'm trying to write a thesis." Liz hung up. Never mind the two heads are better cliché. Two heads just muddle up the situation. She had her outline; she knew what she wanted to get done in what little remained of the summer. Another quilt show was not on her agenda. Sam didn't have to write anything and he already had the pictures. Couldn't he understand she didn't have the luxury of time he had?

Sam arrived the next evening with the catalog. "We have to see this. I spent the morning studying my photos of Geneva's quilts and thinking about them and my reactions to the quilts when I saw them for the first time. They become something different when they're photographed. The photos are good, the best I could do. Maybe there are tricks I could learn to make them better, I know they're good. But they're not true. The overall sense of the collection is not true. I want to see if these photos are true. I'm sure they had top notch photographers, people who do this for a living. I assumed a two-dimensional object—?" Sam shook his head.

"Really three. Even fine paintings are essentially three dimensional because of the surface textures," Liz said. "Especially a lot of modern art."

"I know, I know. That's part of the problem, but there may be lighting problems or size problems. You know how the pictures in books make you always expect the Georgia O'Keefe flower paintings to be big, but they turn out to be 20×30? That probably happens with quilts. I've got to see this show and compare the real quilts with the photographs. That has to be part of my thesis. We've got to go see it, Liz."

She argued, "Like you said. we're essentially two know-nothings in a field we don't understand. We're learning from scratch, and we have to limit ourselves to what's relevant."

"Fools rushing in?" Sam asked; although he didn't believe it, he was trying to copy Liz's uncertainty.

"That's us. Why is Professor Simmons letting us do this? We're probably walking into academic disaster."

"Relax, Lizzy, relax," Sam said. He sprawled in her only comfortable chair to make her laugh. She smiled and shook her head at him. He said, "We don't have to sew but we've got to know what we're looking at. Dance critics don't have to dance, and drama critics don't have to act. I'm really excited. Look, here's one that's like sculpture—I mean, it is sculpture; it's three-dimensional. It's a person and something. I don't know what."

He closed the catalog. "I'm going home to study my photos some more. We've got a busy few days ahead of us." He kissed her on the forehead. "No fever. You'll be alright. We're off to see the wizard, the wonderful wizard of Oz," he sang as he went out the door.

Liz sat down at her kitchen table and tried to get her bearings. She had been trying to refine the version of the first chapter that her mother had preferred. The other versions each had some information that she felt needed to be integrated into her final first chapter. She couldn't just describe the discovery of a naïve, outsider quilt artist; she had to give some quilting information and some biographical information. Whatever she added took a page or two or five and then the whole chapter became dull and academic. Nothing she wrote was suitable for the introduction to a picture book. Her thesis should be one thing and Sam's book another. She had handbooks about how to write a thesis but none of them had answers to her problems. How do you write something exciting without sounding like Indiana Jones discovering a dragon guarding a hoard of priceless quilts?

She occasionally sat down in a bookstore and browsed books about creative writing. She did not want to write a deadly dry thesis. But, of course, she couldn't fictionalize anything. "Writing is the discovery of what you really believe or feel about the subject," one book said. Bullshit, she thought. I really think lots of things—which one is true? Which one will work? Which is serious enough for a Ph.D.? Which will attract readers? Should I even think about attracting readers? She printed her latest version and then began editing it. She wondered what unbiased person she could give the draft to for an opinion. Not Prof. Simmons, not yet, she didn't want him to know what a muddle she was in. Not Jack and not Sam and not Marjorie, they all knew too much about Geneva's quilts. Her mother had been helpful, but now she knew both too much and not enough about what Liz wanted to write. I've got to learn to write, Liz told herself. I've got to have a clear vision of what I want to say. Seeing a bunch of art quilts won't help me with that. But she understood Sam was looking for how to display his expertise in the same way she was. She would give up a couple of days and go to this quilt show because, if it became a book, the photographs would sell the book. Her writing would be secondary. He damned well better have smashing photos, she thought.

When they pulled into the drive, Geneva came out the front door to meet them. Two puppies came with her and bounded toward the car, but they stopped beside the drive. "She's got them trained," Liz said.

"Only two?" Sam asked.

"Robina took the lazy one," Geneva said.

Sam greeted Geneva with a hug. She was a little stiff and looked surprised. "What'd I do to deserve that?" she said.

"Came out to say hello to me," Sam said.

"Thought you were gonna say hello too," Geneva said.

"That was my hello."

"Hugging hasn't caught on out here like it has in the city," Liz said to Sam.

"I'm sorry, Mrs. Gardiner. I can't take back the hug. You know once hugs or kisses are given, they're returnable but can't be canceled."

Geneva laughed. "You're somethin' else, Sam. You really are a sassy young man."

Sam laughed. "I like hugging people. And being hugged back."

Geneva looked away for a minute; she did not seem inspired to give him a hug.

Geneva asked, "Did you get a new car, Liz?" The car they came in was a red Passat that Sam rented in Bloomington.

"I'm treating her to an upgrade for this trip," Sam said. "We'll tell you all about it."

Liz had stooped to pet the puppies, which were yipping and bouncing around her bare legs. The day was hot, and she and Sam were both wearing shorts and t-shirts.

"How have you been? Has the weather been too hot and humid for you?" she asked Geneva.

Sam got a couple of camera bags from the trunk of the car.

"I like hot. But not humid. Hasn't been too bad," Geneva said. "When it gets bad, I can't do much quiltin', just simple piecin' and cuttin', but nothin' with fabric piled up in my lap. But I made a couple new quilts since you were here."

"You must have a bunch I haven't photographed," Sam said.

"Four, five, I 'spect."

"Can't keep up with you," he said.

"But I give some away too," she said.

"Liz told me. I'd love to talk to the people who have them and photograph the quilts on their beds."

"Don't know if they'd care for that," Geneva said. She led the way into the house.

"Oh, everyone likes to feel they're special enough for someone to want to photograph them," Sam said. "Don't tell me you hate all this."

"Once I got over the surprise and got to like Liz and you it was okay," Geneva said. "Too hot for some coffee?"

"If you've got ice cubes, I'd like some iced coffee," Sam said.

"I know people drink it, but I've never tried iced coffee," Geneva said.

"I'll make you some if you want to try," Liz offered. "I bought some donuts, too. Sam, could you get them from the car?" Sam went out. "Geneva, Sam's full of ideas. You don't have to agree just 'cause he's cute when he's excited, you know? You can just say you'll think about any idea he throws your way."

"Don't you worry. I can think for myself," Geneva said a little tartly.

"I know that, but I know Sam's the kind who can sell ice cubes to Eskimos."

Geneva laughed. "I would'a said that if you hadn't."

Sam came in with the donuts and his portfolio. They sat at the table with the iced coffee and donuts. Sam pulled a picture out of his portfolio. "This funny-looking young woman—" he said. He showed Geneva and Liz a picture that Liz immediately realized must be Melanie, the film student.

"She is funny looking with those glasses," Geneva said.

"And the hair," Sam added. "She does that so people won't forget her. She could look entirely ordinary, but she doesn't want to." Geneva shook her head, not to disagree with Sam but at the young woman so eager for attention. "Her name is Melanie and she's in film school at New York University. She saw pictures of your quilts and thought she'd like to meet you and make a film about them—a short film, maybe half an hour."

"So you're talkin' 'bout me all over the place," Geneva said, wiping powdered sugar from the corners of her mouth with the back of her hand.

"I am, that's true. I think you and your quilts are special. They make fantastic photographs. I'll tell you how I got to telling Melanie about you. A bunch of people I was with for brunch one morning were talking about organic food, and I said I'd had eggs still warm from the chicken."

"No, you didn't," Geneva said. "No such thing."

"Well, Liz said she did. She was so impressed with your fresh eggs, I felt like I'd had them too. And I wanted those city people to know about chickens that lived the normal way chickens are supposed to live on a farm."

Geneva shook her head. "Sayin' you did somethin' you didn't is an outright lie. It's a bad habit." Geneva might have been lecturing a grandson.

"You're right. I just wanted to impress those people; none of them have ever seen a live chicken."

"Now you're exaggeratin'."

"No. That's the flat-out truth." Geneva looked at him as if she didn't believe it.

"What do you think of iced coffee?" he asked.

Geneva shrugged. "Won't replace iced tea in my house. So then you told them 'bout my quilts."

"At first I just said I'd visited a real farm. Anyway, Melanie was interested in seeing a real farm. A funny thing is happening—I thought about this the other day, Liz—some of us are starting to get tired of all the stuff we're supposed to love. It's like Liz saw so much great art in Europe she ran away to Mongolia for a couple of years." Liz wondered what point he was trying to make with his tale. "I know when I was trying to think what I would photograph for my thesis, I didn't want to do the same kind of gritty urban photos everybody else has been doing. I didn't want to do nudes."

"You didn't, huh?" Liz said.

Sam answered her seriously even though he knew she was teasing. "I'd have enjoyed it, but I don't think I have anything new to say that hasn't been said many times before by better photographers. Mrs. Gardiner, when I saw your quilts I just kept thinking about the colors and patterns that weren't like others that I'd seen anywhere. They were personal and I could take photographs, good quality, good details, I could do something none of the others in my class were doing."

"So this girl with the hair and glasses wants to come to the country and get away from the city," Geneva said.

"Yes. She does. But there's something more exciting."

273

"I hope so, 'cause that's not excitin' a-tall. Liz has got family 'round here so she's not an outsider. She doesn't think farmers like Ben are ignorant country clods," Geneva said, looking at Liz for confirmation.

"Right," Liz said. Yes, Geneva could think for herself. Good. She had an ally against Sam's approach.

"Melanie doesn't know what to think, but she knows it's a different world than she's ever lived in," Sam said.

"So I go to Mongolia and Melanie comes to Friendship, Indiana," Liz said.

"I've got a couple video cameras. I could make a film. That's partly what I want to start doing today if you'll let me. Just film you working on a quilt, spreading the fabric out, cutting it up, whatever steps there are. I don't need Melanie for that. And that's fine if that's all we want to do. But the thing is Melanie is in film school and she knows a lot of people who can help her get the film into festivals so other people can see it. She can be the producer; she doesn't have to do the filming. Now here's the point where it gets expensive. So Melanie's mother comes into the picture."

"Well, aren't you the busy beaver?" Geneva said.

Sam didn't pause. "Here's the wonderful thing, Mrs. Gardiner, when I told Melanie's mother—who happens to be a businesswoman who makes tons of money—about your purpose, about how you plan to give them to African people, she got very excited and said if Melanie was going to produce a film it should include showing you going to Africa with the quilts and actually meeting people in their villages and giving them the quilts."

Liz saw that Geneva had caught her breath and her face was becoming excited. "Well, I don't think it's all that easy," she said tentatively.

"Right. You need to find out from your minister who the connections are in Africa. But after that it's not very hard. Carla—that's Melanie's mother—would buy the airplane tickets and see that the quilts were properly sent with us. Melanie would want to come along and that's fine. She could deal with getting a guide and a van and a driver and arrange hotels and things like that."

"Sounds pretty complicated," Geneva said.

"The big picture is complicated. But with the Internet, people can arrange travel very easily. I guess the money actually isn't very much to people who make something like five million dollars a year."

"Between the three of us, I would do what I could to convince Carla"—Liz raised her eyebrows as Sam glanced at her—"that once we were there, since none of us have ever been to that part of the world, we ought to have a few days to go to an animal reserve and see what elephants and lions look like in the wild."

"We could do that?" Geneva sounded like she had been told she could sprout wings and fly. "Sam, you're just telling us a tall tale."

"Really, honest to God, Mrs. Gardiner, I would never do that. Truly, I respect you and would not even suggest something that was impossible. I might exaggerate about your fresh eggs and pretend I know all about cows—which Liz knows I don't—but I'm being a hundred percent honest with you."

"Well, that's a lot to think about," Geneva said. "I'd just love to put the quilts into the hands of the women over there who'd use them. But I don't know 'bout uprootin' myself and goin' way off to Africa."

"You don't have to say anything right this minute," Sam said. "Now that I'm fueled with coffee and donuts, I'm ready to get to work. Is it okay if I bring some lights in and set them up in your sewing room?"

"Yes, you're welcome to do that."

"The lights are going to make it hot. Do you have an electric fan?"

"I got one in my bedroom. I move it 'round from room to room. You can take it into the sewing room."

Sam tried to tape Geneva's sewing process in little segments. First she chose fabric from boxes and plastic bags. She pulled out a Ziploc baggie with three fabrics printed with sunflowers, all different; the colors were different enough to look odd beside each other. "Been saving these," she said. Then she dug into a box of blues and pulled out four pieces: one plain, the others prints. "Sunflowers and blue sky" Geneva said. "And a bunch of earth and leaves and stalks and stuff." She added greens and browns to her pile of fabrics. "Might'nt be enough," she said. She added yellow and orange scraps of various sizes.

"Then it's all gotta be ironed," she said. Sam photographed her ironing.

"That's a lot of work before you even get started," Liz said.

"I just love to iron. Always have. Turn off that machine of yours,

Sam, you too, Liz, and I'll tell you something that'll make you smile."

"A secret?" Sam asked.

"Not 'xactly. Well, I guess it is sorta. Alma's the only one I ever did tell this to. Like I said, I like to iron. My favorite chore in the house. I liked it so much, back when I was a girl and my mom put me to ironin' the family clothes, I used to iron my underwear. All of it. And when I got married and Alf found out I ironed my underwear and then I ironed his underwear, he just about fell off a chair laughin' at me."

"Did you starch your panties?" Sam asked, grinning.

"No, just ironed them." Geneva started giggling like a schoolgirl. Her face became rosy with a blush.

"Do you still?" Sam asked.

"No, there's a different kind-a underwear these days, don't need ironin'. But I still iron those sheets that say no-iron on the package."

"What's the next step after ironing? The quilting fabric, I mean," Sam asked.

"Cuttin'. Sometimes I know I want all squares or some regular old pattern like a split rail fence or pinwheels and I cut out all the fabric, and sometimes I see that part of the quilt'll be one thing and part something else and maybe I'll put the parts together with stripping so I just cut some and sew some and then cut some more, 'til I got the quilt as big as I want it to be."

"What are you going to do with this?" Liz asked.

"Think I'll put most-a the sunflowery part in the middle. I might put some brown in for centers—'cause the seedy part gets brown, you know. I'll probably sew a bunch for the middle and work my way out, kind-a let it grow a little bit wild, if you know what I mean. Sunflowers turn their heads—real slow, a-course, not really like a pinwheel. But..." She shrugged. "I don't know yet."

Liz and Sam watched as Geneva folded a piece of fabric and cut several layers at the same time into strips that became rectangles and squares, and then some of the squares became triangles. She cut with the assurance of a chef chopping vegetables for a stew. Then she cut up other fabrics into the same size pieces by folding them and laying a bit of the sunflower fabric on top and using it as her template. "It'll all come out even," Geneva said to Sam's camera. "I'll cut it up and make it even if I have-ta."

They took a break for lunch and went out into the yard to eat under the shade of the big beech tree near the garden. Sam told Geneva that they were driving to Athens, Ohio to see Quilt National and would be gone two days and then come back. "We could take you with us, if you want to go," Sam said. "Would you like to see a really important quilt show?"

"I might like to see it, but I don't think I'd like to ride in a car for two days in the middle of summer," Geneva said.

"This car's got air conditioning," Sam said.

Liz was surprised by his invitation. Geneva had certainly never seen quilts like the ones in the catalog and would have no idea how they had been made—for that matter, neither she nor Sam have any understanding of how art quilts are made. But it would be very interesting to see Geneva's reaction. Geneva's immediate negative response was exactly what Liz expected.

"Thank you kindly, but I'll stay home and probably have that quilt pretty well put together by the time you get back—I mean the top sewed together," Geneva said. "I 'spect I'll have to piece a back too. But I won't feel like workin' with the batting in this heat. Lots-a times I just do the tops and put them aside 'til the weather's cooler."

"Perfect," Sam said. "Let me take a couple of pictures of this picnic. Not for the film, just for me. A nice picture of two of my favorite women talking in the shade of a summer day with those flowers—what are they called?"

"Hollyhocks," Geneva said of the tall row of pink and purple flowers behind them that bordered the vegetable garden. "The low orange-yellow ones on the other side of the garden are marigolds."

"Then maybe I'll take a picture of you in the garden, just a quick one so you don't have to stand in the sun more than a minute or so."

Geneva was about to go into the garden when they heard a car in the drive and the puppies yipping excitedly. Then they heard a voice shout, "Get away. Get away!" followed by a different, surprised, yipping from the puppies.

"It's Robina," Geneva said, getting up. "She's still makin' sure those pups learn not to come near cars in the drive."

"By shouting at them?" Liz asked.

"No. She'll show you."

They went around the house where Robina was getting out of her car. She was wearing denim shorts and a t-shirt.

"I'm gettin' 'em trained, Mom. You won't have to worry 'bout them gettin' hit. Hi, Liz. Thought you'd be here." Then she saw Sam carrying the chairs to take them back in the house. "Oh, here's our hero."

"Show Liz how you train the pups," Geneva said.

Robina reached inside her car and held up a mister. "It's three quarters water, one quarter ammonia. I spray it at them when they get too close."

"And it works?" Sam asked.

"They don't like it. If they get it every time a car comes, they'll stay away."

"What about other cars?" Sam asked.

"We'll have to see. But I think they're learning," Robina answered. She opened the back door and out jumped the third puppy. It ran to play with its brothers.

"We just ate but if you want something, I can make you a sandwich," Geneva said.

"No, no, Mom, I ate. I just wanted to say hello to your friends."

"I think you wanted to check out the famous Sam," Liz said.

"Well, sure. Good lookin' guy. But I had another reason." When Sam took Geneva to the garden for a photo, Robina said, "Let's go in out of the sun." In the kitchen Liz turned water on in the sink to wash the dishes. "I wanted to thank you for talking the way you did to the preacher when you were here before," she said.

"I was afraid I was meddling where I shouldn't," Liz said.

"I'm glad you did. Mom's not been as happy with him as she was with the one before. She liked that young black man a lot and his wife too. But this one's a different kettle of fish. And sometimes he smells kind of fishy to me. Ben and I don't want to say anything either, just like you. But from what she said he wasn't very Christian and downright bigoted to boot."

"I didn't like that but I mostly I didn't like his acting like he had the right to say what she should do with her quilts."

"She didn't tell me anything about that."

Liz explained the conversation.

"Well," Robina said as she was drying the plates, "that explains why she said the other day that she was starting to wonder just what would become of her quilts. We told her we knew what she wanted and would make sure they got sent to African missions like she always said."

Liz told Robina that she had mentioned a do-it-yourself-will to Geneva and had brought a print-out. "Should I give it to you?".

"Good idea," Robina said. "Mom's just real penny-pinching 'bout lawyers and doctors, you know. She doesn't trust their ideas and thinks they're just trying to get rich easy. I'll type up the will and take her up to Versailles court house and find a notary to autograph it. I intend to nag her 'til she does it. I don't want that preacher getting his mitts on anything of hers."

"Strange they had such different ministers," Liz said.

"Cryin' shame. These here little churches don't really belong to the big Baptist organization. They hire their own preachers. Don't know how they find them. I think this here church had some people who weren't comfortable with Redburn and his wife being black. But Mom liked them a lot. Guess nobody asked her opinion."

"That's interesting. So maybe Redburn was independent and not really connected either." Liz had assumed all the Baptist churches belonged to some national organization.

"I don't rightly know. We've never been ones to get into anyone else's business. Ben took a dislike to that preacher at some funeral he preached at. Thing was he preached and didn't talk about the man that died hardly at all. Ben won't go to his Sunday services and I'm sure he won't let him do her funeral if he's still here when that time comes 'round."

Sam and Geneva came in.

"Well, look at that, you got the dishes done in no time," Geneva said. "Thank you both."

"I'd like a picture of you, too, ah—"

"Robina," Liz said

"Sorry, I forgot," Sam said. "Maybe if Mrs. Gardner could stand like she had been doing dishes and Robina was drying..." They posed but Sam did not take a picture immediately. Robina pulled at her t-shirt and fluffed her hair and stood stiffly. "I wish Ben was here. I'd like his picture too," Sam said.

"He's baling hay. Maybe next time you're around."

"That'll be Tuesday. We're going to a quilt show in Ohio, but we'll stop here on the way back." Sam chatted with Robina until she forgot he was taking a picture and then he snapped several very quickly.

"I imagine you've got an afternoon all planned out," Robina said. "I don't want to interrupt. But I wanted to let Lay-Z-Girl have a little time to play with her brothers."

"I'll bring the fan in here," Sam said. "And we can turn on the recorder and Liz can get more information about how you pick out which fabrics you're going to use. She didn't record it when you were showing us."

"Oh, darn, I didn't," Liz said.

"I have to keep her on track," Sam said.

"I'm sure you crack the whip," Robina said.

"It's tough work, but somebody's got to do it," Sam said.

Robina and Geneva laughed as if they had never heard the line before.

"I wanted to ask you, Mom," Robina said. "Did you get a name and address of people in Africa to write to?"

"Not yet," Geneva said. "I asked Rev. Wheeler a while back, but he's not mentioned it, probably forgot. He forgets quite a bit that he says he'll do. Got a lot on his mind, I 'spect."

"Maybe you should ask if he has an address for Rev. Redburn; that's who knew about the people in Africa," Liz suggested.

"That's a good idea. I'd like to know how he's doin'. He was just about the favorite minister I ever did know. I always kind-a thought he must feel like a little petunia in an onion patch," Geneva said.

"I never heard that expression before," Liz said.

"Not an expression, part of a song my mama taught me when I was a girl. We'd sing it if we were peelin' onions. Another line is 'and I cry and cry all day.' Mama would sing that to me if I was crying from choppin' onions."

"I don't think you ever told me that, Mom," Robina said. "You recording this. Liz?"

"Can you sing the song, Geneva?"

Geneva sang part of the song. "If I could 'member all-a the words, we could make a recording of my singing, like all those people on TV.

Think I'd get rich and famous like they are?"

"Have to get you a shiny dress and some high heel shoes," Robina said.

They sat quietly a moment. Liz remembered she was supposed gather information. She asked Geneva, "When did you start accumulating the quilts for Africa?"

"A couple years after Alf died. People wanted to help me fill my time, so they started bringin' more quilt fabrics for me. Then Rev. Redburn brought the missionary couple, and they talked 'bout the need in Africa."

Robina said, "You could'a watched TV all day long."

"Those shows don't mean nothin' to me. Even the news, 'cept for the weather, don't interest me. I could just 'bout throw the TV out, you know."

Geneva had become accustomed to talking for the recorder. She had a simple confidence now and none of the confusion and defensiveness Liz sensed in their first conversations.

"People bring me National Geographic magazines when there's things 'bout Africa. Older I get the more I think 'bout how important life is. It's a God-given gift we can never give back once we take it away."

Robina sat at the table leaning her chin on the palm of a hand, her eyes drooping.

"I'm borin' Robina right to sleep," Geneva said.

"I'm sorry, Mom. You know some nights I just can't get comfortable—if it's not my hips hurting, it's my back or if not that, then my shoulders. And I hate to dope myself up with a ton of Tylenol PM."

"You want to go in the other room and take a nap?" Geneva asked.

"I think I'll go home. I've got to stop at the store on the way."

She picked up her puppy and said goodbye to everybody.

"It's too hot to keep you busy," Liz said to Geneva. "What if we take you down to town for some ice cream?"

"No. I thank you kindly, but I got ice cream in my freezer, and I think I'll have a nap like I 'spect Robina'll do when she gets home."

———

281

As they drove to Marjorie's Liz said, "I think Geneva feels the heat and it wears her out. We need to be careful not to take too much of her time."

"I just don't know what film is going to be useful and what's not. You know in a proper film shoot they get multiples of everything."

"You can't do that here. It's got to be good enough in one shot and if it's not, then it just doesn't get included."

"I think we should let her tell us when she's had enough," Sam said.

"No. You heard, when I suggested we stop she agreed right away. I don't think she would have said anything if I hadn't."

"You treat her like she was your grandmother."

"I try to treat her like the treasure she is," Liz said.

"Maybe that's the same thing."

"You're suddenly philosophical." Liz glanced at Sam. She smiled and he smiled back.

"You know, I wish we were staying at a motel with a pool. Isn't there one around that we could go to?"

"You really don't want to stay at Marjorie's, do you?"

"I've got nothing against it—except there's no pool, if I understand right."

"Tomorrow we'll be in Athens, Ohio staying at a motel with a pool."

Sam sighed dramatically. "We'll get two beds tomorrow if that's what you want."

"That's what I want." She put a hand on Sam's arm. "I'm not the kind who can sleep with different guys on alternate weekends."

"I don't see anything wrong with it myself." He glanced at Liz as she shook her head. "Or have you made promises?"

"No promises. Just my feelings about what's right."

As they neared Dillsboro, Liz thought of her mother complaining about the spare bed and her own discomfort curled on the sofa. "Second thoughts: it's only about fifty miles to the airport and it's on the circle road around Cincinnati. I'm sure there are a couple of big hotels there. Then we'd get an earlier start. And a pool, of course."

"Thanks, Darlin'."

"Two beds." Liz said. Marjorie would understand their desire to be in Ohio early in the morning.

Chapter 12

❧

They were at the edge of Athens asking directions to the Dairy Barn before 12:00. "Hey, look at that!" Sam exclaimed. They had followed a sign to a narrow street and suddenly arrived at a huge white barn. "It really is a barn."

"The picture's on the last page of your catalog," Liz said.

"Oh, I didn't notice." Before they went to the entrance, Sam pulled out the catalog and wrote his name in it. He showed the woman at the desk that he had the catalog. "I just want you to know I came in with it so when I go out you won't think I lifted it."

They paused just inside the door to a very large space that did not suggest it had ever housed cows. Quilts hung on all four walls and others were displayed on standing partitions down the center of the area. "It's an art show," Sam said.

"Of course. Shall we go clockwise?" Only five or six people were looking at the show, mostly women and one man who paused before each quilt.

"Look at this." Sam sounded like a child who has never been to a museum. "This is the one I was wondering about." A sculptural piece was immediately opposite the entrance, an animal figure hulking over a human figure. He walked around it, pausing. "Liz, this is fantastic. You were wondering what it was. Look. It's called 'Not My Reflection.'"

"Oh, my God!" Liz said. "Sam, it's that chimp that tore off a woman's face." She felt chilled, closed her eyes and turned away.

"Right," Sam said. He was flipping through his catalog to find the photograph.

"The catalog photographer didn't show that ragged red splotch where a woman's face would be. Amazing," Sam said.

"I can't look at it." Liz quickly walked to the first quilt on the wall behind her.

Sam came over. "It's brilliant," he said. "I didn't realize either. Are you alright?"

"I can't imagine an artist living with that vision as long as she must have to make the piece. How could she stand it? Or was it a man who made it?"

"A woman. Artists are strong people. Think about Goya." Sam put an arm around Liz's shoulders.

"He went crazy."

"True. Do you like this one?" Sam asked about the quilt before them.

"Sort of so-so." She hugged herself, rubbing away the chill; then she was able to study the design which seemed to be thread painting on hand painted fabric.

"Let me find the photo," Sam said. "The quilting doesn't show in the photo, just the design. Do you think that's okay?" They walked slowly, looking at photos and comparing them to the actual quilts.

They came to a quilt that showed a scene of children playing in a pile of autumn leaves. "How did she do that?" Liz wondered aloud about the pointillist effect with many, many tiny bits of color making up the picture. She got as close to the quilt as she could without touching it. She saw a fine, almost invisible, netting over it.

A woman who was looking at the next quilt turned and said, "She used very small pieces of fabric, overlapped them randomly, you see here? She also sprinkled bits of thread clippings around. Then she probably sprayed it with a fixative and overlaid very fine tulle on top of the whole thing before she quilted it."

"Close meandering," Liz said. Meandering was the pattern Jack had taught her on the long arm machine.

"Yes," the woman said.

"On a long arm, do you think?" Liz asked.

"Probably not. She probably has a wide throated machine and did it little by little."

"Wouldn't the pieces shift as she worked?" Sam asked.

"It depends on the fixative she used, I guess," the woman said. "Actually, I read an article about this woman's technique not very long ago. Some people put fusible backing on the fabric before they cut it into little pieces, but this woman uses a fixative."

"You're a quilter, I presume," Sam said.

"Yes. Nothing like this. I do contemporary quilts. I'd love to have something in Quilt National, but I've never done anything good enough to submit." The woman seemed to be in her forties. She wore glasses and no make-up. Her dark brown hair was curly with random gray scattered through it. She had a soft accent, somewhat like Marjorie's.

"So these are all art quilts?" Sam asked.

"Yes. If you read the catalog you've got there, I think there were over 700 submissions and they chose 84. That's a lot of competition."

"Actually I bought the catalog to look at the photographs and, I admit, I didn't read anything," Sam said. "I should have."

"Are you a visitor here or a docent?" Liz asked, hoping the woman was a docent who would explain techniques to them.

"Just a visitor; they don't have docents. I live in Charleston, West Virginia—a good drive but not too far. This is my second time. I came for the opening but there were so many people then, I couldn't see the quilts properly. I wanted to look at them on a quiet day."

"We're sorry to interrupt you," Liz said.

"Oh, it's okay. I teach and I love explaining things to people."

"You teach quilting?" Sam asked.

The woman nodded. "I teach quilting classes at a shop. I also teach high school chemistry."

"We're art majors at Indiana University and we don't know much about quilting," Liz said. "We're trying to learn. Sam's a photographer and I'm writing my thesis about quilts. I went to the show in Paducah last April."

"I had a quilt in that show. Of course, you won't remember. It didn't win any prizes; but I was proud it was accepted. By the way, I'm Emily Marcus."

Liz introduced herself and Sam.

"I took photos of ones I really liked. Can you describe your quilt?"

Emily described her quilt, but Liz did not remember it. Emily walked through the entire show with them, explaining what she knew about the quilters and their techniques.

Emily was fascinated that Sam was comparing the catalog photos with what he actually saw.

"It's a totally different experience, looking at the photos and at the actual quilt. It's as different as looking at a photograph of a person and then meeting the person in the flesh," Sam said. "The likeness is obvious. Here, in this one there are variegated threads."

"Like looking at brush strokes on a painting," Liz interjected.

"But in the photograph they blend into one color." Sam showed them the photograph. They all stood farther back and then closer to look.

When they had been through the entire exhibit and were back to the sculptural piece, Liz said, "This is so upsetting. A medium that should be warm and comforting, like the relationship that chimp's owner says she had with him, turns to total horror."

"You can't take anything for granted," Sam said.

"You can love someone or something and totally trust them, but all the awful possibilities are somewhere buried inside," Emily said. "This has haunted me since I first saw the show. I think it's very brave of the quilter and also very brave of the curators. Most of these quilts are expressions of joy, really. Joy of creation, joy in the material, in the skills, the color—and then this..."

"Do you mind if I write that down to remember it?" Liz asked.

"What I said?" Emily asked. "You want to remember what I said?"

"Yes. Joy of creation and then you said...?"

"I'm flattered," Emily said. She laughed self-consciously. "I don't think I remember what I said."

Liz pulled her notebook from her backpack. Emily repeated what she had said as best she could remember and Sam filled in her words.

"Thank you so much for spending your time with us," Sam said.

"We learned a lot from you," Liz added.

"And I learned a lot from you," Emily said. "I guess I always used the photographs just as reminders. Now I'll think much harder when I look at a book of quilt pictures or on an Internet site. It was my pleasure."

Liz and Sam went into the gift shop and purchased a few little things. Then they walked through the exhibit again. A trio of Asian women were looking at the quilts. Liz asked them if they were Japanese because she had read several articles about how popular quilting is in Japan.

They talked briefly about the major annual quilt show in Tokyo.

"Maybe next year," Sam said to Liz. "Would you like that?"

"I'd like to have my thesis finished by then." She thought it was entirely possible he would not let her forget about the possibility. These were so different from Geneva's quilts and he had seen few others.

His assumption they would go to Tokyo together was a little too much like Jack suggesting they could go into business together. Why were assumptions piling up?

They walked through the entire show again paused to consult with one another about which quilt would get their vote for viewers' choice. Finally they both voted for the sculptural piece because they decided the artist would not get many votes but deserved recognition.

It was mid-afternoon before they left the exhibit and drove a short distance to a hotel owned by the Ohio University branch in the town. They had quick sandwiches in the coffee shop and settled beside the pool. "Thanks for discovering Quilt National, Sam, and for badgering me to come," Liz said.

"My very great pleasure," he said. "It puts Geneva's quilts in a whole different light, doesn't it?"

"Considering this show and the one I saw in April, she really is an outsider. She doesn't fit into either category. She doesn't even know this kind of quilting exists. I wonder what she'd think of it. She probably wouldn't even call it quilting—well, a few, but not many."

"I'll show her the catalog," Sam said. "I've got to do a really good job, but I really think a film will be the best way to show what she's doing, especially if we can take her to Africa. It'll be a great story."

"She's an old lady, remember? And she's never been anywhere."

"They fixed up her heart, didn't they?"

"I don't really know. She seems to think so, but they didn't do any surgery."

"Maybe she didn't need it. Maybe she'll hit a hundred. Lots of people are making it these days."

"I hope she does."

"I've got to go in the water, the sun's too hot," Sam said. Sam swam, then went to the hotel's exercise room. Liz napped in the shade.

——

As always, Liz felt underdressed when she was with Sam in a public place. She never thought about looking out of place with Jack. Her jeans and t-shirt had felt fine at the Dairy Barn, but in a restaurant with white tablecloths and candles, even though they weren't lit because the sun was only then beginning to set, she felt her plain white shirt at least needed a necklace or a scarf. It didn't matter that Sam also wore jeans and a white shirt. On him it looked like the uniform of a Hollywood mogul.

When she was putting on make-up she almost told him how self-conscious he made her but decided to say nothing. He would apologize and it certainly wasn't his fault, it was simply who he was, his looks, his posture and an attitude that was not the smug celebrity attitude. He always seemed comfortable, whatever he was doing.

Only three other tables had guests. They could tell one table must be quilt show visitors, and the three Japanese women sat at another table. The Japanese women were so elegantly dressed Liz felt even more self-conscious.

Sam ordered a bottle of wine. When he had sniffed, tasted and approved it, he asked, "Tell me, what do you see yourself doing five years from now?"

Liz was surprised; she was not sure she had an answer. She didn't want to answer. "Are we playing party games?"

"No, I really want to know."

"So do I." Liz tasted the wine and smiled. It did not have the slightly sharp edge against her tongue that red wine did.

"Do you like the wine?"

"Yes. You said you didn't know about wines, but I think you actually do. I don't know anything about wines, but even I can tell it's really nice."

"Actually I kind of guessed, but I think it's good. I like it."

"I guess we like the same kind of wine," Liz said. They had talked about quilts off and on all afternoon. They could watch a movie on TV this evening, she had read aloud the list of available movies. They found three or four they either had not seen or would be happy to see again. But at dinner, was the topic to be the future? Their future?

"Okay, I'll put it differently," Sam said. "What do you want this whole project to lead to beyond the Ph.D. ?"

"An interesting job. I'm honestly not terribly ambitious so it doesn't have to be a prestigious job or a high-paying one. I want to get up in the morning and think about how interesting work is going to be that day."

"Like in a museum, a classroom?"

"I don't want to teach. Museum or a magazine. Working with quilts some way." Jack would be very happy if she became a partner. But she didn't want to stand all day working on someone else's quilts. She could run the business end if it grew that big. Maybe she could combine freelance journalism with working with Jack. But she was not going to talk about that with Sam. Maybe she should... No, she wasn't sure at all. Thoughts of working with Jack gave her a claustrophobic feeling. On a quick tour of Paducah Jack had pointed out art galleries and said the town publicized itself as an art center. Hardly, Liz had thought, not to anyone who's seen New York and Paris and Berlin and any other true art center.

"What about freelance or writing books?" Sam asked.

"A very iffy way to pay the rent," Liz said. "I'm not a good writer as working on my thesis is proving."

"Has it occurred to you there are quilting TV shows that must need writers or even moderators?" Sam asked.

"No, I hadn't thought of it. I haven't watched any. I think they're all cable and maybe not big enough budget to have writers other than the teachers who are the stars. Editing books about art quilters would be interesting, but we'd have to have a big success with the Geneva book—"

"*The Friendship Quilts*. That's what we'll call the book and the documentary," Sam said.

"Maybe too good for a title."

"I like it a lot," Sam said. "Sometimes you have to hit the public over the head."

"I don't know..." Liz thought about the overly obvious pun as she ate olives that had been placed on the table with Italian bread and dipping oil. Sam refilled her wine glass.

After a pause Sam said, "I'd love to see what else that woman who did the ape quilt has done. I wonder if she has a website."

"Me too. I'd love to know her art background and her personal background, how she thinks. Now that I've been interviewing Geneva, I think I could learn to be a decent interviewer."

"She may never be able to top that piece. I think she'd have to do something very different. Her process of making that piece would have been an interesting film."

"So now you're really thinking in terms of film instead of still photography? Is that what you want to do?" Liz asked.

The waiter brought salads; they were interrupted by the gigantic pepper mill he wielded like a weapon. "Thanks," Sam said. He seemed to be thinking. "I don't know, I guess I'm as undecided as you. I don't know how much longer my modeling will last. I'm not that hunky 19-year-old any more, but men have more staying power than women.

"Really, I'd rather be behind the camera instead of in front. But, of course, I like the money. I'm investing. I hope wisely but then you read so much about these advisors. But you didn't ask that. Photography or film?" He ate more salad and thought. "I have more to learn about photography. I want to make Geneva's quilts irresistible, you know, innocent and complex at the same time. And I'd like to do a truly good portrait of her. I've got some good pictures and maybe I'll get some good outtakes from the video I've got so far. But that's not the same as a portrait. Do you think she'd be willing to spend a couple of hours just letting me take pictures?"

"First, I think you ought to really look at the pictures you've taken. Something truly candid may be a lot truer than anything you can get making her self-conscious about sitting for a proper portrait. I told her that you're a dangerous person."

Sam laughed. "Nobody ever called me dangerous before."

Liz sipped the wine liking it even better after a few bites of salad and bread. "Oh, I'll bet they have—behind your back."

Sam laughed, loving the idea. "Geneva thinks for herself. I'm kind of surprised she agreed to a film," he said.

"I'm not sure she did exactly. She let you do some video. I don't think the documentary genre is meaningful to her."

"I think I've got most of what I need; maybe a couple hours tomorrow. Maybe we'd open with you talking to Prof. Simmons—just ninety seconds on the definition of Outsider Art."

"If you're working with Melanie, she might have ideas about that.

Film school must teach about format."

"Yeah, I guess. I hope she won't be a pain with all kinds of artsy ideas," Sam said. "Maybe I should take some film school courses." He gazed out the window where trees behind the pool were purpling with shadow. He drank wine and read the label. "Chile. Have to remember this brand..." They were quiet for a few minutes. "Won't it be exciting to take her to Africa?"

"Do you really think that will happen?"

"Yes. Carla wants to make it happen. We just have to pack up the quilts, maybe FedEx them. And then we all get on a plane. I don't know if Carla will spring for business class, but that's a real possibility. Geneva is an old woman, she needs more comfort than coach, don't you think?"

"It would be wonderful to see her meeting people in a village. The look on her face when I first suggested it was beautiful. I wish you'd been there to photograph it. She looked like the kid who got a pony for her birthday. She said she'd feel like 'Santy Claus.' You know what I just realized? December is summer in South Africa—if that's where we might go."

"It's a big continent," Sam said. "Do we know what country we're talking about?"

"I hope she can get in touch with the missionary she liked so much. I don't know how to go about searching. I'll have to find someone who can help. That awful preacher isn't going to be any help at all."

"Then the quilts will all disappear. All the more reason I want really good photos and a book. They deserve to be shared."

"She deserves that kind of payment for her years of work."

"If I can make her that happy..." Sam paused, holding Liz's gaze, "Okay, I'll say it—it would be worth having an actual affair with Carla."

Liz just shook her head. "The end justifies the means? No, no, I don't think so."

"I mean, nobody would be unhappy. Melanie thinks I'm gay, so..."

Liz bit her tongue, frowned and sighed. Sam became busy with the rest of his salad. The waiter brought their dinners.

"It's just dishonest," Liz said.

"Not really. She's very attractive."

"She could be your mother."

"Well, not quite. Anyway, to her I'd be a boy toy."

"And you don't mind?" Liz thought they were sounding like a trashy novel.

"I do and I don't. I guess I make her feel good about how attractive she is. But she doesn't have any designs on me. She's a very sophisticated woman. And she's sincere about wanting to help an artist who needs help."

"I don't understand you," Liz said. After a moment she added, "Geneva would be shocked."

"Fes up. You're shocked."

"Okay, I'm shocked. Let's not talk about it."

Liz had ordered trout and now had to figure out how to eat it. She knew there was a method. She had picked up her knife and fork but was simply holding them, wondering how to attack the fish. Should she cut off its head first? Did it matter?

Sam said, "What you do with that trout is cut along the backbone so you fillet it."

"I don't understand."

"Let me." He moved her plate toward him, took her knife and fork and neatly laid the upper filet out, ready to eat. "When you've finished that, the spine and bones will peel back all together and, viola! You have the other half."

"Thanks. I feel like a country bumpkin with you." Liz surprised herself by admitting this so easily. It's the wine talking, she thought.

"You are a world traveler, my dear. I am totally provincial compared to you."

"That's not true," Liz said.

"It is true. Don't assume you know my feelings." She heard a hard edge on his voice.

"Sorry," Liz said. What was she supposed to think about a man who didn't mind prostituting himself to make a movie but suggested he had deeper feelings than she suspected?

They ate in silence for a while. "Let's go back to the original question. Photography or film? After your modeling career."

"Or along with. That's a possibility—in fact, probable." He paused, staring out at the pool. "I'll tell you the current daydream—if you can handle it."

Liz's intuition said they were getting into territory she and Sam had never been in before. "Maybe I don't want to hear."

The waiter interrupted with the usual "Is everything satisfactory?" They assured him everything was delicious. "The veal is very good. I hope your trout is good too," Sam said.

"It is." Liz looked at the deepening shadows beyond the window. The waiter returned to light the candles on all the tables in the restaurant although it was late enough no other diners were likely to arrive.

"Here's my current daydream." Sam paused as if making up his mind whether to continue. Liz barely nodded her head. "A smashing apartment in a building with a great water view. Not one of those apartments in the tombstone high rises along the Hudson. Maybe something in an older building on Riverside Drive. Not a big apartment, but the view has to be of the sunset, because I don't want the sun waking me up. That means looking at New Jersey with the river at my feet. I'd have to continue doing a few modeling gigs so the money keeps flowing. We work together on books about art quilters. You interview and write, I photograph."

Liz noticed the easy shift to "we" in his fantasy. Exactly where, she wondered, was she supposed to be? Sharing that great apartment? Drinking wonderful wine as they watched the sunset over Hoboken-Upon-The-Hudson?

Sam continued. If Liz's face showed what she was thinking he didn't react. "I don't even know if there's a market, but if we can make a big enough splash with *The Friendship Quilts*, I think there will be. And if not then it becomes people in different parts of the world with their crafts, maybe ancient ways or maybe women in impoverished villages turning their lives around with micro loans and help from NGO volunteers. We will be a team, you and me." Sam paused to let the idea sink in. He added, as an afterthought, remembering her answer about what she wanted after her Ph.D., "Getting up every morning excited about the work that we'll do that day. The artisans we'll meet and help publicize."

Liz liked the idea. Her own imagination was taking her into South America or India or Indonesia. Or maybe those elegant women of Japan who pursue quilting with the same dedication with which their grandmothers had pursued ikebana or the tea ceremony, possibly like the three women who had just left the dining room, all of them smiling and very slightly bowing to Liz and Sam.

Sam took another bite of food and refilled their wine glasses, emptying the bottle. "We'll be partners. The apartment might not be big, but we'll each have our office space."

"Oh," Liz said. Somehow living together was being taken for granted. Liz closed her eyes, swept by the feeling of claustrophobia. *Why are these men pushing me? Why can't I just live my life? It's biological,* Barbara would say. The thoughts were not new, and they did not all go through her head just then. They had been haunting her in those minutes, sometimes half hours, before she fell asleep at night, or when she had hit the snooze button after the alarm buzzed in the morning. The feeling was of walls closing around her, being in a room without doors or windows.

Sam put his hand on top of hers. "You're not about to pass out, are you?"

She opened her eyes. "No... I really, really can't talk about this."

"I can see us working together."

"We are working together," Liz said before he could say more. "Let's get this project complete, however it turns out, book, film. Get our degrees, I hope. I can only take one thing at a time."

"Why?" Sam asked.

No one had asked Liz why she chose to live her life in well-defined chunks, why she had marked this part of her life: Get the Ph.D. Why she not only wanted, but needed, to apply all her energy to the thesis. Yes, she gave herself little breaks when she spent time with Jack, but it was connected to quilting. Jack was a connection to the Paducah American Quilters Society world, a museum, a magazine, an organization, a possible career. Jack's question about marriage had brought on an anxiety attack. Dealing with a second one seemed a little easier.

"I just need to direct my energy at one thing at a time," she said.

"I don't think that's a real answer," Sam said. "We're made for multi-tasking like the articles say. Love and work can go together— even Freud thought so, if I understand right. They could for me. I think you're smarter than I am and could handle it unless there's some psychological trauma you just can't deal with."

"Now you're a shrink?"

"No, that's just reasonable. If you have a hang-up, there's a past problem you're not dealing with. Are you waiting for that guy to get enlightened that you are more important than Buddha?"

"No!" Liz said very quickly. She was horrified that tears had sprung to her eyes. Oh, shit, she thought. What's going on here? Maybe he's right. She couldn't hide the tears, so she dabbed her eyes with her napkin. "It's over forever," she said.

"But it still hurts," Sam said.

"And haunts," Liz said softly. They ate in silence. Liz concentrated on flipping the bones away from the other half of the trout. She did a neat job of it. "Thanks for teaching me that."

"De nada. Can you handle another question?"

"I doubt it."

"Did your parents have a nasty divorce?"

That was easier. Liz could answer like a pop psychology quiz. "Yes and no. It was long ago and it doesn't seem pertinent. I don't think about it."

"You said your mother kind of leaned on you."

"She needed an unconditional friend. I wasn't old enough, really, but now I don't mind that she leaned on me. I learned about finances early."

The waiter came to clear their plates. He asked if they wanted dessert. Sam asked to see the dessert menu. "Do you want another bottle of wine?" he asked Liz. "I liked it a lot."

"I sort of do but I don't want to just sit here and drink wine," Liz said. She also didn't feel ready to spend the next twelve hours in the same room with Sam, even though the room had two beds. On the other hand, more wine would put her quickly to sleep, especially if they started watching a film she'd seen before.

"There's hardly any customers, I'm sure we can stay until they close. If we had a cheese plate we could nibble along with the wine." The dessert menu did not list a cheese plate so Sam asked the waiter if the chef might put one together.

Liz laughed. "That is so New York."

"What? A cheese plate?"

"No, asking for something that's not on the menu. Midwesterners just don't do that, but in New York I've heard people doing it all the time." Liz had been shocked by what she thought was arrogance.

Sam shrugged. "They go into a deli and they tell the guy exactly what to put on the sandwich, never mind what's on the menu board. Makes sense to me."

"I'll bet you wrapped your mother around your little finger," Liz said.

"I was a spoiled brat, until she got divorced and I wound up with a stepfather who wasn't about to be upstaged by a kid. I hated him fiercely for a while, but he brought order to the family we hadn't had."

"Meaning?" Liz asked. She and Sam really had not talked about their pasts and very little about their families. During their drives to Friendship they talked about their project or about the countryside. Sometimes they sang along with the car radio. Sam had said during today's drive that he had meant to bring some CDs.

The waiter reported that, yes, the chef would put together a cheese plate. He opened the second bottle of wine.

Sam explained, "Dad wanted to be a rock musician; he was in a band, but they weren't successful so he sort of drifted from job to job and Mom did too. They managed to scrape by, but they were pretty miserable, and I guess he did drugs with his musician friends and she hated that. He's a fun guy though. He's down in Austin, Texas nowadays, still playing with a band, and he's got some kind of Internet job. I think he's a professional blogger about rock bands. Anyway, my stepfather eventually bought my friendship."

"Bought it?"

"With computers and cameras and photography vacations."

"Where did you go for photography vacations?"

"First a two-week course in Santa Fe. I was kind of sulky about that even though after I was home I had to admit it was pretty cool. About six months later we did a three-week hike in Copper Canyon." Liz wrinkled her brow. "In Northern Mexico. That was before the digital revolution. I was determined to get better pictures than he did. We went home and developed our films together."

"How were your pictures?"

"So-so. He spent the developing time teaching me about photography. It's a hobby for him. He's a tax lawyer, but he's one smart man. My best critic. I've emailed him the quilt pictures. Some he okay-ed, some he told me to retake. I've got a list. So, now that we're getting past who we are in everyday life, what's your secret inner life story?"

The waiter brought the cheese plate. "The chef is sorry he doesn't have anything French except Brie. He even talked about sending his assistant to a store, but the only store in town with a good cheese department closes at 7:00. He's sorry. It's only five dollars."

"This will be fine," Sam said. "You don't mind if we stay here and talk while we take our time with the wine, do you?"

"Oh, no, stay as long as you want to—I mean, 'til ten."

Liz looked at her watch. It was twenty after eight.

Sam said, "Thanks. You can bring a check any time, we're putting it on our room bill. Then if they let you go home you won't have to wait for us to finish."

The waiter thanked him and pulled the bill out of his apron pocket.

"I guess you're right about the divorce," Liz said. "My brothers were in high school and doing fine, David played football and Brian was in the chess club and played tennis, really just because his girlfriend did. Their grades were good enough Mom wasn't worried about them. And they were pretty much straight arrows. I didn't pay much attention to them, and they didn't pay much attention to me.

"I was Mom's confidante once she was on her own. She'd come to my room to help me with homework, but really to tell me about her day, her money worries, her ideas for making money. For a while she did temp work—crud jobs, answering the phone, inputting boring lists of numbers or addresses or whatever. She hated it and didn't want to work for any of the kinds of businesses where she temped. She'd end up crying into my pillow and I'd get her glasses of water. She wanted to have a job she could enjoy, meet people she liked, be her own boss."

"I think I've heard that line," Sam said.

"Right, Dr. Freud. Dad would be late with the support checks and Mom had panic attacks, went on Prozac, caught every flu that came along."

"So you didn't get to be a kid, you had to be a best friend."

"Ja, mein herr doktor."

"Vell, vaat did you feel about dat?"

"When she started doing parties, she'd take me along to tell her how well the party went. She had a checklist for whether the kids had fun, whether the mother was relaxed and happy, how the cakes and ice cream were, how the decorations were, how the entertainment was. I'd fill it out after the party and we'd discuss every point. I hated all those greedy kids who wanted better parties than their friends had, the demanding mothers who wanted impossible things. One wanted an elephant. An elephant in a backyard in Indianapolis, Indiana! And mom spent two weeks nagging someone at the zoo to bring one to the party. They didn't. It was her big failure. I hated those parties. She'd ask me if I wanted a birthday party and I'd tell her I'd rather die than have a birthday party. I didn't even want my brothers to sing Happy Birthday to me, but if they were home at the time Mom made them come into my bedroom and wake me up singing."

"That's nice," Sam said, smiling.

"I didn't think so. I just wanted to have a quiet little life of my own. I wanted to wear jeans, not frilly party dresses. And now she's going to deck me out in some designer thing for her wedding!"

"You're making more sense all the time, Liz. So as soon as you could, you ran off to Europe to be yourself."

"I did. Exactly. I got the hell out of there and she had to hire an assistant."

"Then Europe wasn't far enough..." Sam ignored Liz's irony; he wanted the whole story,

"She came to visit me in Italy and bought shoes for herself and some for me that I still have in a closet in her house."

"So off you went to the most god forsaken place you could find where you didn't need Ferragamos."

"Right..." Liz laughed a little. She paused. Hadn't she said enough? But Sam waited for whatever she was hesitating about. Liz said, as she knew he knew but which she needed to say, "I was in love. Now I've got some perspective about..." She let her voice trail off.

"Once bitten, twice shy." Liz made a face about the cliché and waved her hand, dismissing his easy response. Sam said, "You know, clichés are clichés because they're true."

Better to explain than listen to more clichés. Liz knew she would never tell Sam so much if she hadn't had more wine than she had ever had at one meal. "At first it was all the flutter and excitement and thinking he was as perfect as any human could be. He is a really admirable, a deeply moral and philosophical person."

Sam nodded. "I'm not surprised."

"Two years living in a ger with him...I discovered he's much more..." She paused and sipped some wine. "More something. Ethereal, or maybe spiritual is the word. He lives in a different mental world. When we put fine art off to one side, his thought process was just entirely different. I couldn't follow him. I like ordinary things, like camping out, having bacon and eggs over a simple fire, maybe hiking for a week. I like Geneva's simple quilts better than these arty things we saw today." Sam raised his eyebrows. "Some were really fine. But really, they're a long way from fine art."

"Craft is sometimes fine art, isn't it?"

"Mostly it takes a century to answer that, don't you think? Isn't there a finite number of true geniuses?"

"That's territory I don't think much about. Philosophy more than art, wouldn't you say?" Sam asked.

Liz paused, listening to herself as Randy had taught her to do. Those were mental habits of his, but they had become hers. "I'm sorry, these are graduate semester ideas. You talked about feeling schizophrenic with your two lives. I'm not sure who I am."

Sam nodded. Liz cut up cheese and gave him some with a cracker and cut a different cheese for herself. "I get brie, you eat cheddar. Don't tell me you don't think that way." Sam looked at the food in his hand and smiled an "ah-ha, elementary, Dr. Watson" kind of smile.

Liz felt her face become hot. Damn this delicious wine and damn Sam for pushing her buttons. "I did that, didn't I?"

"Yes, my dear, you did that. Do you really prefer cheddar?"

"I like them both. What I'd really like is goat cheese."

"Shall I ask for some?"

"No. If they had goat cheese it would be on the plate."

Sam refilled their glasses. He looked sad and puzzled until a new thought came. "Should we go back to the Dairy Barn for another look tomorrow before we leave?"

"Do you want to?" Liz asked.

"Sort of. I like to spend time with new art. In New York I go to openings at galleries and if I like what I saw, I go back. If you really aren't interested, we can get an early start and have more time with Geneva. I have the catalog."

"It doesn't open 'til ten and we could be back to Cincinnati by then," Liz said.

"Okay."

"Do you mind?" They were here so he could study the quilts and the photography. "If you really want to see them again..."

"No, really. I never imagined a quilter would take on a subject like that chimp piece. My respect for the field shot up about 200% when I realized what I was looking at. I'd love to seek out people like that woman and do what I could with photography to make them well known. Tell the world: Listen up! Take these people seriously."

"You just may do that."

"Without you, my dear Lizzie, I'd still be ignorant about the whole field."

They were silent as Liz thought about Sam's ambition, the film, taking Geneva to Africa, so enthusiastic he was willing to sleep with Carla Checkbook. Or maybe "willing" wasn't the word—maybe eager was more appropriate. Who came on to who? she wondered.

After their silence began to extend too long, Sam said, "I have to smile every time I think of Geneva's face when we take her to a village or to a church in Africa where she can give the people her quilts. Doesn't that make you feel warm and melty inside?"

"I'm not sure I believe it yet. But the idea—yes, I love it. It's giving back to her because she's really giving me so much."

"The last shot in the film will be her face. She's got a good face, it's photogenic you know. Beautiful."

"Feeling like 'Santy Claus,' as Geneva said."

Liz could see the final shot of the film too. She thought of newspaper photos of philanthropists dedicating a new building, a hospital wing, an art museum, a university building. They were usually men; they did not look like Santa Claus. They looked, maybe, self-satisfied. Or maybe just ho-hum; it had been years since they wrote the check.

A camera would follow Geneva getting off an airplane—well, maybe not, what's to see in modern airports with enclosed jetways? Getting into a Land Rover to go to a village, being welcomed by men, women and children standing outside a little white church—yes, it would have to be an American style church, maybe not too different from the little church in Friendship where Geneva listened to Rev. Wheeler's sermons. Would they be singing "Amazing Grace" or "The Old Rugged Cross" or chanting something in their native language?

"What are you thinking?" Sam asked.

"About your film and Geneva. She's making my career possible. It will be wonderful if we can make her dream come true."

"You and me, Lizzie, we'll make her dream come true." He framed a picture with his hands. "I can't wait to see that happy smile."

Chapter 13

Sam had searched Google maps and found a route to Friendship they did not know existed. As they drove into Indiana in the early afternoon, they were in hilly country on a road that closely paralleled the Ohio River which they had crossed at Lawrenceburg.

"I love this countryside. It doesn't feel like Indiana at all," Sam said.

"Doesn't feel like Gary," Liz said.

"Right, or anything between Gary and Bloomington."

They had told Geneva they didn't know what time they would be back. When they arrived at a quarter before two, the dogs came bounding off the little front stoop but did not approach their car. They yipped excitedly.

"They've learned," Liz said. "Good for Robina."

Geneva came to the door before they were out of the car. "How was your great trip?" she asked.

"Very worthwhile," Liz said.

"It was fantastic in its way," Sam said. He hugged Geneva and she hugged back, no longer surprised by his habit, smilingly enjoying it.

"So you're not excited and he's excited," Geneva said to Liz.

"He gets excited easily," Liz said.

"Double entendre?" Sam whispered as they followed Geneva into the kitchen.

"How would I know?" Liz whispered back.

"Whose fault is that?" he said quickly.

They had stopped at a grocery store and bought cookies for Geneva. She opened them and poured iced tea.

"Has anything new happened since we were gone?" Sam asked.

"Well, sort-a," Geneva said, sounding hesitant. Her back was to them as she put the pitcher of tea back in the refrigerator. Sam glanced at Liz and made a gritted teeth face. She nodded and pursed her lips.

"You're going to tell us, right?" Sam asked.

Geneva sat down at the kitchen table with them. "Have-ta explain a little." They waited for her to go on. "Betty Wheeler come in early Wednesday and later the Reverend come to pick me up for prayer meeting. She explained they were having a hard time findin' out where Rev. Redmond was because the church that he was a part of had broken off with our church people, not just here but the whole bunch of our churches, all through this part of the country. Or maybe it was the other way around, that our people left the bigger group. Of course, I guess neither part actually asked the people, meanin' people like me, what we thought 'bout it. But the thing is the connection with the people in Africa is not somethin' our church knows anything about. They have missions in Central America, but they don't have any African missions. Betty asked if I might, maybe, want to give my quilts to their mission."

"There must be other ways to reach the needy people in Africa," Liz said.

"That's what Ben and Robina said too. Said we probably need to ask you-all to find out from your computers. Ben said people who know how to use them can find out just about anything on a computer."

"That's basically true," Sam said. "We can try."

"Well, but the thing is, once I heard all that, and even 'fore I talked to Ben and Robina yesterday, I kept thinkin' 'bout this idea of mine." Geneva was turning her iced tea glass around and around, making the ice cubes tinkle.

"All, meaning all of what?" Liz asked very softly.

"About CherryLee and the people down where she lives and the people all over America like her family. Down and out but most of them not the bad and dangerous people some others think they are. Not what Joshua Wheeler paints them all to be."

Liz nodded emphatically but didn't say anything.

"I always believed in helping your neighbors and I still do, a'course. What I was thinkin' 'bout, kind-a for the first time is I don't really know anything about Africa much. They just might not like havin' white folks comin' in and decidin' what they ought to have. I don't like for people to come in and tell me what I ought'a do. If a bunch of African people who were a lot richer than me come in to tell me how I ought to live my life, maybe tell me I ought to raise goats instead of chickens or somethin' like that, I wouldn't like it one little bit. And you know, maybe even tellin' me I ought to take up their religion and give up my own that I've believed in since I was a tiny little girl. That's somethin' I never thought 'bout 'til now. What if I was them?"

Geneva had been talking mostly to the middle of the tablecloth where salt and pepper shakers stood beside a lidded glass sugar bowl. She looked up at Liz. "Do you know what I mean?"

"I understand what you're saying, but maybe not really what you mean," Liz said. "I think it would be sad to give up your dream. You don't have to just because it's hard to reach Rev. Redmond."

Sam said, "I imagine he's got a computer and an email address. We could probably track him down." He looked at Liz with a smile. "He might even be on Facebook."

"It's all a mystery to me," Geneva said.

Sam smiled at her. "Never fear, Sam is here." Geneva chuckled but immediately looked serious again. Sam said, "I'm sure he'd remember you and be happy to hear about you again."

"Well, I'd be happy to hear 'bout him too," Geneva said. "You-all goin' to eat any-a them cookies?"

"I am," Sam said. "What about you?" He handed her the cookies first.

"How'd you know I like Lorna Doones?" Geneva asked.

"You had them before and you said it was getting hard to find them," Sam said.

"It's nice of you to 'member that."

"You're one of my favorite people, Mrs. Gardiner," Sam said. "I want to make you happy, 'cause I feel responsible for you since I saved your life."

"I'm grateful. And I'm grateful that you think you could find a way to take me to Africa, but when I got to talkin' to Ben and Robina 'bout it, we got to tryin' to figure out what it would be like. I never been on an airplane and they're kind of dangerous, it seems like, people trying to blow them up and all that."

"But the truth is it's much more dangerous to ride in a car. A lot more accidents and more bad drivers to look out for than there are possible terrorists on airplanes." Sam repeated the usual sales pitch for airlines.

"Well, Ben and Robina went down to Mexico for a vacation a couple years ago, or maybe it was more like five or six years ago—anyway they were tellin' me 'bout all the long lines and things you got to go through even before you get on the airplane and all the changin' planes and the tight little seats and the tiny little bathrooms. They didn't like it. They weren't scared like I think I might be, but they said the seats are so little they couldn't move, and you're all squeezed together with a lot of people—"

Sam put his right hand on top of Geneva's hand. "Mrs. Gardiner, I'm on an airplane at least twice a month. I have to fly to places where I'm having my picture taken for advertisements. In part of the airplane the seats are pretty tight, especially for people built like Ben and Robina, but when you travel in business class it's a lot more comfortable. The seats are bigger and they're farther apart and softer. We would make sure you went to Africa in business class. Several airlines have seats that are a little like your La-Z-Boy over there. You can put your feet up and lean back to sleep. The food's even pretty good. We'd make sure you could travel that way because it would be a long time in the air."

"I guess that's not really what I'm talkin' 'bout," Geneva said. She paused and turned her iced tea glass around. Liz and Sam quietly listened to the ice chattering as they waited for Geneva to go on. "I woke up this mornin' and I said to myself, you've been a silly and selfish woman, Geneva."

Sam's left hand gripped Liz's knee under the table. Geneva was going to tell them something she thought they would not want to hear.

"I don't know, really, what them people in Africa would like. I just know what kind of quilts I like to make. Seemed like I got sick and tired of the kind-a quilts I was makin' all my life and that ever'body I knowed was maken'. I wanted to put together colors and designs that I liked to sew and that made me smile while I was workin' on them, and even while I was workin' on one, my mind would be plottin' and plannin' 'bout the next one. Sometimes I wouldn't finish one 'fore I was cuttin' out pieces for the next one. Somebody'd give me a piece-a print that I just wanted to start usin' right away and I would. I'm like a kid at Christmas with new toys, I couldn't just play with one, I'd have to go from one to another and another. Just for fun."

No recorder, Liz thought. I can't interrupt. I have to remember exactly what she's saying.

"Oh, I told people—and I told myself too—that it was all for the people in Africa. But it wasn't for them a-tall. It was for me. And I got that whole closet full of quilts and I'm jus' like a miser, keepin' them all there and sometimes I open the closet door and just stand and look at them and love them almost like they was my grandbabies."

"I understand that, Geneva," Liz said. "I know what you're talking about."

"But they're not children or people, they're just things I made outta scraps."

"They're beautiful things," Sam said. Liz patted the hand gripping her knee, trying to tell him not to argue, just listen to what Geneva was trying to tell them.

"But now that you're telling me I can really give them to the people in Africa, I don't know...I think it's not right. I think maybe I should give them to Americans who need them. You know, I never 'magined myself goin' to Africa. You two go all kinds of places but this here is where I belong."

Sam's grip tightened. He was thinking, Liz knew, that this would not be the ending for Melissa's documentary. Sam pressed his lips together, telling Liz he understood her message. He would not try to change Geneva's mind.

"They're yours, you can do anything you want with them, or nothing but keep making them and give them away whenever the time is right." Liz felt she had to tell Geneva she agreed with her wish to make up her own mind.

Sam said, "You do give quilts away when you know there's a need."

Liz had a lump in her throat. She felt as if she had shopped for a perfect gift, had been to all the stores on Fifth Avenue and had found, yes, thanks to Sam, the perfect gift, the way to make Geneva's dream come true. Together they had wrapped it beautifully and tied it with a gorgeous bow and now it was being rejected. She knew Sam felt the same. But Geneva had not asked for the gift in the first place. Liz had been excited by Sam's excitement and it had become their dream. Geneva was rejecting it when she realized the fantasy had been more real than she could understand. She did not belong in that far-off African world.

"Ben reminded me that you talked 'bout maybe havin' my quilts in a show. He said it was all right to be proud of the work of my hands. It would even be all right to sell the quilts if I wanted to give money to people who need things worse than me."

"Geneva, I'd love it if you would let me arrange a show of your quilts," Liz said. "I'm afraid it will take a while, maybe a year or even more. It would be best if we could do the book of pictures like Sam wants to do..."

"The Dairy Barn," Sam said. "Wouldn't it be fantastic full of Geneva's quilts?"

"What dairy barn?" Geneva asked.

"The place we went yesterday is a place that shows quilt art. It had about eighty quilts on show," Liz explained. "It's a dairy barn that people turned into an art gallery. Sam, they have a lot of events planned already. There was a list on a bulletin board."

"But wouldn't it be fantastic?" he said.

"It would be fantastic," Liz agreed.

"We've got a book about it, Geneva. We'll show you the kind of quilts we were looking at yesterday. There's a picture of the outside, you can tell it was a barn," Sam said. His look of dread was gone now that another new idea was taking over his imagination.

"There are a lot of venues," Liz began.

Sam interrupted. "She's using a fancy word for places to have a quilt show."

Liz continued, "Geneva, if you really don't want to give the quilts away, you know, very soon..." Liz stopped; she didn't know how to express the conflicting ideas going through her mind. She was trying to convince herself, yes, there would be time to write her thesis, publish a picture book. She had no doubt Sam would find a way to pull it off.

Liz wanted to respect Geneva's feelings, but she had feelings too. Geneva was being honest, and Liz needed to be honest also. "I'm sad, Geneva. I was imagining your happy face when you went to an African village and met the women there and saw their little children and visited in their homes. I thought that would be a beautiful thing."

Geneva shook her head and looked down at her hands clasping one another on the flowered vinyl tablecloth. Liz wished Sam were filming the hands and that she were recording Geneva's slow, thoughtful voice. When Geneva looked up at them there were tears in her eyes, too. "I don't want to make you sad, Liz, or to mess up Sam's plans. But I thought and thought 'bout it. The idea made me real happy and I thank you for wantin' to make it come true. I prayed 'bout it Wednesday night. The others were prayin' for the people we always pray for, and they were giving thanks like we always do. But I was givin' thanks for you two and your good wishes for me. And I was askin' God what was I really doin' with these quilts? And I didn't get an answer. Not then. But yesterday after talkin' to Ben and Robina and thinkin' 'bout all the things that's going on in the church and then thinkin' 'bout how people are people and lots of times just don't get along even when they're all Christians and believe in the same things..." Her voice had become softer and softer. She shook her head.

Sam said, "It's not our place to give you advice. But if we can help at all..." He took Geneva's hand. "You shouldn't be sad."

"Sometimes it's hard to see the foolishness of a dream," Geneva said.

"I don't think it was foolish," Liz whispered. Her sadness was ballooning in her chest; she was struggling not to actually cry. She wanted to be proud of Geneva, but all she could really feel was that a dream had turned to dust—a dream they had all shared.

"It was a foolish dream in a way and then, when you talked 'bout goin' to Africa, it got to be a selfish dream. I'm not Santy Claus or some rich person givin' to the poor. That's not my place in life. Right here, this house, this farm is my place. I need to spend the rest of my days, however many they might be, right here doin' somethin' that makes me feel happy to get up in the morning, my mind plannin' what I'm goin' to sew even before I'm out of bed. So I get up and do my chores to start the day and go make somethin' that I can leave behind. And the quilts can go to people who need them and want them, and maybe will even like them. They don't have to be African people, they can be my own neighbors who don't have enough. Ben and Robina would see to that. That's what I want."

"That's what you should have," Sam said.

"And if you want to bury them for a show someplace, I'd be real pleased to let you, and I'd like to go see what they look like in some barn or whatever place. That's what I been thinkin' 'bout telling you since I woke up this morning 'round 3:30. I couldn't get back to sleep and I been wanderin' 'round the house, like a cat in a round barn, all day 'til you got here, feelin' sad and 'fraid to tell you and knowin' I had to do it."

Liz lost her battle with tears. They were trickling down both sides of her nose

"I'm sorry, Liz, I'm sorry to disappoint you. And you, too, Sam."

"It's all right," Liz said. "It's really all right. My brothers always called me a cry baby. And I haven't outgrown it."

Sam pulled a paper napkin from the holder in the middle of the table and wiped the right side of Liz's face. Liz took the napkin from him, wiped the other side of her face and blew her nose.

"She's not sad. She's happy," Sam said.

"Don't look like it," Geneva said.

"That's true," Liz said. "And I'm going to work extra hard to get the thesis written as fast as I can and to find a place to show your quilts. I don't want to be the only person besides Sam who knows how wonderful they are. I want other people to know about your work."

Geneva seemed about to speak; she hesitated. Liz and Sam waited. "Do you really think they're wonderful?" she asked.

"Yes," they both said together.

"Then how come nobody else does?" Geneva asked.

"Sometimes people have to be told before they can see what's under their noses," Sam said. "Sometimes they need to see something in a book or on television to understand."

Geneva nodded thoughtfully. "That may be so."

They sat silently until Liz was able to say, "Can I go just look at your closet full of quilts for a couple of minutes? And then I think we should get on our way back to Bloomington. It's been a week full of more things than I can handle all at once."

Just outside Friendship they met Ben and Robina. Ben honked and waved for them to stop. They stopped on the side of the road and all got out of their cars. "I guess Mom told you what she's been thinking about," Ben said.

"You look like you've been crying," Robina said to Liz.

"Do I look that bad?"

"It shows," Ben said.

"I was just saying to Ben that her feeling about not sending them to Africa should be a good thing for you. They'll be here and not lost on the other side of the world," Robina said.

"But she had a dream that was keeping her interested and excited. And Sam's just found a way we could make it come true for her. We could really take her to Africa. Giving up your dreams is the saddest thing," Liz said.

"She'll keep on making quilts, that's part of what she said she'd been thinking about. It's because of you, really," Robina said.

"I don't understand," Liz said.

"She said you made her think about why she liked making them so much. She says she decided she makes them because she just likes the making," Robina said.

Ben added, "The poor people in Africa was the reason she started, but she says it stopped being the reason she was doing it a while ago. She's happy when the colors and the patterns all come together the way she wants and when she has one done and lays it on the bed and looks at it."

"Did she tell you she sleeps under every quilt she makes at least once, usually the night of the day she finishes it?" Robina said.

"No," Liz said. "I'll have to remember that."

"She never talked to us much about them, you know," Ben said. "And I guess we didn't talk to her about them either. We always just thought she was sewing to keep herself busy."

"She didn't want idle hands to do the devil's work, so she was doing some good work with her hands," Robina chimed in. "But lately she's been talking about her quilting to us, and we got to understand her better. It's 'cause of you and your questions."

"And loving the quilts. No one else ever told her they loved them, just you two," Ben said. "So we were surprised but kind-a glad when she said she thinks she'll just pile them up and when she dies I'll see that they go to good causes."

"Showing them in a museum could be a good cause," Robina added. "But it'd be better if it could happen while she's still with us."

"I'm going to work hard on that," Liz said.

"I'm working on it too," Sam said. "We're sad because we thought it would be wonderful to make her Africa dream come true. We wanted to put her on a plane and let her meet the people there."

"You didn't get tickets or nothing yet, did you?" Ben asked.

"No, but I've made connections with people who were willing to pay for it."

"Well, we didn't know that," Robina said.

"I guess she didn't tell you that part," Sam said.

"No." Ben looked thoughtfully up the road. A car slowed as the driver saw them parked leaving one narrow lane, he gawked at them and apparently decided nothing was wrong so speeded up after he was past. "But she's already made up her mind, partly because of the troubles in her church. Mom's a stubborn old woman. When she decides something there's no point in putting up an argument."

"We just had an example of that," Sam said.

"Don't cry, Little Lizzie." Ben patted Liz on the back. She laughed a small laugh. "Bet you didn't know Mom calls you that sometimes when she talks about you. Says that's what your aunt called you."

Liz said, "I'm glad we met you. I think you've got my phone number. I'll be back, probably, quite a few times, but when the new school year starts I'll be really busy teaching and working on my thesis and trying to find a museum. Sam will be working on his photos for his book. If anything happens, I hope you call me."

"Sure. And I'll give you our number too," Ben agreed.

Ben and Robina got back in their pick-up and went on toward Friendship.

"They sounded like they had that rehearsed," Sam said.

"I guess they've been talking about it and they thought we'd be at Geneva's."

Liz played over the many things Geneva and Ben and Robina had said in the last couple of hours. She seemed to have spent many days climbing a mountain, reached the top and then had been blown off by a great gust of wind and found herself at the bottom, surprised, bruised, confused. Sam drove calmly and quietly. How could he be so serene when his plans for a documentary had just been destroyed like a sandcastle when an unexpected wave swept over the beach? He had been so calm with Geneva even when Liz knew from the way he gripped her knee that he felt as fearful as she was.

Now they had to go back to step one. Liz did not understand how Geneva could have changed her mind so completely just because the church had had some kind of schism. If they could find Rev. Redburn would she change her mind? Should they try? How was it possible to just give up such a long-held ambition? It was like falling out of love. But you can't fall out of love all of a sudden. Or maybe some people do, people who found out their spouse had been having an affair. Then a feeling of betrayal instantly converts love to hate. But even that Liz couldn't believe: turned from love to hate with the snap of the fingers.

As they approached Versailles, Liz asked, "Sam, what do you think of trails in the woods?"

"I like the trails on the dunes at the Dunes State Park," he said. "I used to pretend it was the Sahara." He laughed. "The Sahara on the edge of Lake Michigan."

"Would you walk through the woods with me for a little while? There's a park, if you turn right at the stoplight and we go about half a mile out of town."

"Sure."

Liz directed him to the lake and the trail she had walked along the day of Aunt Alma's funeral. "Will it bother you if I take a camera along?" Sam asked.

"Not at all but I don't think there'll be any animals around to photograph."

"Paths in the woods make nice photographs," he said. "My stepdad made a whole album of Copper Canyon trails and paths. He called it Invitation to Adventure. Tried to sell it to magazines but didn't get any takers."

They walked into the mid-afternoon shade of the wooded trail. They crossed the little stream with stepping stones. Sam saw a large water bug and photographed it and then photographed the stream in both directions. He asked Liz to walk across the stepping stones and photographed her going both directions. He began to follow a butter-fly flitting down the trail. Liz sat down on a fallen tree and waited for him. She loved being in the woods. She loved being with Jack in the woods. She loved being with Randy in the forest the time they went to Lake Kosovo and visited the reindeer people's camp and met a woman shaman who seemed not at all mysterious as she played with a chubby little grandson. Liz loved being in the woods with Sam as he found one subject after another to photograph. For her being in the woods was an escape from the rest of life.

But today her life intruded as she tried to escape. How could Sam just shift into his fascination with photography when his documentary had just been torpedoed? It would have been better if he had never become involved with this whole quilt project. He had a very comfort-able double life and might have given up photography to pursue his New York career, buy that apartment he talked about with the view of the sunset over New Jersey and share it with some gorgeous model or actress or even a film maker like Melanie. Could they salvage any-thing from the videos he already had and her interviews? It wouldn't have a strong, appealing story line. It would be only an informational little film about an outsider quilter, not a human interest story. He seemed to care about Geneva, but then he always seemed to care about any woman he was with, no matter if she were 86 like Geneva or 18 like the receptionist at the hotel in Athens, Ohio. Sam came back and sat down beside her. "Feeling better?"

"Feeling worse."

"About—?"

"Messing up everyone's lives," she said. "I messed up Geneva's peaceful working toward her goal of giving her quilts to Africans. And because of that I've messed up your plans to do a documentary. And because I...because of Jack, I'm messing up your life even more. I think I'm about to mess up Jack's life, too, because I can't live in Padukah, Kentucky. I'm a walking virus. And I'm doing this thesis not because I know a lot about quilts but because I had to find something to do to forget about Randy and all the dreams I gave up when he fell in love with Buddhism and I just didn't want to know about it. I'm totally selfish; I'm sorry, Sam."

"You're so wrong about so much of what you just said."

"Don't tell me, because I don't believe it and I don't want to argue."

"I'm as mute as a stone," he said. Sam held her. She felt sheltered and forgiven.

They slowly walked back the way they had come. Sam held her hand and did not take photographs. It seemed a very short walk to the car. Sam drove the eighty miles back to Bloomington. Liz stared out the window on the left side thinking about Geneva and about Ben and Robina. She knew she would not see Jack again; she would never be able to share his life; she needed to end the relationship that had gone farther than she imagined it would. About Sam...she didn't know. He seemed strangely to have the kind of Buddhist acceptance and calm that Randy had talked about for so many hours, trying to define in words what he knew had to be experienced. Sam would go to New York in a few days and then be gone for another four or five weeks, including a trip to Switzerland where he would pose on glaciers for advertisement for winter ski outfits.

Liz had these last summer weeks to write as much as possible about Geneva and her quilts: the idea, the making, the donated materials, her artistic excitement every day about her work. Liz wished she could express all this both clearly and with the excitement she heard in Geneva's voice. Wouldn't it be wonderful to be able to use the actual recordings, parts of the interviews, perhaps as footnotes?

Make mine an Outsider Thesis! She smiled to herself. This is the age of multi-media, she thought. Why not? Yes, she would talk to Tom Simmons about it. Not that she expected for a moment the Ph.D. committee would even so much as hear of the idea.

How did I get into all this? Liz thought. But of course, she knew the answer: She had to leave Mongolia, leave Randy exploring the spiritual side of his life. What was the inner harmony, the serenity, the spiritual, meditational peace that he talked about? Why did he think he needed it? Maybe it came naturally to some people without all that angst, ancient Tibetan vocabulary and self-consciousness. Maybe Sam had it; maybe because he had two lives and was successful in one of them and gained from that the confidence that anything he tried would be successful.

Why was she thinking about Randy and his quest? That was past. Was it? Last night she had nearly fallen apart just because Sam asked her about it. Better to think about Geneva's sudden change of heart. What was it inside people that pushed them to change? Were the changes for the better? Or were they meaningless? Why couldn't Geneva allow herself the pleasure of giving her quilts to a group of Africans? Why is that so important to me? Liz asked herself. Did I buy Sam's dream, hook, line and sinker? Did I want to feel like Santa Claus giving Geneva something as amazing as a trip to the moon might have been? Am I upset just because I can't be the angel in the whole business? She moaned.

"Are you alright?" Sam asked.

"No, I'm a fucking mess. I am so confused about everything; I want to dig a hole and pull in the lid and never come out."

"You'll be alright." He patted her knee as if he were petting a dog on the head "Really. Just do what you've got to do. Write and research and read and go back to see Geneva whenever you feel you need to. You'll need to keep each other company sometimes."

"My God, Sam, where are these ideas coming from?"

"You're not the only one whose brain keeps churning while the scenery passes. I think it must be a wonderful thing to realize you're an artist when you're eighty-six years old."

For the next several miles Liz thought about what being an artist might mean to Geneva, who had always just made quilts, not to treasure for themselves but only as utilitarian objects to give away. Ben and Robina said she seemed happier now. Were artists happier? Was it better to be an artist and value your work? Or to be full of charity and give to others? This was a question for ministers, not Ph.D. candidates.

"You can be an artist," Liz said to Sam.

"If I work hard enough. If I have what it takes, the eye, the technical know-how, the perseverance, maybe," he said.

"I'm not the stuff artists are made of," Liz said. "I'm all right brain."

"Maybe and maybe not. Maybe you have something inside you haven't tapped. Maybe it's not the right time."

They drove through the increasingly rolling countryside toward Brown County. Liz smiled as she always did when she noticed the small sign announcing they had entered Gnawbone. It identified not so much a town but, as Barbara would say, as a wide place in the road. A few houses scattered along a half mile of road, no commercial center, no post office. None of the few people who lived here had an address: Gnawbone, Indiana. They approached Nashville. "Shall we get something to eat in Nashville?" Sam asked. "I'm hungry. You know all we've had since breakfast was the candy bars we got when we stopped for gas. And a couple of cookies at Geneva's."

"Oh, I'm so sorry, Sam. I didn't even think about lunch."

"Why are you apologizing? Suddenly you're responsible for everything? Suddenly you're God, or you're Satan, and you caused all the problems in the world."

"Are you trying to say I'm a mere human being?" She tried to smile, but she knew her joke was weak.

"Exactly."

They went into a touristy "Ol' Country" type restaurant on the main street of the arty little town. A sepia toned traditional quilt hung on a wall. Liz examined it and realized it had been quilted with a long arm machine probably in a Chinese sweatshop. It was not an antique as the setting suggested but a relatively new quilt. It was well made, and the colors and design were attractive. "Chinese," Liz said. "I hate that, commercial dishonesty. They could have found a true antique, or they could have displayed an honest new creation."

"I wonder if there's a niche called quilt critics that you could fit into," Sam said. "Or maybe you'll invent it."

The menu was quaintly worded. "Look at this," Liz said.

"The owners are trying to make a living," Sam said.

Liz shook her head. "I'm in such a bad mood."

"Food helps," Sam said. They studied the menu until the waiter came. After he left, both were quiet, letting the experiences of the last few days settle in their minds like loose leaves settling in a teacup.

"When do you think you'll see Geneva again?" Sam asked as they waited for their dinners.

"I'm so shell shocked, I don't know anything." Liz felt more wrung out than she had after the long weekend of Aunt Alma's funeral.

"Don't let her feel abandoned just because she changed her mind."

"I can't abandon her. I need her too much."

"And she needs you, Liz. I really think she does. I'm going to be gone for six weeks; don't abandon me either. I'll be living my schizophrenic life, but I'll be thinking of you." He picked up her hand and caressed one finger after another as if he were a blind man memorizing what made her hand different from any other hand he had ever held. It made her so peaceful she thought she might cry again.

Chapter 14

Liz called Geneva every Monday morning. She asked Geneva what she was sewing, what was going on in her life, how her garden was growing, if her chickens and puppies were all right. Liz reported on the progress of her research. Geneva always asked about Sam and Liz told her where he was. Sam emailed her several times a week and called her at least once a week. He said that Melanie had gone away for August; he could not find out if it was to Long Island or to Santorini or first one and then the other. She did not answer emails or phone messages. Mutual friends reported she was with a lover but wouldn't say whether it was a man or woman.

The documentary idea was on hold, but still viable. During the summer months, it seemed to exist like forgotten eggs in a refrigerator in three Manhattan apartments, Sam's, Melanie's and Carla's. Sam was sure it would be rediscovered when fall came and mother and daughter got together again. They might decide it had gone rotten like the eggs or was simply forgotten. He had some good footage, perhaps not good enough; he didn't know. He wouldn't know until he could show it to Melanie. He thought a shot of Geneva seeing her quilts hanging in a museum might replace the dreamed of African picture. Meanwhile he was spending two weeks in Switzerland shooting winter fashion spreads on stunning, but melting, glaciers. Then he would go to Lake Como for a resort wear shoot and then to Tunisia for next summer's fashions.

Liz worked hard at writing, researching and pursuing museum leads. She was fascinated to learn from Prof. Simmons that a large percentage of Outsider Artists were older people. They seemed to have bursts of inspired creativity after age sixty. If they had previously pursued their artistic bent in traditional ways, suddenly a new idea or technique, often very creative, often characterized by either vivid and bold expression or a new serenity entered their art. They produced breakthroughs that were unexpected leaps rather than progressions of previous work. Liz spent an evening with Tom and Cynthia Simmons looking at slides and talking about various artists who were gaining recognition in their later years.

"You've opened my eyes to a phenomenon I didn't know about," Tom said.

Geneva fit this outline. Liz followed Prof. Simmons' leads and researched outsider artists' ages and progression. She outlined a chapter about other artists and put Geneva in their company. As she struggled to write the chapter she wondered whether to send Geneva a copy of it. Geneva would not be familiar with the other examples and was not able to go to a computer and look up references. Liz decided to paraphrase the chapter, print a few visual examples, and send it to Geneva and a second copy to Ben. She was careful to include Ben in any of her discoveries. She thought of him as a gatekeeper, the person she needed in case anything happened to Geneva.

Ben and Robina took their gatekeeper role very seriously and often, when Liz called to chat with them, which she did every couple of weeks, they asked questions showing they had been thinking about Geneva as an artist. She had become a more complex person in their eyes, more precious and important since her importance to Liz and Sam seemed so large. In one conversation Robina said, "You've made our world bigger."

Liz was so surprised she could only reply, "Thanks for saying that." She was elated and immediately emailed Sam about it.

Liz did not tell Geneva about breaking up with Jack. At first she thought she could tell Jack on the phone; but she decided that was cowardly and unfair. She visited him in Paducah, strolled the streets, stopped at art galleries, some of which showed small size art quilts along with other art. They gathered cards and names of people to approach about an eventual show of Geneva's quilts.

Finally, over dinner, Liz explained to Jack that her life was turning an unexpected corner. She did not know what she would do when she had finished the thesis, but she felt she could not commit to his way of life. He needed and wanted a wife. She wanted him to feel free to find someone who was clear about being the person he needed and wanted. Perhaps a partner in his business. The talk was difficult for both of them. They cried together, they held each other and assured one another they would find their path, whatever it was.

Most of the time Liz felt as if she were in a not very good chick lit novel. She tried to be honest, but everything that came out of her mouth sounded like a cliché. She should never have gotten so involved with Jack. He was a sweet, good man, but she was the wrong woman for him. And he was the wrong man for her.

Liz did not talk to anyone, not Sam and not her mother, about the weekend with Jack. She felt she had done something stupid and dishonest, almost as if she'd pulled some scam although she had always been honest with Jack. She was embarrassed to have made such a selfish mistake. Finally, when Liz met Barbara in Indianapolis to shop for a bridesmaid's dress, she talked about saying good-bye to Jack. Barbara said matter of factly, "That's good. His life is not your life."

"How can you say that?" Liz demanded. "You never met him; you don't know anything about him."

"It was an interlude, Sweetheart. I'm not discounting it or saying you didn't feel deeply. You explored a kind of life and you learned it's not for you. That was very worthwhile."

"Jeez Mother, you make it sound like a business transaction."

"Come on, Liz, you know I don't mean it that way; even if that's what it's like." She changed the subject. "We probably should have gone to Chicago to shop. I should have thought of that." Eventually they found a dress Liz agreed she might wear a few times after the wedding if the hem could be taken up. She could wear it to dinner with Sam and feel appropriately dressed in a fancy restaurant.

Randy emailed at the end of August that he and a friend from the Naropa Institute were driving to Baltimore, Michael's home, after a stop in Pennsylvania at Randy's home. Randy wanted to stop in Bloomington. "I need to see you."

"Why?" Liz emailed immediately, with no other comment. Then

she felt guilty about being so abrupt but she hesitated to write anything more.

Randy telephoned an hour later and said he needed to talk to her about "a life changing decision."

She responded, "Is it really that important? I don't know how much mental and emotional energy I can spare right now." No sooner had she said it than she hated herself for sounding like the New Agers whose jargon she despised and tried to avoid. What a load of crap! She just didn't think she could handle seeing Randy when she wanted to put all her energy into the thesis.

She was waking up at 3:30 at night, replaying her last visit with Jack, feeling guilty about having enjoyed being with him and letting him dream they could be together forever. Once again she thought of pursuing her needs as a virus infecting other people's peaceful lives.

Randy said, "Liz, I've never known you to be so cold. I wouldn't ask anything of you if it weren't very important to me and, I think, for our—not just my—mental balance in the future."

"I'm working so hard to get the thesis done as quickly as possible. I'm dealing with an old lady, and I want it done while she's still alive and able to enjoy being appreciated. I've been totally focused, and I'm afraid to interrupt my focus." This was, of course, a lie, a selfish excuse.

"Honestly I wouldn't ask if I didn't feel we must have this discussion."

"Is this going to be a forty-eight-hour conversation? If it is, I just can't handle it."

"No, no, no. We'll have dinner and talk for an hour afterwards. I really must have your insight, you understand things no one else does. We've shared so much." Tears blurred her vision and she knew, without a doubt, that Randy was tearful too. They gasped for breath in unison; they knew each other so well. Who's messing up whose life now?

He'll always be part of my life. He really needs to see me... She agreed.

She could not possibly concentrate on her work now, not until after the visit. What was it he wanted? He knew she would not become a Buddhist and go with him to meditate under a bodhi tree. Oh dear God, she thought. "An hour" means three or four. But maybe we'll finally finish whatever isn't finished. Maybe this is the summer I find out what I can do on my own.

Liz turned off her computer, closed the books, neatened the carrel. Her mind might as well have been wrapped in duct tape; she couldn't think about art quilts now. She walked across lawn from the library to her apartment on the south side of the university campus. The August heat and humidity was at its worst. These were what she called four-shower days even when she spent eight to ten hours in the air-conditioned library. The ancient air conditioner in her apartment roared like a lion protesting a thorn in its paw and barely cooled two rooms. She was going to be unable to think about anything except Randy until he had come and gone.

In the first second of the telephone conversation the familiar sound of Randy's voice had kick-started a set of flutters in her chest, mostly it was the memory of the first night they had spent together when she became convinced this was an extraordinary man whose fate was connected to hers. She had not seen Randy for over a year, their emails had become infrequent. He wrote of Buddhist practices and philosophies and teachers, the rimpoches he had met and his search for a teacher of his own, someone with whom he would have an instant rapport, a spiritual recognition that came from generations of reincarnations as student and teacher.

"You actually believe that?" she asked in an email many weeks ago.

"I do. Deep meditation brings forth these age-old connections."

Liz was stunned; she had never heard such an idea. It sounded so much like Randy; he truly believed it. She knew he did. He had said, more than once, that he truly believed their meeting in front of St. Peter's was deeper than serendipity. They had a karmic connection of many lifetimes. She had believed it; despite all their differences, now she still believed it.

Even early in their togetherness he said he had so much yet to learn but that was dependent upon finding this one special person—worse than a needle in a haystack, one human among the billions on earth—not a romantic soulmate, a karmic, ageless connection. Randy's communications left her muttering, "too much, too much." She had learned about his emotional neediness during their four years together. For a long time he had needed her. Then he realized, or so he parroted, that all needs were ego needs. He had found a path he had to follow alone. Why was he coming? To ask her permission? Her blessing?

For most of a year, thank heavens or thank Buddha or whatever, he no longer seemed to need her. Now, apparently, he needed one last thing that he could get only by seeing her in person. Maybe it was as simple as needing to see her—her physical self. They had felt such an immediate physical attraction five years ago in Rome. What if he said he couldn't live without her? At that thought her insides tied into knots.

Randy and Michael would start tomorrow morning; arrive the next afternoon. Liz knew she would barely be able to eat until he had come, they had talked and he had left. Her mind played an always changing loop of visual memories...and physical memories, in European cities, standing before Rembrandts, DaVincis, endless Piccassos, Cezannes, Monets, every great painter that ever lived it seemed. The sometimes smelly hostels, the nights on trains so they wouldn't have to get a hotel, walking the Philosopher's Way near Heidelberg, the visions wouldn't stop. The long flight to Mongolia via Korea, the long, long drive from Ulaan Baatar to the small town near the western border, the sound of the otherworldly Tuvan throat singers, the little boy who visited them almost every day, asking the English name of this and that. And the moment of epiphany during the long flight home to Chicago. They'll always be there—the memories—somewhere among the neurons of my brain. Four years I could never have imagined no matter what romance books I read.

Randy was thinner. "Have you shaved your head?" Liz asked as soon as she saw him. His hair was very short, merely a stubble all over his head. She remembered freshly shampooed, unruly curls that made him look younger than he was. Now he looked older, more mature and somewhat monkish. Oh, my, he had had his twenty-seventh birthday last December. "Are you going to be wearing maroon or saffron robes the next time I see you?".

"That may be in my future—maroon, of course. But I just wanted to see what it felt like." Michael had taken Buddhist vows but he was wearing ordinary shorts and a t-shirt. He was small, frail-looking and wore glasses with Coke-bottle lenses. He had a spacy, gentle smile and quick wit. Michael was quiet except when Randy made a point of including him in their dinner conversation. After dinner Michael said he wanted to explore the campus and would be back in a couple of hours. Liz knew, of course, Randy and Michael had agreed on this plan.

After the dinner table talk about his courses and discoveries at Naropa, about teachers and influences, when Michael left them at the door of Liz's house, Randy settled in the living room where the air conditioner growled. He paused and then quietly asked Liz if she would give him her blessing if and when—not so much if as when—he decided to take vows and become a lama. He had discovered a teacher, a rimpoche, whom he had not yet met. Something about the rimpoche's picture and a tape of a lecture spoke so strongly to Randy he knew he had to meet this man, that, actually, he may have known him through a number of lifetimes. The rimpoche lived in a monastery in southern India. Randy was going there after spending a little time with his family. If his gut feelings were accurate, he might remain there for many years. Randy seemed especially to need Liz's agreement that it was all right for him to take a vow of chastity although that was not a necessity in the school of study he expected to enter.

Liz felt she was with a mutation of Randy; he looked so different with almost no hair and ears that seemed much bigger. She pictured him in a lama's maroon robes—a Tibetan lama, not a Southeast Asian monk in saffron. Briefly she wondered if he had actually lost his mind or had hit his head in such a way to damage whatever part of the brain contained his lifelong sense of identity. This was not the Randy she had lived with for nearly four years, always long-haired, a blue topaz ear stud, a young man who blazed with excitement over Bernini or Leonardo. The Randy who later laughed like an eight-year-old with some of their youngest Mongolian students, sliding down a snow packed slope using a plastic potato sack stuffed with straw for a sled, whooping with delight.

He had become a different person so slowly during those months in Mongolia that she had not realized what was happening, but his appearance had not changed until now. Only on the plane as they returned, flying over the north pole did she realize Randy had changed in major ways, while she changed in only very small ways.

As Randy ran out of descriptions and explanations Liz thought, what a relief that he wants so little from me. Even if he imagines I still love him. Of course I do, but in a different way. His instinct was right; we need this evening together. Something wasn't finished...some of it will never be entirely finished. I'm glad he's going his own way. Randy had needed her as much as she needed him. He would never have gone to Mongolia alone, and of course, it wouldn't even have occurred to her. They had indelibly marked one another's lives.

Michael returned; his forehead was covered in sweat from the still humid night. Liz asked if he wanted to take a shower, but he simply washed his face. He refused a beer as Randy had; they both drank ice water while Liz drank beer. It was not yet ten o'clock; they plugged in a small fan to augment the air conditioner and spent another two hours reminiscing about their two years in Mongolia. They told Michael funny and sad and peculiar incidents. Their stories tumbled out, more for one another than for Michael. Only they understood what an intense experience it had been, what an important interlude in their lives. They had accomplished much that was positive for their students and for themselves. Their stories affirmed how important it had been for them to share those experiences. Michael listened intensely, as people rarely listen to other's reminiscences. He mirrored their emotions. What a rare and wonderful skill, Liz thought.

When the men left for Day's Inn where they had rented a room, Liz sat across from her wheezing air conditioner in her dark apartment, playing over the last six hours in her mind. She felt as high and satisfied as if she had smoked very good marijuana. She was barely aware of stretching out on the sofa as she fell asleep.

Liz felt light and sweetly happy in the thickening morning heat when she went out to the sidewalk to wait for Randy and Michael to come say good-bye. Only Randy got out, but she leaned in and wished Michael a good trip and peace on the path he had chosen. She wished Randy a wonderful life; she asked him to keep in touch at least a few times a year. "If you don't have email in your monastery, send me an address," she said. "I'd be sad if it seemed you'd dropped off the face of the earth. And I'll want to crow a little bit when I get my Ph.D."

Randy looked at her a long time. Tears blurred his eyes and she didn't try to fight back her tears. He gave her a long, painfully tight hug. "Namaste," Liz said, tenting her hands in front of her face and bowing her head to him before he got into the car and closed the door. He returned her blessing—both knew it meant more than a ritual parting gesture. Then he was gone.

Liz walked past the sprinklers on the campus lawns on her way to the library; one swung around and sprinkled her. The water felt wonderful, but it released more tears. She sat down on the grass under a tree, out of reach of the sprinkler's arc, and let herself cry for a little while. Then she went on to the cool library and the computer in her carrel. She was able to pick up the thread of the section of the thesis she had been working on. She typed for three solid hours until she had found a way to include all the necessary information and data in a dense description of the growth of quilting in America. A necessary craft became a hobby and then began again to emphasize craft, new techniques, hand dyed fabrics. For many it became a hobby, a communal craft and for those with artistic talent it became a fiber art of endless possibilities.

Liz managed a quick trip to Dillsboro. She and Marjorie went together to Friendship. Geneva showed Liz and Marjorie four new quilts that she had made since Liz and Sam were there. "Sam's going to have to come back in October when the leaves have changed," Geneva said. "I'll have 'bout eight new quilts for him to photograph by then. If I keep quilting," she said with an almost twinkling smile, "Sam'll have to keep coming to photograph them, don't you think?"

"I'm sure of it. You've got him hooked," Liz said.

Marjorie laughed and said to Geneva, "My mom always said you were a flirt."

"I guess Alma knew me better than most anybody 'cepting Alf," Geneva said. "I'll bet you miss knowing she's here on the earth even more than I do." Marjorie nodded, seemed about to say something, then sighed and said nothing.

They were all quiet for a moment until Geneva changed the subject. "You know, I used to set down and make a quilt and say to myself, maybe I ought'n'a be makin' these quilts that nobody 'round here 'preciates. Could be I'm just bein' selfish 'cause I don't really know what people in Africa need or might like? Maybe they're civilized like us and would be insulted by my idea of what they want. I think 'bout that a lot. Sometimes I feel bad."

Liz shook her head, no, and was about to say something when Geneva continued. "I don't think that way no-more. I tell myself, Liz likes them and says they're good and wants to put them in a book. Then I think I'm bein' vain and vanity's a sin, you know. I 'spect I've always had my share of it."

"You shouldn't think that way," Marjorie said. "You're sharing something you love with other people. I don't think that's vanity."

"Mostly I think to myself, I've never been a really selfish person. I always believed in helpin' others and tryin' my best to live a good Christian life. I don't have much chance to do good works, but there's not much I'm sorry 'bout in my life. And now I found out that makin' my kind'a quilts makes me happy. I like watchin' them come together and see'n how they turn out. It's a kind'a little sort'a happiness. I figure most old women like I am don't get half the enjoyment out of whatever they do that I get out of my quiltin'. And enjoyin' ain't a sin when it don't hurt nobody else."

Liz smiled and nodded her head. She didn't want to interrupt Geneva, who went on, "I was talkin' to Ben and Robina 'bout that a while ago and they said I should just be happy 'cause it's a reward I earned for all the earlier part of my life. I was kind-a surprised to think that I'm getting old and maybe I've earned a little satisfaction." She laughed like a kid who had just discovered some new natural wonder like baby birds or tadpoles. "I think they just might be right."

"Maybe no one's really old until the pleasure goes out of life," Marjorie said. "I hope I can feel half as good as you feel in another twenty years."

"Oh, dear," Liz moaned. "Geneva, I still forget to start the recorder, so I miss some of the best things you say."

"You think of Geneva as a friend, and not a research subject, that's the problem," Marjorie said.

"I do, you're right." Liz smiled at Geneva. "You'll have to excuse me a minute while I make notes about that." She pulled out the steno pad Marjorie gave her months ago. It was nearly filled.

"Now tell me 'bout your mother's wedding," Geneva said after she and Marjorie had chatted while Liz wrote.

"It's next Saturday, I'm the maid of honor and Phillip's two sons are both best man. The ceremony will be just family in a friend's garden, but the reception will be a big deal at a country club."

"I'm going to go to the wedding," Marjorie said. "It'll be the fanciest party I've ever been to. Barbara is a professional party giver."

"Then she must be raring to throw a wedding for Liz," Geneva said.

"I keep telling her she has to wait. When the time comes, I just might elope and not tell her about it for a few weeks."

"You're good at making people happy," Geneva said. "You ought to give your mother that much of a present."

Liz was surprised. "I'll remember that, Geneva, if and when the time comes."

"Better write it down in your notebook there," Geneva said. "Write advice from Geneva." Liz wrote it and underlined it as Geneva watched and nodded her head.

Phillip called Liz on Tuesday. He asked her if she had printed photographs of any of Geneva's quilts, or were they all in a computer file?

"The good ones, the ones Sam took, are all on our files as far as I know," she said. "Why?"

Phillip said he had mentioned the quilts to Caroline Dunham, an interior decorator who was currently working on a new pediatric wing of Children's Hospital for children with cancer. She knew about Project Linus and that many of the children would be given quilts. She thought she might like to use somewhat more sophisticated quilts in the public areas to be enjoyed by parents as they walked the halls or sat in a waiting room while the children underwent procedures. "I know Caroline has a fairly decent budget to work with. Do you think your lady down in Friendship could be persuaded to sell a few quilts to the hospital?" Phillip asked.

"She's been against selling her quilts," Liz said. "But this might be different. I could go to a Walgreens and get some photos printed."

"I don't want to rush you, but if you could bring them up Friday when you come for the non-rehearsal dinner—that's what we're calling it—just family. You are coming, aren't you?"

"With my arm in a sling from having been twisted so hard by Mom," Liz said. Actually she was looking forward to the dinner. She hadn't seen her brothers and their families for five years, and she was curious to meet Phillip's sons. Phillip had reserved a private room in his country club for the dinner. Barbara was decorating the club's much larger function room for the reception. The wedding itself would be only family and some of Phillip's relatives, including his eighty-one-year-old mother.

After the phone call Liz looked at the file of Sam's photos. This woman might not like Geneva's quilts, Liz thought. I'll show her the most conventional ones but I'm sure there are art quilters, or very good contemporary quilters, in Indianapolis with more immediately likable quilts. The woman probably doesn't know anything about quilts. Liz Googled Project Linus and found that the quilts made for hospitalized kids by volunteers all over the U.S. were extremely simple. She wished Sam were around to help her make a few selections. She chose a dozen quilts, put them on a flash drive to print. She decided not to mention the idea to Geneva until she knew the extent of the decorator's interest.

Caroline Dunham and her husband were guests at the reception. Phillip explained that Caroline had worked on many of his real estate projects. She reminded Liz very much of Barbara. She was chic, well preserved and business was always at the edge of her mind. She led Liz to the relatively quiet settee outside the lady's powder room and asked about the quilts, their size, how many more were available, what would Geneva Gardiner want for them?

"She might not want you to have them," Liz said.

"Phillip told me about her idea of sending them to Africa," Caroline said

"That's become problematic. A hospital, especially a cancer wing, is a good cause, but it'll be a totally new idea to her."

"Grieving parents. People scared out of their wits that their child is going to die—and I understand many of them, unfortunately, do die." Caroline sounded like a bad actress on a local TV commercial.

"Are the parents wealthy or poor? Are they all white people or—?"

"Of course the hospital serves everyone. I want to make the whole wing feel homey, not juvenile, not Sesame Street-ish. Not over bright cartoon colors. I want something comforting on the walls, not stereotype Disney-ish. I understand how much people love Disney but, between you and me, I can't stand that stuff. That's why Phil's idea appeals to me."

"What if some quilts were available in the waiting rooms for parents to wrap themselves in?" Liz asked. The idea had just popped into her head.

"That would be a big logistics problem. I mean a hospital deals with sanitation issues. No, I don't think that could work. But it would be wonderful, wouldn't it? You're worried to death about your kid having a bone marrow transplant, say, and you could huddle with a quilt wrapped around your shoulders while you watch the god-awful crap on the TV. I love the way you think, Elizabeth. That's brilliant."

"You're right. It's impossible." The quilts would have to be washed regularly. They wouldn't last long. Caroline's husband came to take Caroline back to the party.

"Yes, yes, Darling. I'll be right there," Caroline said. Her husband planted himself nearby, signaling he would give her only a few more minutes.

"What do you think of the quilts in the pictures?" Liz asked. "They aren't run-of-the-mill quilts. They're more eclectic. It's more like putting a Rauschenberg on the walls than a Mary Cassett."

"Now I'm embarrassed because I don't really know modern art," Caroline said. "They look cheerful to me. I suppose I'd need to see them."

"Sweetheart," said her husband, "May I have the next dance?" He bowed exaggeratedly.

"I don't want to keep you, but I need to know pretty firmly if you really are interested in them before I talk to Geneva. She's too old and naïve to be tugged this way and that about her quilts," Liz said.

"And you're the gatekeeper?"

"I feel responsible."

"I'll email you Monday," Caroline promised. Her husband took her hand as if to help her stand up—or hoist her if she hesitated.

"All work and no play," he said to Liz, "ruins a husband's day."

Liz sat for a few minutes before she went back to the reception. She felt brow beaten. Were businesswomen of her mother's generation all so single-minded? She certainly would not talk to Geneva until Caroline Dunham made some kind of commitment. She resented this distraction from her work...but then, quilts sold to a big hospital would be a good resume point when she and Sam were looking for exhibition venues.

On the other hand she was irked that others co-opted her discovery. Phillip was probably trying to win some brownie points with her. He had no idea he had given her a new problem. She liked Phillip but wished he had not interfered with this idea. Geneva's quilts weren't the sort people hung in hospitals, why hadn't she just said so and ended it right there? But even a few thousand dollars could make a big difference if Geneva needed a house repair, medical help. I'd be wrong to deprive her of that without even asking.

Liz went back to the reception. Phillip asked her to dance; he was a much better dancer than she was. "Are you and Caroline going to work something out?"

"I don't know. These aren't ordinary quilts, Phillip. They may be all wrong for a hospital."

"I understand they're special," he said.

"They are. If you keep talking to me, I'm going to step on your toes," she said.

"That's okay. The only faux pas is if I step on your toes."

Liz drank champagne and watched her mother going from table to table during dinner, getting hugs from everyone, laughing, being kissed on the cheek. This party was her ultimate coup. Barbara would never again throw a party she enjoyed more than this one. She looked young and beautiful in a sea foam green gown. Liz had had tears in her eyes when she saw her mother's face as she said, "I do."

Liz also danced with David and Brian. Both seemed to recognize her, at last, as another adult, not a bothersome baby sister. Their wives had become friends who did not see each other often enough.

They sat side by side and talked to one another ignoring their husbands and almost everyone else. The children were better behaved than Liz expected. Liz posed for photos over and over, everyone seemed to have a little camera or a cell phone in their pocket and wanted pictures. Liz forgot about feeling a little ridiculous in the fancy dress, the make-up Barbara had applied and the hair-do arranged that morning in a salon. The photos might be historic; she might never again look like the "after" version of a make-over.

When Barbara and Phillip left in a limousine for the airport, Brian said good-bye and left with his wife and three children for the first leg of their four-hundred-mile drive home. Liz with David, Amy and their two sons spent one last night in Barbara's house. It was now on the market. When Barbara and Phillip returned from their honeymoon on Nantucket part of the furniture would be moved to their new house and the rest sold. Liz was not sentimental about the house, but it felt strange to stay there with David and his family as if it were an Air B&B. Liz and David watched news while Amy put the overtired children to bed. David said, "I've been to plenty of weddings, and I thought this would be like all the rest, but it wasn't. How often do you get to see your mother looking like the happiest twenty-year-old bride in the world? It really kind of knocked me for a loop when the judge said, 'I now pronounce you man and wife.' I don't think I felt that way even at my own wedding."

"At your own wedding," Amy said. She had come in as he was talking, "you heard that and were scared shitless. I thought you were going to run right out the door."

"And you were grinning like you'd won the lottery," he said.

"What an innocent lamb I was."

"Seriously," Liz said, "I know what you mean. I had to try hard not to break down during the ceremony. I kept telling myself, it won't do for the maid of honor to start bawling."

"You're next," Amy said.

Liz shrugged. "I'm writing a thesis."

"Mom says you're still recovering," David said. "From the Mongolian adventure, I mean." Liz shrugged again. She had talked to Barbara after Randy's visit. "I used to get a kick out of telling people, 'My little sister's in Mongolia.'"

"He did a lot of research just so he could be the center of attention at parties talking about you in Mongolia," Amy said.

"You did that?" Liz asked.

David shrugged and looked embarrassed. "Well, you never wrote letters."

"I answered every letter you wrote, which was zero."

"So tell me something I didn't read on the Internet about Mongolia," David said.

"I thought about writing my thesis on their erotic paintings," Liz said. They sat up and talked until after midnight. Amy fell asleep with her head in David's lap.

"I wish Brian had stayed," David said. "We three have never had a talk like grown up people. I don't have a clue what his job's all about."

"You'll both come to my graduation and we'll plan a day together," Liz said.

"Deal," David said.

When Liz got into bed, thinking about the day, the realization that her mother had a totally new life with a new person and that she barely knew her two brothers and their families, she remembered Barbara telling her before Aunt Alma's funeral, "You'll get a Ph.D. in Family." This summer she was gathering experience in family...and that included sorting out how and with whom she might spend the rest of her life. She would never again spend a night in this bed in this house with even one relative.

Chapter 15

Liz had emailed Sam about Caroline Dunham's idea and asked what he thought Geneva would say, and what he thought about the idea.

He responded, "That's a double whammy to explain. Go for it, it's only fair to let her decide. You're on your own, Babe. I'm moving on to Tunis Wednesday."

Liz put aside thinking about Caroline Dunham until she was driving back to Bloomington after saying good-bye to David and Amy and walking through the house where she had grown up. Was there anything in her bedroom she wanted to keep? A birthday gift musical jewelry box with a twirling ballerina statuette on the top and a box of diaries she had partially kept during her high school years? She probably would never read them, maybe she would put them in a dumpster eventually. Barbara's wedding was a turning point, possibly more important than walking across a stage and accepting the Ph.D. diploma.

She had a week of restless nights, thinking through different ways to explain Caroline Dunhan's idea to Geneva. Probably, she would drive to Dillsboro Friday night, stay with Marjorie, talk about the wedding and about how to tell Geneva about the offer. She worried that the quilts were too bold and confusing for a hospital. She didn't want to bother Geneva with an idea that would collapse when the decorator realized what a powerful impact Geneva's quilts made when not confined to a 4×6 print, but rather full size on a white wall. Liz felt they actually were too bright and bold for a pediatric cancer area. She was certain Caroline's enthusiasm would evaporate when she saw the quilts. She called Caroline hoping she could put the kibosh on the scheme. After brief greetings she asked, "Do you have time to listen to my thoughts about Geneva's quilts?"

Caroline said, "Of course, you know them better than anyone."

"They are heavy on reds, oranges, browns," Liz said. "The photos soften the impact somewhat. A full-size quilt on the wall will be pretty overwhelming."

"I think they're bold and wonderful," Caroline said. "They're modern art."

"Much modern art is meant for very large open spaces. They might overwhelm people who are in a fragile emotional state. These average 50×70. That's a big piece of art."

"Why are you trying to talk me out of this?" Caroline asked.

"Two reasons. My gut feeling is they're wrong for a hospital. Geneva has found that most of her neighbors don't like her quilts. I think the people who will see them hung there won't like them either, neither the parents of patients nor the nurses and doctors. I hope you don't owe Phillip any favors because he really shouldn't have got involved in this."

"Do you dislike him for marrying your mother?" Caroline asked.

Now she's going to analyze me, Liz thought. "No, no. I like him. But I don't think he understands the quilts. And my second reason is that I don't want to talk to Geneva about this if it's not going to actually work out. She's always said they're not for sale; they're going to poor people who need them. For me to talk to her about money is almost an insult."

Caroline said, "So you think Phil's idea is a crummy one?"

"That's what I'm afraid of," Liz answered.

"What if I bought them, and if they don't work in the pediatric wing, I put them in a bigger, more public space in the hospital or even in an office building I happen to be working on?"

"If you bought them, they'd be yours, of course, but I feel a strong ethical commitment to Geneva. She made these quilts for poor people. She never had a thought about selling them. And she may refuse outright." Liz knew she was repeating herself, but she felt she had not been heard the first time she said it.

"It sounds like she could use the money, say fifteen hundred a quilt. Or we could say twelve-fifty for her and a commission to you of two-fifty per quilt."

"No!" Liz hung up. She was shaking with anger. What did Caroline owe Phillip? Or was money her usual approach to a problem? Liz went into the kitchen to get the last of the coffee in the carafe. The phone rang. She knew it was Caroline. She was ashamed of herself for being rude; she couldn't let the phone ring and ring and be even more rude.

"I'm sorry, Elizabeth. I didn't realize it's a delicate situation. Phillip is a major client of mine and I don't want to disappoint him. That's all there is to that, nothing more. If it won't work, then it won't work. From what he said it sounds like she could use the money."

"She has very little, but she wants very little."

"Old people can run up serious medical expenses," Caroline said. "Couldn't you at least approach her about selling them and let her make the decision? Isn't it arrogant of you to summarily deprive her of a tidy little sum she would never have any other way?"

"What happens if you really hate the quilts?"

"I like the pictures. I won't hate the quilts, I know that. You may be right about their inappropriateness for that hospital wing, but there is an insurance company's headquarters being redecorated where they could work brilliantly now that I think about it."

Liz couldn't answer—she had run into a woman who was determined to purchase a few quilts if Geneva would sell them. Caroline was looking out for her future decorating projects. It didn't matter what she thought of the quilts.

"Liz," Caroline said after a pause as she waited for a response, "You've been looking for a museum venue. An office building lobby doesn't have the prestige of a hospital, but there could be an opening as if it were a gallery. I might be able to get some media coverage. Ask her about it, please. Just ask."

"I'll see her Saturday. I'll ask," Liz said.

"Thanks. If she says yes—or even maybe—I think we can work together."

"I'll ask, that's all I can promise."

If it were anybody else, I'd phone or email, Liz thought as she drove to Geneva's on Saturday morning. She wished Sam were with her, but she was also glad he was now in Tunisia. He had suggested the quilts could be on loan. Many artists did that sort of thing, why not Geneva? The loan could extend until she or her estate wanted them returned or until the hospital decided to replace them with something else. Liz didn't bother calling Caroline to relay that idea. She would play it by ear when she talked to Geneva.

Geneva's kitchen was full of vegetables from her garden. Robina was expected to come to help can tomato juice and to freeze packages of corn cut from the cob. Small cucumbers were pickling in a big crock of brine. Zucchinis were piled on a counter. The kitchen smelled wonderful with baking zucchini bread. Geneva had a film of sweat on her forehead and her apron was floury and stained with tomato red blotches. She looked like a Norman Rockwell grandmother. Liz took several pictures with the old camera Sam had given her last spring.

They sat at the kitchen table with glasses of iced tea. Liz began by telling Geneva about the wedding and her brothers. Then she said. "There was a woman at the wedding who decorates office buildings Phillip manages. Phillip told her about me, and that led to telling her about you. She took me off in a corner after dinner and asked me if you would be interested in having a maybe four or five of your quilts hung in a new section of a hospital that she's going to decorate."

"Hung?"

"Yes, on the walls as decoration. They're opening a new part of the hospital for kids with cancer. Other people give individual kids little quilts. A lot of women make them for something called Project Linus. But this decorator thinks the parents need something bright and cheerful to look at when they're waiting to see their kids. Do you like that idea?"

"Where is this?" Geneva was frowning. Liz wondered if she was speaking clearly.

"It's a hospital in Indianapolis."

"She doesn't know anything 'bout my quilts," Geneva said.

"She's seen pictures. Phillip asked me for some and I printed some. I should have asked you first. I'm sorry."

"Which ones?"

"I can show you on my computer, but that doesn't mean they're the exact ones she might want. I don't want to waste time with her if you don't like the idea. She would like to buy them. The hospital gave her a budget for decoration, and she could give you fifteen hundred for each quilt."

Geneva leaned back in her chair and looked at Liz. "That much? For how many?"

"For each one."

"I never wanted to sell my quilts," Geneva said.

"I told her that. But she nagged me to ask you. That's why I came here today, really. Would you like to see your quilts decorating a waiting room or a hallway in a hospital? They wouldn't be keeping anybody warm, but they might make people feel a little better at a time when they're worrying about their kids."

"Let me think on it a little while," Geneva said. "You got a way of usually givin' me a wad of ideas to think 'bout."

The dogs broke into an excited burst of barking as a car pulled into the drive. They did not approach the car until Robina opened the door and let Lay-Z-Girl jump out and dash toward the house. Robina said hello to Liz and looked around the kitchen. "Jeez, Mom, you've got enough vegetables here to feed most of Friendship for most of the winter," she said.

"It was a good year. Right amount of rain, not too hot either. These are the best tomatoes I've had in five or six years," Geneva said.

"Yeah, my tomatoes are real good this year. We've got our work cut out for us."

"I'll give you a hand," Liz said, "if you tell me what to do. I don't know anything about canning and freezing."

"You don't have to do that, Liz," Geneva said.

"Now Mom, don't look a gift horse in the mouth. What she doesn't know, we can teach her," Robina said. "Didn't expect you this weekend. Where's Sam?"

"He's in North Africa," Liz said. "I wish he were here to learn something about country life."

After Robina heard about the wedding and they were busy cutting corn from the cob to package for the freezer, Geneva told Liz to explain about the hospital to Robina.

"Four or five or six quilts? That adds up to a lot of money," Robina said. "You know, Mom, you ought-a do it. It'd be a little nest egg for you. The older you get the more things come up. Me and Ben will always be here for you, but it seems like a good place to have a few of your quilts. If you wanted to give the money to an African mission, of course we'd do what we could."

"I'm thinking 'bout that and 'bout the nest egg idea too. I could buy a funeral like a lotta people do. And I'd still have some money left over."

Liz knew Aunt Alma had prepaid for her funeral several years ago when she sold the farm and moved in with Marjorie.

"You think that woman wants-ta come out here and pick out the quilts she wants?" Geneva asked.

"I think she would," Liz said. "I can always tell her you don't want to sell any. It's really up to you. I only said I'd ask."

"You know, not very long ago I'd'a said no, but when I think 'bout a hospital 'specially for kids, that changes things some. They're pretty plain places generally, I 'spect"

Liz said, "That's why they hire people like this woman and give her a pot of money to buy art for the walls."

"Well, bring her down here one of these days and we'll see if she likes the real thing—might not look so much like the pictures, you know. Not to say anything against Sam."

"Sam and I talk all the time about how the real quilts will always look different than the photos," Liz said.

Liz met Caroline Dunham in Columbus; they drove in her Lexus to Friendship and spent two hours looking at quilts. Caroline had tentatively decided on four from the photos. She chose ones with large amounts of floral fabric—the prettier ones—not surprisingly. They talked about art during the drive. Caroline had done some research. She knew she was ill-informed and her clients knew even less. She had met with the hospital administrator and showed him photos. Liz tried to explain the growth of the quilt art movement. She told Caroline there were art quilters in central Indiana whose work might be more appropriate. "I'd have to educate my clients about art quilts and sell them on a new idea," Caroline said. "Get your book written, Liz. It'll be a big help. People want credentials for everything."

"It would be nice to think I could educate others," Liz said.

"I'll hang these quilts and the corporate decor in Indianapolis will never be the same again." Caroline laughed with delight.

"Fiber is serious art," Liz said. She thought, Phillip certainly has a taste for ambitious women.

"I believe things happen when they're supposed to happen," Caroline said.

"I don't think I agree with that. It sounds like there's some grand plan and I believe chance is the real force in the world—blind, unexplainable chance," Liz said. "That's how I arrived at writing about Geneva's quilts."

"You're not religious then?" Caroline asked.

"No. I don't want to insult you if you are. We could talk about something else," Liz said.

"No, talk to me about chance," Caroline said. "I don't have talks with serious thinkers very often. I really enjoyed a philosophy course in college, Aristotle and Plato and all that, you know? I admit I wasn't a very serious student, really. Tell me how chance brought you to Geneva Gardiner."

Liz talked briefly about how she met Geneva and that giving up the African gift idea had been both a surprise and a milestone. She tried to speak succinctly because she felt Caroline was hearing very little of what she was saying. Caroline seemed like a pond duck, quacking one idea. Any new ideas Liz could offer were like the proverbial water running off her back.

Caroline said, "You've come into that woman's life in the eleventh hour and turned her around 180 degrees."

"I hope it's not the eleventh hour. She seems like she could live to a hundred, and I hope she does. And I never meant to change her life or her way of thinking."

"I meant when it seemed everything about her life was set in stone you changed her attitudes about her own life. Most old people are stuck with nothing but their family who see them one way. And that's how they see themselves. They're not going to change. That's what I've observed—at least in my own family. My mother is 76 and nothing is going to change any of her habits." She began talking about her mother's idiosyncrasies and talked for the remainder of the drive about her family and herself.

When they reached Versailles and turned off U.S. Route 50, Liz felt

340

she should prepare Caroline for tiny Friendship and for the very simple little farm and Geneva's house. She described Geneva's sewing room and the treasure trove of the cedar closet.

"It's like a fairy story," Caroline said. "She's the wise old woman guarding the pot of gold."

"If there's a pot of gold it's all the work of her hands."

"I can't wait to meet her. I admit I'm really, really excited."

The second weekend of October was as perfect as autumn weather can be in Indiana. It had been crisp with a few unseasonable snow flurries a week before, a shock to the trees. The maples had become a scarlet rarely seen mixed with the gold and yellow of other trees. The drive to Geneva's was so beautiful Liz had to pull onto the shoulder four or five times. "They all look Photoshopped," Sam said. "I may have to Photoshop them to make them look un-Photoshopped." Liz was glad the scenery demanded her attention. She had barely slept the night before wondering about seeing Geneva's quilts hung in a hospital and about Geneva's reaction. And even more problematic, how would people respond? What if everyone both misunderstood and disliked the quilts?

Sam brought the video camera because the hospital showing would probably have to be the climax of his film. Melanie had said she would not be able to work on the documentary until the second semester, so Sam was spending most of his energy on the book. His financial advisor had helped find a literary agent who was shopping the book around. Liz had submitted edited portions of what she had written. Sam's agent suggested many changes to make the writing less scholarly and more "reader friendly." Liz struggled to write simple sentences. Didn't people need to know what she could only tell in clauses and complex sentences? She kept parallel copies of each chapter, scholarly and commercial.

Everything now took twice as long to write. Sam relayed the agent's message: "Readers don't want to think as much as they want to feel. We have to make Geneva a wonderful character from a place and time readers never have known but fervently believe once existed in a finer America. Play up the rural aspects and play up her independence, her spunk. Be sure to get the skeet shooting in and the incident with the dog and her tenderhearted treatment of the puppies."

"Barf!" Liz had said. "That's not thesis material."

"Right. We're talking about a coffee table book. We've got to make people want to shell out thirty or forty bucks for a book. Pictures aren't enough, not from an unknown nobody like me," Sam said. "Three unknown nobodies are better than one," he added.

When they arrived at Geneva's home she was waiting for them in a new dress and shoes. Robina had taken her shopping. Her outfit included a new pocket book and a string of fake pearls. Sam kissed her on the cheek and told her she was beautiful. Then he asked, "You're going to wear your church-going hat, aren't you?"

"Do you think it goes with this dress?" she asked.

"Put it on and we'll ask Liz's opinion." Geneva put her hat on. Liz knew Sam wanted to make Geneva appropriately picturesque for the video. Without the hat she might be many older women. Her new dress and sweater were plain deep blue with a simple floral design on the front of the sweater. With the hat she became a rural lady with a sense of dignity that had almost disappeared from American life.

"I give it two thumbs up. There's a touch of Jackie Kennedy about you now."

"No there ain't," Geneva said. "You don't have'ta tell me no tales like that."

"I guess I mean people haven't dressed up for serious occasions since Jackie Kennedy's time. I think that's sad. The pearls and the hat remind me of her. I appreciate elegance when I see it even if I'm not the most fashionable woman around."

"You look real good today," Geneva said. "Is that what you were wearing at your Aunt Alma's funeral?"

"You've got a good memory."

"I'll thank your mother for making sure you know how to get properly dressed up when you need to," Geneva said. Liz smiled. Lately, it seemed, Geneva was treating her like a granddaughter.

They stopped at Ben and Robina's house so that Ben could follow them to Indianapolis. He wasn't confident about finding the hospital on his own. Ben would also take Geneva home so Liz and Sam could return directly to Bloomington.

Liz telephoned Caroline as they approached the hospital to ask about parking. Geneva, Liz and Robina got out at the hospital entrance and the men parked the cars. Caroline Dunham was waiting for them. "I'm glad to say I ain't had too much experience with hospitals," Geneva said. "And I hope not to get too familiar with them in the future."

"We hope so too, Mom," Robina said.

"You've been a very fortunate lady," Caroline said. "What's your secret for living a long healthy life?"

"Minding my own business and working hard and being as good a Christian as I can manage," Geneva said.

"Sounds like I might not be the first to ask you that question," Caroline said with a laugh.

"No, you ain't. Sam asked me to come up with an answer for his movie," Geneva said.

"A movie?" Caroline's voice lilted with curiosity.

"First it was just pictures for a book and now it's a movie," Geneva said. "He says I'll be a big star. I told him Liz would be a better star than me."

"Sam is working on a documentary," Liz explained. "It's still tentative."

"Does he have his video camera with him?" Caroline asked. Her hand had automatically begun to adjust the scarf she wore.

"He does, and he has consent forms for everybody," Liz said.

"Then it's real." Caroline sounded even more delighted than before.

"It's a project in process. We don't know what will come of it," Liz said. "He's working with a student producer who insisted on consents from people here today."

"Oh, a student," Caroline deflated but regained her bright smile when she saw Phillip and Barbara approaching. Sam and Ben were behind them. They had met in the parking lot.

"Hail, hail the gang's all here," Phillip said.

"I'm glad to meet Sam, finally," Barbara whispered to Liz as she gave her a quick hug. Sam wore an expensive sports jacket with a black silk turtleneck. The outfit announced he was a movie star, but the camera bag over his shoulder defined him as a movie maker. Caroline was as impressed as Barbara was.

Inside they met the hospital administrator and the chairman of the pediatric department; upstairs they met the nursing director as well as a photographer and a reporter from the *Indianapolis Star*. The president of the hospital's Board of Directors came in a little late with the donors, Mr. and Mrs. Starnheim, for whom the wing was named. Sam quietly asked everyone to sign his release forms. Caroline talked to Geneva about Sam's photos of her quilts. Barbara and Liz talked to Robina and Ben. They were the tallest and largest people in the group and seemed the most uncomfortable. The Starnheims were introduced to Geneva and said they were eager to see the quilts. Sheldon Starnheim was a nearly bald, paunchy man in a very good suit. Marion Starnheim's hair was an unreal platinum. She wore sparkling rings on each hand. She looked about twenty years younger than her husband but, Liz thought, at least a decade had disappeared in a plastic surgeon's office. She was not a young trophy wife but the original one taking good care of herself.

Caroline said to the Starnheims, "I'm so excited to show you the quilts. They add so much comfort to the public areas."

Liz realized the Starnheims had no idea what they were going to see. A stab of panic filled her stomach; nausea felt only a nanosecond away from disaster. She had to turn away from the group and breathe deeply. They're going to hate the quilts, she thought. She wished she had asked Caroline if they had seen pictures. She was positive they had never heard of art quilts and expected something traditional, or certainly no more unusual than a dramatic Amish diamond in a square quilt. Her hands were sweating. Barbara left Phillip's side and came to Liz. "Are you okay, Sweetheart?" she whispered. Liz shook her head slightly but couldn't say anything. Barbara squeezed Liz's hand. "Do you want to go out for a minute?"

"Can't," Liz whispered.

When everyone had signed Sam's forms, the doctor led them up an elevator, down a hall and through a set of doors to the new wing. Immediately at the end of the hall a view into a waiting room almost vibrated with a big orange, yellow and green quilt on the wall. Sam photographed the view then quickly went ahead to find a place to stand and get both Geneva's expression and the quilt in the picture.

"Well, I'll be. My goodness..." Geneva looked at her quilt on the wall. "I thought it'd look 'bout the same as on the barn door when Sam took his picture of it, but it looks real different here where the walls are all white."

Liz watched the Starnheims. They did not know what to think. Mr. Starnheim seemed about to say something but tilted his head this way and that as if he were at an art gallery studying a complex painting. "Perhaps it reminds you of a Sol Lewitt painting," Liz said. "He's done several paintings that are very quilt-like, mostly geometric. Of course, Rauschenberg famously used a real quilt in a very important painting. I'd say these are a bit more like Jasper Johns or, well, many of the post-Abstract Expressionists." She threw out famous names, hoping that they might at least have heard of the painters.

"Someone actually glued a quilt—a real quilt—in a painting, didn't he?" said the doctor who had heard Liz's comment.

"Rauschenberg," Liz said. "It's a wonderful painting. Iconic, really. It's in the Metropolitan Museum." She thought she sounded hyper.

"Of course, Norman Rockwell..." Barbara said. "Not quite the same league, I know. And I think Grandma Moses included quilts...maybe. Liz is the scholar; she's been trying to educate me but I'm not good with names."

Liz might have laughed at Barbara if she wasn't feeling desperate and grateful at least for the distraction of her mother's desperate chatter.

"I didn't realize we were getting real art," Sheldon Starnheim said. "Caroline tried to explain, but I guess I just didn't make the leap."

Mrs. Starnheim was frowning either from perplexity or she simply didn't like the quilt and wasn't impressed by her husband's face-saving comment.

"Come, you must see the others," Caroline said. A smaller quilt that was blue, green and old gold in which many pieces were various sunflower prints hung behind the nurse's station.

"I remember when you started that one, Mrs. Gardiner," Sam said. "It turned out brilliantly."

"Thank you, Sam," Geneva said.

"I like that," Sheldon Starnheim said. "Isn't that nice, Marion?"

"I like it better than the other one," she answered, but had the grace to keep her voice low so only those near her heard.

The *Star* photographer wanted Geneva to pose with the nurses in front of the quilt. "We just love it," the head nurse said to Geneva. "We've got one little girl who saw it and started singing that sunflower song."

"I guess I don't know that song," Geneva said.

The nurse sang, although she did not have a good voice, "I'm your sunflower, I'm your one flower, and I'll... Well, I don't know all the words, but Bethanne does."

"Is she still here?" Geneva asked.

"Yes, she'll be here quite a while, she's having a bone marrow transplant Monday."

"I'd like to hear her sing that song, if I could visit her," Geneva said.

"Perhaps you could bring her out," Sam suggested, "if she's well enough."

"I think she'd love that," the nurse said. She sent two others to bring the child.

"Meanwhile, let's see the other quilts," Caroline said, cheerful now that this quilt was more of a success than the first one.

The hospital administrator led the way down a hall where another quilt hung and into a comfortable waiting room with a refrigerator and buffet for snacks as well as a TV and four cozy seating arrangements. The quilt here was red, gold, dark green and brown with various autumn leaf prints in many triangles. "It's like an autumn lawn. Just like at our house," Barbara gushed. "Isn't that true, Phil? I love it."

"I like this one," Marion Starnheim said to her husband. She turned to Barbara. "You're right, it's like our lawn too."

"Liz tells me sometimes people talk about fiber art instead of art quilts because we think quilt means the kind our grandmothers used to make. But things have changed a lot in the last fifty years or so," Barbara said. Liz wanted to hug her mother.

"Do you mind if I quote you?" the reporter from The Star asked.

"You know, it's Elizabeth you should quote, she's the expert," Barbara said.

Marion Starnheim turned to Liz. "I guess I didn't know quilts could be like art. I understand you're working on a book."

"You are?" asked the reporter.

Liz spoke a little about what she and Sam were doing.

The reporter turned to Geneva. "Mrs. Gardiner, how do you feel seeing your work displayed here?"

"I'm real pleased," Geneva said. "If I didn't know I made them, I'd want to make some like them."

"Mrs. Gardiner," said the head nurse, "if we can go back to the nursing station I'll introduce you to Bethanne Cooper. She said she'd love to sing the sunflower song for you."

Bethanne was a long-haired redhead whose pallid face was a field of freckles. She sat in a wheelchair that a nurse had wheeled in with an IV stand. Sam made quiet suggestions about where Geneva and Bethanne might be in front of the quilt. There's his closing shot, Liz thought. He even has a photogenic little girl. Oh, my goodness, Liz realized, he's got film of Geneva picking out the fabric for that very quilt. Sam must have been blessed at birth by all the good fairies while Carabose, the bad fairy, got lost in the forest and waited around for me to be born.

Finally everyone left, Geneva with Robina and Ben, Caroline with the Starnheims. The hospital personnel dispersed to their regular jobs. "We're taking you two out to lunch," Barbara said. "I've waited a long time to meet the famous photographer."

Liz knew this was Barbara's idea; an opportunity for them to get acquainted. Barbara had complained that she had not met either Randy or Jack. A mother is always a mother, Liz thought. Lunch was a pleasure at a very nice restaurant. Liz enjoyed the hour of quiet conversation and was glad to explain to Phillip and Barbara why Professor Simmons agreed she should label Geneva Gardiner's quilt Outsider Art and why they were worthy of a Ph.D. thesis. "And a coffee table book," Sam emphasized.

Sam had been oblivious to Liz's fears about the Starnheims' attitude about the quilts. Liz explained how Barbara had helped her in what now seemed like a very tiny drama. "You pulled it off like a pro," Sam said. "I wouldn't be surprised if they decide to buy some quilts for themselves."

"Then they'll have to find a different quilter. I don't like that woman," Liz said. "I hope you'll edit her out of any shots she's in."

Sam laughed. "You're such a WASP," he said.

"That is a politically incorrect thing to say to me."

"She's always been the feisty one," Barbara said to Sam.

"How about an old fashioned Hoosier?" he said.

"Whatever that means," Phillip said. "You either insulted or complimented all of us, including yourself."

On the way back to Bloomington Sam said, "You can relax, Lizzie, this was a coup. We have our ending and, come spring, when Melanie and I start editing, I can go back to Geneva's and fill in anything that's missing.

Liz sent Geneva copies of the article that appeared in the *Indianapolis Star* with a note: "Now you're getting famous." The article was very short, but it showed Geneva with the Starnheims in front of the quilt that looked like autumn leaves, although very little of the quilt was in the picture. She also sent Geneva a copy of the book about the Gees Bend quilts, a gift from Sam. When Liz called Geneva the next Monday, Geneva said, "I'd'a rather he give it to me in person."

"We're both working our little tails off with our classes and getting everything in order. You've got some new quilts for him to photograph, so we'll be out there as soon as we can."

Liz was auditing a journalism school writing class to learn to write more descriptively than the straightforward historical material she had been writing. The class did not help much. Gradually she began to feel freer as she described Geneva and tiny Friendship. She wanted to add a paragraph of history and facts about the town. She asked Marjorie to do some historical research.

Marjorie admitted she had begun to write some family history, especially about her mother, father and grandparents. She was flattered and excited about contributing to Liz's thesis and the photo book. "I'll see if I can find out when Friendship was first settled, where and when it got its name and how did the town grow?" Marjorie said. "It's good for me to have an assignment."

"You don't have to think of it that way," Liz said.

"Of course I do. I'm a teacher. I'll ask Geneva about when her family moved to the area; what was their background? Thanks for asking me, Elizabeth Jane."

"I'll give you a footnote." Liz was glad she had thought of asking.

The weekend of the hospital quilt viewing ushered in three weeks of photogenic autumnal glory. The next Saturday she and Sam drove to picturesque Brown County State Park. They saw several deer and more visitors than expected. The following weekend the brilliant leaves were torn from the trees by gales of wind and rain.

In mid-November when Liz called Geneva as usual, Geneva said. "I been waitin' this mornin' for your call 'cause I don't know just what to do." She explained that CherryLee had called her and asked if it would be possible to give half a dozen quilts to people in need. She talked about a couple of families who would have a very hard time getting through the winter.

"No work, no income, just food stamps and a little bit of help from family," CherryLee explained. "They're not going to have enough heat or enough to eat unless I can scare up some help." She was calling local churches and the United Way, but she wasn't sure they would be willing to help the few individuals that CherryLee knew and cared about.

"I told her, 'Sure, I'll give them to you.' But now I'm wonderin', Liz, if there's some particular ones you think I should be sure to keep in case you need them for a show sometime. I got plenty to spare, but now I'm wonderin' which ones are best to give. See, you give me new problems to think about."

Liz was astonished that Geneva was thinking about a show, about how to choose among the pieces. "I'll look through the photos right away and call you back later today," she said.

"You got the photos?"

"All on my computer. Remember? We looked at them once?"

"Oh, that's right. I forget you can do things like that."

"It makes our work a lot easier. Sam and I write notes to each other practically every day on the computer."

"I knew you could do that. Well, it's all too much for this old dog to try to understand. How's Sam? Is he there or off wanderin' around like he does?"

"He's here right now. In fact, if you want us to, we could probably come down next weekend, just come on Saturday and then come right back."

"Well, you don't have-ta make a special trip if you can really just explain which quilts. I 'member I gave you some names but that was just what come to me. I don't recall...I'm gettin' old and forgetful."

"I've got notes."

"Tell you the truth, Liz, I don't want to put you and Sam to a lot of trouble, but I would feel better if you could maybe come for a couple hours middle of the day Saturday when CherryLee can be here."

"I could, and I think Sam will want to come too. Would the two of you mind letting Sam video tape you giving them to her?"

"It's okay with me, I'll ask her. I 'magine it'll be okay."

"So how have you been since I talked to you last week?" Liz asked. They chatted another ten minutes as Liz explained how her work was coming. She did not talk about her long days, often getting up at 5:30 to prepare for the class she was teaching that day because she had been in the library, or at her computer until 10:00 or 11:00 the night before. Liz had never worked so single-mindedly at one thing. She felt she would not have been able to concentrate and work so well if she were not living alone with no pressure from a man in her life. She found energy in the job, at last the form of the thesis made sense and the writing was flowing more easily. Sam was working equally hard since the agent had found a publisher who had produced other books about quilt artists and knew how to position them in the market. He was studying every photo to make choices.

They did not get to Geneva's that weekend. A blizzard began Friday midday. It quickly blanketed a four-state area in what became eighteen inches of snow carried by furious winds that threw snow-burdened trees down across power lines and closed highways. On Friday evening Robina called Liz. "Don't worry about Mom," she said. "She's got the fireplace in the living room and already brought in a good bit of wood that was by the back door, so she won't have to even go out if her power goes off." Robina explained that Ben had a snowplow blade on his pickup. He was, at that moment, clearing their driveway and would probably work well into the night clearing drives for neighbors. Snows like this, and less extreme ones, gave him a winter income that they needed.

Robina assured Liz that when the storm ended they would get to Geneva's house, and if there were any problems they would bring Geneva home with them. "Would you believe," Robina asked, "Mom even has a couple old fashioned lamps and a gallon can of kerosene stashed in the store room?"

Liz had weathered storms and extremely low temperatures in Mongolia. The Mongolians were prepared for such winters. They had dried meat and grain, they had corralled their sheep and horses. She hated the long days of cold, but, like their neighbors, she and Randy bundled into all the clothes they owned and went out to gather snow to melt for water. It was an adventure. Randy inspired Liz to think of it as a personal test of endurance. She sometimes played solitaire for whole afternoons while he read or meditated or went out with the local men to tend to the animals.

That kind of hardship from weather seemed behind her in her small apartment. Her electricity did not go off. She had ramen and boxes of mac and cheese and happily had bought a big bag of apples. The refrigerator held a variety of odds and ends. She barely thought about the blizzard as dangerous until Robina's call. She imagined Geneva in her small house amid snowy fields. She had the dogs for company and she was used to such storms. She would have to hand tie a quilt if the electricity was out. She would read her Bible.

Saturday morning the television reported widespread overnight power outages. Liz tried to call Geneva and got only dead silence. Then she tired Ben and Robina, but their telephones were also out. So was Marjorie's phone. Although the television showed virtual standstill in all of southern Indiana and Northern Kentucky as well as parts of Illinois and into Ohio, she took this as a time to continue her writing, which was nearing the end of the full first draft.

A text from Sam asked if she thought Geneva would be alright. She texted back with the information she had. He said he would take her out to dinner if she wanted. The storm was abating, the late after-noon ought to be a good time for him to go out with his camera for snow pictures, especially in the blue-gray light of dusk just as the streetlights were coming on, creating golden halos and long interest-ing shadows. He said he wished they were at Geneva's because there must be wonderful expanses of snow with small houses and barns, almost buried in drifts. It must be very picturesque.

"You're not a nature photographer," she said.

"Not at present. Who knows what the future holds?" he said.

"The Shadow knows," she intoned. "If I put on the parka and boots I wore in Mongolia, I can go anywhere in this piddling little storm. Give me a call when you think you'll get here." Sam's enthusiasm about the snow had kindled her sense of adventure after so many hours star-ing at a small laptop screen in her close little apartment. She would show him Liz the snow bunny.

Sunday afternoon Ben called. "Liz," he said. "Maybe you need to be sitting down." His words took her breath away. She was sitting; she let her head fall back against the chair as she held the phone to her ear. Ben explained that he had been unable to get to Friendship until an hour ago because the two-lane road had not been plowed until that morning. Friday he had called and advised Geneva to "just stay in 'til I get there." But by morning the phone lines and the electric lines were down and he couldn't reach her. He had not been worried; they had weathered storms and tornados over the years. When he finally plow-ed through her drive, he saw a path in the snow going toward the chicken house. He found her in the snow, nearly covered over. She had been there, possibly, since the day before. With no working phone, he had to drive to the police station in Versailles to report that he had carried her into the house. The county coroner would come to assess the cause of death or maybe she'd be taken to a hospital.

"I don't know if it was a heart attack or a stroke or maybe she fell but it didn't look like she struggled to move. There was a lotta snow." His voice got thick and low and slow. "I think it mighta been sudden, I kinda hope so."

"I do too," Liz said. "Thanks for thinking to call me." She was also choking up.

"I don't know when the funeral'll be," Ben said. "I called Robina and she said to call you 'cause she was going to start calling relatives, so you're the second person I told 'cept for the deputy. I don't know what to do now but wait." Liz heard a sound that she assumed was a stifled sob. "I gotta hang up. We'll let you know more later."

Liz called Sam and told him about the talk she just had with Robina when she called to ask if there was anything she could or should do. Then she called her mother.

"Do you want to talk about it?" Barbara asked.

"Right now I'm going to meet Sam. I'll probably need to talk to you later."

"I'm here any time you want to call. I'm so sorry."

Liz put on her parka and boots and met Sam near the Student Union. They held each other for a few minutes and then went in to drink coffee and try to talk. Neither were able to speak in complete sentences. He walked her back to her apartment. "Come in with me," she said.

Sam spent the night. They needed the comfort of embracing and making love. They awoke in the morning's blaze of sunlight face to face, slowly blinking, surprised to finally be entwined in one another's arms in bed.

Liz called while Sam made breakfast. Robina said they should come on Tuesday for the funeral. "You don't need attend the viewing Monday evening. There's nothing you need to do. But I gotta tell you—" She chuckled.

Liz was surprised that Robina could sound cheerful. "But what?"

Robina explained that Ben went to see Joshua Wheeler yesterday afternoon. He told the minister that Geneva wanted a very simple service. Ben had said, "I want to talk about my mother 'cause I'm the only one left, the grandkids have never come around much and probably won't come through the snow for the funeral. Robina will arrange for music. We called a woman we know's got a good voice and she's got a son who plays the keyboard. She'll sing "I Come to the Garden." That was Mom's favorite hymn."

Robina explained, "Ben very firmly to Joshua Wheeler, 'All I need you to do is say a prayer. A short prayer mainly about my mother. I don't want no sermon. I want it short and sweet, just like my mother was. The ground's too frozen to dig a grave, so she'll be in the vault until we can have a little family burial. Then we'll need another little prayer.'"

"You think he can keep it short?" Liz asked.

"If he don't, Ben'll speak up or signal the kid with the keyboard to play something."

"That's perfect," Liz said.

Robina added, "It'll be short, but I hope you'll have time to go the house and give the nurse some quilts afterwards."

The roads were mostly clear on Tuesday when they left Bloomington at seven, giving themselves three hours to drive the hundred miles. Sam had rented a Subaru with snow tires. The sun shone in a perfect blue sky, brilliantly, blindingly. As if that sky could never have dumped this frozen blanket of cold on the fields and trees and roads.

They stopped a few times for Sam to take photos. "I think you're an all-purpose photographer at this point," Liz said.

"Beautiful things just ask to be photographed," he said.

They drove to Marjorie's home because they had agreed to meet Barbara and Phillip there. Barbara hugged Liz. "You don't remember when your grandmother died, so this must feel like that."

"It just feels awful," Liz said.

The little church was nearly filled. Most of the congregation had known Geneva for many years. CherryLee and her daughter, Shawna, were there. Liz introduced herself and asked them to sit beside her. Ben had said to CherryLee before the funeral, "Mom wanted to give you half a dozen quilts. Robina and I put some aside so if you can come to her house afterwards, we'll give them to you. But one thing, she wanted Liz to say if those were the ones you should have." CherryLee looked confused. "Liz and Sam are writing a book and they want to have a show of some of Mom's quilts. There's some they might want to be sure to keep. We just don't want to mess up Liz's plans."

The minister had probably never officiated at a shorter funeral service. Ben spoke slowly, glancing now and then at a paper he had in his hand. When he paused, he looked at Robina, and sometimes at Liz. He ended with, "I'm sorry I'm the only one of her children still here; I've missed my sisters and I know Mom did too. I did not understand her very well until lately, but Elizabeth came and loved her quilts and taught me to appreciate my mother like I never did before...appreciate and, I guess, understand her in a way I didn't. And my wife feels the same. Mom's life was happier when she found out somebody liked the work of her hands. That was a blessing no one else could give her. Thank you, Elizabeth. I hope you'll say a little bit about my mother."

Liz was stunned. She stood slowly and said, "Please give me a minute..." She closed her eyes and took a long breath, exhaled slowly. "Geneva Gardiner was a fine, fine woman. She had little and she gave much—little, I mean, of worldly things. But she had a warm and generous heart. And she had many friends, who I think are here today. Many of you fostered her quilting talents with your generosity by giving her the fabrics to make her many quilts. She spoke often of the generosity of her friends at this church, and she mirrored that generosity with the wish to share the quilts she made with others less fortunate. She was a natural artist but didn't know it, and yet it gave her pleasure. She was a very wonderful woman. I hope I brought some gladness to her. She brought gladness to my life. I was blessed to know her."

Liz sat down, stunned that the words had come almost as she might have written them.

Ben nodded to Rev. Wheeler, who stood and said a short prayer that astonished him, and many in the room, because he looked at Ben and forgot several bits and bobs of scripture he meant to say.

The singer sang, "Just As I Am." Many people sniffled and wiped tears that had escaped to unknown trails over weathered aging faces.

Several, including Marjorie, Barbara and Phil, followed Robina to her house for lunch.

Liz and Sam, Ben and CherryLee went to Geneva's house, which sat surrounded by drifts piled high by Ben's snow plowing. As they walked toward the house, Ben said, especially apologizing to CherryLee, as he kicked at a yellow spot in the snow, "The dogs are still here and there might be some smell of dog shit in the house. I've been coming by and feeding them and letting them out and taking care of the chickens but, you know, they really oughtta be out more than once a day. So I'm sorry if it's going to stink. We'll get it aired out soon as we can open windows."

"Are you going to take the dogs?" Sam asked.

"I guess I have'ta. I'll put an ad in the paper, but I can't say I expect any takers," Ben said, unhappily resigned to keeping the promise Sam gave Geneva months ago.

The minute the door was opened the dogs rushed out. The house was cold. Ben had closed all the doors to other rooms and left newspapers all over the kitchen and hallway. It was very cold in Geneva's sewing room. The quilts Robina and Ben had chosen at random were piled on the cutting table. Liz and Sam saw only one they felt was important to keep for a possible show.

"What if we make it eight?" Ben asked. "So CherryLee can keep a couple for herself. She's the one that changed Mom's mind about sending them off to Africa."

"Sure," Liz said. "Pick out what you like."

CherryLee hugged Liz. "Mrs. Gardiner spoke real fond of you, you know," she said. She gave Sam a hug as well. "She thought you were the coolest thing and so do I."

"I'm plenty cool at this moment," Sam said, caressing her face with his icy fingers. She gasped, pulled back and laughed.

Sam videoed Ben handing the quilts to CherryLee and Shawna. They didn't mind doing the presentation a couple of times for him. As they were about to leave Shawna said to her mother, "It'd be kind of nice to have a dog."

Ben quickly said, "They're real sweet dogs. I'd be happy to give them to you."

CherryLee looked at Shawna for a moment as if she were going to say, "No way." But she said, "If YOU had a dog, one dog, YOU would have to walk it and feed it and take it to the vet and get shots with your babysitting money."

"I would. I'd take good care of it."

"And what about if you go away to college in a few years?"

"By then you'll love it so much you'll think it's a good trade-off when I'm gone."

CherryLee laughed, shook her head. "You hear that girl?" she said.

"I didn't want none," Ben said. "But now we've got two—unless Liz or Sam..."

"No," both said. "We can't."

They helped CherryLee and Shawna put quilts and the black and brown dog in the car. The other dog looked confused and whined when he wasn't allowed to get in the car with his brother.

"You're coming with me now," Ben said to it; he quickly put it in his pick-up truck. "You've got a sister at my house." CherryLee thanked them again and drove through the tunnel of snow toward her home.

Ben said, "Robina's taking care of people at our house for lunch. I didn't tell you, but she called up the lawyer in Versailles who's got Mom's will. You know she filled out them computer will papers you got for her a while ago, Liz. I wanted to make sure it was all legal, so I took it to the lawyer I use."

"She didn't say anything to me," Liz said. She thought that was so long ago, it was before she changed her mind. She looked at Sam. "Oh, shit," she said. "I guess it says to give the quilts to her church to give to Africa. I suppose that's going to be a problem."

"No, she changed it," Ben said. "The lawyer called me about it 'cause, you know, I've got power of attorney. I took Mom up to Versailles, just after the Indianapolis hospital thing. Anyway, since you're here and don't know when you might get back, I thought we could go to Versailles after lunch, if that's all right with you two."

Barbara and Phillip left after lunch. Liz and Sam followed Ben and Robina to Versailles. They had driven the edge of the town on U.S. Route 50 every time they came to see Geneva, but they had never been in the center of the little county seat. Sam immediately loved the town center with its brick courthouse standing in a square surrounded by buildings mostly a century old. A Civil War cannon, never used, protected one corner of the square with a small historical plaque about Morgan's Raiders. A slender tree had toppled across a sidewalk and had not been removed.

"The snow on the trees makes it look monumental," Sam said. "I can take photos without that fallen tree." He walked around the square, photographing the courthouse and the town square from different angles.

Mrs. Parker was a pert but not very pretty woman with a long face and unbecoming glasses. She looked like a small-town cheerleader grown gray and negligent of using sunblock. She chatted with Ben, Robina and Liz while they waited for Sam to come in. She asked Ben to bring an extra chair from a colleague's office. She said the will had been amended on September 23rd.

Mrs. Parker read the preliminary legalese, then the formal language that gave the farm and all its buildings and contents to her only living son, Ben Gardiner, except for the quilts in her sewing room. She willed all the quilts to Elizabeth Jane Lissome "because she made me see that they are beautiful and valuable. I know she will find the right place for them whether it be in the homes of the needy or museums or whatever she believes is right. I want her to give at least two to Sam Goldman in case they don't get married like I hope they will."

Liz was stunned the second time today. She stared at Mrs. Parker until she had to breathe. Her gasp turned into a sob. She put her hands over her face and cried the way she had felt like crying all through the funeral service. She had stopped herself then and merely wiped away the tears that rolled down beside her nose. Now she cried as if she had indeed lost a grandmother. Sam lifted her from the chair and held her until she was able to stop crying.

Liz said to Ben and Robina, "You should have them, not me."

"Mom knew what she wanted to do with them," Ben said. "There never was any arguing with Mom when she had her mind made up. They're yours. We trust you to do what's right."

END

About Atmosphere Press

Atmosphere Press is an independent, full-service publisher for excellent books in all genres and for all audiences. Learn more about what we do at atmospherepress.com.

We encourage you to check out some of Atmosphere's latest releases, which are available at Amazon.com and via order from your local bookstore:

Twisted Silver Spoons, a novel by Karen M. Wicks

Queen of Crows, a novel by S.L. Wilton

The Summer Festival is Murder, a novel by Jill M. Lyon

The Past We Step Into, stories by Richard Scharine

The Museum of an Extinct Race, a novel by Jonathan Hale Rosen

Swimming with the Angels, a novel by Colin Kersey

Island of Dead Gods, a novel by Verena Mahlow

Cloakers, a novel by Alexandra Lapointe

Twins Daze, a novel by Jerry Petersen

Embargo on Hope, a novel by Justin Doyle

Abaddon Illusion, a novel by Lindsey Bakken

Blackland: A Utopian Novel, by Richard A. Jones

The Jesus Nut, a novel by John Prather

The Embers of Tradition, a novel by Chukwudum Okeke

Saints and Martyrs: A Novel, by Aaron Roe

When I Am Ashes, a novel by Amber Rose

About the Author

Almost as quirky as Liz, author June Calender, a quilter for forty years, has traveled widely, including to Mongolia and Tibet. She published a travel book, *Phantom Voices in Tibet* (2003, Creative Arts). After being invited to the annual Playwright's Conference at the Eugene O'Neill Theater, she moved to NYC to pursue a playwrighting career. Many of her plays were produced off-Broadway, as far as Alaska, San Francisco, and Milwaukee. She has now retired to Cape Cod, where she teaches a writing course, Telling Stories, for retirees who want to write about a lifetime of experiences in the Academy for Lifelong Learning.

Made in the USA
Middletown, DE
11 February 2022